The
Black F

Run for your

Gordon Bickerstaff

To
Cassandra
All the very best!
Gordon x.

Lambeth Group Thriller #3

The Black Fox
Run for your life...

Zoe Tampsin is resourceful, smart and Special Forces-trained, but she has been given an impossible mission.

She has to protect scientist, Gavin Shawlens, from assassination by the CIA, and discover the secret trapped in Gavin's mind that the CIA want destroyed.

As the pressure to find Shawlens escalates, the CIA send Zoe's former mentor to track her down and her fate seems sealed when he surrounds Zoe and Gavin with a ring of steel. With each hour that passes, the ring is tightened, and the window for discovering Gavin's secret will shut.

Zoe is faced with a decision that goes against all of her survival instincts. If she is wrong, they both die. If she is right, she will discover the secret and become the next target for assassination.

Also by the same author

Deadly Secrets *The truth will out ...*
Everything To Lose *The chase is on ...*
Toxic Minds *The damage is done ...*
Tabula Rasa *The end is nigh ...*

This book is a work of fiction. Names, characters, businesses, organisations, places and events are used fictitiously or are the work of the author's imagination. Any resemblance to actual persons, living or dead, or actual events or locales is not intended and is entirely coincidental.

*

Acknowledgements

Special thanks to Emily, Pamela and Natalie for all her inspiration, support and coffee. Thanks also to the readers who have given me feedback on the first two books. I am humbled by the readers who took time to write comments that have helped me to improve my stories.

I am grateful to the following for their work on the production of this book: Alex, Clarissa, David, Helen and Julia.

*

*

'If you are going through hell, keep going.'
Winston Churchill

*

One

Marysville, St Clair County, Michigan, USA

Joe Koswalski's fingers squeezed the black leather armrests of his swivel chair. He felt angry with the high-handed attitude of the CIA agent leaning over him and invading his personal space. They had waltzed right into the operations control room, waving their creds in the air, and assumed command as if they owned the place.

When had the CIA leapt to the top of the pile of government agencies? Arrogantly expecting everyone to run after them, like good little government employees.

The CIA agent scanned the surveillance screens at Joe's workstation while a noisy face-to-face argument raged behind them. His long neck pushed close to Joe's face for the perfume in his extra triple hydration deodorant to sting Joe's nose like a hot needle. Joe didn't need to listen carefully to find out what the CIA wanted.

'All you need to know is there is an imminent threat to our national security. I have orders from the President. You'll do exactly what I tell you or you'll stand aside and I'll find someone who will,' Ertha Odeele shouted.

'I will not,' Marty Candose shouted back.

'Damn you!' Ertha screamed and pulled a handgun from inside her coat.

'Listen, lady, you have no idea what you're asking. If we have a border incident with Canada, we will catch a barrel load of shit,' Marty argued.

'Do as I say or I will charge you with treason,' Ertha lashed back.

'Get outta here, lady. You have no business being here.'

'Do what I tell you to do.'

'No way, lady. I'll not provoke an international incident with Canada. Not without written orders. No way in hell,' Marty replied, and stared down the gun pointing at his head.

The CIA had arrived just after six-thirty in the morning just when the shift had moved into its final hour in the operations room of the US Customs and Border Protection Station at Marysville near the border with Canada.

Border patrol supervisor, Joe Koswalski, had worked for CBP since 1998. A portly figure bulged out of his oversize uniform with chubby cheeks and a shiny bald head. Like his waistband, his mind bulged with big ideas.

At the start of his shift, his boss Marty had given him good news. He'd chosen Joe to organise the celebrations, to mark ninety years since the border station opened in the summer of 1924 at Port Huron. Its role back then had been to catch rumrunners smuggling contraband liquor into the United States. Its role ninety years later had changed markedly.

Initially, the station had been located at the railroad terminal near the mouth of the Sarnia-Port Huron railroad tunnel. In 2007, the station moved to a high tech surveillance complex in Marysville as part of the air and maritime domain awareness project.

As unofficial historian and curator, Joe managed all the journals passed down through the decades, detailing stories of border incidents over the years. Some real humdingers he felt sure people would like to hear about.

He'd not long started to tell Marty about some of his grand ideas for the celebrations when the three CIA people burst into the operations control room.

Ertha Odeele led the CIA team and immediately ordered all other CBP agents out of the room, leaving only Joe and Marty to control the surveillance equipment. The argument behind Joe escalated and the swearing got more intense. Joe glanced back to see Marty and Ertha standing toe-to-toe, finger pointing and posturing.

Still wrapped in her outdoor clothes, gloves and hat, Ertha wore a black trouser suit with the jacket buttoned over her potbelly. Long collars from her white blouse lay on the lapels of her jacket.

A forty-six-year-old African-American from Texas, Ertha's accent had long since been smoothed out during her time in Washington. She kept her hair short and wore small gold earrings that matched a gold crucifix pendant. She'd been in New York visiting her sister, when she got an urgent call from her boss, ordering her to report to the CIA office in New York.

Although a whole head shorter than six-foot Marty, she postured aggressively and argued vociferously with the uniformed Marysville Operations Supervisor. She demanded total surveillance blackout on her command.

Marty refused, and argued that the Canadian Border Services Agency would react to any incursion across the border.

Just when Marty thought she'd backed down, a call came through from Border Patrol Headquarters in Washington. Marty's Division Chief lectured Marty about the need for cooperation in matters of national security.

After a few short but intense words, Marty received assurance that any border incident would not be his responsibility, and not on his record. Reluctantly, Marty ordered Joe to prepare for the blackout. They stood ready to respond to calls from border patrols in the area.

The matter now settled, Ertha raised her radio to her head and said, 'Nighthawk-5, this is Nighthawk-2. You have a green light. Get it done quickly and quietly.'

*

Garristone Gate in Sarnia, a quiet residential cul-de-sac of twelve detached houses, looked idyllic with perfectly manicured lawns and white concrete drives. At ten minutes before seven, two black Chevrolet SUVs with all round darkened windows drove onto the lot, heading for house 2089.

The lead SUV carrying the first team moved fast up the sweeping concrete drive and screeched to a halt at the front door. The following vehicle carrying the second team stopped at the bottom of the drive.

Two men, Peters and Modamo, and two women, Heskan and Amster, quickly piled out of the first vehicle and ran over to the house. They all wore black leather gloves, boots and dark winter coats with collars pulled up to keep out the cold. The men were over six-foot tall, clean-shaven with short hair and muscular builds. Modamo carried a door battering ram.

Heskan, the Nighthawk team leader, looked confident and determined. A trim, red-haired, fresh-faced twenty-seven-year-old, confident and bossy, and aiming for the next big tick on her résumé.

Amster had tucked her shoulder-length blonde hair into a brown fur and suede trapper hat. She carried six more years and ten more kilos than Heskan. Although more experienced, she had less ambition than Heskan.

Two other similarly dressed men, Coleman and Miles, slipped out of the second SUV and took positions facing the road. Coleman appeared to be a clone of the other two heavies except he wore a black beanie over his bald head. Miles had a medium build with short hair and a thin neat beard. He wore a flat cap and stood a little shorter that the others at five-seven.

Coleman had worked with Peters, Modamo and Amster on previous operations. They knew and trusted each other. Heskan had joined them fresh out of Langley with lots of theory and simulation training, but not much field experience.

Coleman had criticised Heskan's plan and warned her that it needed more preparation. He had wanted the front door or the back door. They had argued and Heskan ordered Coleman to guard the driveway. He stood ready to block interference from passers-by although he didn't expect any.

The sun would soon start to rise on this crisp but dry mid-November morning. Rain had fallen overnight, and the ground proved slippery underfoot where crunchy ice had formed. The temperature had dropped below zero but not low enough for hard ice.

In the late spring, Garristone Gate had welcomed new neighbours when two women moved in to number 2089. They soon discovered the women preferred to keep themselves to themselves. They weren't Canadians and didn't appear to have jobs or any kind of work.

For the first month or so, a Canadian cousin or friend helped them settle into the area. Brought groceries and chauffeured them around in a Toyota Highlander with blackened windows.

Some neighbours found the younger woman friendly and approachable, and she often played alone in the back garden with their white West Highland terrier dog. The older woman seemed nervous, and wary of talking to strangers.

It took five hard bangs with the battering ram for Peters and Modamo to smash through the front door. Normally two or three from these two heavies would have been enough. The door had been well secured.

They didn't announce who they were, and the only sounds heard in the house were their frustrated curses at not entering the house quickly. Modamo ran upstairs to the bedrooms followed by Heskan and Amster. Peters covered the front door.

The young woman, dressed in pyjamas and slippers, had been in the kitchen feeding her dog, Whiskers. When the door banging started, she switched off the light in the kitchen, and stumbled over the dog's food bowl as she hurried to the hall.

She did exactly what she'd been told to do if the house came under attack. She ran into the hall and hit the silent alarm button on the wall at the bottom of the stairs. She darted back to the kitchen, emptied the cutlery drawer onto the floor, and then ran out of the kitchen back door. Whiskers ran after her. Everything seemed like a game to Whiskers.

Anyone else attacked in their home would be in shock, but the young woman appeared calm and focused, just as she'd been in rehearsals. She knew the plan, run fast to first base, and stop for nothing. In the back yard, she ran past their swimming pool to the Howard Watson Nature Trail.

She planned to turn east on the trail, run to Telfer Road, and then over to first base, Sarnia Fire Station 5. An escape plan she'd rehearsed every week for the first six weeks since she arrived in the house.

Coleman paced impatiently beside the second SUV. He looked up the drive to the house and watched the first team struggle to break the front door. He clapped his gloved hands together and puffed out warm breaths into the cold air, like cigarette smoke.

Just after the first team crashed into the house, he caught a glimpse of a woman in light-coloured clothes running to the wooded trail at the back of the house.

'We have a runner. I said we should cover the back door,' Coleman said to Miles.

'What will I tell Heskan?' Miles asked.

'Nothing is going to happen here. Tell her I've gone after the runner.'

Coleman grabbed a flashlight and ran after her. He took off his gloves and stuffed them inside his jacket pockets.

The woman had turned too sharply onto the trail, skidded on light grey compacted gravel and fallen down onto her knees. She rested for a moment as Whiskers sneaked under her arms and licked her face. She knew he wanted to be picked up as usual but it wasn't going to happen this time.

She pulled the leg of her pyjamas up past her knee to see blood oozing from small cuts. She heard someone running and saw a flashlight pointing in her direction. Like a sprinter taking off from a starting block, she launched her body down the track.

Coleman lit her body with his flashlight and shouted, '*Stop. Stand still.*'

Whiskers ran back to the man and barked. The woman stopped and looked behind. She saw the man standing with a gun and flashlight clasped between his hands. She put her hands in the air to surrender, bowed her body and inhaled deeply to catch her breath.

She looked at a blood patch on her pyjamas then at her foot and confirmed what she already knew, she'd lost a slipper. She smiled when she saw Whiskers walking behind the man. Her slipper in his mouth, flopping back and forth as Whiskers shook his head from side to side.

'I'm not going to hurt you, just relax. You need to come with us. For your safety, that's all. Everything will be good,' Coleman said to her.

The man walked toward her, holstered his gun and drew a pair of handcuffs from his belt. Whiskers ran back to the woman, her slipper still in his mouth, and then circled her before he ran back and dropped the slipper at the man's feet.

*

A Sarnia police cruiser had responded to the silent alarm. Headlights and roof lights flashed but no siren. Miles ran over to the police cruiser waving what looked like a badge in a pocket wallet. Short hair, flat cap, good coat, expensive scarf, shirt and tie, he looked official.

The Sarnia officer lowered his door window and saw two official-looking SUVs at the house. He expected to hear that first responders had everything under control. His eyes focused on the badge, and he didn't see a handgun moving to his head until too late. The Sig handgun pushed so close to his face, he could see scratches and dints on the black nitron finish.

'Call it in as a false alarm. *Do it*.' Miles demanded.

The officer looked back at the house and tried to grasp the whole scene as fast as he could. Then he stared at the man to get a good look at his face.

'Okay, buddy, easy. Control, this is Adam one-niner, responding to silent alarm B-37. Show me at Garristone Gate. *Abduction in progress*!'

Miles smashed the butt of his handgun into the side of the officer's head to knock him unconscious. The radio operator shouted back for more information.

Miles ran back to his vehicle to grab his radio from the driver's seat. He reported loudly into his radio, 'Nighthawk, be advised, LEOs have been alerted. I repeat LEOs are rolling.'

Coleman walked toward the woman on the trail. A dozen more steps and he could grab her. He stopped and looked down at the dog at his feet, and said, 'Hey there, little guy. I ain't gonna hurt you.'

He leaned down to stroke the dog. He didn't see the woman allow a kitchen knife to drop down her sleeve into her hand. She threw it straight at him. It buried in his chest and cut his aorta. In less than a minute, he would bleed out. He grasped for his radio, but passed out and died before he could speak. He slumped backwards onto the ground.

If Coleman had been given the file on the women, he would have found out that the younger woman had been classified as highly dangerous. She had killed on impulse twice before. Once when a burglar planned to attack her sister, and once when her own friend tried to kill her sister. Both of them killed with a two-pronged fork, the type used for carving meat.

Neither the blood nor her knife in the man's chest bothered the woman as she collected her slipper and put it on her foot. Without another thought, she turned and ran down the trail. Whiskers stood beside the man and started to sniff around his body. The woman stopped and slapped her hand on her thigh for Whiskers to follow.

Two

Sarnia, Canada

At the house, Modamo pushed the woman from behind while Heskan dragged her through the front door. Local law enforcement officers were *en route* so there wasn't time for the woman to dress. They hauled her out in her pyjamas, large baggy dressing gown and slippers.

Amster got into the driver's seat and fired up the engine. Peters informed Heskan that he'd cleared the house and Miles told Heskan that Coleman had gone after the other woman.

'Move your butt,' Heskan said to the woman.

Frightened, the woman screamed, 'Who are you? What do you want?'

'Shut her up,' Modamo said to Heskan.

The woman saw that her sister wasn't in their vehicle. She panicked and said, 'Wait. Where's my sister? I can't leave her here.'

'Get inside,' Heskan ordered and pushed.

The woman resisted Heskan and pleaded, 'PLEASE. Not without my sister. You don't understand. She can't cope.'

'Move,' Heskan said.

'I haven't done anything wrong,' the woman pleaded.

They ignored her protest that the handcuffs were too tight. Heskan hurriedly slapped a piece of duct tape over the woman's mouth. The edge of the tape covered more than half of her nostrils, making it strenuous for the woman to breathe.

Approaching sirens in the distance raised Heskan's blood pressure. She didn't want her team, or her first extraction to end up with a shoot-out involving Canadian police. She dragged the side door open. The woman struggled to take steps for fear of slipping on ice. Modamo pushed the woman hard in the back. She tripped over her slippers and fell into the vehicle.

Her belly crashed onto the sill of the SUV and her head banged on the metal floor panel. She lay unconscious when Modamo heaved her inside. He bundled her onto the back seat as Peters closed the side door.

Heskan leaned out of the passenger door window and told Peters to go and help Coleman find the other woman. She turned her head inside, threw an anxious look at Amster, and said, 'What are you waiting for? Get moving.'

Heskan said into her radio, 'Nighthawk-2, this is Nighthawk-5. I'm rolling with parcel-one.'

Amster grunted as she spun the steering wheel and reversed violently onto the adjacent lawn. The SUV slipped around on the frosted grass, tearing up the lawn. She gunned down the lawn, past the police cruiser at the bottom of the drive, and out of the cul-de-sac.

Peters hurried down the drive to join Miles and slipped off his feet when he tried to stop at the second SUV. Miles told Peters that he couldn't raise Coleman on the radio.

Peters tried, 'Nighthawk-9, come in. Nighthawk-9, respond.'

No reply.

'Hang tight, we're on our way,' Miles said into the radio as Peters revved the engine and made a fast three-point turn to push onto the road.

He drove to the point where the trail opened onto Telfer Road. Peters parked three car lengths back from the opening. Tall trees and large bushes lined the opening, so his vehicle wasn't visible from inside the trail. Both men got out, looked around and waited.

When the woman came running out of the trail, she stopped when she saw the two men standing at their vehicle. They watched her walk backwards into the trail. She beckoned her dog Whiskers to follow her. Both men saw puffs of moist air around her face as she panted heavily into the cold air.

Miles fetched a twelve-gauge shotgun from the back of the SUV. He settled it in his arms and took aim. He waited a few seconds for her to react.

When she saw the shotgun, she turned and started back into the trail. He fired and the shell pounded into her back, knocking her off her feet. She fell forward onto the ground.

Miles ran to her with his shotgun ready to fire again. Peters followed and they watched her try to crawl forward, but her arms and legs jerked in an uncontrolled spasm. Miles hadn't fired pellets or a slug at the woman.

He fired a wireless Taser shotgun shell. When the shell slammed into her back, four electrodes penetrated her skin and delivered an electric charge that scrambled her muscle coordination. The sharp noise from the shotgun frightened Whiskers, and he ran back to the house.

Miles lifted the woman up in a firefighter's lift and took her to his vehicle. Peters reported that he had the second parcel. He ran along the trail until suddenly he stopped short. Shocked to see a knife sticking out of Coleman's chest.

'*Geez*. Fuck. Coleman is *dead*!' he shouted into his radio.

'No names.' Heskan fired back.

Sirens announced the arrival of Sarnia police at Garristone Gate as Miles and Peters carried Coleman out of the Howard Watson Nature Trail. Just before they drove off, Miles called in to report the recovery of Nighthawk-9. Peters drove to the rendezvous point.

The first team had raced toward Lake Huron along Huron Shores Drive to Old Lakeshores Road. A speedboat called Nighthawk waited with its engine revving, ready to whisk the captured women six miles south to Lakeside Park on the US side of Lake Huron.

The driver of the speedboat spoke to Ertha Odeele, and told her one of the parcels had arrived. Ertha told Joe Koswalski to prepare for surveillance blackout.

The woman appeared to be semiconscious when Modamo and Amster manhandled her out of their vehicle. They saw a lot of blood on the seat, and on her clothes and legs. She had a gash on the side of her head, and blood had run down her neck but not enough to explain the blood on her lower body.

They laid her on her back on the ground beside the vehicle, and quickly realised she wasn't obese as they'd thought. She was pregnant. They looked at each other, confused. No-one had told them to expect a pregnant woman.

The fall onto the vehicle's sill had ruptured her womb. She had lost a lot of blood, and they had no idea whether the bleeding would stop or get worse.

Amster fetched a first aid kit from the vehicle. Heskan ran back from the speedboat to the vehicle to find out why the woman lay on the ground.

'This is a fuck-up. She's in a bad way,' Modamo said to Heskan.

Amster said to Heskan, 'She's pregnant. Why didn't you tell us?'

Heskan knelt down and checked the woman's pulse.

'She's still strong. Get her up,' she said.

Modamo threw up his arms in frustration and said, 'We can't take her on the boat like this. She'll die for sure.'

'We need to take her to a hospital,' Amster added.

Heskan ordered, 'This asset can neutralise a risk to our national security. Get her on the boat.'

'Bullshit, she won't neutralise anything if she's dead,' Modamo said.

'What are we going to do?' Amster asked.

Heskan walked away from the vehicle, raised her radio to her chin and spoke to Ertha Odeele. Her voice edged with concern as she explained the asset's condition. She confirmed that Nighthawk-9 had fallen and that LEOs were closing on her position.

'I need that asset alive,' Ertha said.

The captain of the speedboat stepped out of his cabin and shouted to Heskan, 'Canadian patrol boat on the lake has turned around. Heading our way. ETA six minutes. We need to leave now.'

'Can you outrun it?' Heskan asked.

'If we go *now*,' the captain replied.

'I think she's losing her baby,' Amster called to Heskan.

Heskan called into her radio, 'Team two, ETA?'

'Three minutes,' Miles replied.

'One minute or you remain here to face the Canadians,' Heskan said.

'Go faster for Christ's sake,' Miles said to Peters.

'Nighthawk-2, the main parcel is damaged, transport could break it. What do you want me to do?' Heskan asked.

After a long pause, Ertha replied, 'Stick to the plan.'

Three

Darlington, County Durham, England

Zoe Tampsin sat at her kitchen table with a mug of black coffee between her hands. She ran her hand over her head, sighed loudly and looked longingly at the clock. Ten minutes past four in the morning. The room felt cold and dull with a stale smell. Yellow light from the street streamed through a grey net curtain and lit up one side of the room. The other side remained dark.

She sat in the middle of the room facing the dark side. She clasped her hands around the coffee mug for warmth while she reflected on the call she received from the head of the Security Service, the previous night.

He gave her new last-minute orders. He ordered her to abandon her current operation, take Dr Gavin Shawlens with her, and go dark. He warned her to hide deep because an intensive search would be launched to find Shawlens. He had organised an unmarked Astra car for her and she drove through the night to her doghouse in Darlington.

If she stuck strictly to the go dark protocol, she would not contact anyone and keep off the grid until he contacted her again, but she felt riled. She had serious unanswered questions about the previous operation, called SLIPFIRE, and she wanted them resolved.

Now, she had unexpected orders to go dark and prepare to be hunted like a fox who'd stolen the farmer's prize lamb. It felt unreal, out of control and suspicious. Preparation, planning and organisation were her trademarks. Her new orders unsettled her to say the least.

She took her coffee and went through to the living room. Very little street light penetrated the old dark brown curtains. Her eyes had adjusted to the dark and she stared at the picture on the wall opposite her sofa. Darkness and silence were old friends she knew well.

She put her coffee on the floor near her feet, and opened her mobile phone. She had drunk too much coffee while she deliberated and agonised over the past five hours. Finally, she made up her mind, and decided to break the go dark protocol.

*

Michael Tampsin's mobile rang and woke him up from a pleasant dream. It took him a few moments to engage his brain. He noticed his wife Stella's perfume. Her indirect way of telling him she would like to make love, but he'd got into bed forty-five minutes after her.

Stella groaned a groan. *Too late, mate*, she meant as she pulled on the duvet and turned over. He switched on the bedside light beside his cabinet, and turned his head to the bedroom door when he heard the heating boiler cycling. The central heating prepared itself for another cold November morning.

His mobile phone lay on top of the bedside cabinet, still fast asleep. He reached inside the cabinet drawer for an old prepaid Nokia phone. It flashed with new importance. He sat up and sharpened up. Only three people in the world knew his Nokia phone number.

'Michael,' Zoe whispered.

'Zoe. What? Are you overseas?' Michael asked as he looked at the time.

'No. I'm at the doghouse.'

'It's four in the morning. I thought you must be overseas. Why are you at the doghouse?'

'How's Mum and Dad?'

'Fine, they're fine.'

'Stella?'

'Everyone's fine,' he said.

'How's my baby?'

'Amy is fine. She had a great time in Disneyland Paris with Alec. They just got back the other day. She's brought you back a lovely present. It's a gold-coloured—'

'Good. I'm glad she had a good time,' she interrupted and he heard tension in her voice.

'I truly love you, sis, but what are you doing at the doghouse, and why have you pulled me out of a perfectly lovely dream?'

'Michael, I'm stuck between a bullet and a bomb.'

'Oh, that sounds like a bugger of a job.'

'Yes, it is. It's been sprung on me. You know how much I hate that.'

He picked up strained concern in her voice, and he knew she'd landed in a bad place. She thrived on danger and faced fear head-on. Combat-hardened and Special Forces-trained, she had faced death many times. Her confidence weakened only when she faced something she couldn't control with smart planning and preparation. She could hide her concern from others but not from her brother.

'What can I do?'

'Nothing.'

'Do you need new rings?'

'Rings are good. Michael, if this job goes tits up, I want you to tell Dad not to believe anything the top brass say about me.'

'That sounds really bad,' he replied, and became concerned.

'No matter what they say about me, tell him to keep his powder dry. You know he thinks he has more clout than he does. He'll try to rattle the brass,' she added.

'I don't know ... he's still got powerful friends in the army.'

'This isn't an army job, it's a spooks job.'

Michael shook his head and sighed as he arranged the duvet around Stella's shoulders. He thought, *oh no, here we go again. What has she done now?* Many times, when they were at school, their teachers had called him to the staff room to tell him he needed to deal with his sister. As if he had any control over her.

She wasn't a bad child but she didn't like restrictions. Her teachers didn't like pupils who vaulted over the boundaries. Not that Michael had ever been a teacher's pet. In a fight, he got his fists out just as quick, but he had the nonce to step away from trouble at the right moment.

'Zoe, you asked me twice what they were like. I told you not to work for those clowns. It's always a chess game to them and you are nothing but a pawn in their wicked playground games.'

'Michael, when do I ever do what you tell me? Maybe you should've ordered me to go and work for them.'

'Copy that.'

The sound of her husky voice, saying his name, brought comfort to his thoughts. From her lips it sounded more personal. He loved how she always called him Michael and not Mike, Micky, Mikey or Mick as others did. He replied to those names but didn't like them. His mother called him Mikey from day one, and ever since aged two, his father called him Captain. Zoe always called him Michael.

'I'm still on the good side. It's just that people will tell Dad, I'm a traitor.'

'A traitor? Shit. Zoe. What have you done?' He forced the words out under his breath.

'I'm babysitting a boffin until my boss can figure out what to do with the baby. In the meantime I have to go dark and get the blame for kidnapping the baby.'

'What's the game plan?'

'I keep the baby in my doghouse. I'll be hunted like a wild fox. It's likely you and Dad will attract surveillance, so be on your guard. Better not warn Dad in case he kicks off.'

'Do you have backup?'

With a low sad voice she replied, 'Nada. Lonesome fox here, hiding in the blind.'

'Get some backup. That's an order.'

'I have few options on that score. When I'm branded a traitor, there will be an all-out alert on me. I can't trust anyone in Special Forces. People who know me will not believe it but they'll follow orders.'

'What about OTRs?'

'Do you know of any?'

'I'll see what I can find out from the On The Run unit. I'll let you know.'

'Phones will be risky when this kicks off.'

'Okay, if we can't talk, we'll just have to use Aunt Mary,' he said.

'Gosh. Is Mary still working?'

'Of course, I always keep her ticking over. Do you remember the protocol?'

'I'm not going to forget that in a hurry. Okay, when I've got Aunt Mary operational, I'll send a text,' she replied, and her voice lifted a few notches.

When she worked deep undercover for Special Forces, she kept in contact with her brother via a fictitious aunt.

Michael had used friends in army intelligence to create Aunt Mary with a full life history, including her current location in a large government-run retirement home.

Anyone who searched a database would find Mary Blundell allocated to room C225. In fact, she'd been double-booked with the real occupant of room C225, but since Mary remained invisible, it didn't matter for computer-based checks.

'How long will you be stuck in your doghouse?'

'Don't know for sure, maybe a week. With any luck my boss will get what he's after, and I can return the baby.'

'When is the kick-off?'

'Probably within a day, two at most,' she replied.

'Okay, I'll think of something to tell Dad and stop him going ape-shit.'

'Maybe he should go ape-shit. The spooks will be expecting it,' she said.

'I'll see how it plays. Look after yourself. You're the only sister I've got. I love you.'

'I love you more,' she replied.

'No, you don't.'

'Yes, I do. Look, Michael, thanks for this little chat. I needed it badly. Now go back to your dream, big boy.'

Zoe picked up her coffee and relaxed on her old sofa. Speaking to her brother and knowing she could open a line of communication through Aunt Mary, had eased her concerns. Even though she oozed confidence, she still touched base with her brother to recharge her self-belief. A ritual they had done for each other since they were young kids when they had to look out for each other in unfamiliar schools in foreign parts of the world.

Their father had dragged the family around the world from one military base to another, until finally their mother put her foot down. When Zoe reached her mid-teens, she insisted on a stable home in the UK.

They had been baptised in the army, brought up on base camps, and taught to be fearless. So with a feeling of inevitability, they'd followed their father into an army career. The Tampsin family could trace their military history back more than 180 years.

Zoe's career had been hard on her marriage, and she'd divorced Alec Haymarket after ten years. In their dysfunctional family, Alec had taken the role of parenting their daughter Amy while Zoe went away on active duty. For Amy's first ten months, Zoe had been a good mother, and then the parental roles were reversed.

Her career took off, and she spent long periods away on duty. Alec looked after Amy and became an expert in baby and toddler training. The inevitable downside meant Amy became a daddy's girl and always sided with her father, which Zoe found hard to accept.

Zoe took another sip of her extra strong coffee and remembered the night she said she wanted a divorce. Alec had tried desperately to talk her out of it but she remained determined to set herself free. The conversation echoed loudly in her mind.

'Why won't you give me more time?' Alec had said.

'Time waits for no woman,' she had replied harshly.

'This is so unfair. I've loved you since the first day we met. I don't know what else you want from me. It's unfair on Amy.'

'Leave Amy out of this. We move on, and she'll be the better for it.'

'You know that's not true. She wants us both, together. I want us to stay together. We're a wonderful family. You've said that.'

'Amy wants what you tell her. I'm not blind. She'll understand my reasons when she becomes a woman. End of,' she had said, and then stormed off.

Looking back, it had been a horrible chapter in Zoe's life. Now, one year on, the intense fireworks she'd wanted in her personal life hadn't materialised. Slowly, as if reluctant to admit defeat, she allowed Amy to bring them closer together. She and Alec had remained close friends after all. They both knew her plan. Amy didn't hide her motive and they played along to keep Amy believing in her dream.

Amy wanted them to get over their personal problems and re-marry. Others in the family believed they would reconcile, especially with head bridesmaid, Amy, actively planning their second wedding and their second honeymoon.

Zoe believed she would be the lead parent when Amy started to develop into a woman. Zoe had plans for Amy's teenage years and she looked forward to the challenges. After all, she'd been a rough-tough, knife-throwing, tree-climbing, harum-scarum nightmare. Who better to understand the trauma of adolescence and show Amy the ropes?

*

Zoe's doghouse, a small two-bedroom mid-terraced house stood inconspicuously in a quiet part of Darlington. It had a light red brick face and had a dark green front door. The front door opened into a narrow hall where doors on the right led to the living room and the dining room. At the end of the hall, stairs led to the bedrooms and the bathroom.

A door in the dining room led to the kitchen at the back of the house and the back yard. The house appeared dowdy, dull and had been furnished with old second-hand furniture. Perfect for making the house unattractive to house burglars.

Enclosed with high walls on all sides, the back yard had a bottle-green wood gate that led to a narrow service lane behind the houses. A secret doghouse didn't need to be pretty, it just needed to be safe. A simple place no-one knew about, where she could disappear to when necessary. In her doghouse, she had the company of a safe old friend.

She climbed the stairs to look in on Gavin Shawlens. She found him still fast asleep on the bed in her spare room. She fetched two old army blankets from a cupboard, placed one over Gavin, and one around her shoulders as she returned to her sofa in the living room.

She couldn't sleep. She opened the backpack her boss had left for her in the Astra car. The conversation she'd with her boss, Sir Milton Johnson, not more than seven hours ago, still rang in her ears.

An image of Johnson popped into her mind. She had seen Johnson a few times at briefings. A sixty-four-year-old, medium height at five-six and carrying thirty kilos overweight. He had a round doughy-looking white face.

He'd spent too many years stuck in an office chair. His hair had receded and he persisted in combing the remaining thin strands of side hair back over his bald head. She remembered thinking, *if he'd been my dad, I would wait until he fell asleep, and then cut off those stupid looking strands of hair on his head.*

When he called, he'd told her that Dr Gavin Shawlens would soon be in grave danger. She already had Shawlens under her protection, so he ordered Zoe to take him and go dark. He told her the Prime Minister had informed a meeting of COBRA that Shawlens had something, probably knowledge, worth tens of billions of dollars to the US.

He'd said the Americans wanted to buy Shawlens 'as if he was a bloody pizza pie' and that the PM had agreed to sell him to the CIA. Johnson told her to hide Shawlens, to allow him more time to find out why Shawlens had such a high price on his head.

Johnson had said she couldn't have a safe house so she had used her own doghouse. He'd organised an untracked car and a basic field pack plus cash. He alone would be her contact. He'd put a ghost phone in the pack for direct contact and told her to deactivate her standard issue secure encrypted mobile (SEM) satellite phone.

Johnson warned her that when the shit hit the fan, all the security sisters and cousins would hunt for her and Shawlens. He told her not to trust anyone in the Security Services, not even her friends.

He'd said she would be labelled a traitor, an enemy of the country, to be killed on sight. Unusually for a covert operation, he'd given her formal written orders. He wanted to assure her that her backside and her exemplary career were covered when she completed the job.

Johnson had insisted she should avoid a confrontation. He told her to go dark and deep until he told her she could reappear. She'd discovered to her shock why he insisted on no confrontation. He hadn't supplied any weapons.

The only weapons she had were her own Browning 9mm she carried with her and another Browning she had hidden in her doghouse. In total she had six rounds of ammunition.

Johnson had foisted the operation on her without an opportunity to re-equip. In her book, meticulous planning and preparation were essential for any operation. Poor preparation made her feel cautious, and no preparation made her feel vulnerable.

Michael told her to get support and she knew he'd made the right call. If she did find people to help her, what could she give them to defend themselves? Not much more than swear words and threatening behaviour. Unacceptable in her book.

She checked the empty clip in her second Browning, hoping it had somehow re-filled since the last time she looked at it. Still not full. She imagined her doghouse surrounded by CIA agents. Windows smashing, door crashing, flash bangs, an intense firefight to protect Shawlens, and then those awful four words. 'I'm out of ammo.'

Four

Later that morning, Gavin Shawlens woke and felt disorientated. They had arrived in the middle of a murky night after a long drive from Cosham, Hampshire. He didn't do any driving but he went to bed and straight to sleep.

Still half-asleep, he trundled down the stairs with heavy footsteps, through the dining room to the small narrow kitchen.

Zoe had made fresh black coffee. He discovered the damp, dusty smell of a cold and unloved that hadn't had a visitors for five months.

Zoe hadn't slept and although she didn't look fresh and bright, her mind still a sharp razor edge. His clothes had creased and curled at the edges because he'd slept in the ones he wore the day before.

Light brown cord trousers, blue shirt under a crew neck sweater and soft brown boots. His hair on one side stood up because of the way he'd lay his head on the pillow. She greeted him with a smile.

'Good morning, sleepyhead.'

'Morning, Zoe. You've got thirty-six messages on your machine.'

'I know, I've checked the caller IDs, they're just the usual spalls.'

'Spalls?'

'Spam calls, solar panels, surveys and the like.'

She noticed him staring. 'What?'

'Nothing, I'm still not fully awake.'

She had changed out of the rugged, dark blue military-type clothes, and looked more like a woman than a soldier. She had changed into a short skirt and long sleeve grey turtleneck top. She wore her black hair in a smart tousled pageboy style.

She ran her hand over her head and most of her fringe stayed up, revealing more of her face than he'd seen when her hair sat neatly set around her face.

He liked her new domestic look, especially her bare legs. It wasn't as if he hadn't seen her legs before. He'd seen them many times in the Cosham flat when she wore her pyjama shorts in the evening.

He could even point out the scars from her war injuries. But he had never seen those sculptured legs under a sexy tan-coloured suede skirt.

The suede looked stiff, and probably hadn't been worn for a long time as it stood an inch off her legs. Each time she moved or turned her body, his heart skipped a beat.

Zoe Tampsin stood five-eight in a slender and athletic-looking body. During the short time he'd known her, she had proved her intelligence and determination. That much Gavin knew. He didn't know that the forty-three-year-old had joined the OTC at her university and went on to receive the coveted Sword of Honour as the best officer cadet during the Sovereign's Parade at Sandhurst. A glorious day for Zoe and her military family as the first ever Tampsin to receive the Sword of Honour.

It wouldn't have surprised Gavin because he'd seen the sharp end of her power during the SLIPFIRE operation. Like a highly driven blue-chip businesswoman, she had an intense field of awareness and unquestionable self-confidence. In the last week alone, she had saved his life twice.

'Why did we have to bail out of Cosham?' he asked.

'While you were having your shower last night, I received word that the people who had us under surveillance were planning to attack the flat. So, I've brought you to my doghouse. It's a safe place I keep in case I need to disappear for a few days.'

'I thought Toni and the Special Forces guys were waiting outside the flat to deal with any trouble.'

'I received new orders from the head of the Security Service to move you to safety,' she said.

'Why me?'

'If a firefight broke out at the flat, he didn't want you in the middle of it.'

She lied convincingly but remained conscious of his childlike tendency to unleash a barrage of questions when he felt out of the loop.

'Where are we?'

'Darlington, County Durham.'

'I've never been in Darlington. Is it a nice town?'

'Afraid you won't see much. We need to remain invisible.'

'Why?'

'Johnson has ordered us to go dark.'

'For how long?'

'Not long.'

'Why go dark?'

'Orders. Johnson has taken direct control of our situation. I have direct contact with him. When he says it's safe, we will surface. No more than a few days, a week at most. By the way, I've deactivated your SEM phone.'

'What about Alan Cairn? Does he know where we are?'

'No-one knows about my doghouse. That's the point. It's secure from enemy peekers and friendly leakers.'

'What about our debriefing in London?'

'The SLIPFIRE operation is over for the moment. We are in a different situation. Johnson is in control of this one. We have to trust him. We have to sit tight and wait until he issues further orders.'

'Is that normal? I mean for the head of the Security Service to take operational control. I don't wish to speak ill of him but is he any good? Wasn't he a career civil servant? Is he a safe pair of hands?'

'Yes,' she said, loudly enough to let him know she felt annoyed with the questions.

Her voice and expression were clear. Enough questions. But he didn't allow that to hold him back. He paused only for a few minutes to stare at his coffee. The aroma had gone six months ago when the jar had first been opened.

Gavin stood the same height as Zoe and he kept his body lean and in good shape with jogging and occasional visits to his university judo club.

Zoe liked his laid back and unthreatening manner, and she found his boyish looks and occasional incredulous gaze or huge grin pleasing to watch.

When they first met, she'd been jealous of the extraordinary blue-green gems he had for eyes. His hair had changed from a light straw colour in summer months to a darker colour in November. She liked men's hair to be short and neat, and since his hair had grown an inch over his collar, she reminded him almost every day that he needed a haircut.

She also told him to stop trying to look like a student. She had marked him down as a hopeless academic whose apparent naivety of basic things had proved unhelpful and irritating. She hadn't decided whether his naivety appeared genuine or put on for effect.

'When did we arrive last night?'

'Just before four this morning. You've slept for five hours,' she said.

'God, it feels so much longer,' he said as he stretched his arms in front of his body.

'You had a noisy nightmare but you settled down so I didn't wake you.'

'Thanks. I had a really bad dream, that's all. Any milk?' he said as he stirred his coffee.

'The cupboard is bare. I'll pick up some supplies later. How long have you been having nightmares?'

'Since I went on meds after my transplant,' he replied.

'I read about your scrap with James Barscadden. You're lucky to be alive.'

'They gave me a new stomach and put me on anti-rejection meds. The nightmares started soon after I left hospital.'

'The drugs have probably loosened your brain. We'll just have to wait and see if that provides an improvement or not,' she said, and smiled.

'Any chance of a hot shower?'

'Any chance you know how to service a central heating boiler?'

They both went through to the dining room and she finished ironing her jeans while he watched. He sat at an old square dining room table that had lost its shine decades ago. None of the four dining chairs matched each other or the table. His hands gripped around the cup for heat.

He'd had a few nightmares during their stay in Cosham and Zoe thought they were nothing more than a nuisance, until Johnson told her they could be significant.

Zoe recalled the instruction given by Johnson when she told him about Gavin's nightmares. He had said, 'Zoe, this could be very important. Tease out his nightmare. It might be the key we need.'

'Is it the same nightmare when you're freezing cold and you don't know where you are?' she asked.

His voice quivered as he replied, 'Yes. It's dark and I can't see anything. I have a terrible feeling of being lost. I think I'm inside the cabin of a boat, there's not much room to move about. I'm stuck and sinking fast. Water is flooding in everywhere. There's a door I keep reaching for but I can't get to it. I know if I can only reach the door, I'll be able to get out. I can't reach it; the water covers my head. I panic and wake up.'

'What else can you remember before you wake up?'

'The boat hits the bottom with an almighty bang of metal. It sort of bounces up and I bang my head on the roof. I feel I'm going to pass out and swallow freezing water. I panic when the water covers my head, and then I pass out,' he said.

She saw that just telling her the story had freaked him out. For him, the experience had become too real and too frightening. For her, something significant lurked in there, something worth billions of dollars according to Johnson, but she couldn't see it.

'I know it's painful for you, but rewind the images and look around to see if there is anything else that might explain what happened. Do you know how you got into the cabin?'

He looked as though he held something back when he said, 'No, I don't know. I don't want to think about it.'

She moved closer to him and said, 'Gavin, you need to concentrate and spit it out. Trust me, you'll feel tremendous relief and the nightmare will dissipate. It won't bother you anymore.'

She put her hand on his shoulder to reassure him. He took a deep breath as if about to plunge his head into water, and then he let it out slowly.

'It doesn't make any sense to me,' he said.

'Of course it doesn't make sense. It won't until you let each piece of the jigsaw rise to the surface. When you have all the pieces, you'll have a picture. Tell me what you have.'

'In previous nightmares I've heard voices. I'm underwater so I thought it to be nonsense. Last night, after the water covered my head and I passed out, I woke up with bright lights on my face. I can't see anything but I can hear people talking. I think they are the same voices as before. They sound relaxed and casual but I sense they're talking about me, not to me. I can feel someone has a hold of my arm then I feel a cold needle lifting the skin on my arm. Then I pass out again.'

'The voices, are they familiar or foreign? Are they English? Do you recognise the accent?'

'They're faint but not Scottish or English. Canadian maybe?'

'American?'

'I'm not sure. It's as if I'm just waking up and hear the voices in the distance. It's difficult to focus on them. It's only a dream so it could be anything.'

Zoe felt a rush of exhilaration. At last, she had something to tell Johnson. Something that sounded significant. Maybe, the key Johnson wanted to find. She saw Gavin's face light up as though he'd remembered something important.

'What else?' she asked.

'Nothing else,' he said, but she saw in his eyes he had lied.

'What have I told you about nothing ever being nothing?'

'It's probably more nonsense.'

'I'll be the judge.'

'It's the first time I've ever had this happen in the nightmare.'

'Come on, Gavin, spit it out.'

'I opened my eyes and I'm on my back. I felt extremely sad, heartbroken, like I did when my mother died. I don't think I've ever had that feeling in a dream before.'

'Are you in an ambulance?'

'Not an ambulance. I don't think … it doesn't move but then maybe an ambulance doesn't move in a dream. I don't know. Uugghh, I hate this nightmare. I don't want to think about it.'

'For God's sake, man, get a grip of yourself.' She raised her voice aggressively.

Gavin got up and went into the living room to be alone. He stood at the window and looked at the rain falling in sheets outside. He watched a woman across the road pushing a baby buggy with one hand and dragging her young child along the street with the other. Her long hair soaking wet and clumped together like rat's tails. He'd seen the look before and his eyes welled up.

She sighed loudly. He wasn't one of her obedient soldiers so she couldn't boss him around so easily. He'd recently lost the love of his life, Emma Patersun, and his grief still felt raw, which made him fragile.

Zoe brought him a fresh cup of black coffee. He hadn't touched the first cup. Zoe's coffee looked like liquid tar. She stood beside him and saw water in his eyes as he watched the woman outside.

'Does she remind you of Emma?' Zoe asked.

'Yes. It's as if I'm still walking around with a gaping hole in my body. It won't heal. I can't make the grief go away. I met her when I turned sixteen and I always believed we would grow old together. It's just terrible to know she's not here.'

'It's a mixture of anger and sadness. They don't go away quickly but you'll come through it. You know she wants you to come through it, don't you?'

Emotion strained his voice as he said, 'I'm living in a terrible blank space. I don't know how to get her back.'

'You can't get her back. You need to accept that before you can move on,' she said.

'I can't, if I see someone with her look, memories flood back. I fall back and I feel worse than before.'

He looked ready to burst into tears. She drew him close and gave him a hug. He wasn't a tough soldier. She couldn't snap a soft academic out of his thoughts by getting in his face and shouting the odds.

'In the army, we have bereavement counselling. They tell you that crying can help the recovery. Have you cried for

Emma?' she said as she released her hug and held his wrists in her hands.

His head remained down while he shook it gently. He looked distraught as he confessed, 'I can't cry. I want to cry. I can't do it.'

'You shouldn't bottle it up, you must let her go. Emma wouldn't want you to be trapped like this. I believe if you don't let them go, they cannot find rest.'

Her grip on his wrists tightened. For a moment, it felt like she wanted to shake some sense into him, but she released her grip and let him go.

'I know, but I can't help it,' he said, and gave her a watery smile.

'I wish I could help you move on quickly, but it takes time. You'll never get over her death, but you must learn to live again. Come on, get yourself straightened up.'

She boiled two kettles for hot water, and he headed upstairs to the bathroom. Thirty minutes later, he emerged, washed, shaved and with his hair neatly combed. He found Zoe in the living room. His state of mind as near to normal as possible.

Five

Zoe headed through to the kitchen. Gavin followed then turned back to sit at the dining room table. He sat with his fingers steepled on the table, looking like a humbled schoolboy, waiting for his breakfast. She fetched a can of pineapple chunks, two plates, a can of peach halves, a can opener, and plonked them on the table.

'Make yourself busy,' she said.

He feigned a struggle with the can opener, then shook the can of pineapple in his hand.

'What?'

'Both of these are past their sell by date,' he said.

'So?'

'Nothing, they're okay, they haven't blown.'

'I may not be a top scientist, but I do know about botulism.'

'Sorry, of course. I'm cautious because I've worked with the botulism toxin and it made me wary of out-of-date tinned food.'

'You've worked with botulism toxin?'

'Yes, I've used it as an enzyme inhibitor.'

'Now, you see, that's interesting. One day you'll need to tell me about that work. I'd like to know more about botulism toxin.'

'Do you mean the Botox stuff?'

'Cheeky beggar. Never mind my face. I'll Botox your tongue for you.'

They both laughed and their tension eased for a few minutes. The back of her mind had been working on a plan to deal with their situation.

While she paced back and forth across the room, she wrote out a list of the equipment that she needed.

'Won't Alan Cairn be worried that we've just dropped off the grid?'

'Johnson will tell Cairn we're off-line. The SLIPFIRE debriefing will be rescheduled for a later date. So don't worry about it,' she said, and her tone told him to be quiet while she concentrated on her list.

Zoe and Gavin had completed an investigation for the Lambeth Group into illegal research at the University of South England.

Their controller in the Security Service (formerly MI5), Alan Cairn, Head of the Centre for Protection of National Infrastructure (CNPI), had headed back to London.

At the end of their operation, Zoe had discovered the flat they shared in Cosham had been under covert surveillance.

To discover who lay behind the surveillance, Zoe had set a trap with Gavin Shawlens as bait. Before the trap had been sprung, Sir Milton Johnson called Zoe at the flat and ordered her to take Gavin, go dark and wait for further instructions.

'Okay, I guess my job is not to reason why.'

'That's correct. Good man, and for God's sake stop staring at my arse, unless you want a clout across your face,' she said when she saw a reflection of his head and shoulders on the glass panel of a wall cabinet.

Zoe felt disengaged by the strange circumstances. One minute, she'd been the team leader at the centre of an important operation, and then as if a switch had been flicked, she'd been sent to a dark corner with orders to hide and remain hidden. Her discomfort made worse by the fact she had six bullets for her handgun. She felt totally unprepared for any action.

She hated lack of preparation because in military operations it put people at risk. In a surge of determination, she decided to trust her instinct and work around her orders. She thought, *things go wrong in this business and I'm not going to be the one unable to save our skins if the job goes pear-shaped.*

Gavin dispensed tinned fruit onto dinner plates for their breakfast. After they'd eaten, Zoe used her landline phone to call an ex-soldier she knew well and trusted.

William Carrhage owned a garage in Faverdale, an industrial area on the outskirts of Darlington. Known as 'Spock', on account of his pointy Vulcan-like ears, he'd helped Zoe out with equipment and transport on previous occasions.

In fact, she chose to locate her doghouse in Darlington to be close to Spock's garage. Zoe had saved Spock's life twice, and he would do anything for her including give up his own life if she asked. They shared a soldier's secret that would bind them together until death parted them.

Zoe and Spock had served together in Afghanistan. Spock had been on patrol and as he returned to Camp Bastion, he came under a mortar attack that hit a building near his position. The building blew out and covered him with rubble.

Other members of his patrol returned fire. Zoe and two American Special Forces soldiers out of Camp Leatherhead rushed to the building. They found Spock and started heaving lumps of rubble to the side with their bare hands. They worked in total darkness to avoid giving their position to the enemy.

Spock's groans guided them, and after what felt like ages, they found his face and wiped the dust out of his mouth and nose. When they pulled him out, covered in blood, he had crush injuries and a piece of metal rod from the building embedded in his back. He suffered a stroke as they stretchered him to the Camp Bastion medical room.

It had been the second time Zoe had saved his life, but this time his injuries were so severe he'd been medically discharged out of the army. Whenever they talked together, or with other people, they would never talk about the first time she'd saved his life. Zoe didn't want to remember it, let alone talk about it.

She had bleached it out of her mind but Spock remembered every second as if it happened yesterday. Spock should have talked it out with a therapist to help him recover from post-traumatic stress disorder. Zoe made him promise never to discuss it with anyone and he'd kept his word.

Gavin went upstairs to stretch out on his bed and be alone with thoughts of his childhood sweetheart, Emma Patersun.

Zoe called up to the bedroom, 'Make yourself at home. I'm going out to get supplies. I'll be back in an hour. I might have a little job for you to do.'

'What job? I thought we had to stay dark,' he called back.

He got up and walked to the top of the stairs to find out more, but arrived just in time to see the front door closing behind Zoe.

'What job?' he said to the door.

Gavin stared at the door for a minute, and then sighed with frustration as he went down the stairs and into the living room. He strayed over to the television in the corner, an old cabinet box at least twenty years old with a portable analogue aerial on top. TV signals were digital, so the analogue television wouldn't work. Still, he switched it on and off several times but it didn't produce a picture or sound.

In the living room, the furniture comprised a three-seat sofa, one armchair, one dining room chair and one small coffee table with a rack underneath for newspapers. Some of the newspapers were five years old. In all of the rooms, the original floorboards were stained dark brown.

No chance of anyone sneaking around the house without the floorboards making an announcement. He creaked over to the coffee table and lifted an old newspaper then returned to the sofa. He stared through the newspaper and brought back memories of Emma Patersun.

*

Zoe drove the black and silver Astra to Spock's garage. She handed the keys to Spock and told him it needed a new identity. Johnson had provided the Astra for her escape from Cosham but it wouldn't be long before it became too hot to drive in the streets.

Zoe sat in Spock's garage office as they discussed how to source her list of equipment. She explained to him why she had moved to her doghouse and that she would be the subject of a massive hunt.

'My boss has dropped me into a hole. I'm not equipped,' she complained.

'Let me cover your back. I'm still good. I won't let you down.'

'No, Spock. I need to know I have a safe port here if the weather becomes murderous,' she replied.

'Sure?'

'Yes,' she said, and handed him her list. 'How much of this can you get for me?'

'Most of this I can get easily but weapons and ammo are tricky at the moment. What about your own contacts?'

'Normally, I could access black market equipment, but when the word goes out that I'm rogue, I'll be exposed.'

'If the word is out on you then I can't use the black market either. The black market network can provide anything for a price but loyalty is thin. For a better price, a seller will give you up in a heartbeat. I could try—'

'Don't sweat it, Spock. I have another plan for weapons and ammo. I know of a private stash hidden in Morpeth.'

'Can I help?'

'I know the layout like the back of my hand. I'll be able to slip in and out before anyone has time to think,' she said.

Zoe had a lot of time and patience for Spock. Although a man in his early fifties, army service had taken its toll, so he looked older and more infirm than he should for his age. He stood a few inches shorter than Zoe, and he'd become twenty kilos overweight since his medical discharge.

He kept his white and downy hair short, and he had a white moustache to hide a horrible looking shrapnel scar over his top lip. His nose had been smashed and his nostrils had flattened out.

Spock gave Zoe the keys to a dark-red, ten-year-old, Ford Transit van. He said the van would get her to hell and back. They laughed when she asked him how he knew her travel plans. While Zoe finished her coffee, Spock applied a coat of special clear lacquer to the windscreen. He said the lacquer contained special nanoparticles to produce light reflection defects to distort images taken by facial recognition cameras.

Before she left, they went through their little ritual that only they knew about. They hugged and he held on to her for dear life. While she held him, his body shook and he apologised repeatedly for his tears and his weakness. She hugged him tightly.

For a few minutes, he would relive the night in Bosnia when she saved his life for the first time. Water filled his eyes, ran down his cheeks and he sniffed to stop it running down his nose.

Holding Zoe as he'd done that night brought him great comfort and reassurance. When a bout of depression gripped him, he felt trapped in the darkest corner of hell, surrounded by the enemy as they prepared to tear his body apart, organ by organ.

In Bosnia, she had reached down like a giant angel, grabbed his collar and pulled him out. His vivid memory would never let him forget where he'd been, but a hug from Zoe reminded him what she'd done that night. He owed her a debt he could never repay, but he would die trying, if only she would just ask him to do it.

At her insistence, they made a pact never to talk about that night to each other or to anyone. His pact with Zoe meant he refused treatment for severe post-traumatic stress disorder.

When she felt his body ease, she kissed him gently on the side of his face and relaxed her hug. This hug gave him emotional release, and peace of mind.

'I wish I had your strength.'

'Spock, you're still alive. You have Pat and she's a wonderful wife. Start from there and don't look back.'

'How do you deal with what we went through?'

'I just do, Spock. What else can I do? I know that it's hard for you but you must never speak of that night. You understand, don't you?'

'Of course. Watch your back,' he said as she got into the red van.

Six

White House, Washington, USA

General George Schumantle, Chairman of the Joint Chiefs of Staff (JCS), waited patiently in the Oval Office in the White House. He sat in civilian clothes with Director CIA Katherine Kaplentsky. He didn't know how much President Cranstoun had told Katherine about the POINT-K issue, so he didn't speak of it.

Instead, they discussed Bill Maverack, a former CIA Director of the National Clandestine Service who had crossed swords with George Schumantle, and came off much the worse.

Katherine had removed Maverack from office, and had his memory redacted to clear his mind of national secrets he had no right to possess. With that awkward discussion out of the way, she picked up some of her paperwork and started reading.

George watched her as she flicked through a briefing paper. He would never say it, but he admired her greatly. She had a strong self-confidence that came from her rapid rise through the ranks to the top of the CIA. She had striking and disarming good looks.

Tall with long slender legs, Katherine had flawless lightly tanned skin, sparkling sea-green eyes and strong dark red hair that any model would be proud to have. She kept her hair long and free. But at work, she wore her hair in a neat chignon, so her full face remained visible for those pointed facial expressions to make their mark.

In another life, she could have been a successful model or a great lawyer. Her work suits were expensive, tailored and decorated her body with finesse. All of this and the IQ of a mastermind.

They both knew the President had taken a call from the British Prime Minister, and they were anxious to find out the outcome.

A door opened, a Secret Service agent scanned the room, and then stepped aside for President Cranstoun to pass without altering his stride.

He walked straight to his desk and sat down. He slammed both palms on his desk in frustration. His face twisted with anger. The Secret Service agent closed the door.

Cranstoun blasted, 'These fucking useless Brits. They've not kept to the deadline because Shawlens and his minder have disappeared. Damn them.'

'Brits. Unreliable as ever,' George said.

'We need to take total control of this situation,' Cranstoun urged.

'Maybe they just need a bit more time,' Katherine said.

'Time has run *out*.'

'Yes, Mr President.'

'Katherine, I want you to go to London. Suspend all other European operations and focus on the capture or removal of this man. I need this done yesterday, please, for God's sake. Flood their island with your people and coordinate the manhunt. Find this man before—'

'Before what, Mr President?'

Cranstoun shook his head. 'All you need to know, Katherine, is this. If that man reveals a POINT-K secret then this administration and this country will drop straight into hell. Everything we have, everything we cherish, will be burned. That's not going to happen, Katherine, because *you're* going to do whatever it takes to eliminate this threat.'

Bill Maverack had lost his CIA job because he insisted that he as Head of NCS should know everything about POINT-K. Katherine had warned him that some secrets were beyond a security clearance. She understood POINT-K sat squarely in that category, and she wasn't going to ask questions. She wasn't going to follow Bill Maverack into the waste bin.

'Understood, Mr President.'

'George has forty-three military intelligence personnel in London, and another sixty-two arriving from Europe. The NSA has been re-tasked. They are waiting for your London station to feed them input. Resources are in place. Use all of them to get the job done quickly.'

'Can we access the British surveillance service at GCHQ?' she asked.

George answered the question. 'No need. They're already linked into Prism. They don't know that we've set Prism up as a one-way mirror with GCHQ. Everything the Brits get is already mirrored to NSA. We control what is reflected back to them.'

Cranstoun got up and came around to lean against the side of the desk. He looked solemn and determined.

'Listen to me carefully, both of you. I know the military and the CIA have serious issues dating back to Vietnam. You must put these to one side. I want both of you to impress upon your people that all US personnel will work as one body on this matter. Any inter-agency rivalry or non-cooperation, from any person at any level, will be dealt with severely. Gloves off. This is bare knuckle stuff,' Cranstoun emphasised.

They both nodded, and looked at each other for agreement.

'Tell your people this is a direct and potent threat from me,' Cranstoun said.

'This Shawlens disappearance can't be a coincidence. The Brits must be up to something,' Katherine said.

George said, 'Obviously, they want to know why we have put such a huge price on Shawlens. If the positions were reversed, I would be desperate to find out. They still want the deal. They're trying to interrogate Shawlens off-line. We just can't allow that to continue.'

'My contact in the Security Service has passed on details of an asset that could be very useful. Can I sanction an incursion into Canada to collect it?' Katherine asked.

'Do it. I'll speak to the Canadian PM if there are any ruffled feathers.'

'Okay, I'll move on it right away,' Katherine said, and stood up.

She looked sharp and focused as though she wanted to get into action as soon as possible. Cranstoun walked with her with his arm open to guide her to the door.

'Thanks, Katherine. Please keep me updated. Remember this is a tight ship. People only need to know that Shawlens is a threat to our national security. Nothing more, you understand.'

Cranstoun opened the door for her. They faced each other as they stood in the doorframe. He patted her on the arm and said, 'You can go where others cannot. You can succeed where others have failed. Strength to your arms, Katherine. It's time for you to show me how great you are, and how smart I've been to appoint you Director CIA.'

Katherine bowed her head deferentially to Cranstoun, and then turned to face her deputy waiting outside. They walked hurriedly along the corridor.

Katherine asked, 'Where is Ertha Odeele at the moment?'

'She's in New York.'

'Good, get me her number, I have an urgent job for her.'

Cranstoun sat on a chair opposite George. The strain on his face seemed even more marked than when George first told him of the existence of POINT-K secrets.

George asked, 'How much have you told Katherine?'

'Not much. Don't forget she has a legal background. I don't want a debate about the legal ramifications of POINT-K. All I want Katherine to do is focus on Shawlens and resolve that issue. It's her job to keep the secrets secret, not to wrestle with their significance.'

'I do believe she understands the distinction clearly,' George replied.

'When she has done that job and POINT-K is secure. I want it to remain in place. It must again become totally secret. I've thought a lot about the original premise and I want to keep that option in reserve.'

'What do your Chief of Staff and the cabinet think about it?' George said.

'I haven't told them about the POINT-K secret. I told them we have a serious threat to national security. They need to know something is responsible for all of this activity in England, but I've said nothing about the real reason. Apart from you, I'm the only one who is aware of the POINT-K problem.'

'Until the end of your presidency, then that knowledge will be redacted,' George said.

'I look forward to that. I certainly don't want to dwell on the circumstances that will necessitate the use of this resource. That's a nightmare I'm happy to leave for a future president.'

'You can envisage a future scenario when we'll need this POINT-K?'

'Yes, George, I'm certain it will save our country and our people. I want it to be waiting there, ready to come to our aid.'

'As you wish, Mr President.'

They both stood and shook hands then Cranstoun said, 'Shawlens cannot be permitted to set this country back a hundred years. Give Katherine anything she needs. No matter the cost or the collateral damage in England.'

'It won't happen, Mr President. The Brits are simply stalling to find out why we want Shawlens. I'll force them to hand him over sooner rather than later.'

'I hope so, George, because I spoke with Jack at the Treasury last night. What he told me kept me awake all night, and made me physically sick this morning. Hypothetically speaking, his current estimate is that people and banks in countries all over the world are holding over eight hundred billion dollars in banknotes. If a crisis precipitates a run on our currency, then he estimates he can cover no more than five hundred billion from the Federal Reserve.

'After that, the country will be bankrupt. If it runs to the full eight hundred billion then the country will never recover. You do realise, George, if that is allowed to happen, then every scrap of military hardware that can be sold, will be sold, to generate cash to keep the country afloat. Our military as we know it will be finished. There will be another president after me, but you, George, will go down in military history as the last Chairman of the Joint Chiefs of Staff. Make sure that POINT-K does not end our way of life.'

'I hear you loud and clear, Mr President. Loud and *crystal* clear.'

'One more thing, George.'

'Yes, Mr President.'

'I don't want another of these damn POINT-K secrets popping out of the woodwork during the remainder of my presidency. One is quite sufficient for my nerves to cope with.'

*

George Schumantle came from a family with a long history in the military, and he fitted the picture perfectly. As Chairman of the Joint Chiefs of Staff, he'd reached the highest position possible in the US military and his family were immensely proud of his achievements. As a trim fifty-nine-year-old, George stood proudly at five-ten with short salt and pepper hair neatly parted on one side.

Only rarely did he venture out of his highly decorated uniform. But when he did shed his uniform, he liked to dress in expensive tailored clothes and designer shoes. Off duty, he liked to laugh and he travelled around the country to hear top comedians. He'd seen his favourite, Louis C.K., more than a dozen times over the past twenty years.

In his military version of the President's state limo, 'The Beast', George Schumantle relaxed and told his driver not to hurry back to the Pentagon. His PA read out a series of matters and communications that had arrived in the office while George met with Cranstoun.

While his PA talked, George thought about the desperate situation that had unfolded on his watch as Chairman of the JCS and guardian of the POINT-K secrets. He had always hoped that in his period of service as Chairman, he would not be called upon to deal with a POINT-K secret. Then Gavin Shawlens surfaced and his hopes crashed out.

The POINT-K scheme had been instigated in the 1950s to protect the most vital US secrets. A small group of powerful men had acknowledged that politicians came and went with the seasons, and some of them were little more than shallow attention seekers. Some were hollow weaklings, who couldn't keep a real secret even if their life depended on it. Good front men for voters to exercise their democratic rights, but not safe pairs of hands for the most critical state secrets.

Top military commanders and heads of intelligence services had worked with some politicians who were careless, indiscreet, and open to blackmail. While service personnel and security agents were more trustworthy, they were human beings who could be turned, blackmailed or fooled into revealing secrets.

So, the most vital of the USA's secrets were held securely by one person, the Chairman of the Joint Chiefs. The POINT-K secrets remained in the Chairman's vault until events unfolded that necessitated engagement with the President of the day and government agencies. George had informed Cranstoun of the existence of POINT-K secrets and explained that the acronym meant 'president only informed if needs to know'.

All of the POINT-K secrets had remained safely hidden with no chance of exposure except for POINT-K4. A single act of compassion eighteen years ago had created a loose end, Gavin Shawlens. For eighteen years, Shawlens had been loosely monitored by discreet surveillance, and until recently the POINT-K4 secret had remained secure.

Then Gavin Shawlens became involved in a fight for his life with the criminal James Barscadden. The fight had nearly ended Gavin's life, and he required emergency medical treatment. The treatment had altered his memory patterns.

Old memories started to drift back into his mind and became manifest as nightmares. In time, Gavin would recall his memory of POINT-K4 and the US would face a global threat to their national security.

When the special agent monitoring Shawlens reported her concerns about his nightmares, George Schumantle ordered preventative action to ensure POINT-K4 remained in his vault. George figured it would not be too long before Shawlens posed an unacceptable risk. Shawlens had to be sacrificed for the greater good.

An early attempt to capture, interrogate then execute Shawlens had failed. Then a second attempt to execute him in Prague also failed because Shawlens had been placed under the protection of a Special Forces team led by Zoe Tampsin. George believed another assassination attempt would have resulted in a massive firefight with UK Special Forces on the streets of England.

The two failures had eaten into the timescale, and increased the risk that Shawlens would recover his memory. George had no option but to confide in Cranstoun. He told Cranstoun about the existence of POINT-K secrets, and explained why he required the President's personal intervention with the British PM to head off exposure of POINT-K4.

George told Cranstoun that if his intervention proved successful then he would decide what happened to the POINT-K4 matter. He warned Cranstoun that if his intervention proved unsuccessful, then the country would face unprecedented anger and hostility on a scale never before known. A cataclysmic crisis that would bring the country to its knees.

In a private conference call with the British PM, Cranstoun requested the immediate surrender of Gavin Shawlens to the CIA. In exchange for replacement of the ageing British nuclear deterrent with newer existing US submarines, and resolution of the UK dispute with Argentina over the ownership of the Falkland Islands.

A package with an estimated loss of income to the US Treasury of forty billion dollars over twenty-five years. The British PM agreed the deal, negotiations were conducted, contracts were exchanged, and then the deadline passed without Shawlens being handed over to the CIA as promised.

Seven

Darlington

Zoe Tampsin stacked two bags of grocery supplies onto the passenger seat of the red Transit van Spock had given to her. She had fed and watered Gavin Shawlens while they shared a flat in Cosham, so she knew what he would eat and drink. She bought the groceries from a small supermarket store and paid cash.

During the drive back to her doghouse, Zoe's secure phone rang. Her mind raced around in circles and she pulled over to answer it. The secure phone Sir Milton Johnson gave her for direct communications. Her heart lifted with anticipation.

When the line connected and she heard him breathing heavily, her hopes rocketed. Might Johnson be excited because he'd found out why the Americans wanted Shawlens?

'Zoe.'

'Yes, sir, thanks for calling.'

'Have you found a safe place to hide?'

'Yes, sir, Shawlens is safe and secure.'

'Good, I'm relieved to hear that, Zoe. The deadline for handing over Shawlens has passed. The Americans are going ballistic and the PM is screeching like a four-year-old. Soon everyone will be searching for you. It won't be long before they find out what I've done. If this weren't serious, it would make great circus. It's such fun watching these politicians in a crisis.'

She listened to his voice. He seemed to enjoy his mischief and the antics of the headless chickens running around frantically wondering what to do. She became concerned and wanted to tell him someone would notice his bizarre attitude.

'Sir, are you any further forward?' she said with harshness to bring back his focus.

He took a deep breath, let it out slowly. 'I've pulled in every favour I can with friendly Americans, Russians and Germans. No-one knows anything about Shawlens or why the US is so desperate to have him. He's definitely not associated with any major security issues or secret developments. I've drawn a complete blank. Makes no sense.'

Damn, she thought, 'Sorry to hear that, sir.'

He said, 'I hoped you might have news of a development in his nightmares?'

'He's still having them. He had another one last night. It's the same story and places him under water. But dreams can use images to mean something else. He may not be under water, it may be the opposite. Dreams are so bloody unreliable,' she said, and her frustration entangled her voice.

'I don't believe it's a dream. I believe he has recalled a memory,' Johnson said.

'That did occur to me, but Shawlens is certain they are dreams. He doesn't associate what he has remembered with any of his past or existing memories. There's no match.'

'Bugger, I hoped he would shed some light on what this is about,' he said.

'Sir, what do you want me to do with him?'

Her voice rang with urgency and she wanted to hear him say she should bring Shawlens back to London.

'We can't hold out for long, the pressure from the Americans and the PM is at bursting point. I'm waiting for a reply from the Israelis. They say they have an idea what this is about. Problem is, they want to bargain for something in return, and there is no time to mess about. If that doesn't tell me anything. I'll have to hand him over.'

'We lose Shawlens and whatever he knows, forever,' she said, and her voice signalled she didn't like that option.

'Yes, I'm afraid so. Look, Zoe, is there any way you could use drugs or mind manipulation techniques to loosen his mind and push his memories along?' he said, and made the request sound like his last hope.

'Sir, that's a job for a qualified MO. I don't have any drugs or facilities to conduct that type of process. Doing it too fast will kill him. We don't have time to do it slow. If you want to go down that route, sir, it will have to be done at a secure medical facility. I know where they are of course. I can deliver him if that's what you want.'

'No, probably not a good idea. Just a desperate thought in a desperate moment. We don't have enough time for anything, I suppose.'

'Understood, sir.'

He didn't disguise his feelings. She sensed his anxiety and she heard the strain in his voice. She sensed he wasn't thinking judiciously, and that meant he could easily make a bad decision. The hairs on the back of her neck sprang rigid.

She realised he really didn't know what to do. Typical of a civil servant trying to play hardball with people who didn't have rules.

'The Americans are on a deadline so whatever they are worried about should begin to surface. We just need to hold on a bit longer and give this issue a chance to show itself.'

'Yes, sir.'

'We are not going to be robbed again,' he said.

'Robbed?'

'Long story, Zoe. It dates back to the Second World War, and the movement of the British Empire's huge stock of diamonds and gold bullion to the USA and Canada for safekeeping. It didn't work out well for us. In today's money, hundreds of billions are missing.'

Silence hung while Zoe thought, *you're clutching at straws.*

'Sorry, sir, I've never heard anything about missing bullion.'

'The topic is taboo with the Yanks. They refuse to talk about it. I don't know how, but I think Shawlens may have stumbled on a secret that would lead us to the missing bullion.'

Silence again as he seemed to be disappearing down his own sinkhole.

She decided she would not follow him.

'In his dreams he is under water, terrified, facing death. Could we reproduce that scene and unlock this thing that's troubling his mind?' she asked.

'What do you suggest?'

'I could deliver him to a large safe house with a pool. Put him in the water. Force this dream into his conscious mind.'

'You may be right. This dream is the only thing in his life I can't interpret. Are you certain this water drowning episode is the only thing troubling him?'

'Yes, sir, certain. Tell me where to deliver him. You might have an answer by tonight,' she said, and then closed her eyes and hoped he would go for it.

'I don't know if there is enough time. Leave it with me, I'll look in to it.'

'I could deliver Shawlens to a safe house today, sir. Get things moving?'

'No, you must keep your head down for a few more days. Countless teams are preparing to scour the country for you. I can't protect you.'

Uugghh, she thought. 'Sir, I have a serious problem. I have very limited weapons and ammunition if it comes to a fight.'

He raised his voice. 'You'll just have to make do with what you've got. I told you to make sure it doesn't come to a fight.'

'I don't function well when I don't have sufficient equipment to do the job, sir.'

He raised his voice a notch further. 'I'm sorry, but we are where we are. Don't get in to a fight and you won't need to worry about weapons.'

Zoe cursed under her breath. Typical head civil servant response. Become invisible, hide in the dark and keep a low profile. Ignore the fact that determined people will find you, and when they do, you must be equipped to protect yourself.

'Easier said than done, sir. If everybody and their uncle are looking for me, and a team turn up at my doghouse. What am I supposed to do—tell them to go away?'

'*You* will do your duty without question. *You* will keep Shawlens safe. That's an order,' he said, loudly.

'I'm sorry, sir. I'm used to planning, organising, briefing my backup and getting my men in place before I kick off.'

In a softer voice he said, 'I wish things could be different, Zoe. But there we are. You are a clever and resourceful soldier who has demonstrated time and time again that you can deliver under great pressure and danger. You will do so once more. Understood?'

'Yes, sir.'

'You need to trust me, Zoe. When the crunch comes, I'll either know what Shawlens has and I'll have control of it or I won't and I'll take the fall. I'm on the firing line here in London, not you. I'm taking a huge risk to discover what Shawlens has to give up. I have taken steps to ensure you will be exonerated for your part. I assume you've read the written orders I gave you,' he said.

She closed her eyes tightly. He still had the gravitas to put her firmly back in line.

'Yes, sir, I'll keep him safe until you contact me again. If anything significant comes out of his dreams. I'll call you immediately.'

'No, I'll call you when it is safe to do so. Hopefully, that won't be too long.'

Disappointment and frustration filled her thoughts. She didn't believe Johnson would organise a safe house. She didn't believe Johnson even had a plan. He sounded like a stupid old man playing a dangerous game of chess. With her as his queen, and Shawlens as his pawn, but they were the only two pieces on his side of the board. The other side had all their pieces and all of his pieces as well.

Listening to Johnson had settled one thing in her mind. She wasn't going to cower in her doghouse like a sitting duck, waiting for a posse of CIA agents to track her down and kill her. She'd had an incompetent boss once before, and that didn't work out well—for him.

Eight

London, UK

In the large split-level CIA operations room in Grosvenor Square, a group of fifteen section heads and other senior members of staff had gathered on the upper level. Collectively the heads managed and supervised eighty UK-based CIA staff. They expected a briefing on the unfolding of a national security threat.

The much larger lower level had subdued lighting to reduce reflections on numerous flat panel screens on rows of desks, computer workstations and other communication consoles. Dozens of analysts, technicians and agents worked the desks. Others delivered files and updates to people around the room.

Director CIA, Katherine Kaplentsky, swept into the upper room followed by her deputy and two others. They stood in front of a large screen showing pictures of Gavin Shawlens and Zoe Tampsin. She stepped closer to the group to engage with them, and close enough to the people at the front to be in their faces. Katherine had always been a high-vis director who made time to visit every corner of her domain.

An only child, born in Chicago, in the prosperous middle-class suburb of Park Ridge, Illinois, she graduated from Yale Law School. Some of her contemporaries described her as brash and arrogant while others described her as too scary. Not long after graduation, the CIA recruited her into the CIA Office of General Counsel.

Within months, she not only gave legal advice to the CIA, but policy guidance to the Director. It didn't take long for the political executives and senior Washington bureaucrats to recognise that Katherine would become the sharpest and sleekest scalpel on the tray.

The CIA have a sound recording made during the immediate aftermath of the 9/11 attack. A recording of a Langley office in panic with many people screaming and shouting in the background. In the foreground, a voice could be heard issuing instructions in a cool, confident and determined voice. In a period of chaos, Katherine Kaplentsky remained as cool as an ice cube fresh from the freezer.

'Quiet down. Listen up everyone. This is a special situation, national security imminent threat, category 1, priority alpha. All other work is suspended until this situation is resolved,' Katherine announced.

'We have thirty-two personnel locked in current operations,' one of the group said.

'I need everyone here. Bring your people in, if it's safe to do so,' Katherine replied.

She acknowledged the two men at her side. 'Let me introduce Len Park from NSA's National Security Operations Center, and Colonel Steve Hutcher from Military Intelligence.' The two men signalled their presence to the group.

'Steve has over one hundred military intelligence officers at his disposal in the UK. He will coordinate military support. Len has three thousand analysts at Fort Meade waiting to process every scrap of information you can find. They'll coordinate with an alpha task force of two hundred at Langley. They are ready right now to support your efforts here on the ground.'

A buzz of questions and comments flew around the group as they realised the sheer scale of the operation put in place to find two people.

Katherine continued loudly to quieten them down, 'Work effectively with everyone. This is not a competition to see which agency bags the prize. We'll all work as one body of Americans on this matter. Complete transparency across the board.'

She spotted looks of disapproval, smirks on some of the faces, and rumblings of dissent at the back of the group.

She looked stern when she said, 'Be warned and warn your staff. Any lack of cooperation from any desk will be reported to me and will be dealt with severely. We all have one priority. Find these people. Get a lead, pass it on, and the analysts will run it down for you. You'll have resources at your disposal to look into every crevice and every hole in this rain-sodden country. Trace and question every living person known by these two. If anyone has seen either of them recently, I want to know about it. Tell your people to squeeze their assets, and their assets' assets. They have my permission to throw money at them, *if* it will give us a lead.'

'This is going to take five minutes with all our resources in play,' someone said.

Katherine turned to look at the speaker. 'Do not underestimate Tampsin. She's an experienced Special Forces officer, one of their elite. Very smart and very driven. This is her home ground, and she'll be tough to track. Shawlens is an academic. He's her weak spot in this situation.'

She paused for a drink of water.

'Are we working with the British or against them?' a section head asked.

'Officially, they agreed to hand over these people. Unofficially, they have *misplaced* them.'

A loud roar of laughter erupted and many comments about British competence swirled around the room.

'Be careful to keep these comments to yourselves. British security is sending liaison officers to assist. We need to play them to find out what they know,' Katherine said.

'Would it be easier if we just shut them out?' another asked.

'Let them play along, but do not let them impede your search. I want the intelligence flow to be one-way. Get what you can from them. Give them nothing,' Katherine replied.

'What if we hit resistance? It's their country,' someone at the back asked.

'If it's low level, run over them. If it's high level, contact me. I'll deal with it.'

'This will cause a massive rift between us and them. Future cooperation will be difficult if not impossible,' said another.

'Tough bagels. By the by, all leave is cancelled. Order your people to tell their families they won't be home for a few days. In a few weeks, it will be Thanksgiving. I'm determined the President and all of us will celebrate Thanksgiving knowing we completed this job successfully, and protected our national security and our way of life.'

'Will you lead this operation from here?' someone at the front asked.

'Yes, I'll be riding shotgun on this task. Expect me or my deputy to be asking you for updates every twenty minutes. If anyone fails to put one hundred percent into this task, I'll personally ship them home in total disgrace. If we do not find these people in time, they'll damage irretrievably our country's national security. We will have failed. Every man, woman and child in our country will pay a heavy price for that failure. We are on the front line here, people. Get this job done. Get this job done. *Now.*'

Katherine's deputy looked at a message on her phone and then stepped up and whispered something into Katherine's ear.

'That's all for now. Updates please - every twenty minutes.'

Katherine and her deputy walked smartly around the people and down the steps to the lower level. They left the operations room and headed to an office on another floor.

Waiting in the office were Ertha Odeele and Division Chief Spencer 'Spence' MacAllisin. Spence had flown to a private airfield in southern England by company jet. Ertha Odeele met him as soon as he landed, and drove him straight to Grosvenor Square.

During the drive, Ertha told him she had arrived in England two days ago. She updated Spence on her new work at Langley. Work she had to drop when Katherine ordered her to supervise an incursion into Canada. Although Ertha and Spence were old friends, she said she couldn't brief him on the national security emergency that had unfolded. He knew her well enough to understand she meant she didn't know anything.

'Katherine is briefing key people personally,' she said.

'I guess that says it all,' he replied.

Katherine and her deputy entered the room and they all shook hands like long-lost friends at a funeral. They sat around a circular table and drank filtered coffee. Better quality coffee than the bitter tasting dark fluid flowing down throats in the operations room.

Spence had been pulled out of a major operation that he had developed meticulously for months. But when Katherine called him, he sensed something much more important had happened in London. He felt privileged that Katherine had selected him to lead the search, and so without hesitation he flew to her side.

Spence had become Katherine's most experienced hunter in Europe. With unlimited backup at his fingertips, she felt certain he would find the fugitives. He also brought a significant value to the hunt. He had worked with Zoe Tampsin in Bosnia when she supported American-led operations to capture war criminals.

Spence MacAllisin had made East European Division Chief before Katherine took control of the CIA. A well known character who'd served the CIA in various parts of the world for over thirty years. A man known for integrity and loyalty, he hadn't climbed over or backstabbed anybody to get up the ladder.

He waited a long time to get his position, but everyone working for him respected and trusted him. They viewed him more like a supportive father than a boss. His agents had often gone the extra mile for him.

Spence had the utmost respect for Katherine. He admired her meticulously planned climb to the top. He predicted she would make director. A fifty-five-year-old linguistics graduate, Spence could speak Russian, French and German comfortably, like a native. He stood five foot eight, clean-shaven with short neat hair and a good build.

He always dressed casual with an open shirt and no necktie. He preferred dark coloured jackets and light coloured chinos. Unmarried and not in a relationship, Spence had married the job and he loved his job. His family were the people in his office. His French housekeeper believed he earned a living as a political commentator. She kept his house neat, she taught him to cook, and she kept his body from wilting.

Katherine told them the official cover story. Gavin Shawlens had information that would cause catastrophic damage to US national security. Zoe Tampsin had kidnapped Shawlens and planned to deliver him to Russian agents.

Katherine asked, 'Ertha, is the Canadian asset on ice?'

Ertha nodded, 'Secured in a country house as you instructed. Ready to be interrogated when you specify the line of questions.'

'No interrogation. Just keep her on ice. What about her wild sister?' Katherine asked.

'I've left instructions to keep her sedated.'

'Good work, Ertha.'

'What happened with Canada?' Ertha asked.

'Cranstoun smoothed it over. No fall-out,' Katherine said.

'Anyone know why Tampsin has turned traitor?' Spence asked, because traitor wasn't a label he would attach to Zoe.

Katherine said, 'We believe Milton Johnson gave her direct orders. He's the traitor. She's carrying out his orders without fully understanding the consequences.'

Spence thought for a moment. 'Okay, that makes sense. Unfortunately, it doesn't make it any easier. She'll follow orders and complete her mission no matter what. Surrender is not in her vocabulary.'

Ertha asked Spence, 'How serious a threat does she pose to our field agents?'

'Very serious. Zoe is at the top of her game. She holds a black belt, expert grade two, in krav maga.'

Ertha said, 'Krav maga. Sounds like a type of goulash. What is it?'

'It's a system of close contact combat developed by Israeli Special Forces. Now used by elite Special Forces all over the world. In Bosnia, I saw first-hand what she can do. She's a lethal animal,' Spence said.

'Really?' Ertha said, and didn't sound convinced.

'Let me tell you about Zoe Tampsin. With the confidence of a tigress she sauntered unarmed into a fortified Bosnian safe house, protected by five heavily armed guards, posing as a battered drunken hooker. She lured three of them to a back bedroom where she killed them silently before they started on her. She dropped the other two before they knew what hit them. Then calmly opened the back door to let us take over. All without a single shot being fired.'

Katherine raised her eyebrows. 'Impressive.'

'I had told her before she went in that I wanted two for interrogation. When I got in the house, two were alive, barely. I don't know of anyone who could have done what she achieved. The woman has nerves of steel.'

'Thanks for that, Spence. We should post a warning to all team leaders,' Katherine said to her deputy.

'Can she stop a bullet?' Ertha asked.

'Of course not.'

'That's fine. We avoid close combat, and like any lethal animal, shoot it from a distance. We'll find her and we'll deal with her,' Ertha said.

She made a face to Katherine that showed she wasn't impressed with Tampsin.

Spence knew that Ertha didn't get on well with Special Forces people. She believed they were too full of themselves, and unbearably rude at times. Too often, they demanded unrealistic backup and intelligence gathering before they would lift a finger. A few years back, she'd lost four good agents when Special Forces progressed too cautiously into a hot zone.

Spence raised his voice a notch. 'Ertha, don't underestimate Zoe Tampsin. She's very good at blending and making herself invisible. When I said "battered hooker", her make-up looked fantastic, worthy of an Oscar. If she's hiding—'

'Tell me. Where can she hide in this tiny back end of beyond?' Ertha asked.

'This is her home ground. She'll know all the dark corners,' Katherine said.

'We'll never find her quickly if she's down a rabbit hole. We need something to flush her into the open. We need a carrot,' Spence said.

'I have a copy of her file. All the carrots you need are in there,' Katherine said, and handed the file to Ertha.

'We'll only get one chance at this. It will need to be the sweetest carrot in the bunch,' Spence said.

'Time is of the essence. I need this done now,' Katherine said with emphasis.

Spence sat back in his chair and held his gaze on Katherine's eyes. He realised the significance of this mission. Sometimes, CIA Directors used excessive hype to ram home their message.

Whatever had happened, it had Katherine by the throat. He had seen some of her predecessors distraught but he believed the queen of cool couldn't be rattled. Today proved him wrong, not only had she been rattled, she allowed others to see her distress.

Over the years, he'd witnessed several serious threats to national security. None of them produced this scale of response. If he'd been alone with Katherine, he would have asked her for details about the threat. He sensed she could say more, but now wasn't the right time to ask.

'No holds barred?' Spence asked.

Katherine nodded. 'None, whatsoever.'

'What about the laws of the land?' Ertha asked.

'For this mission, ignore them, they don't apply to us,' Katherine said without hesitation. Spence and Ertha looked at Katherine with astonishment on their faces.

'Are you saying we have a free pass to run around Britain and do whatever is necessary to eliminate this threat? Ride roughshod over law enforcement and Security Services?' Spence asked with incredulity in his voice.

'Yes,' Katherine replied.

'They won't just stand by and watch,' he added.

'Yes they will. Do not let them get in your way. If they do, inform me immediately and I'll deal with it.'

'Jesus, this must be the biggest threat we have ever faced in our entire history.'

'Yes, Spence, by a very large order of magnitude.'

'So—'

'The scale of the threat is all you need to know,' Katherine cut him off.

Ertha had skimmed through Zoe's file and picked out a photo. She looked at it carefully, twisted it in her fingertips then handed it to Spence.

'Sweet enough for you, Spence?' Ertha said.

'Aww for God's sake. *No,*' Spence said.

Katherine said, '*Spence!* No holds barred. If you have a problem with that, you need to let me know, right now.'

'No problem,' he replied as he returned the photo to Ertha, and thought, *what on earth is at stake that needs us to stoop this low?*

Nine

MI6, Vauxhall Cross, London

Toni Bornadetti sat in the outer office of Sir John Steelers, Head of the Secret Service (formerly MI6). She waited more than twenty minutes in the smart, light oak panelled office. She wondered why she' been summoned to a meeting in the bowels of Babylon House as the building had become known because of its resemblance to a Babylonian ziggurat.

Before her promotion, orders were issued by her boss at the Regiment. She felt a little anxious appearing at Babylon House for her first briefing. She assumed her boss had attended a meeting with Steelers, and that she would be brought in at the end to receive her orders.

Toni had never met Steelers but she'd heard about him. A career diplomat who'd worked in Europe and the Far East. He'd worked at the British Embassy in Washington DC before he took up his appointment as Head of MI6 and then the Security Service. Although in his early fifties, he appeared trim and fit. He and his wife enjoyed hiking, skiing and cycling. They had no children to bring up, and so they enjoyed a rich and entertaining high life, mixing with ambassadors, foreign dignitaries and wealthy executives on the diplomats' party circuit.

The middle-aged and well-groomed secretary guarding Steelers' office, raised her head and looked over her spectacles at Toni. When their eyes met, she smiled so sweetly that Toni wondered if she'd clicked with a fellow gay.

A green light flashed on her communication console. She lifted a handset, flicked her shoulder-length auburn hair and slipped the handset to her ear, listened and nodded. When she replaced the handset, she looked up and smiled brightly.

'Captain Bornadetti, follow me please. Is it Antonia or Toni?'

'Toni.'

'Lovely name.'

The secretary led the way, opened the door and announced Toni to the people inside. As she closed the door on her way out, Sir John Steelers stood up, and came around his desk to shake her hand. He introduced the others in the room. Boyd Collans from the Security Service, and Ertha Odeele from the CIA. Toni shook hands with them both.

'Sit down please, Toni, and congratulations on your promotion by the way. I understand you'll take over W-Troop,' Steelers said.

By the time Toni sat down, she'd decided she didn't like Steelers. She didn't like poker-faced men in pin stripe shirts wearing wide red trouser braces. In her mind, only fat men wore braces because they couldn't wear a belt and Steelers wasn't fat so he didn't need braces.

She might have sensed that he didn't like her. Steelers liked women to be frightfully fluffy and delightfully frilly. Just as if they'd walked out of an Emily Brontë novel. Toni walked like a man, shook hands like a man and sat up straight like a man. If she punched his face, he would feel like he'd been punched by a man.

'Yes, sir.'

'How much did they tell you about that?'

'Next to nothing. The CO said Captain Tampsin is no longer with the regiment. I'll take command of W-Troop with immediate effect.'

'Let me put more detail on that.'

'Thanks, sir, I would appreciate any further information.'

Toni looked closely at Steelers. He looked handsome with engaging eyes and a relaxed charming manner. Skills he probably learned in the diplomatic service. She'd met smarmy types before. She didn't like them. Normally, she would let them know very quickly but not this one.

An attractive and rugged thirty-six-year-old, Toni looked as fit as she'd been when she joined the army at eighteen. She looked like the twin sister of Michelle Rodriguez who played Letty in the *Fast and Furious* films.

She had tied her black shoulder-length hair in a knot at the back of her head. Her Mediterranean skin had a light tan and appeared blemish-free. She stood five-seven and her weight hadn't changed since the day she joined the army. She looked strong, muscular and capable of looking after herself.

Many times, she'd been asked why she'd joined the army when she should have been in the movies.

Steelers said, 'First, I want you to tell me about your role in the SLIPFIRE operation for the Lambeth Group.'

'Lambeth Group?' Ertha queried.

Steelers turned to answer her. 'A small section in the Security Service that investigate fraud and crime in the research and technology sector.'

Toni said, 'Scott Bradwood and I were deployed to support Captain Tampsin. The Captain had orders to protect Dr Shawlens. He'd been asked to investigate a group of scientists suspected of developing an energy product based on old Nazi research. The trail led us to a factory in Prague where we were involved in a firefight. Dr Shawlens found evidence that effectively closed the SLIPFIRE investigation. Prague is where I got this,' she said, and pointed to the plaster above her eye.

'Dr Shawlens gathered the evidence needed to close the investigation?'

'Yes, sir, mission accomplished.'

'What happened when you returned to the UK?'

She told them Scott had remained in a safe house to guard a Bulgarian informant and liaise with Secret Service in Bulgaria. After the Prague operation, they received news that Scott and the informant had been executed. When they arrived home, they went straight to the safe house to see Scott for themselves.

In reply to a question from Ertha, she added that she meant herself, Captain Tampsin and Dr Shawlens, and they were met at the safe house by Alan Cairn, Head of CNPI.

'What did you expect would happen next?' Steelers asked.

'Back to London with Alan Cairn, debriefing, then back to the regiment.'

'What did happen?'

'Captain Tampsin and Dr Shawlens returned to the flat they shared during the SLIPFIRE investigation. She ordered me to set up round-the-clock armed cover on the flat.'

'Did she say why?' Steelers asked.

Toni shook her head. 'Only that there were loose ends to deal with and she expected they would show up at the flat. We were camped outside, and we prepared for action at a moment's notice.'

'Did she say who?' Ertha asked.

'No, sir, but in Prague we were attacked by a professional mercenary, Herman Vindanson. The Captain killed Vindanson. I assumed she expected repercussions.'

'Then?' Steelers asked.

'Then both of their SEM phones went off-line. We rushed over to the flat but they were gone.'

Ertha interjected aggressively, 'You saying Tampsin snatched Shawlens from under your damn nose? Is this how people get promoted around here?'

Toni looked surprised. 'I'm not sure what you mean.'

'Their SEM phones were disabled to avoid tracking?' Steelers asked Toni.

'Yes, sir, I believe so.'

'Why did Tampsin take this action?' Steelers asked.

'I have no idea, sir. I know she'll have a very good reason.'

'Have you tried to contact her?'

'No, sir. She's gone dark. All communications with friends, colleagues and family are severed. That's the go dark procedure. She'll stick to procedure.'

Ertha leaned forward to face Toni. 'Why did she take Shawlens and go dark?'

Toni shook her head. 'I have no idea but there will be a good reason.'

'Yes, so you've said,' Ertha said.

'I understand you and Tampsin are close friends,' Steelers said as he looked down at a file in his hands.

'Yes, sir. It has been my pleasure to serve and compete with the Captain.'

'This may come as a shock,' Steelers started.

'Sorry to interrupt. You said compete. What do you mean?' Ertha asked.

'For fun, we challenge each other in extreme sports.'

'Explain,' Ertha said.

'On our last challenge, we went river sledging in the Scottish Highlands. I raced her down a white-water river course. You lie down flat on a plastic sledge, and skim the rapids at high speed. I won that one,' she said, and smiled.

Steelers swung his gaze over to Ertha to check if he could continue. She nodded.

'This may come as a shock but I have to tell you that Tampsin has turned her back on her country. She *is* a traitor.'

Toni sank back in her chair and looked stunned. She quickly scanned the other two faces before she returned her look of astonishing disbelief to Steelers.

'That's … impossible, sir. She's as British and as straight as they come.'

'I agree, it's hard to believe. She has served our country with great distinction and honour. One of our modern day heroines without any shadow of doubt. I'm equally shocked because I know Sir Milton Johnson ordered her to take Shawlens off the grid. He's now under arrest and will face the music.'

Toni heard what Steelers said but didn't believe him. No-one knew Zoe Tampsin better. Toni thought there would be a greater chance of the moon being made of cheese than of Zoe being a traitor. A massive mistake had been made or something had been falsified against her.

She decided she would get to the root of it for her friend and mentor. Thoughts of Zoe's grateful hugs and kisses filled her mind and fired pangs of exhilaration down her spine. But first things first, she knew she would have to play along with Steelers.

'I don't yet know what Johnson has told Tampsin but the facts are clear. Tampsin has abducted Dr Shawlens and is preparing to hand him over to Russian agents in the next few days. Thankfully, our friends in the CIA became aware of this plan. We arrested Johnson quickly but Tampsin escaped with Shawlens.'

'Shawlens? Sir. I don't understand. In Prague, when we discussed why Vindanson had attacked the team; the Captain said Vindanson wasn't after Dr Shawlens because he is a worthless idiot. Her words.'

Steelers said, 'Did she indeed? Did you know that earlier this year Shawlens had been taken captive on a cargo vessel heading for Russia? We had to dispatch a team to storm the boat and recover him. He had secret Lambeth Group technology with him. Did you hear about that operation?'

Steelers lifted another file and plonked it on his desk in front of Toni but she didn't lean forward to look through it. She hadn't been a captain long enough to know he'd offered her a chance to examine the file.

'Yes, sir, I did hear about the raid on the Russian boat. The SBS lads have been crowing about it for months, but obviously not any details about Shawlens and Lambeth Group secrets.'

'Tampsin is most likely following direct orders given to her by Johnson. It doesn't really matter how she has been played. What matters to me is that she must be stopped and Shawlens must be prevented from giving anything to the Russians. No matter the cost.'

'Copy that, sir.'

Toni sat up straight in her chair.

Steelers said, 'I have issued kill orders on Tampsin and Shawlens but I would prefer to have them back alive. You know her best. If anyone can draw her out of this mess—it's you. Bring them in alive if you can or eliminate them if Tampsin will not comply. Do you have an issue with those orders?'

All three of them scanned Toni's face to detect her real reaction to the orders.

'No, sir. I'll do my best to keep them alive but if there's a fight, she'll shoot to kill. If I have to take her out, I'll do my duty without hesitation.'

'Good. You'll work closely with Boyd and Ertha. There are ten teams scouring the country for Tampsin. Five from the Security Service and five from the Secret Service. You'll support Boyd's team. Ertha will coordinate with the other teams. She has knowledge of Russian personnel and Russian procedures. Time is not on our side, Captain Bornadetti, any questions?'

'No, sir, I'm clear.'

'Then, I won't detain you any longer. Boyd will keep me informed of his team's progress,' Steelers said as he rounded his desk and walked toward the door to open it for them.

Toni smiled briefly at Steelers as she left, and he reciprocated. She felt elated with her first briefing as captain. As Zoe's sergeant, she received scant details and simple direct orders. Wait here, do this, be there, pick up that, or deliver this. At last, she felt so much more involved with a free rein to think and plan for herself.

She felt liberated as if she'd been plucked from the shop floor, and dropped into the executive suite at head office. At last, an opportunity for her to use her brain to plan, prepare and give orders to her sergeant.

Toni always expected she would succeed Zoe to lead W-Troop, the first all female Special Forces troop in the regiment, but not in her wildest dreams did she ever anticipate taking over in these circumstances.

They'd first met in the Special Reconnaissance Regiment (SRR) when Zoe provided the opposition in a grading contest to decide Toni's level in krav maga. Brown belt against black belt. An intense needle match that drew blood from both of them, but Toni moved up a grade and they became close friends.

Boyd escorted Toni and Ertha to the operations floor. As they walked, Boyd said, 'Tampsin has an outstanding military record. I guess that means she'll not surrender.'

Toni said, 'She won't surrender under any circumstances. The chances of a non-lethal outcome are slim at best.'

'Shoot to kill is the safest option for everyone on the search teams. Do you agree?' Ertha asked.

'Yes, because that is exactly what she'll do. If her orders are to make sure Shawlens is not taken alive, she'll kill him before you get anywhere near him,' Toni said.

Ertha had studied Toni's file and watched her closely from the moment she first set eyes on her. She suspected Toni might be too close to Tampsin to be trusted. Steelers said her personal knowledge of Tampsin offered the best hope for finding Tampsin quickly.

Steelers gave Toni a good grilling and she responded with detached and professional answers. Ertha sensed that Toni had been waiting for the opportunity to fill Zoe Tampsin's boots. Ertha didn't object to Toni joining Boyd's team but she would keep a close eye on her.

Boyd guided Ertha and Toni around the operations room to show them how the Secret Service had coordinated their search. Teams of analysts worked at wallboards and computers to collate everything known about Gavin Shawlens and Zoe Tampsin.

Boyd didn't quite have thirty years on the clock. He stood six foot tall with short black, and had gained an attractive row of neat front teeth thanks to a rugby boot that took out seven of his front teeth during an inter-university game. He'd been recruited directly from Cambridge after a private cheese and wine party hosted by a group of civil servant scouts. While smart and keen, he had little experience in real tradecraft.

Boyd introduced Toni to each of the backroom team. As she walked around the computer workstations, she glanced up at the large summary screen to see photos of Gavin and Zoe staring back. She realised the scale and determination of the hunt to find them. They wouldn't be deploying all of these people and all of this effort if there weren't an immediate risk to US national security.

'We're hacking into her office computer,' Boyd said to Toni.

'How long will that take?' Toni asked.

'Hours, no more. When we're in, I want you to dig for anything that could lead us to her bolthole. Understood?'

'Of course.'

'If you find anything, you bring it straight to me. Steelers will liaise with the Yanks. Clear?' Boyd said, in a low voice, and his eyes darted cautiously to Ertha.

Toni got his meaning. 'Yes, sir.'

Ertha stood with a CIA colleague in direct contact with CIA operations in Grosvenor Square. He told Ertha that as far as he could see, the Brits were cooperating, but nothing had turned up. He confirmed that the Brits had no idea where

Shawlens and Tampsin were hiding. She told him she had pretty much come to the same conclusion.

Toni listened to one of the analysts giving an update on his progress to hack into Zoe's desktop computer. Computer jargon and unfamiliar terms washed past her. The full impact of what Steelers had told her began to hit her like a sledgehammer.

When Steelers called Zoe a traitor, Toni didn't believe him and shut the idea right out of her mind. They were mistaken. Now she'd seen all the people and resources frantically trying to find Zoe, she felt overwhelmed and claustrophobic.

She wanted to run to the toilet and throw up. The analyst carried on talking about Zoe's computer but his voice faded as Toni thought, *oh boss, these bastards are planning to kill you, what the bloody hell have you got yourself into?*

Ten

Cabinet office, Whitehall, London

Sir Milton Johnson sat alone in an anteroom near the main cabinet office briefing room. Well, almost alone, ignoring the guard standing at the door. The windowless room felt warm and stuffy, and overhead lighting didn't extend much beyond the rectangular table in the middle of the room.

His clasped hands rested just in front of his groin as he twiddled his thumbs clockwise then anti-clockwise while he waited. He seemed remarkably calm, although he knew of the argument raging in the COBRA room along the corridor about his refusal to hand Gavin Shawlens to the CIA.

He smiled at the irony in the fact that he as head of the Security Service, had made a piss-poor effort of covering up his tracks when he assisted Zoe Tampsin to go dark. He'd always been first to criticise others for poor tradecraft. Now, everyone would know his tradecraft had proved to be the poorest of them all.

He expected the meeting along the corridor wasn't going well. The deadline for handing Shawlens to the CIA had long passed, and they were furious with him. They'd taken his watch so he had to guess he'd been waiting in the room for more than an hour. He heard a gentle knock on the door as the guard outside signalled the guard inside that a group of people were making their way to the room.

A few moments later the door opened. Sir John Steelers breezed into the room followed by Katherine Kaplentsky and Maureen Broadway, Chair of the Joint Intelligence Committee (JIC).

When Katherine found out she had a meeting in the COBRA room with Maureen Broadway, she called her deputy to find out what she could about the woman.

Katherine's deputy had replied, 'Broadway has a reputation as an effective troubleshooter. Political opponents agree she is the right person to chair the Joint Intelligence Committee. She stands no bullshit from anyone. She frustrates the British security heads because they can't pull the wool over her eyes. They say she can cut through their techno-terrorist crap like a laser through skin.'

'Strong points?'

'Unusually for a senior politician, she's fair and willing to buck the party line when her conscience dictates. She speaks her mind, always. She has a smart enough tongue to tear up any politician or civil servant who dares challenge her strongly held views. And has done on many occasions.'

'Weak points?' Katherine asked.

'When they vetted her for her first security post, they found no dirty laundry, and no unfortunate family skeletons. In fact, nothing that the security heads could use for leverage. She's not the prettiest politician but she's clean. Her biggest weakness—milk chocolate.'

Maureen's short body had an apple-shape, and she carried forty kilos overweight. To hide her shape she wore oversized clothes. Hair style didn't interest her so she kept her hair cut short like a man, and she dyed her own hair a shocking dark brown.

As the three sat down to face Milton, he looked past them to watch the door being closed. An expression of disappointment slipped onto Milton's face. 'Oh dear me, is the Prime Minister late for a constituency luncheon? Or is he having his eyebrows done?'

'Very droll, Milton, very droll indeed. The PM has asked me to resolve this Shawlens business, and that is exactly what I intend to do here,' Maureen said as the three of them sat opposite Milton.

Milton sat back in his chair, folded his arms together and grinned broadly, like Anthony Hopkins' grin as Hannibal Lecter. Maureen wore a loose, short-sleeved top and her bat wings flapped as she moved her arms.

Milton could have said something unpleasant about her bat wings, but he didn't. After all, he wasn't Pierce Brosnan, and Maureen gave back as good if not more than she took. No point going there with Maureen.

'Well, Maureen, I wish you all the very best and I do mean that most sincerely,' Milton said, and then smiled wildly.

Maureen dropped a thin folder onto the table and slid it over to Milton. He picked it up, looked inside for no more than ten seconds, closed it and slid it back to her.

'John's people have strong evidence that you assisted Tampsin to abduct Shawlens. What do you have to say?' Maureen asked.

'John's people have been looking for evidence to push me out of my post for years. He wants to amalgamate the two services. I imagine he'll call his combined group the Secret Security Service, and I understand the cabinet is attracted to the cost saving like dung flies to a pile of crap,' he replied.

Maureen said, 'I have successfully argued against that proposal and—'

Katherine showed her impatience. 'Can we please keep our focus on Tampsin and Shawlens? Is Tampsin acting on your direct orders?'

Maureen immediately furrowed her eyebrows and flashed a disapproving look at Katherine. It clearly signalled, *do you mind? You're here only as an observer.* Maureen held her gaze until Katherine acknowledged it with a nod.

Milton smiled as he watched them. He'd seen Maureen do that look in many meetings. He enjoyed watching high-flying K2 as he called Katherine, put down by ground-hugging Maureen. He knew K2's sharp legal mind wouldn't be so easily deflected.

Milton didn't reply. If it took them half a day to get an answer to that question then that gave Tampsin an extra half day to find out why they wanted Shawlens.

'When we were in this building not long ago for the COBRA meeting, we collectively accepted the decision to hand Shawlens over to the CIA. Did we not?' Maureen said.

'For goods I recall you guessed were worth forty billion dollars.'

'Yes, I did say that, and when the PM asked if there were any objections, you said nothing. Is that correct?'

'Do you recall the PM's final words?' Milton asked.

Maureen replied, 'Of course. He said, "What we do here today is covered by the collective COBRA responsibility agreement and the Official Secrets Act. I sincerely hope all of you understand the scale of the shit-storm that will engulf each and every one of us if this decision goes public. Because it will block out the sun for the rest of your life." Word for word, I believe.'

Milton added, 'He said something after that.'

'I don't recall anything else,' Maureen said, and she looked at Steelers for confirmation.

Steelers added, 'He also said, "Milton you have forty-eight hours to find out what the bloody hell I'm selling for forty billion dollars." I have a transcript here.'

Katherine interjected. 'Forty-eight hours have long passed. We need to—'

Maureen fixed her with a fierce look, and said, '*Please*, Ms Kaplentsky, I must ask you to contain yourself. He is a British citizen and he is entitled to be questioned by British officials. If you are unable to observe then I'll ask you to leave.'

Katherine scowled at Milton's grin. He smiled at her increasing frustration.

Looking at Katherine, Milton said, 'Katherine, you know that in our business timescales are flexible, if the prize is worth the wait.'

Steelers gestured his hand to Katherine, and said, 'I take it you haven't found out why our cousins want Shawlens.'

Milton shook his head. 'I'll give him up this very minute if Katherine is prepared to tell us why President Cranstoun is willing to pay a god's ransom for this man.'

Both Steelers and Maureen looked to Katherine for an answer. She didn't know, other than the fact it involved a POINT-K secret, but she wouldn't let the Brits know she wasn't in the loop.

'All *you* people need to know is our national security is at stake,' Katherine emphasised.

'So, you want us to blindly accept a bland statement and hand over something worth forty billion dollars?' Milton asked Katherine.

'Look, for God's sake. He's *not* worth forty billion dollars. Get that idea out of your head. We are upgrading your nuclear deterrent, which we both agree you need but can't afford. We are getting rid of your Argentine problem, which you didn't fully resolve in the first place,' Katherine replied loudly.

'Just like you fully resolved the troubles in Korea and Vietnam,' Milton hit back.

He wanted to provoke an argument. Decades of vitriol were lined up ready to fly. He hoped if he fired enough back at K2, she just might say something to explain how Shawlens became a risk to their national security. Maureen allowed a few more national insults to be traded before her patience ran out.

'Enough. Okay, Milton, you've made your point. Back to square one. The PM did ask you to find out what Shawlens had that would be worth forty billion. You gave it your best shot, and the PM wants you to cough him up. We must complete the deal with the Americans. Now, I want you to give him up and then we can all relax with a nice cup of Earl Grey. Does that seem fair to you, Milton?'

Milton shook his head. 'You know something, Maureen. I've always thought it so incredible that politicians are quick to make life and death decisions about an individual, but don't have the balls to deliver the message themselves. Why is that do you think?'

'Where is Shawlens?' Katherine demanded.

'I have absolutely no idea,' Milton fired back with a smirk.

'*Milton*, for God's sake—playtime is over,' Steelers said.

'John, old friend, playtime hasn't started yet. I'm sure you already know that,' Milton replied, and fixed his gaze on Steelers.

'What can you possibly hope to achieve with this pointless prevarication?' Maureen asked.

'Truth and honesty among friends for a start. Is that too much?'

Steelers threatened. 'You're gambling, Milton. It's a risk not worth the life of the head of the Security Service. This is a serious error of judgement that will have unfortunate ramifications for your Service.'

'It *is* a gamble, John, quite right. They are on a clock for a reason. If I can give Tampsin another day or two, I believe she'll find out what Shawlens has that's so vital. If she does and she can't contact me then she'll go public with it. At least the world will know, even if I don't.'

Katherine flashed her eyes at Steelers and said, 'That's *not* going to happen.'

'What if this is a grand bluff? A stupid ploy by spooks unknown. You could be sacrificing yourself for no good reason,' Maureen pleaded.

'Risk is the name of the game,' Milton replied.

Steelers shook his head in disbelief and said, 'You are prepared to die for this thing, which could end up being nothing of great significance? We both know of issues when the Yanks have got their knickers in a twist over the most trivial piece of useless intelligence.'

Maureen commanded, 'Milton, as chair of the JIC, I'm your immediate line manager. I order you to call Tampsin this minute, and instruct her to bring Shawlens to London.'

Steelers placed a mobile phone on the table.

'I certainly will not,' Milton replied with a tremble in his voice.

For the first time in the meeting they noted his confidence begin to weaken.

'Milton, think about the consequences, will you? If I leave this room empty-handed, these people will be brutal with you. You know what they will do. You are too old for this bloody nonsense, Milton. Come on now, do as I ask,' Maureen pleaded.

'I'm thinking of the consequences of not knowing what Shawlens has and probably belongs to us but they are determined to keep from us,' he said, pointing an accusing finger at Katherine.

'What do you mean by that?' Katherine demanded.

'The British Empire's gold bullion and diamonds shipped to North America for safe keeping during the Second World War. Hundreds of billions didn't make it back.'

Katherine looked surprised and said, 'That's old crap, just like you.'

'Oh, Milton, not that old chestnut again. You've banged on about this nonsense for far too long. I'm sick to the back teeth of it. It's a boil festering in your brain and it needs lancing,' Maureen added.

'Do you know what you're doing?' Steelers asked.

'Very last chance, Milton,' Maureen said, and slapped the palm of her hand on the table.

'Bugger off, Maureen. Let them get on with their so-called enhanced interrogation techniques.'

Steelers said, 'Milton. They're not bluffing.'

Milton looked at Katherine and said, 'I'd like the waterboarding first, please. I like my water lukewarm with a twist of lemon if you could. Followed by not less than twelve hours of hypothermia. Ten degrees C would be just perfect for my complexion. And I must have at least forty-eight hours of stress positions to get rid of those awful wrinkles on my back. Then I'll be ready for the drugs, but please, Katherine, not more than three at a time or I'll get confused. I'm afraid it's an age thing.'

'Is he raving mad?' Katherine asked Maureen.

Milton said, 'You know, Katherine, you really should re-write the memorandum. Change it from enhanced interrogation techniques to harmful interrogation techniques, then the acronym could change from EIT to HIT. Everyone will then know exactly what it means.'

'I've heard enough. He's all yours,' Maureen said to Katherine as she picked the folder off the table and got up from her chair.

'Goodbye, Maureen, old dear. Thanks for those occasions when you did support my position in the JIC. Please don't be concerned if you hear me screaming in your dreams. It's not me. I can't scream,' he said as she walked to the door.

Eleven

Morpeth, Northumberland, England

A day later than she'd planned, Zoe and Gavin drove to Morpeth. In keeping with old-fashioned military strategy, Zoe didn't reveal her plan to the lower rank, i.e. Gavin. It wasn't that she didn't trust him, she didn't want to spend the entire journey answering pointless questions about her plan.

Like a new recruit, he wanted to drive the red van. She agreed and hoped that driving would keep him quiet. He hadn't driven a large van before, so his driving skills had to climb a steep learning curve. He'd crunched the gearshift five times, and stalled the van at two sets of traffic lights before he mastered the pedals.

He must have said *sorry* a dozen times and his apologies were becoming tedious. They arrived at their destination at eleven-thirty in the evening. Gavin had yawned so many times in the last hour, she began to wonder if he would fall asleep at the wheel.

It had rained all day and the roads were sodden but at least the rain held off while he drove the van. The temperature outside would fall to zero, and weather forecasters had warned drivers of the risk of black ice on untreated roads.

Zoe looked up at the sky. She saw fast-moving broken clouds high in the sky, and through intermittent breaks in cloud, a bright moon.

Zoe didn't need a map or satnav to find the row of lonely industrial units on the outskirts of the town. Gavin cruised around the area and Zoe looked out for a suitable place to park the van.

She found a small lane used by farm tractors to access fields. Overgrown bushes and small trees on either side hid the lane from view. No-one would spot the van parked off the road, and it offered a good view of the row of warehouses on the opposite side.

Zoe told Gavin to park their red van in the lane. She had allowed him to drive to keep his mind busy. After his fourth attempt to reverse into the narrow lane, and not end up in a ditch, she took over and reversed it in first time.

While she surveyed the area, she told Gavin that she needed to re-equip for the mission. She planned to break in to an industrial unit to pick up some weapons and ammunition.

He'd made his third excuse as to why he didn't want to break the law, when she told him she would do the theft on her own.

An unwilling academic on a heist is a recipe for disaster, but she needed someone as a lookout, and if she picked up an injury, he would need to drive the van back to Darlington.

A row of five separate warehouses lined the road out of town. Identical units built at the same time. The main road lay on a higher elevation so the warehouses had driveways off the main road that led down to a semi-circular space in front of each warehouse.

The first two didn't have perimeter fences. They were small industrial manufacturing warehouses, one producing car parts and one producing leather goods. They were locked up for the night.

A national distribution company occupied the next two and an old perimeter fence surrounded them. The fence had collapsed or buckled in places, and overgrown bushes obscured large sections.

In the first warehouse, five semi-rigid eighteen-wheel trucks were being unloaded. In the second warehouse, a dozen small delivery vans were being loaded. Large roller doors on the access platforms were open in both warehouses.

Floodlights bathed the working areas for a stream of people loading and unloading the vehicles. Some vehicles departed and others arrived while Zoe watched. *Next day deliveries*, she thought.

Then she turned her attention to the last warehouse in the row. Beyond and behind it were open fields waiting patiently for next year's crop. The fields were surrounded by a low hedgerow that didn't offer much cover for a thief.

She trained her binoculars on the last warehouse. This one had a new security fence topped with razor wire, and well-positioned CCTV cameras. They had recently enhanced their security and she knew why. Two years ago she had inspected the site and warned the owner to improve security, or lose his permit to store weapons and other high-risk items. She must have been convincing because he'd done what she suggested and more.

While she thought about the new security, Gavin used her binoculars to look at the warehouse.

'It looks pretty secure to me,' he said.

'It should be. I told them they had to upgrade their security.'

'Good, you know the layout and what to expect,' he replied.

She shook her head. 'I wasn't expecting a security guard.'

Her tone suggested the job might have to give up on her plan. She had wanted to take what she needed, and leave no sign she'd been there. A night guard changed that plan. Opening this warehouse would tell the hunting dogs where to concentrate their search. She paused while she ran the numbers on the risks.

He handed over the binoculars, and said, 'Don't you have kit stashed somewhere else?'

'I have a small store in London.'

'Let's drive down to London,' he replied.

'London has too many cameras and Toni knows about my London store.'

Gavin looked confused and said, 'Toni wouldn't turn us in.'

She said, 'We don't know who had us under surveillance in Cosham. The fact that Johnson made us go dark means he doesn't know who he can trust in the Security Service.'

'We can trust Toni.'

'Toni is a professional. She'll follow orders. If a corrupt suit has issued orders then she'll not know she's being played. If they order her to find us, then we have a problem.'

'I understand,' Gavin said.

Phew, close call, she thought.

Zoe hadn't told Gavin the real reason why they'd gone dark. She hadn't told him she'd found out the CIA had them under surveillance. She hadn't told him that the CIA and the Security Service had begun a nationwide hunt for him.

If he knew any of it, he would collapse under the pressure and whatever secret he had would likely disappear. She shouldn't have brought Shawlens. Michael's advice had proved right—she needed proper backup.

'Does Toni know about this stockpile?' he asked.

'She knows that some Preppers have stores around the country but not the locations.'

'Preppers?'

'Preppers are people who are prepared for the next world-changing apocalypse.'

'What do you mean the *next* apocalypse?'

'Nuclear war, asteroid strike or the sun throwing huge solar flares at the earth to fry all the electronics. A world-shattering event capable of plunging civilisation into darkness,' she replied.

'You mean when society falls apart?'

'When it comes, there will be no electricity, no banks, no networks, no food, no water, no transport and society will descend into chaos. The only survivors will be those who are well prepared for catastrophe. Preppers have stored enough supplies for a year or more, until things settle down and civilisation is restored.'

'Why Morpeth?'

'It's impossible to predict which continent will suffer the catastrophe, so to hedge their bets, wealthy Preppers have stores hidden around the planet to give them the option of migrating to the safest corner of the planet. This Morpeth stash belongs to an American billionaire.'

As he listened to Zoe, he remembered the novel *I Am Legend* by Richard Matheson. When he read the book, he'd wondered what society would be like after a catastrophe. He looked at Zoe and thought, *shit, if that ever happens. I want to be at your side.* He didn't want to dwell on the horror of a post-apocalyptic society so he quickly changed the subject.

'How did your daughter Amy like her trip to Disneyland?' he asked.

'She loved every minute of it. Alec is having all the fun with her. I'm so jealous, but I'll make it up to her later,' she replied.

'I've got a niece the same age as Amy. I'd like to take her to Disneyland some day. I think children help you to remember what it's like to be a kid,' he said, but she didn't take her eyes away from her binoculars.

She said, 'I can't say I've had that feeling, but I can imagine you having as much fun as the kids.'

'Is she still trying to get you and Alec back together?'

'Oh yes. She hasn't given up on that,' Zoe replied.

'If she's a chip off the old block, she'll succeed.'

Zoe moved the binoculars from her eyes and looked at Gavin with a wry smile.

'You're a sentimental old tart. But I expect she will. I just haven't decided when I'm going to let her have her way.'

'Can I come to the wedding?'

'Let's not get ahead of ourselves. It's time for me to get ready,' she said.

She gave him a two-way radio and told him to keep it switched on and listen but maintain radio silence, unless he felt threatened or vehicles approached the building. She said she would call him when she wanted to leave, and then he should drive the van to the front of the building. He took the binoculars and watched her as she walked quickly along the road to the warehouse gate.

*

The warehouse had modern breezeblock walls and grey metal roofing. Three air-con cooling units on the roof kept the dozens of computer servers at their ideal temperature. A ten-metre lawn surrounded the building surrounded like a huge green collar. Zoe had told them to remove the high bushes and long grass that had blinded large areas of the previous perimeter fence. They'd followed her advice.

She knew they used the bottom floor for storage, and the upper floor housed their computer servers, offices and maintenance. Around the building, there were three sets of stairs and one goods elevator from the ground floor to the upper floor.

Behind the building lay a car park, and the space around the building well floodlit. One nine-year-old car had the whole of the car park to itself. The security guard's car she guessed.

The front of the building had a glass-covered entrance and atrium with stairs leading to the upper floor, and a reception desk manned by the security guard. Access through the entrance door required both swipe card and key code for out of hours. Good security, but then they'd been advised by an expert.

The security guard watched a movie on his tablet, and occasionally scanned the video screens beside his desk. The next time he looked at the front gate monitor, he saw a drunk woman at the gate, staggering and retching as if about to throw up over the entrance.

She wore a black parka coat with the hood up, black cargo pants and black walking boots. She looked like a camper or backpacker. She pulled a bottle of whisky from her backpack and took long swigs from the bottle.

He ignored her. Rain would wash away the mess. Then she dropped her pants to her feet and squatted down as if preparing to shit, pee or both. Her empty whisky bottle rolled down to rest at the bottom of the gate. He cursed her and said, 'Bitch, I'm not having human crap dumped at the gate.'

He paused the movie on his tablet, and pushed his body up from the chair. He grabbed his outdoor jacket and peaked cap that matched his uniform. He opened the glass entrance door and stormed up the drive to the gate.

'What the fuck do you think you're doing. Shove off or I'll call the police.'

He worried about his boss finding shit at the gate and thinking he'd missed it because he'd slept on the job. She ignored him shouting from the other side of the gate.

'Go shit on the grass, for Christ's sake,' he shouted at her.

She ignored him and made deep groaning noises as if she couldn't force the shit out.

He opened the main gate, picked up the whisky bottle, approached the woman and leaned down to grab her arm.

She turned to face him and he saw the barrel of a handgun between his eyes. He dropped the bottle and she kicked it away. She turned him around, pushed the cold gun barrel into the back of his neck, and told him to stand perfectly still. She quickly pulled up her trousers and sorted her clothes.

She pushed the gates wide open, marched him down the drive, into the building and over to his reception desk. She used large plastic ties to secure his hands and feet. She taped his mouth and left him lying on his side under his desk.

For a moment, she looked at the frozen picture on his tablet but couldn't decide what he'd been watching. She took two steps up the stairs to the upper floor, and then remembered the single car in the car park. Well-paid IT jobs on this site, no-one would walk out here to work.

Zoe scanned the monitors. The whole area around the building had CCTV. The building housed records, files and computer servers for the American billionaire's company website and IT system. Zoe knew the billionaire Prepper kept three large transport containers at the back of the building.

As expected, she found the containers parked at the far end wall near to a large roller door for vehicle access. Sensors detected her movement and switched on floodlights to light up that area of the floor. She stood beside the containers, looked all around and listened.

Nothing out of place, no unusual noise, no-one working late. Nothing to worry about, except a large area at the opposite end of the building remained in total darkness. Not the place to be when all the lights were out. She took off her parka and hung it on one of the containers. She had a short black leather jacket underneath her parka.

Beside the containers lay a trailer with small boat and outboard motor. She opened up the first container with bolt cutters she had brought in her backpack. Inside, she found a Land Rover Discovery. She read a notice stuck to the windscreen stating the engine had been modified to run on basic alcohol fuel. As she looked along the side of the container, she saw a row of five-gallon cans containing alcohol fuel.

She shone her torch inside, and then raised her two-way radio to her mouth, ready to signal Gavin to bring the van when an instinct made her stop. She turned and walked back to the mouth of the container.

She saw Toni and another woman standing in the firing position, arms outreached with their handguns aimed at Zoe's head. No-one moved and no-one said anything. The woman pressed her earpiece communications bud and asked about Shawlens. Boyd responded from the reception desk. He'd checked the CCTV and reported no sign of Shawlens.

Ertha said in a soft voice, 'On your knees, very slowly.'

Toni looked inside the container and asked Zoe, 'Where is Shawlens?'

'Safe,' Zoe replied.

'Need you down here,' Ertha said.

'Two minutes,' Boyd replied.

Ertha said to Zoe, 'Take your weapon out of your jacket, fingertips on the muzzle and put it down at your side—very slowly.'

Zoe set her radio on the ground then complied with Ertha's order. She kept her eyes trained on Toni until the moment she let go of her weapon.

'Hands behind your head,' Ertha said.

Zoe straightened her body and put her hands behind her head. She had underestimated the speed of their response. She expected them to figure Johnson hadn't given her any weapons. She thought they would stakeout the army weapons depots up and down the country. She got that wrong.

Everything about Zoe's service could be found on her record, including her inspection and approval of Prepper stores. She thought the encryption on her office computer would have delayed them a few days, but with US technology and access to a triple mainframe, they'd cracked it in a matter of hours.

Toni had found the Prepper inspections in Zoe's computer, and only needed to guess which one. In fact, it wasn't much of a guess because the other two stores were hidden in underground locations, and much more secure.

When Boyd arrived, he drew his weapon on Zoe. Ertha holstered her weapon and used a hand radio to contact Spence. He received her call in a mobile command and control vehicle on the other side of the country. She requested more agents converge on her position to search for Shawlens.

Spence immediately ordered all teams in the north of England to Morpeth by road and helicopter. Ertha explained to him that her hunch on Toni's operational knowledge of Tampsin had come good. Spence praised her for making a good call. She said Toni Bornadetti deserved a medal.

Ertha went over to stand beside Toni. She congratulated her on an excellent piece of intelligence work. She told Toni she had achieved in short order what thousands of analysts, geeks and spooks had failed to do with mountains of technology at their disposal.

Before they arrived at the warehouse, Ertha had questioned Toni's reasoning for staking out the building. Ertha had wanted to focus her attention elsewhere. Strong intuition told her Toni could get inside Tampsin's head, so at the last minute she agreed to follow her hunch and support Toni's stakeout. She admitted her concerns and apologised to Toni for having doubted her reasoning and professionalism. Toni nodded her appreciation.

'I don't know if your people will award you a medal but if they don't then you'll definitely receive one from the CIA, maybe a DIM,' Ertha said.

'What's that?' Toni asked.

'Distinguished Intelligence Medal.'

Ertha walked over to Zoe for a closer look. *Not so tough after all*, she thought.

'It's over now, Tampsin. Give him up and I guarantee he will live. If I have to hunt him down, he'll die in a hail of bullets,' Ertha said to Zoe.

In another situation, Toni would enjoy her success, but she didn't feel good about holding a gun on her friend and mentor. She wanted Boyd and Ertha to vanish so she could speak properly to Zoe. Find out what had happened. Toni watched Zoe relax her body. She'd seen her do it before, like a rattlesnake faking a retreat before it strikes. *Oh boss—don't you fucking do it—don't make me fire on you.*

Twelve

Boyd holstered his weapon and while the two women covered Zoe, he handcuffed her hands behind her back. Seconds after they'd lowered their weapons, they heard gunfire and the sound of large sheets of glass crashing onto the ground in the reception area.

'Toni—with me,' Ertha said, and pointed toward the reception area.

'Copy that,' Toni replied.

Ertha shouted at Boyd before she ran to the front of the building, 'Kill her if she moves a muscle.'

As they ran, they heard more gunfire, and more of the atrium glass panels crashed down on the ground.

'*Spence*. I'm under attack. I need backup,' Ertha screamed into her radio.

They arrived at the reception desk, weapons ready to return fire. No-one had entered the building.

Ertha dashed over large piles of broken glass to take cover behind a wooden cupboard between the entrance door and the reception desk. She raised her head above the cupboard and sneaked a look outside. She saw no-one.

Toni took cover behind the reception desk and nodded to Ertha that she had her back covered. Ertha returned a few rounds into the dark night to draw fire. Enable Toni to locate the gunman's position. The gunman didn't return fire.

Ertha gave out a sigh of relief. *Too damn old for this stuff*, she thought as she looked at a rip in her trousers. She thought some glass on the floor had done it but in fact, her trousers had split when she crouched down behind the cupboard.

With her Sig handgun in her right hand, she grabbed it with her left hand to stop it shaking. She stiffened her neck and pressed her head against the cupboard. Closed her eyes for a moment, took a deep breath and let it out slowly.

Four minutes of silence passed, then Toni whistled to Ertha and hand-signalled that she would go back down to the rear exit and circle round. Ertha nodded agreement. Toni inched her body backwards until it seemed safe for her to turn and run.

When Toni reached the three containers, she found Boyd flat on his back. His body looked rigid like a surfboard. His handcuffs and keys lay beside his body. Zoe had gone.

Toni placed two fingertips on Boyd's carotid artery. She noticed a small smear of blood on the index finger of his left hand. She tried to move his arm away from his body.

Her mind leapt back to Prague and the operation Zoe led to rescue Gavin Shawlens. Zoe had fought the mercenary Herman Vindanson in hand-to-hand combat. When they found Vindanson, his dead body appeared rigid with paralysis.

Toni stood up straight when she heard more shots fired into the front entrance. She heard Ertha return a few rounds. Toni looked along the building to Ertha's position, still pinned against the cupboard. When Toni turned her head back, she saw Zoe had stepped out of the shadow inside the container, her Browning aimed at Toni's head. Toni knelt down and placed her weapon on the ground, straightened up and walked over to Zoe.

Toni flashed her eyes back at Boyd. 'In Prague, when we found Vindanson paralysed, I asked you what happened to your ring. Now he's paralysed and I see your ring is missing again. I guess I should be thankful it's not me lying there.'

'Well done, Sergeant, figuring out I'd come here for supplies.'

'The old suits don't dirty their hands with weapons and Johnson didn't requisition any. I remembered you told me to bring ammo to the Cosham flat. You disappeared before I could do it so I knew you were short. I guessed weapons and ammo would be your first priority. In your report on this place, you described unacceptable security,' Toni explained.

'How long have you been hiding in the shadows?'

'Three hours,' Toni replied.

'I should have switched on all the lights,' Zoe said.

'You should have waited another hour. The Yank thought I had wasted her time. She wanted to pack up,' Toni replied.

'I didn't expect you to break my computer security so quickly,' Zoe said with surprise.

'A super hacker with a triple mainframe, cracked it in two hours,' Toni confessed.

'Impressive.'

Toni reached out her hand. 'Let me take you in. Get this thing sorted.'

'No chance,' Zoe replied.

'They've issued a kill order. I can't protect you. I can't stop them. What am I supposed to do when they have you cornered?' Toni pleaded.

'Bornadetti, you'll do your duty to the utmost of your ability,' Zoe ordered.

'Why are they saying you are a traitor?' Toni said, and snapped her mind back to her operation.

'I don't know what they've told you. I'm not a traitor.'

'What about Shawlens?'

Zoe shook her head and said, 'He's just a pawn in a political game. I've to keep him off the board until we know more about the stakes.'

'Until you pass him onto the Russians.'

'Russians? Why would I do that?'

'I understand they want his Lambeth Group secrets,' Toni said.

Zoe laughed under her breath and shook her head in disbelief.

'His Lambeth Group secrets are commercial and domestic rubbish. You should look at his Lambeth Group file. It's all silly science stuff like the SLIPFIRE job,' Zoe said.

'Why then is the CIA swarming the country looking for Shawlens?'

'The CIA want him, not the Russians, *and* it's not for his Lambeth Group secrets. There is something else up for grabs and they're not telling us. That's why Johnson ordered me to take him off the board. Johnson is trying to find out why the CIA want Shawlens.'

'Johnson ordered you to hide Shawlens from the CIA?'

Zoe nodded. 'Yes.'

'Please, boss. Let me take you in. I can't bear to think of you being killed by these people.'

Strong emotion resonated through her voice and reminded Zoe of Toni's deep desire. Toni had made it obvious many times, but Zoe made sure it had never gone beyond really tight hugs and gentle kisses on the neck.

'Turn around. Put your hands behind your back,' Zoe demanded.

No time for a long chat. Zoe used the butt of her Browning to whack the back of Toni's skull. Quickly she caught Toni's jacket to prevent her head hitting the floor. She fetched Toni's handgun and put it on the ground near her hand. She arranged Toni's body to appear as though she'd been knocked out from behind and fallen face-forward onto the ground.

Zoe ran fast toward Ertha. When Ertha heard someone running and turned to look, she saw Zoe. Ertha tried to raise her arm to take aim, but Zoe had already aimed a head shot that killed her. Zoe checked Ertha's neck to confirm the kill. She noticed a wedding band on Ertha's finger and she said, 'Sorry.'

Zoe gently ran her fingers over Ertha's eyes to close them. She felt a little remorse for removing a woman from her family, but Ertha carried a weapon and knew the risk. Many times Ertha would have thought that one day her life could end like this, and still she chose to place herself in harm's way. Her choice.

Zoe crouched down at the reception desk to check on the security guard. Shaking and terrified, he had small cuts on his face from broken glass but still alive. She raised her two-way radio to her lips. Zoe had set it on transmission when she first walked out of the container to face Toni and Ertha. Gavin had heard everything.

'Okay, Wyatt Earp, that's enough. Bring the van around to the back door. Quickly,' Zoe ordered.

Gavin arrived at the back door and waited while Zoe opened the large roller door for him to drive the van inside and park beside the containers.

'Oh God. It's Toni,' he said, when he saw her on the floor.

'She'll be okay.'

He looked bewildered and asked, 'How did she get here? What happened?'

'Someone sent Toni after us. She guessed I'd come here for weapons. We now know that one of the Security Service bosses is corrupt. Lucky I got the drop on them,' she lied convincingly.

'Did Toni say who gave her orders?' Gavin asked.

'They had guns on me. I had no time for a chit chat,' Zoe said.

'What are we going to do now?'

'Stay dark. Wait for Johnson to tell us it's safe to surface,' she replied.

Zoe needed to change the conversation. He would soon have questions she didn't want to answer. She took control of his arm as her eyes searched his body. She removed the handgun he'd stuck down his trouser waistband then spun him around quickly to scan all of his body.

'What?'

'That's good, you didn't catch a stray bullet. You've still got all your toes. I'm impressed,' Zoe said.

Excitedly, Gavin said, 'When I heard them on the radio, I ran to the gate but I couldn't see anything. I thought I should cause a bit of trouble and give you the upper hand.'

'Good initiative. Any problem with my handgun?'

'No problem except it ran out of bullets. Looks like you've been busy all right,' he said.

Before she left him in the van, she gave him her backup Browning HP-SFS (safe-fast-shooting) and basic instructions.

'Come on. We don't have much time. More agents are on their way.'

Zoe opened the other two containers and found stockpiles of food staples: rice, wheat, beans, nuts, sugar and salt. Stacks of assorted freeze-dried meals, canned food, seeds, oils, portable barbeques, and powdered milk. A row of one-week survival backpacks.

Gavin walked around the stacks of shrink-wrapped packs of bottled water. There were hundreds of litres of water. Zoe opened chests, the size of large freezers, packed with survival gear including weapons, solar panels, diving gear, collapsible boats, tents, tools, toolboxes and medical kits. Lots of outdoor survival gear.

Zoe selected and packed the equipment she wanted. Gavin browsed like a big kid in a toy factory, picking up some things, putting them down when he saw something more interesting.

'Let's go,' she shouted as she threw three backpacks into the back of the van.

Both of them went to pull the handle on the driver's door, and he said, 'I'll drive.'

He looked hyped-up, from the driving and the shooting, and the fact they'd come out on top.

'Not this time, sport, just in case we run in to more of them on the road. I'm trained in defensive and evasive driving,' she said as she opened the driver's door.

He said, 'Okay, but I think I should carry a gun.'

He offered an open hand for her to drop a gun into his palm. She glanced down at his hand with dismay.

'You hit large panes of glass. A chimp with a blindfold could have done that, and you didn't put the safety back on.'

'But it ran out of bullets.'

'End of. Mouth shut,' she bellowed.

Thirteen

Faverdale, Darlington

They arrived back at Spock's garage a few minutes after midnight. Spock had waited for them to return. He opened the gate for her to slip the van into the yard. She parked the van in the only vacant bay in a row of six maintenance and repair bays. Spock closed the roller door and switched on the lights inside the garage.

Gavin and Zoe got out of the van and Spock saw in their faces they'd been involved in an incident. They weren't talking or looking at each other. Gavin looked twitchy and ashen-faced.

Zoe's mind had moved a million miles away as she analysed what happened. Spock unloaded the gear Zoe had brought, and transferred it to a storage room he used for tyres and shock absorbers.

'Get everything?' Spock asked.

'Not everything. I'm short of a few items, but nothing critical,' Zoe replied.

'No problem. I've still got pals who deal.'

Spock flashed his eyes back and forth at each of them in turn while he shuffled around them, waiting and expecting to hear what happened. Neither of them spoke.

'Are you going to tell me what happened?' Spock said to Zoe.

'Walked smack bang into an ambush,' Zoe said.

'How did they manage that?' Spock asked.

Zoe pointed to the kitchen area. 'Gavin, can you do me a coffee, please?'

'I'd like tea,' Spock said as he showed Gavin to the small kitchen that the mechanics used for their tea breaks. Gavin grunted with frustration as he walked with Spock to the kitchen.

Spock saw the dissatisfaction on his face. Gavin made his feelings obvious when he tossed a chair out of his way just before he entered the kitchen. Still smarting at Zoe's refusal to give him a handgun.

Spock returned to Zoe's side and said, 'Need to know basis.'

'Exactly. He doesn't need to know,' Zoe replied as she looked over to the kitchen.

'Copy that,' Spock replied.

'Toni turned up with some CIA spooks. She did well to predict my movements. Got to give her that,' Zoe said.

'Toni Bornadetti?'

Zoe nodded confirmation and Spock saw in her expression that they'd nearly died.

'Fuck. How did she get in front of you?'

'They hacked my computer in double-quick time. She found my reports on the Prepper stores. My report on the Morpeth Prepper showed it as insecure. She made the right call,' Zoe said.

'How many dead?'

'Two, but not Toni,' she replied.

'Blimey, so now the CIA is pissed off. They'll want your guts on a plate.'

She smiled at Spock. 'Just the way I like it. Nothing has changed.'

'Does Toni know about me?'

'You were before her time but it won't be long before the CIA run through all my known associates. I reckon a few days, check that. One day before they come here to ask you questions. They'll put you under surveillance.'

'I'll be on the ball, don't you worry about me and Pat. I can spot a Yank at fifty paces.'

'I know you can.'

'You can't do all of this on your own, boss. Let me help you on this job.'

'Thanks. You're right, I need backup. But I need to keep you in reserve in case things get really out of control. My brother, Michael, is chasing down some OTRs for me.'

'OTRs, boss, you must be kidding. The reason they're on the run is because they can't be trusted.'

'They're ex-military. They'll take orders from me,' she replied.

'How did the tea boy handle the fireworks?'

'He's a royal pain in the arse but he coped well. I thought if he saw any action, he'd fall apart when it started, but he came through and saved the day,' she said.

'Does he know they were CIA?'

'No. I've told him there's a rotten apple in Security Services, trying to run us down, and Toni is just following his orders. I think he bought it but best not to talk about it. He asks too many questions.'

'Why is he so pissed?' Spock said as he looked at the chair Gavin knocked over.

'He thinks because he fired a weapon he's now a marksman. He wants me to give him a handgun.'

'Heaven protect us from inexperienced idiots with guns,' Spock said as he walked over to the van.

Spock inspected his van to make sure it hadn't picked up any damage that would need to be repaired. He kicked and prodded each of the tyres to make sure they were still solid.

'Was the van caught on CCTV?' he asked.

'Yes, but I scrapped their CCTV before I left the building,' Zoe replied.

'Good.'

'I'll hold on to it if you don't mind,' Zoe said.

'Not a problem, boss. If you think OTRs would be okay for backup, I know where one is hiding out in Newcastle,' Spock said.

'Someone you know?'

'Someone we both know. Karen Turnbell.'

Zoe thought back. 'I remember Karen, they called her Tinker. She served in the Redcaps, didn't she?'

'Not any more. She's wanted for murder.'

'Murder? Christ, that doesn't sound like her. I recall her as a stickler for the law,' Zoe said.

Spock nodded. 'Certainly an enthusiast in the job.'

'Sounds like the Redcaps' *Exemplo Ducemus* must have slipped her mind?'

Spock said, 'Apparently, the guy she killed had it coming. Doesn't excuse what she did but she's got nothing to lose, and she's as loyal as any you'll ever meet.'

Zoe racked her memory. 'I met her in Afghanistan, when she stepped in to pull Toni off a drunken sapper. Toni came to within an inch of despatching the guy to the cemetery when Karen pulled her off. Smoothed everything over with the sapper's CO and didn't charge either of them. I went to her tent to thank her, and we had a few drinks together. I haven't seen her since. Where is she?'

'She's hiding in a squat not too far from here, Old Benswell in Newcastle,' Spock said.

'How long has she been OTR?'

'Must be near on two years now.'

'Thanks, Spock. I'll pay Karen a visit.'

Zoe thought Karen would be good for backup. As a military police officer, Karen had special skills. Military police have to deal with the same type of criminals as civilian police, but with one major difference. Military criminals were trained killers.

Redcaps went through the same training as regular soldiers, and then they were taught how to overcome a professional killer. As an expert instructor, Zoe had trained male and female Redcaps in krav maga, to give them an edge.

'Here we are,' Gavin said as he brought a tray of tea and coffee, milk, sugar and chocolate cookies. They all went to Spock's office to sit around a table. Gavin must have left his attitude in the kitchen because his mood had lifted and his face seemed relaxed and friendly.

He'd decided he wasn't going to ask her for a gun. When the opportunity presented, he planned to take one and hide it in his jacket. He imagined himself stepping in at the last minute to save the day again, and then she'd be glad he'd taken a gun.

Every corner of Spock's office had been cluttered with piles of papers, car parts, and tools. Along one wall stood a row of grey metal lockers for mechanics to change clothes and store their things. Two four-drawer filing cabinets stood beside his desk, but with a mountain of paper covering his desk, the cabinets weren't used to store his paperwork.

Beside two pictures of naked women on the walls, there were two larger pictures of well-endowed naked men. Two of Spock's six mechanics were women, and one of the men classed himself as bisexual. Spock believed in equality in all things.

Zoe, Gavin and Spock sat at the table in the centre of the room, drank, ate cookies and chatted about the past.

Spock told Gavin he would follow Zoe into an active volcano if she wanted him. He tried to embarrass her and it worked. She went out of the office and into the store where Spock had left the backpacks. She sorted and checked the equipment she'd stolen from the American Prepper.

Gavin lowered his voice so Zoe wouldn't hear as he asked, 'So, what do you think of Toni turning up like that?'

'Close call. You were both lucky to get away,' Spock replied.

'I'm sorry we had to involve you in this thing. It seems some bastard in the Security Service is determined to put us in harm's way. I wish I knew why,' Gavin said, and his expression hoped for an answer.

'I wouldn't worry about it. Zoe is the best. She saved my life in Afghanistan. As I said, I'd follow her into a volcano if she needs me.'

Spock told Gavin about the night in Afghanistan when a mortar attack blew out a building and covered him with rubble as he returned to Camp Bastion.

His eyes well up and his voice weakened as he recalled how Zoe found him and started heaving lumps of rubble to the side with her bare hands.

In fact, Spock's emotions didn't relate to him being pulled from the rubble. At the time, he'd been unconscious and remembered very little of the mortar attack. His memory of *that* incident centred on his hospitalisation and recovery. As he told Gavin how Zoe saved his life in Afghanistan, his emotions began to overwhelm him because his feelings had taken him back to the first time Zoe saved his life, in Bosnia.

Those memories were vivid and terrifying. He didn't say anything about Bosnia because Zoe made him promise never to recount the incident to anyone inside or outside the army. He kept his promise. He told people about the time in Afghanistan, and as he told the story he relived the time in Bosnia.

In Bosnia, when Spock and Zoe served in Special Forces, they were part of a team sent to snatch a war criminal. Their intelligence brief had been incomplete and an intense firefight raged from flat to flat in a residential housing block.

The Bosnian and his bodyguards had an escape route out of the building. Spock had made a wrong turn in the confusing corridors, and collided with the fleeing Bosnian. The bodyguards overpowered Spock and took him prisoner.

Zoe had worked undercover, heavily disguised and dressed as a hooker. In the crowd surrounding the building, she saw the mission falling apart. With increasing enemy firepower on the streets, and a large threatening crowd massing outside the housing block, the Special Forces group had been ordered to withdraw and return to base. The group commander assumed Spock had been killed in action.

Zoe watched her team re-group and get out of the hot zone. She moved to the edge of the crowd to see what had happened behind the building. Just in time, she saw two VW black saloon cars pull away with the target Bosnian in the front car and Spock in the following car.

She ran from the crowd toward an onlooker watching from an old Skoda saloon car. She opened the driver's door, knocked him unconscious, and dragged him out of the car.

In the Skoda, she followed the VWs to another block of flats in the opposite side of town. The Bosnian and his men dragged Spock out of the black saloon and pushed him onto the floor of the lobby in the block of flats.

Several of them kicked Spock while they waited for an elevator to take them to the fifth floor. Zoe watched them from outside.

Inside the Bosnian's flat, his bodyguards prepared Spock for torture while the Bosnian told his family of the attempted assassination and his narrow escape.

Spock didn't know who had leaked information about the Bosnian to Special Forces. He didn't need to know. He expected they would torture him until he died. Zoe knew that as well. He prepared himself mentally for the pain to come.

The Bosnians blasted his ears with rants about what they were going to do to him. They brandished blunt and dirty implements they were going to use on his body.

Despite the shouting and the face slapping, Spock tried to imagine himself standing at the top of Grand Canyon. He'd been there so the memory felt strong. When the pain became unbearable, he would jump off and focus completely on the fall. He would feel the wind rushing past his face, his clothes billowing, and the terror, *his* terror, not *their* terror.

When he finally smashed into the ground, he would be dead. He would have done it, not them. In his mind, he peered over the edge. He felt the wind on his face, dust in his eyes. Block everything out, and focus on the fall. Arms out like Superman, ready to dive off. The vision became powerful in his mind and shut out everything happening to his body.

Zoe walked casually from the Skoda to the block of flats. No point calling for reinforcements. By the time it arrived on site, Spock would be dead. She enticed and then silently killed the two bodyguards patrolling the building. One had patrolled the entrance on the ground floor, and the other outside the Bosnian's flat on the fifth floor.

The guard in the corridor thought his boss had sent him a reward. Until she spun around behind him, rammed her stiletto heel into his knee joint to force him down, clamped one hand over his mouth while she sliced through his carotid artery and half of his neck with the large blade in her Swiss Army knife. Very messy but needs must.

She lifted his sub-machine gun and a hand grenade. She listened at the door and heard the Bosnians shouting at Spock. She heard Spock screaming. In fact, everyone in the building heard his piercing screams.

They'd cut off half of Spock's left hand pinkie, and tried to force him to eat it. He needed her fast. She pulled the ring and placed the hand grenade two metres from the door, and then dashed for cover around a corner.

BANG! The blast shattered the door and Zoe darted into the flat with the machine gun high in her arms and her head looking down the gunsight. She dropped to a crouched position, engulfed in a wall of smoke, dust and debris. No time to evaluate targets. Screaming and shouting intensified as people sounded off.

She spotted Spock's position. His boots, his legs tied to a chair. She killed everyone else in the flat as fast as she could, until silence owned all of the rooms. Any hesitation to identify and select valid targets among the dust and smoke would have given someone enough time to fire on her.

Spock had caught a stray bullet in the shoulder but he could walk. She saw blood streaming from his left hand as she cut him free with her knife. She fetched a kitchen towel and wrapped it around his hand. She grabbed a long winter coat, a scarf and put them on him to hide his Special Forces uniform.

People peeked out through their doors and asked each other what had happened. Zoe repeatedly said, 'Gas explosion,' to the ones who looked at Spock as they hurried past. No-one challenged them as they struggled along the corridor to the elevator and out of the building.

Zoe swerved the Skoda onto the other side of the road, and narrowly missed parked cars. She rammed the pedal to get as far away as possible before friends and family of the Bosnians found out what had happened. As she pushed the Skoda, Spock broke down and cried with relief. He'd resigned himself to more excruciating torture.

When she'd driven a safe distance away, Zoe stopped the car. She turned to face him. He wailed and howled like a banshee. She slapped his face to snap him out of his shock. She looked at his shoulder wound. A flesh wound, or in her assessment, an itch. She pulled a field dressing from his trouser pocket and quickly wrapped it around his hand.

She wasn't delicate with his hand but he didn't react to the pain. The gel in the dressing would soon stop the bleeding. She slapped him again, not a hard slap this time, and he began to calm down. The professional soldier surfaced and returned to duty.

Spock looked out of the back window. 'We need to go back.'

'What?'

'I've forgot my pinkie.'

They both burst out laughing and they laughed for a minute to ease the tension in their bodies. They leaned toward each other and their two foreheads rested gently on each other. She pulled her head back and they both smiled at each other.

They had left behind a horrendous bloodbath in the flat. She had killed the Bosnian, his brother, two bodyguards, the brother's wife, her three children and their grandmother.

If the women and children had dived to the floor and kept quiet, they would have survived. Before they set off for their base, Zoe told Spock it would look like a family feud or ethnic revenge killing, and that would be the best outcome for her and for him.

She made him swear on the lives of his wife and children not to tell anyone what she had done to save him. He bottled up the vivid memories of that night. The screaming rants of the Bosnian as he described the torture he had planned. The severe pain as they hacked off his pinkie. Their grubby, nicotine-smelling hands, pulling his mouth apart as they tried to force him to eat his pinkie. The taste of his blood. All vivid and locked in his mind.

He couldn't talk to anybody about what happened. He couldn't confide in a trauma specialist. He dealt with his deeply repressed feelings by telling people how Zoe saved his life in Afghanistan while he relived the night in Bosnia.

All the seething emotions of the terror in Bosnia came flooding back. It wasn't an ideal coping mechanism, but it worked for Spock. Only his wife Pat knew about his night terrors. She didn't know what happened in Bosnia, but she picked up the pieces when he woke from a nightmare.

Fourteen

Newcastle

The following evening, just after ten-thirty, Zoe parked the red van six blocks away from her intended destination. She looked out through the windscreen at the sky. A blanket of thick cloud overhead with a moderate wind from the north, but thankfully no rain.

No need for a waterproof coat. Cold but at least the temperature hadn't fallen below zero. A full moon his somewhere in the clouds. Maybe it saw Zoe Tampsin had come out and didn't want to watch.

Spock didn't know exactly where the OTRs were hiding. He'd sketched out a rough guide to the Old Benswell area of Newcastle. Zoe intended to take Gavin with her, but when she saw the scale of neighbourhood deprivation, she figured a high risk the van would be vandalised or stolen. She told Gavin to wait with the van.

He hadn't had an opportunity to take a weapon, so he looked delighted when she left him with an unloaded handgun.

Zoe wasn't confident Gavin could even be trusted with an unloaded weapon but he remained her only backup for the moment. He didn't have enough mean-looking aggression to scare off any thieves, but if he kept his mouth shut and waved the weapon in their faces, then with any luck, they should leave him and the van alone.

*

Ten minutes later, she turned a corner into the street that fitted the profile Spock had sketched out. Most of the streetlights were smashed, so the street harboured many dark pockets.

Dark archways led from the front of the street to walled yards at the back. The street looked as if it had been bombed out. Doors and windows on most houses were smashed or stolen and the street had become covered with litter, used fast food containers and bits of broken furniture. The street looked like a scene from a post-apocalyptic movie.

Fly tippers had dumped three large loads of junk on the road, and kids had scattered the rubbish all over the road, searching for something useful to sell. Boulders and slabs of concrete peppered the road to deter police cars and obstruct builders planning to demolish the houses.

Two burned-out cars and a burned-out van made the road look like a war zone. A black and sand-coloured mongrel dog, tagged along with Zoe as she walked.

'How did you know I need backup?' she said to the dog.

Zoe wasn't familiar with Old Benswell, and all her senses racked up a notch. She walked over to a row of abandoned, terraced houses. They looked like the kind of place where squatters might hide. This row of broken houses had been boarded-up with steel metal covers, and every inch of exterior wall had been covered in indecipherable graffiti.

Tall weeds sprouted out in all directions from the walls and guttering. As she got closer, her senses jumped to high alert. She noted every dark place where someone could jump out of the shadows and attack her. Walking slowly on, she found a house that looked less damaged than the rest.

Most of the roof remained intact, an important feature for a squat. The weeds growing around the door had been flattened by numerous footfalls. Someone stayed there. She stood beside the steel door and listened. She spread her fingers on the steel door and pushed to see how much it would give. Then she put her shoulder to the door and shoved it open eight inches.

A pungent smell of human excrement escaped and she felt certain she'd found an active squat. She expected all the squatters would know each other. Someone should be able to tell her where to find Karen.

She prepared to make a more determined push with her shoulder when she noticed movement out of the corner of her eye. Someone behind her watching. She heard shoes crunch against rubble on the road. More than one, possibly three. Someone kicked a stone in her direction. It hit the metal door and when she turned around, she faced four men.

Not old tramps but local thugs, heavyweights and vicious-looking. She felt an attitude in the air as if she'd trespassed on gangland territory. They gave off a strong confidence as if they always got their own way, and took whatever they wanted from anyone stupid enough to walk down their street.

'Welcome ta Big Dag's palace. Are yee lookin far a wee bit of bizzness?' a black man with a thick Newcastle accent said.

He glared at her as if she had just landed from another planet. His angry face, intimidating and frightening.

She shrank back and cowered. Two of the others spread out to her flanks to stop her running away.

Big Dag appeared to be African-English, and Zoe guessed his family were originally from Senegal. She'd been there and recognised the eye shape and face structure.

He wore a long black leather coat over a silver-coloured jacket and black pants with fine silver stripes. A mountain of a man with muscular arms and legs that filled out his coat arms and trouser legs. He looked like a body builder who'd probably pumped steroids and worked weights to produce his bulk.

A smaller but equally massive Nigerian, she thought, in an extra large NFL blouson jacket and XXL baggy jeans, moved to her right. He swung a battered aluminium baseball bat up and down, clipping the road on the downswing.

The third mixed race man had a shock of lime green coloured hair, and a thin lanky frame. He moved over to her left. He wore black Dr Martens boots, black jeans and a dark green parka. Like a juggler, he repeatedly flipped a thick metal tube in the air, and caught it in his hand. A length of old gas pipe as long as his arm. He had a vicious looking knife scar that ran from under his left nostril down and across his cheek.

Standing behind the three men, a young teenager with a strong family resemblance to the Senegalese guy. Probably his younger brother or cousin. Staying behind Big Dag, he looked nervous and agitated as if he had an attention disorder. His body jiggled to some kind of dance. His hands agitated as he encouraged Big Dag to, 'Do the bitch, do her now.'

The teenager served as Big Dag's gofer and carrier, a job that got him the respect he craved for on the street. To get even more massive respect, he pestered Big Dag for a chance to make his name.

Zoe stepped away from the metal door and toward Big Dag. She kept an eye on a large switchblade knife in his left hand that he flipped open and shut. His open coat billowed behind him.

She gaped at the eight-inch blade and terror defined her face. Her lips trembled and her hands shook. She gasped for breath and started panting.

'Bitch, that's me property. Yee dun vandilled me hoose. Yee gotta pay far me rapairs, like,' Big Dag said.

'*Pay. Pay. Pay*,' the teenager shouted.

'Big Dag is lord and master of this whole street. Kneel before your master,' the Nigerian said.

Zoe knelt and pleaded, 'Oh, please, Mister Big Dag, please don't hurt me. I'm lost and I'm looking for my son. I've got money. I can pay you, please take all my money, take the money.'

She clasped her hands as if in prayer for a few seconds, before she swung her shoulder bag around and fumbled in the bag to find her purse. She pulled out her purse to show him the money. She sighed loudly with frustration as her trembling, fumbling hands tried to pull a wad of notes out of her purse. She descended into a pitiful sniffling wreck.

'Oh ahm gunna take yer chinks, hinnie, but us lads has penetrating needs. Weel deal wi thim first, like,' Big Dag said, and the others bayed like frisky wolves.

The teenager behind him became even more agitated and started what looked like tap dancing, except a tap dancer wouldn't agree with that assessment.

Big Dag pointed his knife to a burned-out van in the middle of the road, and said, 'Come ova tae me palace. Let's see what yav got for us, hinnie.'

The teenager ran over to the van and opened the two back doors to reveal a filthy mattress on the floor. He stood on the mattress and kicked beer cans out onto the road. Big Dag looked down at the pitiful wreck in front of him.

He flashed an evil grin to his gang and said, 'Cumon, hinnie, let's party.'

Trembling like a leaf, she didn't move, so he stepped forward and reached out with his right hand to grab her hair.

Before he put his hand on her head, she grabbed his other hand and rapidly twisted it out to make him drop the knife, and shift his balance onto his left foot.

She pushed up strongly on her right leg and leaned forward as her left boot flew up to kick Big Dag so hard in the groin it lifted him a fraction off the ground.

She heard what she wanted to hear. A bone crack, as the reinforced tip of her boot smashed into the pubic arch at the bottom of his pelvis. If his bones were strong, it would just be a hairline crack. If his bones were weak, the pubic arch would split. No way to tell what he got. Either way he would be in severe pain for a long time. He collapsed in a heap.

The Nigerian rushed at her with his baseball bat raised high. She swerved to avoid the downswing, grabbed the bat with her left hand after it hit the ground, and grabbed the Nigerian's jacket with her right hand. She pulled him down to control his head, jerked her head back and then rammed her forehead into his nose.

His nose burst and blood streamed all over his face. She had snapped the nasal bone at the top of his nose and forced the bone fragments to rip into the soft nasal tissue. Painful, but not as much as the groin kick.

She swung the bat high behind her back to connect with the side of the mixed race guy's head as he ran at her from behind. It smashed hard into his ear and burst his eardrum. She picked up the blade, flipped it and raised it high as if she planned to throw it into the Nigerian's chest. When he saw the knife, he backed off, and clamped his bleeding face between his fingers to stem the gush of blood.

She scowled at the mixed race man and saw blood oozing through his fingers as he held his hand over his ear. He dropped his gas pipe and scurried along the ground to get away.

The teenager had tried to run to Big Dag's side. Zoe's eyes locked on to the teenager's face. Her arm still raised high, ready to throw the blade. The teenager stood four long strides from her, too far to reach. His face gawped in shocked disbelief as he saw his idols covered in blood and retreating like cowards *from a woman.*

Clasped between his shaking hands, he had a Colt revolver pointed at her body. Big Dag's gun, which the kid carried for him. The three men shouted at the kid to pull the trigger. His head darted between Big Dag and Zoe.

'*Da-a-a-g*,' the kid shouted.

The kid jerked his body back and forward. He wanted to run to Dag and give him his gun as he had done before, many times. Zoe stood between them.

'Get me, man. Respect me. Do it,' Big Dag shouted.

'Respect you, Big Dag,' the kid shouted and flicked his fist to point at Big Dag.

'Squeeze it like ah showed ya, man. *Now*,' Big Dag shouted.

The mixed race guy saw an opportunity. He scurried over to his gas pipe. He pictured himself thrashing the pipe into her head. Zoe saw his move in the corner of her eye and she sensed he would go for a frenzied attack.

'*Do it* or al cut yur balls off,' the Nigerian shouted at the kid.

The kid's head turned to scan the Nigerian's face. His bulging eyes showed he meant what he said.

Zoe threw the knife. She didn't flick the knife, so her throw sent the blade handle into the side of his head.

The kid stumbled backwards and dropped the gun. Zoe darted forward to pick up the gun and the knife. The kid ran off and didn't look back. With a gun in her hand, the two men ran off.

Big Dag writhed in pain clutching his groin. She noticed a damp red patch on his silver trousers around his groin. *No sex for a month or maybe longer with any luck*, she thought.

From previous fights, she knew the damage she'd inflicted on his body. She'd crushed his scrotum against his pubic bone with such force, his testicle sac would have split and coils of his seminiferous tubules would ooze out of his testicle.

When he tried to get on to his feet, his tubule coils would unravel and slither down his leg causing excruciating pain. When upright, his massive weight would press down hard on his cracked pubic arch to send an additional unbearable pain.

Worse than giving natural birth to eight-pound twins. So bad he would pass out before he could take one step, she guessed.

Zoe leaned over to inspect the side of Big Dag's head as if looking for something lost or missing.

'My coach said if I kicked a man's balls hard enough, sperm would squirt out his ears. Maybe I didn't kick hard enough. What d'ya think? Give it another go?' she asked.

'I'll fuckin' kill-yuh,' Big Dag said.

Zoe wiped the Nigerian's blood from her face. She raised the bat high and piled it hard into Big Dag's ribs.

'When I hear those bones rattling behind me. I'll know it's you.'

Fifteen

Zoe removed the bullets from Big Dag's Colt then broke the gun in two. It had been poorly maintained and looked more dangerous than useful. She thought the teenager probably knew that it could backfire. She kept Dag's knife. It had an attractive handle. The whole altercation lasted a matter of minutes as it should have from a krav maga expert.

Still, she felt disappointed with the outcome. In a textbook move, she would have allowed Big Dag to get closer, until they stood opposite each other, then quickly she would have rammed a powerful head butt through his nose. She would have put Big Dag flat on his back and he would have cracked his skull on the road.

When she saw Big Dag's knife, she figured he could stick her, depending on the speed of his reactions, which were unknown. So, she took the knife out of the equation and kicked him hard in the groin.

In training, Zoe showed her soldiers how to deliver a head butt unexpectedly fast. If done with moderate power, an assailant would be incapacitated and unlike a punch or a kick that can be telegraphed and defended, a head butt could be landed before the opponent could react.

In class, while rotating a model skull in her hand, she told them a woman's skull grew half a millimetre thicker than a man's skull. She joked with her trainees about early cave dwellers when head butting became the choice method to settle an argument.

She told them that fist fights were rare amongst cavemen because broken fingers often led to death through incapacity. If you can't wield your club, you can't defend your cave or bring home the bacon, she warned them.

She told them to assess every situation and if possible avoid violence. But if violence became unavoidable, then they should use the three BFs: be first, be fast, and be final.

*

Zoe returned to the house and pushed the metal door open. Inside the house, she stepped over large stones used to keep the door shut. The smell of human faeces had a powerful presence. She retrieved a pencil torch from her backpack.

She looked around while her eyes adapted to the darkness. The ceiling in the floor above had partially collapsed and a part of the roof above had been exposed. Obscene graffiti covered every inch of wall space. Some of it looked artistic, and some of it simple and crude. It reminded her of the pornographic images she'd seen decorating walls of some houses in the ruins of ancient Pompeii. She and Alec had honeymooned in Sorrento, near Naples.

She stopped near a large cupboard and realised from the smell she'd found a toilet. After the human excrement and rotting wood, she could smell strong human body odour.

Cautiously, she tiptoed up the stairs to the floor above. When she reached halfway, she noticed a large intimidating silhouette standing at the top of the stairs. Undeterred, she continued climbing the stairs.

'Boss?' the silhouette said when Zoe neared the top of the stairs.

'Karen?' Zoe said when she recognised the voice of Karen Turnbell.

With three or more layers of heavy clothes on her body, Zoe hadn't recognised a female shape underneath.

'What the hell are you doin' here, boss?' Karen asked.

Zoe reached the top of the stairs and stood in front of Karen. 'I'm looking for you.'

'Go back, boss. I'm not givin' meself up.'

Zoe shook her head. 'Not why I'm here, Karen. I need your help.'

'Me?'

Zoe looked around. 'Is there anyone else here that's reliable?'

'Sweet's here,' she said as she led Zoe into her room in the squat.

All of the floor spaces in three rooms and the bathroom were covered with bodies wrapped up against the cold. The squatter community had a strict hierarchy in force. Third-class residents were wrapped in paper or cardboard. Second-class residents had multiple layers of winter clothes. First-class residents had layers of clothes and old duvets, blankets or sleeping bags. From what she could see, Zoe guessed at least twenty people lived in the squat.

Harry Nimpea (a.k.a. Sweet) lay fast asleep in an old sleeping bag. He also wore multiple layers of old clothes and a knitted beanie hat to keep out the cold. They shared the room with four other squatters. As Zoe looked around, Karen said they were taking turns to keep watch on their things and look out for police.

Zoe didn't know Sweet, and expected he would also be on the run from military and civil police. The smell of body odour on the upper floor had become strong enough to blot out the human excrement from the downstairs cupboard. Zoe expected powerful smells. They didn't normally bother her but the potency in this squat made her eyes water.

'How did you find us, like?' Karen asked Zoe.

'Not difficult. Newcastle is your home town. You know this area backwards and besides, the MPs know you're here.'

Alarm sprang on Karen's face as she gathered her things. 'Shit, man. I need to relocate.'

'How have you been?' Zoe asked.

'I'm living on a knife-edge, like, with me good eye on the door for thieves and druggies, and me other eye on the street for Redcaps and woodentops.'

'The MPs haven't told the police yet so you're safe for the minute.'

A thirty-year-old and five-seven brunette, Karen Turnbell (a.k.a. Tinker) kept her hair cropped short like G.I. Jane. With short hair, square face and multiple layers of clothes, she could easily pass for a man.

She hadn't always been like that. In the Royal Military Police, she had shoulder-length, hair and a face that needed minimal make-up. In those days, she had an infectious smile and eyes that sparkled with a fiery confidence.

Karen woke Sweet, and when he set eyes on Zoe, he panicked. He thought she had come to arrest him. He relaxed when Zoe said she needed recruits.

Zoe asked Sweet about his CO, his unit, where he served and people he knew. When she'd finished interviewing him, she felt a nagging doubt about him, but she decided she couldn't leave him on the street now he knew about her. She agreed to take him on.

The two of them left their ragged clothes in the squat when Zoe told them she would pay well for their service. When they went downstairs, Karen saw the front door open. She led Zoe around to the back of the building, and out through the back yard into an alley.

Karen looked relieved as they hurried along the alley to the next street. She said, 'You were lucky not to run in to Big Dag. Wandering around here on your own is dangerous, like.'

'Big Dag?' Zoe replied.

Sweet said, 'Local drug lord. Vicious bastard, he likes to slice and dice his victims.'

'Tall, African, sumo wrestler type with a long coat, and fancy threads?' Zoe said.

Karen nodded. 'Yeah, real bad bastard, like. He owns the street, that's why we're getting out down the alley, like. We need to keep off his street.'

Zoe smiled. 'I met him outside your squat. Very charming. Not sure I understood everything that he said, mind you.'

Sweet dismissed her and said, 'Wasn't Big Dad. If it had been, he would have cut your throat with his ivory-handled blade, after he and his gang had raped you.'

'Do you mean this blade?' Zoe said as she pulled the African's folded blade out of her pocket and showed it to Karen.

'Shit, man. Did you take him out, like?' Karen asked.

'Just his balls. I don't think he'll be raping anybody for a while.'

Sweet looked at Zoe with suspicion. He half-expected screaming sirens and vehicles to sweep around them in some elaborate trap.

A tall and bald thirty-four-year old, Sweet had some angry-looking scabs on his head so he hardly ever removed his beanie hat.

Before Karen woke him up, she told Zoe the police wanted him for the manslaughter of an elderly man in a DIY superstore car park. Sweet had started an argument with him over a car parking space, and then Sweet hit the man with so much pent-up rage, the man had died before he hit the ground.

His once-powerful body had become overgrown with excess fat. In the army, he'd been a loner because of his deeply entrenched anger, hard sarcasm, intolerance and very short fuse.

He seemed to have a grudging respect for Karen out of necessity.

Zoe read all of his tells, and knew exactly where he'd come from and exactly where he'd go if he gave her the slightest bit of trouble.

Zoe said to Sweet, 'If you join my team, you obey my orders without question.'

Sweet's eyes narrowed to a fine slit and in a sly voice, he said, 'Boss, you can trust me.'

A smirk crossed Zoe's lips. 'I can do more than that—I can kill you.'

As they walked to the van, Zoe told them she had an OTR scientist, Gavin Shawlens. She told them she had to protect and hide him. She promised them five grand each for their service then told them to get into the back of her van.

Gavin turned around in the front passenger seat to greet them with a smile as Zoe did the introductions. He noticed immediately that they smelled awful. No shower facilities in a squat unless you like alfresco under a hole in the roof when it rained.

Gavin cocked his head and looked at Zoe's forehead. 'What happened to you?'

A bruised bump had started to show on her forehead. Gavin rested one hand on her shoulder and used his other hand to move her hair away for a better look. He noticed faint red smears on the side of her face, where she had wiped the Nigerian's blood.

Zoe flicked his hand away from her face. 'I'm fine, don't fuss.'

'I've got ibuprofen,' he said.

He pulled out a packet and gave her one tablet. She swallowed the tablet then took the packet off him and took another two tablets.

Karen watched them and warmed to Gavin's concern and attention to Zoe's bruise. Karen's eyes lit up like fireflies. She watched his every move and listened to every word. She didn't speak to Gavin. She wanted to wait until she looked clean and presentable.

She admired the soft features in his face. His maleness tempered with female traits of passivity and gentleness. So different from the testosterone men in her circle. She liked his furrowed brow, and his vivid blue-green eyes were magnetic. His grin seemed to be anchored with a tightly clenched jaw with the look of a chastened schoolboy. She loved the whole package.

One thing stuck in her mind when they shook hands. His hands were firm but very soft to touch. The hands of an important intellectual with wealth, status and sensitivity. His hand joined with hers for a second or two longer than it did with Sweet, and Gavin had reached further toward her to shake her hand.

Her heart fluttered. She felt heat under her clothes as her body flushed and her breathing quickened. She rubbed the palms of her hand against the sides of her trousers to wipe off the sweat. She felt a love rush over her body. Her hands tingled and her legs felt weak.

Each time he turned around to speak, she tried to hold onto his gaze. He switched his gaze onto Sweet for less than a second then returned his eyes to meet her gaze. He did that four times and on the fifth time, her gaze triggered a brief smile on his face. Her heart raced.

Zoe dropped Karen and Sweet off at a motel in Stamford just off the main A1 road. She had already booked a room and handed over the keys to Karen. She gave them money for food, clothes and prepaid mobile phones. Zoe had chosen a motel adjacent to a hypermarket store, and not more than thirty minutes' drive from her doghouse in Darlington.

Sixteen

Darlington

The following morning in Zoe's doghouse, Gavin slept soundly in the spare bed. Outside, the weather had taken a cold turn, and inside felt not much warmer. The central heating boiler had kettled then stalled, again. The noise woke Zoe and she got up. She didn't need to check the time. The boiler came on at six and kettled within a few minutes. She fetched a single electric element heater for the living room and switched on the backup electric immersion heater for hot water. She checked the wall thermometer, still in double figures but only just.

Gavin had complained about the cold in the house. Zoe didn't believe he'd ever experience real cold. Next time he kicked off about the cold, she planned to tell him about her cold weather training.

On top of the Brecon Beacons in Wales, in the dark, on snow-covered rough ground with howling fierce winds. Wearing basic clothes with no tent and no equipment, she'd endured one of the survival tests in the SAS selection process with no concessions to women given or requested.

An hour later, under darkness, Zoe slipped out of the house and drove to an open-all-hours supermarket for provisions. While she shopped, she received a text from Karen saying she'd had the first good sleep in a long time.

When Zoe reached the supermarket, she connected her phone to a mobile signal router before she called Karen. Spock had given her the router, and although not new tech, it would delay a trace for seven minutes. When it registered a green light, she made the call.

Karen said she would've liked to steep in the bath all morning but they planned to have an early breakfast and then go shopping for new clothes. Zoe heard a more composed voice from Karen and it seemed her spirit had lifted. Zoe raised her eyebrows when Karen asked after Gavin Shawlens, and then asked if he had a partner.

Zoe had just finished stacking bags of groceries on the passenger seat of the van when she received a call from Aunt Mary. Zoe stared at the ringing phone. The Aunt Mary number had been used for coded text messages between Zoe and her brother.

Michael wouldn't make a voice call unless he had an emergency on his hands. She connected her phone to the router and waited for the green light before she answered the call. She looked at the time on the phone, ten before eight.

'Michael.'

'Zoe, listen. Amy has been snatched.'

'What? My Amy?'

'A CIA team broke into Alec's house. He fought and killed one of them. They shot him in the back. Zoe … Alec is dead.'

'Oh God. Did Amy see this?'

Images of a snatch team fighting and killing Alec filled her mind. Amy loved her dad and the sight of several men attacking and killing him would scar her for life.

'She didn't. She doesn't know he's dead. I've told her he's visiting you.'

Zoe clamped her eyes shut as she asked, 'You've told her. Where is she now?'

'We've been brought to Mum and Dad's house. All of us are under house arrest. Amy is sitting with Mum. They're reading a book together. Only Dad and I know Alec is gone. Mum and Amy don't know.'

'Michael, you did the right thing calling me.'

'I had to. They're planning to make Mum and Dad go before a police press conference to beg you to return home. Face the music for having fought with and killed Alec. To head that off, I told them I could contact you.'

'Fuck. When did this happen?'

'Last night. They brought me here three hours ago and they brought Amy an hour ago.'

'Who are they? What do they want?'

An ominous silence hung in the air as Michael paused and waited for Alan Cairn to step forward and take the phone. Cairn headed a section of the Security Service know as CNPI.

'Tampsin, this is Alan Cairn. I believe you know what the CIA want.'

Zoe raised an angry voice, 'Cairn. Are you telling me you helped the CIA to snatch my daughter?'

The words were alien and she couldn't believe what she'd said. She felt threatened and vulnerable. The most precious people in her life were in danger and she felt helpless.

'Straight exchange. Give Shawlens to the CIA in return for Amy,' Cairn replied.

'She's a child, for God's *sake*.'

Silence for a few moments while the words bombed Zoe's mind. She fought to control the shock rattling through her body. Her daughter Amy in the centre of a hostage exchange surrounded by armed and dangerous brutes.

She heard a conversation in the background then Alan Cairn said, 'Tampsin, your brother has offered to take her place at the exchange. Do you agree?'

'I agree. I'll hand Shawlens over to the CIA. They hand over Michael, and then your people leave my Dad's house,' she said.

'Your family will remain under house arrest until the exchange is over. We want the exchange done today or tomorrow,' Cairn said.

'I want to speak to my brother,' Zoe demanded.

'Zoe,' Michael said.

'I want you to warn them that if Amy is hurt in any way, I'll give them odds of two hundred to one. Understand?'

Michael heard the anger in her voice and understood what she meant. As children they invented many secret communication codes. If anything happened to Amy, she would kill two hundred CIA agents in retaliation. He didn't pass on her threat because the people he'd met were more than likely to inflict their own retaliation.

'One other thing you should know. Milton Johnson is dead,' Michael said.

'Oh, for God's sake. How?' she asked.

'No further information. Cairn told me. He's your new boss.'

'I'm sorry to hear about Johnson. He put himself on the firing line,' she said, and sounded as if she wasn't surprised.

'Where does this leave you?' he asked.

'Did I say between a bullet and a bomb? Feels worse,' she replied.

'Maybe a bullet should be heading elsewhere.'

'What do you mean?'

'Shawlens,' Michael said.

'What has Cairn told you?'

'Cairn says Shawlens has put the national security of the US at serious risk. Maybe you should speak to Cairn again,' he replied.

Zoe looked at the countdown timer on her mobile phone signal router. She expected a trace had run on the call.

'How are your new legs?' she asked.

'Fine, they're a much better fit,' Michael replied.

'So you don't need that expensive wheelchair I bought you?' she asked.

'I'll hold on to it a while longer if you don't mind. Legs do get tired.'

Michael Tampsin had been a promising major with a great career ahead of him until invalided out of the army. He lost the lower half of his legs to an IED. He told everyone that his artificial legs were the most important additions to his life because they made him an inch taller than Zoe. She looked at the timer again. Time to bug out.

'Tell them, tomorrow, seventeen hundred hours, location to follow,' she announced.

'Tomorrow at seventeen hundred. Copy that,' Michael said.

'Michael, I'm supposed to help Mum tomorrow with her physiotherapy. Can you ask Aunt Mary to come over and do it in my place?'

'Aunt Mary will cover for you, sis. Leave it with me.'

'I'll text a location for the exchange, then this will be over, bye for now,' she said.

Zoe threw the phone router into the passenger seat and slammed her hands against the steering wheel. She shook with fury.

In her mind, she pictured her brother Michael and thanked him for taking Amy's place at the exchange. A quick thinker, like her, he'd done the right thing to keep Amy safe.

Her mind shifted to her ex-husband, Alec. As a couple, they had their problems but he didn't deserve to die this way. Someone would pay, she made a solemn promise.

In all of her previous undercover work, she had maintained a clever cloak of anonymity to keep her family safe. Cairn must have handed her file to the CIA so they could find her weakest spot.

A vision of Cairn burned in her mind. No matter what happened from now on, he would regret that decision, one way or another.

The CIA went straight for the jugular, her eight-year-old daughter. Not only had they killed Alec, and taken Amy, they'd put all of her immediate family in danger. Unacceptable, and unforgiveable. Ferocious anger didn't adequately describe how she felt about Cairn's betrayal.

They could have subdued Alec Haymarket with a Taser or a dart gun. Killing him meant they were sending her a message. Telling her they were prepared to do whatever is necessary to kill Shawlens.

Images of Amy struggling in the arms of strange men seared her mind. Tempered only by knowing she hadn't seen her father being killed. Her heart pounded and beads of sweat formed on her brow.

If she'd already had breakfast, she would have thrown it up as her stomach twisted into tight knots. She closed her eyes and regained control. Reasserted her confidence. Reinforced her determination. Moved her mind to the next item on the agenda.

They'd killed Johnson and severed her link back to the establishment. They must have tortured and killed him, but he didn't give them the ghost phone or they would have found her and crashed her doghouse. Johnson's quest had ended for him at least and they expected her to accept follow suit and surrender Shawlens.

To force her hand they put her family in harm's way and set Alec as a warning. People are fallible, mistakes are common and innocent people become collateral damage. To ensure no further harm to her family, she had to do exactly what they want, when they wanted it.

To comply, she had to abandon Johnson's belief that Shawlens had something of great importance for the country. Something stolen during the Second World War. Wealth that rightly fully belonged to the British people. She didn't believe in it anyway. No amount of missing bullion would make her risk her family.

'Options?' she said, loudly, and swivelled her head as if surrounded by a troop of invisible soldiers.

Seventeen

On the drive back to her doghouse, Zoe tried to overcome the stress and get her mind grounded. It hadn't ever been a problem for her before but this time it with her flesh and blood at risk, she struggled to shift her mind off the negative.

At this time in the morning the road wasn't busy, but her driving became so erratic that several drivers had to flash lights and sound horns at her.

Then she drove through a set of traffic lights at a T-junction, swerved and spun out of control. Narrowly missing a small Toyota car. She pulled the van over to the kerb, and a pedestrian hurried over to the van to asked if she needed help. She shook her head and he carried on his way.

She banged her hands on the dashboard and groaned loudly at the windscreen. Her anger felt palpable. It made her eyes water and her hands tremble. She wound down the driver's window and allowed cold morning air to slap her face.

She leaned her elbows on the steering wheel, wedged her thumbs under her cheekbones, and massaged her forehead with the tips of her fingers.

She felt deceived and betrayed. She'd been commended for her service and personally congratulated by heads of departments for her work. Loyalties change, she accepted that, but her family were now pawns at the mercy of the CIA. That thought stuck in her craw and wouldn't budge.

For the first time in her life, her strength crumbled. She had faced death and she had lost comrades and friends. She had lost people in horrific situations but none of it undermined her core strength or her confidence. Death didn't bother her and neither did invalidity. Her brother came through it and she believed it had made him a stronger person.

Many times, she'd seen people die when they shouldn't and others survive when they couldn't. All the death and destruction she'd seen and done told her you couldn't second-guess when death will end a life. So she didn't try and didn't even give it a second thought. But not now. Not with her family on the line. She couldn't do it.

Her family were the foundation of her strength. They were the cornerstones that no-one and nothing could take away from her. She could always rely on them to shine a light on her life when times were dark, and they could rely on her.

When death stared her in the face, she held no fear. She knew her family would honour her, remember her and love her. None of the awful things she'd seen and done haunted her. Her family washed away the worst stains with their unstinting pride, their close happiness and their love for her.

Now, she faced a fearsome reality. Her two worlds were racing to a head-on collision and her own family would become collateral damage. With Alec already dead and Amy about to discover she'd lost the father she adored and loved. Who would be next? She sensed her life draining away like a water barrel riddled with bullet holes.

If any of her close family were harmed because of her work, her life would become empty and pointless. She felt as though she'd gathered her family on top of a tall building just as a violent earthquake wreaked devastation. The gate to her conscience flew open, and all the trauma and death she'd seen and brought on her enemies surged out of the depths of her mind like bats fleeing a dark cave.

She fought to control her thoughts, and return her focus to the exchange. She knew that simple operations like an exchange could go wrong, mistakes are made, accidents occur and people die. Alec had died protecting their daughter.

A sobering thought brought her mind back. Michael had hinted that she should put a bullet in Gavin Shawlens. His words echoed in her mind as she started the van, and continued her journey. The thought dominated her mind all the way back to her doghouse.

The more she thought about it, the more it seemed the right thing to protect Amy. If the choice is Shawlens or Amy, there is no choice, she would protect her daughter. With Gavin Shawlens the only leverage available, she had only one safe option. Give him up and end the situation before any more of her family died.

*

It had started raining when Zoe returned to her doghouse. She leaned forward and rested her head on the front door with one hand on the door key pushed into the lock and two heavy bags of groceries in her other hand. Reluctant to push the door open, she stood at the door in the rain, reflecting, contemplating, before she turned the key, walked into the house and took the groceries to the kitchen.

In the kitchen, she heard muffled laughing and shouting from next door's children. An image of Amy took pride of place in her mind. After storing the groceries, she climbed the stairs and checked on Gavin. She crept into his room and found him still asleep on top of the bed. He wore his day clothes against the cold dampness in the bedroom.

He'd flopped on the bed and fallen asleep with two blankets wrapped around his body. She hadn't switched on the hall light so she stood in the dark just inside the room, listening to next door's children rumbling about in their room.

As she stared at his body, playful scenes of Amy rolled in her mind as if she watched home movies. She could never carry a photo of Amy on her but she could draw vivid images in her mind.

Images of Alec and Amy doing airplanes, him holding her wrist and ankle, and then spinning her on the spot. Soaring up to the sky, and then diving to the ground; she loved every minute. It seemed she would become a tomboy like her mother.

Few people knew about Zoe's miracle baby. A near-fatal stabbing during an operation in Bosnia had ended any hope of children. The blade had pierced her womb and the MO told her she would be unable to carry a child.

The cut had weakened her womb and it wouldn't be able to support a growing baby. He said she would miscarry before three months. The MO's news had been devastating, and typical of Zoe, she asked the MO if that meant she could dispense with contraception.

The MO's prognosis had proved correct. In the first two years of her marriage to Alec, she miscarried seven times. After the first two, she felt suicidal, but she learned to control her trauma with the help of a secret hope. Somehow the pregnancies would repair her womb for her.

Then, against all the odds, Zoe defied her prognosis and gave birth to a healthy baby girl. Apart from the need for a caesarean birth because her womb couldn't contract properly, the pregnancy had been normal. She remembered the moment the midwife put Amy on her chest. Zoe said, 'Hello, little girl,' and right on cue Amy opened her little blue eyes to look up at her.

Zoe fell overwhelmingly in love with the baby the medics had said she could never have. She set out to be the loving and wonderful mother she never had when she grew up. Her glamorous mother remained distant and not the kind of woman who liked to cuddle children.

In fact, her mother found it hard to talk to children. Zoe and Michael bonded more strongly together and parented each other when their father went off on army duty. She vowed Amy would have a wonderful life.

Zoe entered the bedroom and knelt down at the edge of the bed, eighteen inches from Gavin's head. She whispered quietly.

'I can't have my baby put in harm's way. I don't want you to suffer as they try to open your mind. You're too gentle. Better this way for you. Better this way for me.'

She drew her Browning and moved it to within an inch of his forehead. She released the safety with her thumb, and drew her finger to the trigger. Her cold and merciless training kicked in. Certain of the right thing to do.

When her marriage to Alec Haymarket started to hit the rocks, they attended marriage guidance and the specialist had taught them mindfulness. While Zoe embraced it, Alec didn't and their marriage failed.

Mindfulness trained her to recognise the critical moment between a trigger event and the point when control is lost. Zoe closed her eyes for that moment of relaxation and breathing.

She took a deep breath and let it out slowly. She'd done this before. She could blank out feelings of humanity and get the job done.

When you've done it many times before, it becomes automatic. This time would be easier with the sound of children playing next door, and a strong image of Amy in her head.

Eighteen

Gavin sprang upright and shouted, '*Don't do this to me.*'

He sat up erect on the bed facing the ceiling, but his eyes remained closed. He had broken out in a cold sweat and his face looked ashen and drained. His hands pounded rapidly on the bed, like some mad concert pianist bashing down on a keyboard. His body trembled and he panted hard as if he'd been running.

Zoe moved her gun out of sight. 'You're trembling. What happened?'

Gavin opened his eyes and glared. At first, he didn't see her and didn't move his head to her voice.

She said, loudly, '*Gavin.* Are you okay?'

'Uugghh. Bad, bad … really terrible dream,' he said as he looked at her.

She saw undeniable fear in his eyes. The same look she'd seen in her soldiers when they faced death for the first time.

'Same nightmare as before?' she asked.

He shook his head. 'Worse, worse … ever.'

'How?'

'*Ghost.* The movie,' Gavin said,

'What about it?'

'The demons that came to drag Carl to hell. They came to get me. I wanted to die and they came for me. Horrible angry demons pulling and dragging me. I didn't want to go with them. I didn't really want to die. Oh God, I didn't really want to die. They dragged me away.'

'It's just a nasty dream.'

'I've never had a dream where everything is so sharp and defined. I can pick out detail and texture.'

'What kind of detail?'

'I can't remember it now but in the dream it's as if I'm really there.'

His eyes welled up with tears, his restless hands fidgeted with the blankets and his face looked distraught.

He seemed to be having some kind of mental episode. 'What else?'

'I can't understand why I said I want to die? I don't want to die. I saw them coming for me. I tried to get away but I can't move quickly in the water. I can't turn. They grabbed me. Pulled me down under the water. I'll drown - please don't do this to me.'

His voice squealed like a twelve-year-old boy whose voice hadn't broken. Whatever he'd remembered had frightened the daylights out of him. An overwhelming experience from a memory he had recovered.

'Try to calm down. It's over,' she said.

'Something is slipping away from me. I don't know what it is. I think I'm going insane with this. I don't know what's happening to me.'

'Pull yourself together,' she said.

'There is something there, something hiding, and waiting. I need to go home,' Gavin said.

She looked surprised and replied, 'Home?'

'I'm sorry, Zoe, I need to go home. I can't do this anymore. I'm going home.'

She shook her head with concern. 'Wait a minute, you just can't take off and go *home*.'

'I've got to go back home. My sister will kill me when she finds out.'

'Home … where to?'

Gavin glared and replied, 'To my Mum and Dad's house.'

He got up and walked around the bedroom, back and forward, to pick up his things. He wanted to leave that very minute. She got a hold of his shoulders and forced him to face her.

Still trembling, she drew him into a tight hug. She held him until he slowly put his arms around her and hugged her back. It settled him.

Johnson might be right, she thought. Shawlens has seen or done something, somewhere in his past. It's in his head and making its way to the surface. His parents were dead and something had made him regress to the safety of his childhood.

Something the CIA didn't want him to reveal. Something so powerful they eliminate her family to keep it secret.

'I need to tell you something, before you go home,' Zoe said.

'What?'

'Look, Gavin. For operational reasons, I haven't completely kept you in the loop. This whole thing we're in right now. It's going tits up. So, it's time for you to know exactly what's going on. Why we're here. Come with me.'

Zoe kept a comforting arm around his shoulder as she led him downstairs and into the living room. She sat him down on the sofa and made him tea and toast. His trembling eased but still in shock his face remained pale. She allowed him fifteen minutes to settle then she told him everything he didn't know.

She told him the surveillance they found at the flat in Cosham had been put there by the CIA, and that the mercenary Herman Vindanson had been sent by the CIA to kill him. Sir Milton Johnson had ordered her to take him from Cosham and go dark. The PM had agreed to hand him to the CIA for a massive price. Finally, she told him what the CIA had done to her family to force her to exchange him for Amy.

'What the hell have I done?' he asked.

'Whatever it is, it must be great enough for them to use this level of force.'

'Phone your brother and cancel the hostage exchange. I'll hand myself in to the CIA office in London. I don't want to put Amy at risk,' he said.

'Do you have any idea what they want from you?'

'I haven't done any work for the USA. I have an American research assistant, Sharon Bonny, but apart from being useless as a researcher, she's the only connection that I have with the US.'

'What is her research about?'

'Her family own a brewery in New York, so her work is brewing related. She ran a project on reduction of beer chill haze caused by proteins. First base in a project is to repeat existing research in the area, but she's so bad in the lab, she hasn't moved off first base.'

'Interesting. Maybe her training lies elsewhere,' Zoe suggested.

'She's earmarked to be the next Director of Research for her brewery, and they're paying for her to be trained in research.'

'Okay, did you do any work for foreign governments?'

'None. I'm not allowed to. Emma and I were kidnapped by a group of Russians. They tried to steal her SeaPro process for making food ingredients. Special Forces rescued us from the Russian boat.'

'It's not about SeaPro or Barscadden,' she said.

'Then let's go down to London and find out what it is about. Whatever they want, I'll hand it over. You know I'm no good with this cloak and dagger stuff,' he said.

'That's a fact. Have you ever met Sir Milton Johnson?'

'Once or twice at the Home Office, just briefly.'

'Did you ever do any special projects or investigations for him?'

'No, why?'

'He believed you had something of national importance. That's why he ordered me to take you off the grid. If you surrender, the CIA get what they want and we lose it forever,' she replied.

'I don't have anything.'

'If they're after a file or something physical they would have ripped your home, your office and your lab to shreds to find it. If you're sure there is nothing then it must be something you don't yet know about but soon will.'

'Why soon?' he asked.

'Johnson said the CIA is on some kind of clock and time is running out.'

'What the hell? You make me sound like a time bomb.'

'It must be in your head. In your nightmares.'

'My nightmares?'

'What if it isn't a nightmare? It could be a repressed memory trying to reach your conscious mind and soon it will surface.'

'I can't make any sense of it. I don't know what it means. If it's a memory; I would know what it meant.'

'You don't have all the pieces in place yet. Whatever it is, it's supposed to be worth billions.'

'Billions? Really?' he said, and sounded surprised.

'Apparently. Can you think of anything that might fit the bill?'

'There is one thing. A bit stupid really, but it's the only thing I can think of that could be worth a fortune,' he replied.

'What?'

'Julie Blackhest worked for Barscadden as his research director. She gave a seminar at my university. She gave me her personal USB drive to copy her PowerPoint onto the projector computer. I copied the entire drive onto the computer,' he explained.

'You think the CIA is after Barscadden's secrets?' she asked.

'It's all I can think of that might be worth money.'

'If that were true, they would be hunting Barscadden and not you. Does any part of your nightmare connect with Barscadden or Blackhest?'

'Nothing I can recall.'

'The demons that tried to drag you away. Were they Barscadden's men?'

'No, definitely not. It's dark in the cabin of the boat and they just look like the black shadowy figures from the movie,' he replied.

'Trust me. When you experience that part again, go with them. Don't resist. Let it happen and you'll move on to the next part.'

'I don't think I can do that. I can't overcome the fear of going under water,' he said.

'You can do it if you picture yourself with them. Tell yourself not to fear them.'

'That's easy to say but not so easy to do,' he replied.

'Gavin, it's a memory from the past, and look at you now. You're here, fine and healthy, so whatever happens, it isn't going to hurt you. There are no such things as demons. Trust me, if there were, I'd know because I'd be the first one they'd want to take. You probably saw a fleeting shape and your mind tried to recognise it, but came up with shadowy demons from the movie. Next time, look at the demons, then go past them and move on. If you do, you'll reach the end of the nightmare, and it will all be over,' she said.

'I can do that,' he said.

'Believe me, I've done it and it works.'

Nineteen

Zoe thought carefully about what Gavin had told her and quickly dismissed the idea the CIA wanted Julie Blackhest's secrets. No part of his dream related to Barscadden or Blackhest, and Johnson had said nothing about Barscadden.

As far as Gavin could understand, his nightmare felt like a really bad dream. He didn't think of it as a memory because he couldn't relate it to anything existing in his current memory.

Gavin felt guilty that Zoe's daughter had been taken as a hostage. He tried again to convince her they should go to London so he could give himself up to Johnson. She told him the CIA had killed Johnson and that Alan Cairn had taken over as acting head of the Security Service.

'Johnson gave his life to protect us because he believes there is something vital at stake. I say we wait another day or two, and if nothing has come to light, then we travel to Thames House in London.'

'Okay,' Gavin said, and together they made themselves some breakfast.

*

All the possible scenarios ran through Zoe's head. If necessary, she could give Gavin up at any time. Amy and Zoe's parents were under house arrest but safe. She decided to keep Gavin for as long as possible. *His next nightmare could be the one that switches on the light*, she thought.

'What are we going to do?' he asked.

'My brother has a CIA gun at his head. I must proceed with the hostage exchange,' she replied.

After breakfast, she called Karen's mobile phone and told her she had a hostage exchange to set up. Zoe outlined the kind of vacant building she wanted for the exchange. Karen recalled a vacant warehouse in the Team Valley Trading Estate, south of Newcastle. She described the warehouse, surrounding area, access roads and potential escape routes.

As she listened to Karen's description, Zoe sat at her dining room table with her laptop, and looked at the area on Google Maps. She found the warehouse and examined all the surrounding area in satellite mode with high magnification and street view images.

During the afternoon, Zoe and Karen finalised a plan. Karen swung into action, made some calls to her street friends, and arranged to have the approaches to the warehouse watched.

Zoe arranged to meet Karen and Sweet in a fast food restaurant in the centre of Team Valley Trading Estate. At five-thirty in the evening, Gavin and Zoe approached the restaurant, and saw Karen and Sweet sitting near the door.

Zoe nodded to Karen and she nodded back. Before Zoe pulled on the glass door, she said to Gavin, 'I'll do the talking. You back up my story when you can, but do not contradict me. We cannot tell them about the CIA. Are you clear?'

'Yes,' he replied.

Like Zoe, Karen prepared thoroughly for action. She wanted to know who, why, what and when in as much detail as possible. Zoe couldn't tell Karen the CIA and UK Special Forces were after Gavin. Karen pushed for detail about the opposition so she could judge their capability and determination.

Karen needed a focus for her aggression, so Zoe told her about James Barscadden, Julie Blackhest's USB drive, and Barscadden's bodyguards called WRATH. Zoe had led a Special Forces team that engaged Barscadden's men off the Scottish coast at Ardwell bay. She had interrogated one of the men, and she fed Karen most of the detail she had gathered about WRATH.

Gavin saw an opportunity to support Zoe's story. He told them that Barscadden's people had brutally killed Emma Patersun, her sister Donna and her husband, Jim. He depicted everything he knew about WRATH.

He described in detail what he saw at the WRATH base in Miltonbrae Street, Glasgow, including a pile of Special Branch officers, stacked like cattle in a meat-grinding machine, ready to be rendered. Gruesome details helped convince Karen and Sweet that the enemy were ruthless bastards.

While Gavin told his story, Karen saw his pain and found it easy to believe him. Karen had taken a fancy to him when they first met. Having heard what had happened to him, she decided she'd look after him. Both of them had trauma they needed to get over, and she thought they should support each other mentally and physically. She would become his bodyguard, and loving partner.

Zoe scanned Karen's tells, and knew that their story about Barscadden and WRATH had taken hold. Even better, Karen seemed keen to give them payback for what they'd done to Gavin.

Against her better judgment, Zoe allowed Sweet and Karen to have a few drinks while they ate. In the squat, they'd missed the routine niceties of normal life. She reminded them she wanted them sharp and steady tomorrow.

Sweet held his pint glass in his hand, laughed her warning off, and made a comment about not being in the army any more. Zoe warned him that if he turned up with a hangover, then she would put him out of his misery, permanently.

Karen reassured Zoe that Sweet would be fine, and her reassuring expression meant she would take care of it.

Karen engaged Gavin's eyes. 'So you survived one attempt by Barscadden's people, like?'

Her voice soft and sympathetic, her face relaxed and not quite doe-eyed, but getting there. Both Zoe and Sweet cringed at the thought.

'I lost Emma. Barscadden burned Emma and Donna to death in their home.'

'How awful for you. I can't imagine how painful that must have been,' Karen said.

Is she wasn't sitting across the table from him, she would have cuddled him.

'Her funeral became the most devastating day of my life. Every minute of that day is seared into my thoughts,' he said, and his voice broke.

She reached across the table, lifted Gavin's hand and caressed it between her own. She had noticed before that his hands were firm and soft to touch. She wanted to feel his hands once more.

She rubbed his hand gently. He didn't flinch, frown or worse, withdraw his hand. She knew some men interpret over-familiar touching as sexual invitations, and she didn't care.

'Revenge is—' Sweet said.

'Shut it,' Karen barked at him.

Karen said, 'I'm sorry for your loss, but don't you worry, pet. Barscadden's people aren't going to hurt you. This time, I'm looking after you. If anyone's going to burn to death, it'll be *them*.'

'Thanks, Karen. Sometimes I wish I had died so I could be with Emma again.'

Karen looked disappointed with him and said, 'Don't talk like that, man. You don't know how it works. If you go before your time, like, you'll not be reunited with her. I believe our loved ones need to prepare a place for us, and only when our place is ready can we join them. You'll have to wait for your turn, pet, but don't worry, it comes along soon enough.'

Karen squeezed his hand then let it go. The doe-eyed look on her face said everything. If he didn't realise she'd fallen for him, then his brain must have gone on holiday.

Zoe looked at Gavin's face and slowly shook her head. Despite Karen's obvious gestures, he still thought about Emma and his troubles.

Zoe said to Karen. 'I've told him a trauma specialist could help with the grief.'

'Oh, pet, it does work. I've seen a good many soldiers get their lives back after some sessions with a good post-traumatic stress doctor,' Karen said to Gavin.

Telling his story had brought memories of Emma Patersun flooding back. He looked vulnerable and distraught as if going into shock. He wanted to leave and be on his own, but Zoe pulled him back down into his seat.

'Come on, Labcoat, you'll be fine,' Karen said.

'Labcoat?'

'That's your handle. Everybody has to have one, like. I'm Tinker, he's Sweet and you're Labcoat. For communications, like,' Karen said.

'Aww, give it a rest, ma arse is bleeding already,' Sweet said as he got up to go to the toilet.

'Ignore him, pet, he's a card-carrying, fully paid-up philistine,' Karen said.

'Are you okay?' Zoe asked.

Gavin looked edgy and began to fidget. Anxious to be on his way; he wanted to be alone with his thoughts.

'I'm fine. I have good memories. I fall back on them when I can,' Gavin replied.

Karen said, 'Don't you worry about tomorrow, pet. This gal has it all planned out. It'll be a breeze. You know what her handle is in the regiment?'

Gavin shook his head.

'It's DP which stands for Diana Prince, you know, the alias of Wonder Woman.'

'Wonder Woman?'

Zoe said to Gavin, 'Don't listen to that nonsense. Soldiers like to label everything and everybody.'

Gavin nodded, 'The face is perfect but the hair isn't right.'

Zoe sighed loudly and shifted around in her chair to signal she felt the conversation had become tedious. Both Karen and Gavin smiled at her. A faint smile creased Zoe's lips.

'That's better,' Karen said.

Gavin smiled and said, 'I thought Wonder Woman had large—'

Zoe said to Gavin, 'That's enough, Labcoat. I want to go over the plan one more time. Go and get another round of coffees and chocolate cookies.'

Gavin turned his head and faced the opposite direction. Zoe saw in his expression before he turned his head that he wasn't going to respond to 'Labcoat' from her.

Zoe conceded with a smile. 'Come on, Gavin, a round of coffees and cookies, if you please.'

*

Zoe waited until eight the following morning before she called Michael. She expected she would have to speak to Alan Cairn and had prepared what she would say. Somewhere in the conversation, she would make it crystal clear that he had crossed a line by exposing her family to risk, and that she held him responsible for the death of her ex-husband Alec.

Michael answered her call. She asked about Cairn, and he told her Cairn had returned to London. She sensed concern in Michael's voice—a warning. If they expected her to confide in her brother then she would disappoint them. She ended the call and sent text instructions instead to be relayed to the CIA officer in charge.

The exchange would take place later that day at seventeen hundred hours in a vacant warehouse on the outskirts of the Team Valley Trading Estate, Newcastle. At that time, the sun would be setting and the roads would be busy with evening rush-hour commuters.

In the text, she instructed the CIA to bring Michael to the north entrance of the building. Zoe and Gavin would enter from the south. The exchange would take place in the middle open space of a large empty hall. They would leave with Shawlens, she would leave with Michael, and then CIA men would leave her parents' home.

Twenty

Letchworth Garden City, Hertfordshire

Michael Tampsin sat alone in the dining room of his dad's house. He'd been waiting for Zoe's call. His parents lived in a large six-bedroom house on Baldock Road in Letchworth Garden City. His parents and his niece, Amy, had been confined to the living room.

Amy sat at a table with her Gran and together they read *Harry Potter and The Philosopher's Stone*. The night he died, Alec had been reading the book with Amy and had told her he would ask her lots of questions about the story.

In the kitchen, Spence MacAllisin and two other CIA agents discussed logistics and operational matters.

Looking through the dining room window and past the trees lining the drive, Michael saw a large command and control vehicle parked on Baldock Road. He guessed there were another eight people inside.

Michael's phone rang and Spence hurried back to the dining room. Michael spoke briefly then Zoe ended the call. She sent a text with her instructions for the exchange. Michael handed his mobile phone to Spence, and as they looked at each other, Spence knew Michael had warned her off to stop the trace.

An analyst hurried into the room and beckoned Spence, who followed him out of the house and into the command vehicle parked outside. The analyst told him he'd been able to pinpoint the source to the greater Newcastle area in the north east of England. Spence gave him Michael's phone and then went back to the dining room.

Spence said to Michael, 'I'm glad Zoe is going through with this.'

'She's got no choice,' Michael replied.

'I have to say I didn't believe them when they said she's become a traitor.'

'Do you know my sister?'

'I worked with Zoe in Bosnia. We caught some notable war criminals. I have the greatest respect for her. I know she's not a traitor. But she's following the orders of a traitor. She just doesn't know it.'

'Thanks for sharing that. I knew it had to be something along those lines.'

'She's working on a scenario Johnson has given her. She's a very smart lady. I'm hoping all of this intensity will make her question the validity of his orders.'

'If Alan Cairn had been here when she phoned; he could have told her,' Michael said.

'That wouldn't work on her. It's the oldest con in the book. A new boss tells you your old boss is a traitor. She would ignore it until she had verifiable evidence. I do think it's a good sign she asked to speak to him. She's having doubts about Johnson, and what he ordered her to do,' Spence said with an optimistic voice.

'I hope so, but killing Alec Haymarket has changed her position,' Michael said.

Spence nodded. 'I understand that, and I expect her to be suspicious and ultra-cautious about this exchange.'

'Alec was a nice guy. She'll be gutted. They were divorced but still a family.'

Spence looked sympathetic and explained, 'What happened to your brother-in-law wasn't supposed to happen. With a child in the house, he should have thought about that, and surrendered. He fought and killed one of them. They had to stop him,' Spence said.

'It is a pity Johnson isn't available to cancel her orders.'

'He wasn't supposed to bug out. I wanted him to call Zoe and tell her to come in voluntarily. He refused, and instead he just buried his head deeper in the sand. None of this should be happening.'

'Good people have died,' Michael said.

'Zoe has already killed one of my people and one of yours. I want it to end before we lose any more friends.'

'Unexpected shit happens. I'm well aware of that,' Michael said, and pointed to his artificial legs.

'I didn't ever expect to lose Ertha Odeele. I've known Ertha for fifteen years. I've spent Thanksgiving at her home every year for the past ten years. I love her family as if they were my own. When this is over, I'll have to tell them she has fallen. Her funeral will mark a very bleak day for the CIA. She had many friends.'

'I'm sorry about Ertha. Informing the family is one aspect of the job I don't miss.'

Spence nodded to Michael's legs. 'Afghan IED?'

'Yeah. The stupid thing is I served in the Royal Engineers. I wasn't supposed to be outside the compound. One of the lads complained about malfunctions in his metal detector, and like an idiot, I said I'd have a look at it. Probably just a loose wire. Bang, it malfunctioned.'

'Unlucky,' Spence said with a look of commiseration.

'As I said, unexpected shit does happen.'

'I know she's following orders but family take priority, right? Above all other things. She'll hand Shawlens over tonight, and your family can begin grieving for Alec. She won't try anything stupid?' Spence said.

'She won't. She'll be there, but maybe UK Special Forces should handle the exchange. With Alec dead, she's going to be on a knife-edge. Familiar faces would reassure her, and prevent any cock-ups.'

'My boss considered that option, and ruled it out. The CIA will handle the exchange. She'll remember me from our time in Bosnia. She knows she can trust me. I covered her back a dozen times. Zoe had Black Fox as her codename and I had White Fox. Together we were a very successful team. When we skulked we were a formidable team,' Spence said, and a wry smile spread over his face as he remembered those times.

'Skulked?'

'A group of foxes skulk. When we skulked, the enemy trembled,' Spence said with pleasure.

Spence's radio crackled loudly then a voice summoned him. He nodded to Michael and then went outside to his command vehicle for an update on the exchange location. Displayed on a large screen he saw the Team Valley Trading Estate.

A CIA technician pointed out the target building. Spence surveyed the area and smiled as he realised she had chosen well. He figured it would be too obvious to roll up there before the appointed time.

He said Zoe would probably arrive early to check the layout, and rolling up too soon would spook her. Spence requested a drone for aerial surveillance and then he discussed the travel arrangements with the technician.

The Team Valley Trading Estate lay four hours north including one short comfort stop at Scotch Corner. Spence told his team they would leave at twelve noon.

Another CIA technician told Spence that Director Kaplentsky wanted a word. Spence sat down at a console for a two-way video link, and gave Katherine a full update on his preparations for the exchange.

He told her about the conversations he'd had with Michael Tampsin. He said he believed Zoe would give up Shawlens before she would put her brother at risk.

Katherine told Spence she had approved his request and that a drone had been deployed.

When he finished briefing Katherine, Spence gathered his team around him to discuss the exchange. He had three field agents from his own East European Division office, and three Delta Force marksmen. Spence had just started to brief them when they heard a loud knock on the back door of the vehicle.

Spence leant over an agent sitting at a console, and looked at the video image of the space behind the back door. He saw a woman holding a CIA agent ID up at the camera.

'Let her in, will you,' Spence said to the agent nearest the back door.

Spence introduced Sharon Bonny to his team.

'Sharon worked closely with Shawlens in his laboratory, and she'll verify that the package on offer is the real McCoy.'

Sharon nodded, shook hands with Spence's team.

She said, 'I've observed Shawlens for several years. I called it in when he became a threat to our national security. I'll know immediately if the offer is not Gavin Shawlens.'

Spence said, 'I believe Tampsin will play ball to protect her family, but she's following orders and she'll not give up that corner easily. I expect her to try something. She may execute Shawlens to prevent him speaking to us. Retaliation for killing her ex would be an option she has thought about.'

Sharon said to Spence, 'We must assume Shawlens has passed his information onto Tampsin. After I have verified that the offer is Shawlens—execute both of them.'

Spence said, 'I plan to interrogate Tampsin and find out what she knows.'

Sharon shook her head. 'Let me be clear. This information is above the security clearance of everyone in the CIA including Director Kaplentsky. If anyone interrogates Shawlens or Tampsin and gains this information, he or she will be executed. Understood?'

Spence gathered his hand-picked team around a large interactive screen showing a map of the Team Valley Trading Estate. They brainstormed, postulated and discussed various scenarios. What if this, what if that, what if when, and Spence gave clear and unambiguous responses to each one.

He said, 'Tonight, regardless of what trick she tries; we terminate Shawlens and Tampsin. No matter the cost to them or anyone who doesn't get out of our way.'

Just as he finished his briefing, an agent intervened and told him the vehicles were ready to head north.

He said, 'This threat to our national security ends tonight. Buckle up and keep it tight.'

Just before twelve noon, Spence went into the house to fetch Michael who got up awkwardly onto his artificial legs. Spence watched as Michael hobbled over to a corner in the room and got into his wheelchair.

Spence looked confused. The service people with artificial limbs he'd seen were much more nimble.

'Do you need the wheelchair?'

'These damn new legs have to bed in. I'll take the chair in case I have to stand and wait.'

Michael's chair looked like a standard wheelchair but he had modified it to provide adjustable tension in the back and seat canvasses with additional padding in the cushions. He had built the frame with the newest blue-coloured, lightweight aluminium and the latest anti-tip castors.

He preferred self-propel wheels and had fitted them with quick release mechanisms. However, his modifications meant the chair couldn't half-fold back for ease of storage and transportation.

Twenty-One

Newcastle

A few minutes before five in the evening, Zoe entered the vacant warehouse in Team Valley Trading Estate. Outside, Karen met with four of her streetwise hoodie friends. She paid them cash, and they told her no strangers had approached the warehouse, but they saw a man creeping about on the roof of the adjacent building. Karen looked at the building. It certainly provided a good vantage over her position.

The warehouse had been stripped of all machinery, but a few built-in structures provided good cover. Long metal gangways criss-crossed overhead. Rows of skylight windows on the roof allowed the last rays of sunset light into the hall.

Many of the skylight windows had been smashed, and pools of water pock-marked the floor where rainwater had fallen. The twilight overhead provided just enough light in the middle of the hall for them to conduct their business. Large areas at the sides and ends of the building were set in darkness.

Zoe checked the building and then signalled Karen to drag Shawlens into the centre.

Gavin stumbled and staggered as he wiped blood from his badly cut and bruised face. His feet were bare, bruised and bloody. His left hand hung limp, and the fingers stuck out at an odd angle.

In the centre of the warehouse, Zoe took control of him, and Karen hurried back to the door at the south end of the building.

Gavin couldn't stand. Zoe pushed him down on an old chair she'd found, and he seemed to have difficulty keeping his body upright on the chair. She steadied his body to stop him flopping onto the floor.

At five on the dot, a group of people entered the north end of the building and spread out. Three men, one woman and Michael propelling his wheelchair. They approached the centre of the warehouse.

Two men stayed behind. Michael got out of his wheelchair to walk with the man and the woman. They stopped when Zoe raised her hand to signal they'd come far enough. She wanted a good space between them.

All of their eyes zoomed in on the battered body of Gavin Shawlens trying to stay on the chair.

'Captain Tampsin, I'm Spencer MacAllisin, East European Division Chief. We worked together in Bosnia.'

'I remember you, Spence, congratulations. Division Chief, no less.'

'I'm sorry we meet under these circumstances. We should be enjoying a drink and a meal to recall the great work we did in Bosnia.'

'I'm following orders.'

'As am I, Zoe. As am I. So, I fully understand your position. I hope you can understand my position.'

Spence looked at Gavin and saw a man badly beaten up and damaged. He looked back at Zoe and said, 'Was that really necessary?'

'Shall we conclude our business? I'd like to be reunited with my brother and have my family released from CIA custody,' Zoe replied.

'Of course. Sharon, will you please verify,' Spence said.

He waved his hand for Sharon to approach Gavin.

'Sorry, Michael, I don't have space for your chair. I wasn't expecting it,' Zoe said to her brother as she looked at the wheelchair he'd left beside the two other men.

'It's the new legs, sorry.'

Michael walked with Sharon Bonny to within hand-shaking distance of his sister. Zoe spotted two red laser target beams play on Michael's head. She expected there would be at least another two shooters not giving up their positions by using lasers.

Gavin looked up to see Sharon Bonny. She peered intensely at his face.

He recognised her and felt betrayed. He now understood she had joined his research group to spy on him. At least he now knew why she couldn't do lab work.

Sharon stood beside Michael with her hand gripping his arm.

Sharon called out, 'Gavin, can you hear me?'

Gavin spat out a mouthful of blood onto the ground. 'You evil spying bitch. Do your worst. I've said all I'm going to say.'

'Gavin, the last time we spoke. What did we talk about?'

'Who gives a shit about the lies you told me? You lured me into your car so your murderer Vindanson could kill me. You must have been cursing your luck when the police car turned up. Ha ha-ha-ha. I'll bet your boss tore a strip off you for incompetence.'

'I did my job and believe me, I hated working in your lab. And by the by, the minute you walk out the lab, they down tools and chatter all day about what they've watched on TV. No wonder your research team couldn't discover shit in a sewer,' Sharon fired back.

'Fuck you,' Gavin replied.

'Doctor Shawlens, you need to focus,' Spence said.

Gavin and Sharon looked away from each other and neither of them wanted to speak. Sharon looked angry enough to turn and walk away.

Spence said to her, 'You're here to do a job. Get it done.'

'Last I spoke to you at Kinmalcolm, after your so-called research group meeting. I asked you a question. Repeat your reply,' Sharon said.

'I don't remember,' Gavin replied.

'Answer her question, or I'll break another finger,' Zoe shouted at him.

Gavin recalled the meeting and answered her question. Sharon turned, walked away, and nodded an affirmation to Spence. She kept on walking to the two men waiting further back in the shadows.

Immediately, the two laser beams switched their play from Michael to Gavin.

Zoe and her brother walked backwards then Zoe pointed to the south exit and pushed her brother in that direction.

Zoe shouted to Spence, 'I got what I could out of him. If you come after me, or don't release my family—that information will go viral.'

Spence turned around, raised his hand high, and shouted 'Wait!'

Zoe nodded to Michael to mean *now*. Michael accessed his mobile phone and pressed a green button. A carousel in the empty seat of Michael's wheelchair dropped to the floor. It gave out a loud escalating scream as if it would explode.

Someone shouted, 'BOMB!'

Twenty-Two

A deafening explosion and a blinding flash ripped the centre of the warehouse. Gavin dived to the ground just as a hail of bullets tore through the back of his chair and sent it spinning across the floor.

He got up and ran after Zoe and Michael. His fake fingers fell off, and although difficult to run in fake feet, he ran as fast as he could.

Before anyone could move, the carousel reached its highest pitch and fired out three hundred ball bearings at high speed in a 360-degree radius. They smashed into the legs of the people nearest to the chair and painfully stopped them in their tracks.

Sweet had taken a high position on one of the catwalks. When the carousel started screaming, he shouted 'BOMB' and yanked on a wire to pull the rings on six M84 flash bang stun grenades, fixed to a long metal rail over the exchange area.

Each one detonated with an ear pounding 'BANG' and an intense blinding flash. Gavin escaped in the confusion when the CIA agents and Delta Force marksmen with night vision binoculars were blinded by the flash.

Outside the south entrance, Karen pressed a red button on an initiator box, and set off a small plastic explosive on the roof of the adjacent building that overlooked their escape route. She had put a small explosive device inside a football, patched the ball up with tape and got one of the kids to take it up to the roof.

The kid kicked the ball toward the sniper. The ball wasn't close to his position, so the sniper ignored it, but the blast stopped him firing on Zoe's team as they escaped.

Karen held the door open while Gavin, Zoe and Michael ran through the south exit toward the van. Sweet couldn't get down from his overhead position and catch up with the others. They couldn't wait for him, so he hid and planned to leave later.

When they reached the van, Zoe caught the keys when Karen threw them to her. Karen and Gavin scampered into the back. Michael froze when Zoe told him to take the passenger's side. He couldn't believe his eyes, an old Ford Transit van. Probably capable of nought to sixty in ten minutes. A dinosaur compared to the SUVs the CIA had.

As he hauled at the handle and threw the door wide, Michael asked, 'Can this thing fly?'

'Not very high,' she replied.

'They have three-litre engines. Maybe they won't notice us in the blur when they fly past doing ninety.'

'Not to worry. This old girl has a few tricks,' she replied.

When Michael closed his door, Zoe rammed the accelerator. Front tyres skidded furiously on loose gravel until they got traction, and then they were off down a pedestrian path. A man out walking with his Alsatian dog shouted abuse at Zoe as he got out of her way. His dog pulled hard against his lead, and barked loudly as the van flew past.

'Did Aunt Mary pick up our jewels?'

'Yes, they're safe and sound,' he replied.

Michael had organised two ex-SAS mates to enter his parents' house. He'd hid a back door key under a pot in the back garden for them.

They overcame the two CIA guards, and took the family to a safe house Michael had rented. He looked at his watch and said they were already in the safe house.

Since childhood, Zoe and Michael had been thick as thieves as they grew up in an army environment. Inside each other's head with room to play around. Always planning, plotting and scheming together.

Michael knew exactly what she wanted him to do when she mentioned Aunt Mary, and she knew she could trust him to get the family to safety. Secret signals and codes helped them to survive a succession of rough schools as their father dragged them around the world from one army base to the next.

Gavin tore off his fake feet and Karen helped him put on his socks and shoes. He didn't need help but Karen wanted to hold his feet in her hands. He didn't object, either he didn't have ticklish feet, or he enjoyed her touching them.

She wiped some of the make-up from his face. It looked too real, and it upset her to see him looking battered.

The pedestrian path led to a tree line, and through a short arch formed by larch trees on either side which led to the sidewalk of a road on the other side. Michael saw the archway ahead. A narrow gap with a gate between two trees meant for pedestrians.

'Karen?' Zoe shouted.

Karen popped up and looked out through the windscreen.

'Shit. Some bloody do-gooder has closed the gate. I opened it five minutes ago.'

Michael braced himself. 'It's not wide enough. *Zoe*, it won't do it. *Jesus*.'

'*Hold on-n-n*.'

Gavin and Karen braced themselves as Zoe forced the van through the archway. The wooden gate snapped and disintegrated into bits, branches hammered both sides of the van, cracked the windscreen and made deep gouges on the driver's side.

Zoe blasted the horn to warn pedestrians as she pushed through. The van flew out of the path in a flurry of leaves, dust, and broken branches as it swerved onto First Avenue.

The van sideswiped a silver-coloured Renault Clio and forced it to swerve away. The van flew out of the pedestrian lane like a big red banshee and the shock on the Clio driver's face added a few more grey hairs. Zoe overcorrected and the van's body rolled back and forth.

'*Aye—yee—jaa*.' Michael squealed as the van nearly overturned.

Zoe gritted her teeth, pressed on, and overtook a larger white van by driving down the centre of the road, causing oncoming traffic to hug the kerb.

Car horns blasted the air. Adrenaline surged through Zoe and Michael like molten lead. Karen and Gavin couldn't see from the back how close they came to disaster.

Pedestrians shouted and pointed at the van, while Zoe snaked the van through one gap between two cars, then another. Michael saw another red van ahead, similar in colour, but a different shape, and thought he'd guessed her plan. Hide their red van among a small fleet of other red vans.

'Nice one, boss,' Karen shouted from the back of the van.

'Good plan, sis, but it won't work. Not now we've got half a tree stuck to the bodywork,' Michael said.

A three-foot branch had wedged into what remained of the passenger's door mirror. Its leaves flapped on the windscreen on the passenger's side. The driver's door mirror hung by the wires and banged against the door, buffeted by the rush of air.

The engine roared past its normal pitch, and Michael sensed it couldn't take much more. His heart dropped to his socks as he imagined the black SUVs catching-up, and the agents spraying the van with hundreds of rounds.

Zoe pushed the van down First Avenue to the bridge over the River Team, heading toward the junction with Queensway. She ignored the Give Way sign, and forced the van straight across the junction to the next one, which formed a T-junction with Kingsway.

There were four bollards on the road around a tarmac repair. Too risky to swerve at speed so she drove through them, crushing two and sending one flying in the air, just missing a nine-year-old boy rolling down the sidewalk on a skateboard.

With tyres squealing, Zoe swept the van sharply left onto the Kingsway dual carriageway. She forced a cyclist off the cycle lane, onto the sidewalk and he fell off his bicycle. He screamed abuse at the van as Zoe regained control and aimed it south.

Traffic ahead had congested on the roundabout with Eastern Avenue. Zoe blasted her horn and flashed her headlights to clear a path as she weaved around cars and vans.

She came up fast on a black Audi A5 hogging the overtaking lane. She expected him to move out of her way, he didn't. She braked but not hard enough, and the van thumped into the back of the Audi.

Still the Audi refused to move over. It braked hard. Zoe swerved onto the grass verge and pushed through between the Audi on her left and the tree-lined central verge on her right.

The van snapped the door mirror off the Audi, and the driver slammed his screeching brakes as Zoe cut him up to avoid a thick branch that would have taken the roof off the van. Karen peered out the back window at the Audi driver's raging face. She stuck out her tongue at him.

'Always wanted to do that,' she said to Gavin.

Karen pulled his arm toward the back door so his face filled the window. 'Come on, Labcoat, have some fun.'

Like a five-year-old, Gavin stuck out his tongue at the driver. Gavin and Karen smiled at each other. He sat back in the van. 'I can't believe I did that. Don't call me Labcoat.'

'Too late, it's all over Facebook and Twitter. From this day hence, Dr Gavin Shawlens will be known only as Labcoat,' she announced.

For a few seconds Gavin believed her until he saw a smile start in the corner of her lips and spread right across her face. He laughed and pushed her shoulder backwards. She grabbed his hand as if they were going to arm wrestle.

She squeezed it for a second. It made him turn his head and look into her eyes. They stared at each other for a few seconds, and to her delight she sensed they'd bonded.

A green Ford Fiesta following Zoe's van slammed into the back of the Audi when it stopped. No-one had been hurt but a lot of broken glass and plastic scattered on the road.

'How many?' Zoe called out to the back of the van.

Karen looked out of the back door window and shouted, 'Nothing.'

Zoe came up fast on the Lamesly Roundabout to exit the Team Valley Trading Estate. Michael reached over and switched on the hazard warning lights.

She swept around the roundabout then turned left onto a long inclined slip road to join the A1 heading south. Although nose-to-tail, the traffic on the A1 moved fast. A forty-ton lorry came up parallel with the slip road.

Zoe's van raced the lorry, but there wasn't enough slip road to get in front. In four seconds, the lorry would be level with her van. She had no driver's door mirror so she snatched a look backwards, but couldn't see properly.

Zoe's foot stood hard on the accelerator. She pulled up on the steering wheel to lift her backside off her seat.

She screamed. '*Aa-gg-hh*!'

'*Brake*.' Michael shouted.

The engine laboured loudly but couldn't deliver more power. She forced the lorry driver to swerve onto the overtaking lane to avoid a collision. Cars swerved, headlights blazed, and furious drivers blasted their horns and swore at the lorry driver. The lorry driver blasted his horn, threw on all of his lights at Zoe, and then punched a clenched fist in the air.

'Risky one, sis,' Michael said with relief as the van picked up speed on the level road.

Michael looked at her knuckles on the black steering wheel. They were drained white and her arms locked rigid. In the excitement, Zoe accidently knocked the wipers on and they scraped the dry windscreen.

Michael reached over and switched them off. He could smell nervous perspiration from her body. He knew her nervous smell, and it reminded him of the games they played when they were kids.

Other kids played dare, double dare and triple dare. They played deadly, near death and certain death. He patted her gently on the forearm as he moved his hand back.

'Karen?' Zoe called out.

'Nothing yet, boss,' Karen said with disappointment as she peered out the back door window.

'Something's not right,' Zoe said to Michael.

'They're not following,' he replied as he reached to switch off the hazard warning lights.

'How many vehicles did they have?' Zoe asked.

'Three that I saw, but I'm pretty sure from the communications chatter they have more in the area,' Michael replied.

'Then they already have vehicles on this road. The old White Fox, Spence, is up to his sneaky tricks again.'

'Maybe we should get off this main road,' Michael said.

'No, that's what Spence wants, less public. We'll be fine on a busy main road. He needs to avoid excessive collateral damage. Too much public reaction.'

Zoe's stress moderated and she eased off the accelerator. She stopped weaving and overtaking, and allowed her body to relax. The engine noise toned down and helped lower the tension. Her mind raced around all the corners searching for something she'd missed.

Something Spence had thought of and she hadn't. It's a horrible feeling for a soldier when a plan is not going to plan. Michael recognised the feeling all too well. He felt it just before he lost his legs to an IED in Afghanistan.

The traffic ahead slowed. Red brake lights flicked on and off as congestion took control of the traffic. Even so, the column of traffic moved along at forty-five miles per hour when Zoe joined the tail end.

Soon the van had become trapped in a long snake of steadily moving traffic. It looked and felt like a normal commute.

Michael couldn't hear or see any police or any other helicopters overhead, and the vehicles all around the red van looked perfectly normal as if they should be there. Might this be the calm before the storm?

He wound down the passenger door window and released the wedged branch. The branch fell on to the road and a Honda Civic following drove over it. It banged loudly on the car's catalytic converter. The Civic driver blasted her horn and flashed her lights at the van.

Zoe expected two or maybe three of their SUVs to give chase along the one and a half miles of the Kingsway. From their perspective, Kingsway should have appeared perfect for a pursuit and arrest.

Karen waited with a few surprises in the back of the van. Ready for action. Enough to slow them down while Zoe raced down the A1 to the large rectangle shaped junction at Scotch Corner.

She planned to go around the junction to the small service track on the south side, slip into the heavily wooded centre, decamp and switch to a car Spock had left there for them. Then calmly join the traffic on the other side and head north back up the A1 to Darlington. That had been her plan, but now she began to wonder if she should stick to it.

Her mind skipped around on the hunt. Spence would have had a response prepared. In Bosnia, she'd sat in on many of the White Fox's briefings. She knew he left nothing to chance. She liked that about Spence, and he liked that about her. She expected him to have a fleet of cars waiting to pursue.

Zoe turned to Michael. 'Why did Spence not stick to their procedures? This stuff is basic pursuit 101. An automatic response should have kicked in. The road layout would have appeared perfect for a classic chase and stop. What else could I have done to make it easier?'

'Maybe you shouldn't have made it too easy for him,' Michael replied.

'The ball bearings wouldn't have killed anyone?' she asked.

'Definitely not. The charge I fitted would fire them hard enough to cause painful bruising, nothing more,' he replied.

'Shit. Karen are you sure no-one got near the van?' Zoe asked.

'No-one came near but I had to leave it for a short while to deliver Gavin. They could have put a tracker on the van. Maybe the banging about knocked it off and they've lost us,' Karen said.

Zoe's mind hunted and hunted for an answer.

'Maybe Spence has been called off. Rush hour traffic is too high profile for an incident. Thousands of cars, vans and people on this road,' Michael said, but he wasn't convinced.

Zoe settled the van down to a normal drive down the A1 except the van looked battle-scarred with its scrapes, dents, cracks and bits of tree camouflage.

'What am I missing, Michael? Please tell me,' she pleaded.

Twenty-Three

Newcastle

Sweet called Karen's mobile. She moved forward in the van until she sat behind Zoe's seat and put the phone on loudspeaker.

'Tinker, did you make it?' Sweet asked.

'Yes, we're clear and free. What's your status?' Karen asked.

'Good. I'm still in position, watching them below me.'

'Have any of them left the warehouse?' Zoe asked.

'No. The enemy are dazed, and taking care of their wounded,' he replied.

'Sit tight. They'll soon be on their way to find us,' Karen said.

'I can take them out. Only four of them sitting around,' Sweet said.

Zoe's ears pricked up to full attention. 'No. Keep your cover and wait.'

'I'm fed up waiting. I can do them and take their vehicle,' Sweet argued.

'You'll obey my order. Sit tight. Do not engage them,' Zoe commanded.

'Fuck off. I'm the one left here to look out for myself. Their vehicle is full of expensive gear, worth a fortune. I'm having it,' Sweet argued.

'*Sweet. Stand down,*' Zoe bellowed.

'Follow orders or so help me, I'll brain you,' Karen said into the phone.

'Karen. End it. Remove the battery,' Zoe commanded when she realised what had happened.

*

Sweet handed his phone to Spencer MacAllisin. Thermal imaging of the warehouse had pinpointed Sweet's hiding place. He quickly gave himself up when CIA agents closed on his position. Without hesitation, he switched sides and volunteered his help for a price.

He told them everything he knew, and then offered to call Karen so her phone could be tracked. Spence called Katherine in Grosvenor Square, and asked her if she'd received tracking on the Black Fox.

Katherine turned around to face a grey-haired thin man in a sharply pressed USAF uniform, mission controller, Colonel Steve Hutcher. A tall good-looking man who stood beside a communications console.

He confirmed hard lock on the Black Fox's signal, and that the coyote had taken up the pursuit. Katherine relayed the news to Spence and told him he should clean up and ship out.

Steve Hutcher had direct communication with a reaper ground control station attached to the 48th Fighter Wing of the USAF based at RAF Lakenheath in Norfolk. The two ground controllers, pilot and technician, prepared their MQ-9 reaper drone for attack mode. The pilot flew the drone, and the sensor technician completed systems and weapons checks.

Steve Hutcher ordered the ground controllers to hold the drone level at eighteen thousand feet, and steady at eighty knots.

He turned to Katherine. 'Requesting approval to go weapons hot.'

The drone pilot, a former F16 pilot, confirmed multiple locks on the target van. He scanned the four screen feeds on his console. The top screen above his head gave him direct line of sight from the nose camera.

At his eye level, he got visual feeds from the cameras and sensors of the multi-spectral targeting system. Below his eye level, the screen showed a large map of the ground area, and at hand level, two flat screens provided weapons systems and instrument readings.

The reaper had IR, visual and phone tracking lock on the van. The highest level of instrument accuracy for pursuit. The pilot requested permission to open fire on the confirmed target vehicle travelling south on the A1 main road.

Katherine Kaplentsky relayed the request to Washington and received an immediate reply. Green light the 30mm cannon.

Steve relayed authenticated approval to the ground control station. Katherine ordered one warning shot, but not for compassionate reasons, she expected to have to justify her decision. Better for her and the politicians if the kill shot followed a warning shot.

Spence relayed Zoe's position to six other CIA vehicles and ordered them to close in from all directions. He told them to prepare for a major road incident. He told them he wanted immediate isolation, clean up and disposal of the van and its occupants.

One of the CIA SUVs approached five miles behind Zoe. Another stopped and waited three miles ahead of Zoe's van. Others raced to the main north-south artery on the east side of England.

'Target designation set. Locked in. All green, check,' the pilot said.

'Check,' the technician repeated.

'Approaching weapon acceptability window in five, four, three, two, one, check. In the zone. Fire at will,' the technician said to the pilot.

The pilot opened small flaps on his console for weapons fire control. The technician called out instrument readings, closing velocity, range to target and time to exit the weapon acceptability window.

The pilot watched the video feed and the gun sight scales. He waited for the right moment. A good space between the target van and the vehicle in front. A gap opened up, and he fired a short burst ahead of the target van.

A warning shot, but also a range and target check for the pilot. He banked the drone to the left to come around for the final killer shot. His burst hit the ground four seconds before Zoe arrived. Bright yellow and white flashes marked the road where the cannon rounds tore up dinner plate-size holes in the tarmac.

Drivers who saw the impact flashes and chunks of flying tarmac pulled up or swerved. Brakes screeched and some vehicles were rear-ended by other cars failing to stop.

When the traffic flow stopped, a major pile-up of vehicles sprawled over the road with ten mangled cars and trucks at the centre. Many were injured in the carnage and it would be a miracle if no-one died.

All of this happened behind Zoe. Watched by Gavin and Karen through the back windows. Zoe floored the accelerator pedal and the van escaped as she veered in and out of a lay-by to cut around a Renault car stopped ahead of her.

'What the bloody hell is going on?' Michael threw a desperate look at Zoe.

'Can you locate their helicopter?' Zoe shouted to Karen.

'When they killed Johnson and Alec, and then took Amy, I thought this business must be massive. But firing on us on a public road. This is above and beyond anything I can imagine,' Zoe said to Michael.

*

Spence watched the drone video feed on a screen in his command vehicle. 'A bloody warning shot,' he screamed at the man nearest to him. He didn't imagine Katherine would order a warning shot.

'What's the problem?' the technician asked.

'We've shown Tampsin our hand. She knows about drones. She understands the weapon acceptability window, and she'll evade the next shot. The cannon is useless.'

Spence called Katherine and told her the van could not be targeted by the cannon. Tampsin would weave the road, brake and accelerate at just the right time to make the shot impossible.

He demanded authorisation for a Hellfire II missile. He repeated his demand. Katherine told him the collateral on a British main road would be too costly. He insisted. She refused. He demanded again.

She scanned the expressions of a dozen military people around her. Their faces told her Spence had told the truth. She relayed his request to Washington although she expected it to be rejected. *Imagine the media coverage the following day*, she thought and expected Washington to back.

*

'Oh mm-yy God. It's not a helicopter. There's a fucking reaper on our six,' Karen shouted to the front of the van as she identified the distinctive V-shaped tail.

Zoe and Michael looked at each other with shock. Zoe weaved in and around cars, vans and trucks. When a knot of vehicles blocked her way, she hurled the van onto the hard shoulder or the grass banking to overtake slower moving vehicles. The White Fox had trumped her with a card she never dreamed he could use in the UK.

'Damn you, Spence.'

'Why didn't he go for the kill shot? Doesn't make sense to give you a warning,' Michael said.

Zoe shook her head. 'I don't know. We should be dead.'

She felt deflated and scared that she'd made the most catastrophic mistake of her life. All four of them dropped into a quiet zone. Unable to speak as their brains took in the depth of their situation.

Their minds filled with thoughts of the video feeds they'd seen of drone attacks on insurgents. Vehicles on the run obliterated, buildings still and peaceful one second and blown to smithereens the next. Mostly those insurgents didn't know what hit them.

They knew what an attack drone would do to their van. Thoughts of the van being riddled with cannon rounds produced a morbid feeling that they were about to die horribly.

The silence in the van felt like the lull before a firing squad. Waiting for the squad to take aim. A firing squad of 30mm cannons. Their little red van now the red dot on the bulls-eye target.

Zoe's thoughts raced forward. This thing with Shawlens just took the elevator up a hundred floors. It must be colossal to warrant a reaper on the roads of England. *I can't cope with this. Pull over and give up, pull over and give up*, sounded loudly in her head like a train announcer at Kings Cross railway station.

Michael frantically searched maps on Zoe's laptop for the next exit off the A1. Hunting for somewhere to provide cover. A tunnel, underpass or somewhere they could hide from a reaper.

'How did they get our position? We must be ten miles away,' Michael asked Zoe.

'Sweet dragged out his call to give them a fix.' Zoe said.

Michael looked outside. 'The banking at the side of the road is too high. We can't get off this road. The next junction is Scotch Corner in five minutes.'

'Fuck it. We don't have *five* minutes,' Karen shouted when she saw the reaper line up behind them.

'Get out of the bloody way. *For God's sake,*' Zoe screamed and blasted her horn at a green Nissan Micra trying to move into the overtaking lane.

'They fired on us. What are they thinking?' Gavin screamed as he craned his neck to see the reaper.

Gavin's mind folded in on itself. He realised that whatever they wanted, it wasn't worth the others giving up their lives for him. He thought of the van ending up like a tin box riddled with bullet holes the size of tennis balls. No-one inside would survive.

'Zoe. Stop the van. Whatever they want, I'll give it up. *Stop the van,*' he shouted.

With steep banking on her left side and busy oncoming traffic on the right, Zoe couldn't get off the road. Anyway, the fields beyond the road were sodden with rain, and she'd likely get stuck in mud and become a sitting target. Michael and Zoe exchanged looks, worried eyes. Eyes of surrender.

'Come on, sis. It's futile. Time to give this up,' he pleaded.

'Gavin, are you sure you want to give up?' Zoe asked.

'*Yes,*' he shouted back.

*

Katherine Kaplentsky shook her head with surprise when approval came back from Washington. Hellfire II missile approved. She relayed the message to Steve Hutcher and he informed the reaper pilot. The pilot and his technician looked at each other with shock and surprise.

'Control. Please confirm last order,' the pilot requested.

'*Fire* the goddamn missile,' Katherine shouted at Steve's console.

*

Gavin and Karen peered through the van's back windows. Karen screamed, '*Incoming,*' as she saw the reaper bearing down, lining up a shot.

Up ahead on the road, under yellow sodium streetlights, Zoe saw a black SUV stopped in a lay-by. She saw a figure standing side-on, beside the SUV, and aiming a shoulder fired FIM-92 stinger missile at her van.

She saw the flare at the back of the stinger when its engine engaged after its ejector motor pushed it a safe distance from the operator. Everyone in the van screamed at Zoe to swerve.

During her service in Afghanistan, Zoe had fired four stinger missiles. She knew the FIM-92 stinger had dual IR and UV sensors.

It would accelerate to twice the speed of sound and lock on to the shape of its target. Impossible to escape and not enough time to stop the van and get out. Death by explosion flew towards them.

'Huugh. Michael ... I'm so sorry,' Zoe squealed as her grip tried to crush the van's steering wheel.

*

Time seemed to freeze. Michael's thoughts moved to an old pew in his local church. He lowered his head to pray.

Gavin stared out through the windscreen and quietly said, 'Emma, I'm coming. Please be there for me.'

Karen stared out the windscreen, and puckered her lips at the stinger.

Zoe's pounding heart leapt into her mouth. Her eyes clamped shut and her life flew through her mind, like a film reel spinning out of control.

From her first memory as a two-year-old in her dad's arms, her mum telling her she would become a clever girl, to school when she'd been surrounded by a ring of squealing and chanting school girls as she beat up two school bullies, to her first kiss, first time making love, university graduation, award of the Sword of Honour at Sandhurst, look of pride on her Dad's face, wedding day with Alec and then Amy, her lovely daughter.

With Amy's dad already dead and now her mum and uncle about to die, little Amy would be suddenly plunged in to a life alone. Pushed onto her grandparents. Safe hands, but unable to show affection or love.

Not what she planned for Amy. If anything happened to her, Alec would take over. If anything happened to him, Michael and Stella would adopt her. How many fallbacks do you need to safeguard your child's future?

Her parents were too old and they had been poor parents to her and Michael. *Not this for my Amy. Not this for God's sake*, her frantic, harrowing thoughts moved rapidly through her head like the violent spurts of blood pumping through her brain.

With crystal sharpness, her last seconds with Amy blazed into the front of her mind. She had packed to go away on a mission and had told Amy she wouldn't see her for a few weeks. Amy told her she had to pack to go to Disneyland Paris with her Dad. She pleaded with Zoe to go with them.

Zoe had pooh-poohed as she'd done many times before. 'I'll see you when I get back.'

Alec had said to Amy, 'That's your mother for you.'

The look of disappointment on Amy's face, and now an intense feeling of guilt for the loneliness her daughter would face. The images almost stopped Zoe's heart and she felt her life spinning out of control. She drew in one last breath and lowered her head. She stood in the firing line waiting for the shout. *Fire.*

Twenty-Four

'*Waaow-jaah. Bastard*!' Karen shouted.

'*Jesus*,' Gavin shouted.

Zoe opened her eyes onto the rear view mirror but couldn't see clearly out of the back windows because of Gavin and Karen. She drove over a pothole and the bounce shoved their heads to the side. She caught a glimpse of a wall of flames in the dark sky.

Zoe flicked her eyes to the front just in time to see a woman standing beside the black SUV in the lay-by with the stinger launcher in her arms.

She saw Toni Bornadetti and they had just enough time to exchange eye contact, and for Zoe to see the SUV driver slumped over the steering wheel as she roared past.

Michael said to Zoe, 'That woman looked like Toni Bornadetti.'

Zoe side-glanced him and smiled.

Toni had decided that no matter the consequences, she wanted Zoe to stay alive. If it meant she had to go OTR, then they would do it together.

Gavin and Karen stared at flaming fragments of the reaper that had crashed on the road. The traffic pile-up had blocked the main flow of traffic and only a handful of cars had followed. They stopped when the road became covered with fragments of metal debris and burning fuel.

The image of Toni standing with the stinger brought an emotional burst into Zoe's mind. *Okay, Toni, I give in, I want to, I'll do it*, she thought. Since the first week they'd met, Zoe felt Toni had wanted to make love to her.

Many times Zoe sensed Toni's feelings and read her tells. In changing rooms, she even smelled Toni's desire. Zoe had always given Toni clear return signals, she wasn't gay and wasn't interested. Now she wanted to devour Toni and savour every part of her.

*

Zoe reached Scotch Corner and swerved into the dense wooded area in the centre. They quickly decamped, gathered their equipment and switched to a silver-coloured Renault Grand Espace.

Slowly, Zoe exited the wooded area on the other side and calmly joined the traffic. She changed her return plan to avoid the congestion caused by the pile-up on the A1 and the reaper explosion.

She left Scotch Corner at Middleton Tyas Lane for a circular route back to Darlington, through country roads to avoid the A1. Michael phoned ahead to Spock and he waited at his garage. The carnage on the A1 had splashed all over the news, and Spock guessed they'd been involved one way or another.

Once under cover, Zoe, Karen, Gavin and Michael got out of the Renault and stretched their legs. Gavin couldn't walk, and leaned against the car. Tension in his muscles weakened his legs and adrenaline shock had drained his blood glucose.

Spock's wife Pat arrived with mugs of coffee, chicken sandwiches, and potato crisps. The four of them devoured the refreshments and didn't speak. They were drained emotionally and physically. Pat didn't speak to any of them while they tried to recover from their ordeal.

Spock busied himself, preparing a new dark blue van for Zoe. Much larger than the Transit, it had a tall roof like a removals van for walking around inside.

He fitted new decals to all the panels on the blue van and changed the registration number plates to match an existing local plumbing and electrical supplies delivery van. The only way to discover Spock's clone van would be if the two vans were parked side by side or the VIN numbers were compared.

Karen went over to the Espace to help Spock remove the equipment they intended to use on pursuing SUVs but hadn't. Spock asked Karen what happened but Karen said very little. It wasn't that she didn't want to speak. Her mind replayed and analysed what had happened.

'Check on Aunt Mary,' Zoe said to Michael.

Michael called the team he organised to rescue his parents and Zoe's daughter. The operation went well. Using Michael's spare keys they had entered his parents' house and overpowered the two guards without any violence. The family had transferred to Michael's safe house and had settled for the night.

'Everything is good. They're safe and secure, and they've got Stella there as well. Dad is kicking off but other than that, everything is cool,' Michael said.

'That takes an enormous load of my mind,' she replied.

'I know. I'm just sorry Alec isn't with them.'

'Take these with you,' Zoe said as she handed over an envelope.

'What's this?'

'My written orders from Johnson. Use them to ensure that I am not branded a traitor, and our family remain safe,' she replied.

'Dad will be so relieved you had these to cover your back,' Michael said.

'Please don't tell Amy about Alec. I need to do that.'

'Of course. I'll say he's still with you. Look after yourself, sis.'

'You look after our family,' she replied.

Michael and Zoe hugged each other as if it would be their last time. Michael wanted to be on his way to the safe house, to be reunited with his wife and take control of the ongoing safety of their family. Zoe fetched her actor suitcase and transformed Michael with a suitable disguise.

He thanked and said goodbye to everyone. Pat drove him to the railway station to catch a train heading south.

When Zoe came back into the garage, Gavin unexpectedly took her in his arms and gave her a strong hug and although surprised, she hugged him back.

'You were awesome. I don't know how you do it. Keep your focus on point all of the time. My brain fizzled out more than once,' Gavin said.

'As a child I had very strong IB. I think that's why my mother found me too difficult to cope with. I still have it,' she replied.

'What's IB?'

'If you had children you'd know. It's strong in my daughter but I understand it. IB is inattentional blindness. I'm sure as a lecturer you've experienced students not listening to you, not paying attention, away in a mind of their own,' Zoe said.

'Yes, I have. I've even done that.'

'Huge parts of a child's brain processes information. Ninety-five percent of what is going on around them is junk. To avoid overload, they must focus only on what's important at that minute, what's essential for their development. That's how you learn.'

'It makes perfect sense,' he replied.

'If I give Amy a phone to play with, and then come along later and ask her to clean her room. I force her to choose, switch her focus from something she thinks is important to something routine. So she turns a deaf ear to the routine job and an argument kicks off.'

'It's not difficult to understand when you put it like that.'

'I still have IB. It gives me sharp focus and it doesn't tire me because I'm not processing all the other junk around me.'

Zoe spotted Karen hovering, flashing daggers over to her, looking anxious and signalling she wanted to talk. She paced back and forth, and she looked angry. Ready to blow her top.

She'd been mulling over what had just happened and adding up what she'd been told by Zoe. Karen slammed her hand against the side of a car to let Zoe know she wanted to speak. Zoe told Gavin to sit down and relax, and then she went over to Karen.

'Walk with me,' Zoe said to Karen, and they walked to a quiet corner of the garage.

Karen said, 'You've taken us for stupid mugs, like. Level with me right now. A reaper in offensive mode over UK roads? What the fuck is going on?'

'I didn't expect a reaper. As you know, we prepared surprises for the SUVs that I thought would give chase.'

'Who the hell are we dealing with?' Karen demanded.

'The CIA with approval of UK Security Services.'

'Oh, Jesus. What have you got us into?'

Zoe told Karen the story from the night Johnson called her and ordered her to take Gavin Shawlens and go dark. She told Karen about Gavin's nightmares and although he believed he'd had a meaningless dream, she believed he'd recovered a memory.

'I'm sorry I deceived you and told you that Barscadden's people were hunting Gavin. I couldn't ask you to face the CIA,' Zoe confessed.

Zoe fetched a wad of money, handed it to Karen and said, 'Here is your money, and Sweet's share. I've asked Michael to use his contacts in military intelligence to produce a new legal identity for you. You'll be able to stay in the country or go abroad. With a new look, some money and legal documents, you can start a new life.'

'What do you think has happened to Sweet, like?'

'Jail or more likely dead. Loose mouth that needs to stay shut. I want you to get clean away, Karen. Your job here is done. My family are safe. You know I'll always owe you big time for that.'

Karen looked at the money and reflected on the new story for a while. She thought about how it would affect her situation. It wouldn't help her if she gave herself up. It wouldn't make any difference in her trial, and she would still go to jail for life. Maybe they would knock a few years off if she talked, but not enough.

If she went to jail then the pig she killed would be laughing in his grave. They both looked over at Gavin, sitting alone with his thoughts. His head resting in his cupped hands and reliving the drone attack.

'Labcoat doesn't look as though he's got anything worth billions of dollars,' Karen said.

'Johnson told me he'd been through Gavin's personal and professional life with a nit comb. He couldn't find anything to explain all this hassle,' Zoe replied.

'The reaper proves there is something. What could that be?'

'I have no idea but I'm burning inside out to know what it is,' Zoe said.

'You say he has this memory and it's coming to the surface.'

'Whatever this is about, it will pop out soon. Then we'll know.'

'Then we'll become primary targets,' Karen said.

'No. I intend to spill this to all the senior people I know in the Security Service. Once the secret is known by a couple of hundred people, there's no point hitting primary targets. It's too late,' Zoe replied.

'Will they scrap the CIA team leader and bring in someone new?'

'No. They have Spence in play because he knows me but he's made a mistake showing himself. It works both ways. I know him. Anyway, his plan didn't fail. Reaper or stinger, one of them would have taken us out for sure.'

'How well does he know you?' Karen asked.

'I worked with Spence MacAllisin in Bosnia. I learned a lot from him. He's very good. I'd been seconded for one op but ended up working with him on more than a dozen. All of them successfully delivered. He's one of the best. He has a brilliant record, and he's clever enough to keep out of the reach of the administrators and bean counters in Langley. They call him the White Fox. Not for his white hair but for his cunning.'

'Can he predict your next move?' Karen asked.

'He's already done that. He expected me to be prepared for a chase and so he didn't chase us. I must admit he caught me out with the reaper. I would never have expected him to get approval for a reaper to fire at us on a British main road. He knew that.'

'Who do you think fired the stinger and brought down the reaper?'

'Toni Bornadetti. I saw her as we drove past,' Zoe replied.

'I hope she has covered her tracks.'

Zoe patted Karen on the shoulder. 'Think about it, Karen. If you hadn't pulled her off that sapper in Afghanistan. If she'd gone to jail for killing him, we would all be dead. You saved us, Karen.'

'I suppose. I do remember her beating that guy senseless. I remember the venom in her eyes.'

'Did you ever find out why they fought? She wouldn't tell me,' Zoe said.

'He called her a blocked-up dyke. In front of quite a few people. One time too many. He thought she would have sex with him to prove she wasn't a dyke. Men can be very stupid. He had it coming, like.'

'That's why he didn't press charges.'

'I told his CO she would get off and the sapper would face charges of sexual harassment. There were plenty of male and female witnesses. His CO decided he didn't want the hassle. Shipped him home. Over and out.'

'Good result all round,' Zoe said.

'So, they don't actually want Labcoat, they just want to execute him to keep his mouth shut.'

'Yes, that's about the size of it.'

'Okay, I'll stay on. Gavin is one of the nice guys. I don't want anything to happen to him,' Karen said, and handed back the wad of money.

'Thanks, Karen. When this is over, I'll work on a new appearance for your new life. What do you think about going grey early? It would mean you could stop dyeing your hair once natural grey comes through.'

'No way, boss. Scrap that. I don't want all the old codgers in their baggy cardies and leather slippers, scuffling about after me. Ugh. Get a grip.'

Karen couldn't go back to her hotel. So Karen, Zoe and Gavin travelled back to Zoe's doghouse in a dark blue electrical and plumbing supplies van, provided by Spock.

While she drove, Zoe wondered if the excitement and stress would draw Gavin's memory to the surface, or bury it for good. When Zoe locked the door to her house, the three of them converged in the kitchen for a three person hug.

Twenty minutes after eleven at night, the three of them finally came down after the intense adrenaline rush earlier in the evening. The food they'd eaten earlier had replenished their blood sugar levels and taken the edge off their anxiety. They could relax for one night at least.

Twenty-Five

London

In the CIA control centre, Katherine Kaplentsky ordered all CIA vehicles to the reaper crash site to secure the area. She abandoned pursuit of the target van, and made containment of the disaster her top priority. She instructed her analysts to flood the media with news of a helicopter that had crashed on the A1 south of Newcastle.

A flexible news story had been prepared several years ago when the deployment of stealth drones over civilian areas became necessary. She ordered her people to get the story out on all news channels and social media sites.

With Katherine managing a large number of analysts and planners, they captured and controlled media comments, on-site photographs and first-hand accounts. Like sheep, the press and the media quickly followed the version of the accident launched by the CIA.

Katherine positioned three tame experts in the spotlight to offer opinions on why a helicopter had crashed on the A1. The circus lasted until four in the morning when the number of new sources and new requests for information dramatically tailed off to a trickle. The story took hold and the truth successfully hidden.

Later on that morning, Katherine waited in the executive briefing room at Grosvenor Square. She drank filtered coffee and ate an avocado chicken club sandwich for her breakfast. It had been a long night, and she had slept very little but she felt pleased that she had put a lid on the A1 crash.

While British emergency services dealt with the car pile-up, military personnel threw a cordon around the downed reaper. They convinced the local authorities they were expert air accident investigators sent to preserve all of the evidence for what would be a major investigation. There were no injured to be moved from the reaper crash site.

The remains of the downed reaper were gathered and quickly removed in two military trucks. The trucks made their way to a crash investigation warehouse. They rendezvoused with another two trucks containing the remains of a crashed helicopter. The trucks containing the reaper made their way to RAF Lakenheath, and the trucks containing the helicopter made their way to the crash investigation warehouse.

The helicopter had been recovered from the airplane graveyard in Arizona, crashed, dismantled and stored in containers on a UK airbase. Ready to be rolled out and used to cover up military hardware that had crashed on civilian land.

Police officers inspected the holes in the road tarmac and received reports from witnesses who had heard the sounds of gunfire. CIA analysts had started a powerful story in the media that a turf-war had broken out between rival gang bosses, resulting in the gunfire that had caused the pile-up.

Police forces were pushed onto the defensive when they were severely criticised for not preventing gang battles on main roads. Katherine congratulated her deputy for that one.

*

Spence travelled by helicopter to London and a car drove him the short distance to the underground car park at Grosvenor Square. During his journey, he wondered how the fall-out would be handled. To protect her position, Katherine would need a head to roll, and he stood squarely in pole position.

He'd let Shawlens slip through his grasp at the warehouse. His escape resulted in a major disaster on a main road causing the deaths of seven adults and three children in the pile-up.

Spence hadn't actively planned his retirement, and with no other interests in life, he worried how he would cope without the daily interaction of his extended family in the East European Division.

Dropping the ball is unforgivable at the best of times, but this particular failure would end his career. He expected the worst as he rode the elevator to the executive briefing room on the fourth floor.

Hindsight is such a wonderful gift and if he'd thought for a second his plans would fail so spectacularly, he would have pulled his handgun and shot Shawlens in the head when he had him in the warehouse.

He didn't do that because he wanted to interrogate Shawlens. He wanted to find out why his country would move heaven and earth to find and kill him. He wanted to know how Shawlens had compromised US national security.

He wanted to know why Britain stood back and let US hounds run riot over their land. Why the head of the Security Service had died during torture while refusing to give him up. So many imperative questions and still no answers.

When the elevator door opened, he looked at the ten-metre walk to the meeting room that stretched out before him. He wanted to turn around, leave the building and have others tell Katherine he'd resigned and returned to his office to clear out his things.

In the warehouse, he had killed Sweet to shut him up but now it looked like he'd burned the only viable lead. Humiliation, disgrace and incompetence were not feelings he wanted to face right now.

A woman analyst came out of a room to use the elevator but she paused when she saw Spence. She looked awkwardly at him for a moment, and then turned back to re-enter the room. He looked at the back of her head as she disappeared behind the door, and thought, *the whole building knows I'm burned.*

Katherine heard the elevator doors and stepped out into the corridor.

'Spence, I'm in here,' she called to him.

Her tone seemed relaxed and not at all what he expected. He knew her angry voice and that wasn't it. Painkillers he'd taken in Newcastle had started to wear off, and the pain in his leg began to throb again. He hobbled as quickly as he could to the meeting room.

'What happened to your leg?' she said when she saw him limp into the room.

He pulled his left trouser leg up to reveal black and blue bruising on the back of his leg.

'Ball bearings. A gift from Tampsin's brother. Sore as hell but nothing broken.'

'Did you get much sleep?' she asked.

'None.'

'I've not had much either.'

He looked at her face and hair. She hadn't showered. She'd washed off her make-up and hurriedly reapplied it so her face looked grubby and gaunt. *I haven't had any sleep and I don't look as bad as that*, he thought.

'Help yourself to coffee and sandwiches,' she said, and pointed to the catering trolley.

He moved with hesitation but she didn't give the impression she would launch an attack on his failure. He took out a packet of painkillers and took a few more before he drank his coffee.

'What's the latest?'

Katherine read from a paper. 'Ten dead, more than twenty injured at the pile-up. Nothing at the crash site.'

'How massive is the shit-storm?'

'Totally contained. My team took control of the media. Our story is now the official story. We have a downed helicopter at the crash investigation warehouse and I'm in total control of the crash investigation team. I just need a body from the morgue to pose as the pilot. Local police investigating the pile-up have been convinced that gunfire during a gang feud caused that problem. The storm has shifted to them.'

'Christ, that's fantastic work.'

'All the components were in place. It went like clockwork. I know you field jockeys think we administrators do nothing all day. I worked on the creation of the original DRVA, and I'm pleased to say it worked exactly as we planned it.'

'DRVA?'

'Downed reaper vanishing act,' she explained.

'I love it already. What about our targets?'

'They got clean away but I'm sure they're still in the area,' she replied.

'Obviously, Tampsin has recruited some help,' Spence said.

'Tampsin changed the rules. She'd been ordered to go dark. No contact, no visibility, remain hidden and wait for orders. I must say it's unusual for a soldier.'

'She has a sharp brain and now she knows Johnson is dead. She's working for herself. Her next move will be in *her* best interests,' Spence said.

'The analysts at the NSA have focused on the north of England and come up with a solid lead. One of her former soldiers medically discharged out of the service. He owns a garage near Darlington. His name is William Carrhage.'

'Spock. They called him. I remember him. I met him in Bosnia when Zoe and I were hunting war criminals,' Spence said.

'You remember him?'

Spence sat down and said, 'Yes, he got left behind when an extraction went sour. Presumed KIA and would have been but Tampsin had been undercover that night. She found him and managed to smuggle him out. If they'd caught him they would have tortured him for hours then buried him alive.'

'Interesting. So, Spock owes her big time.'

Spence nodded. 'No doubt about it.'

'Good, I'll have him and his garage put under surveillance,' Katherine said.

'What happened to the reaper?' Spence asked.

'Brought down by a FIM-92 stinger,' she replied.

'One of ours?'

'The team you had deployed ahead on the road to wait for Tampsin. They were neutralised and someone used their stinger. The stinger meant for Tampsin if the reaper failed,' she explained.

'Has to be British Special Forces. They could listen in on my communications. Do we have any idea who it was?' Spence asked.

'Not at this time. British ranks have closed tighter than a duck's ass. Your plan would have succeeded, if they hadn't interfered. Blame for the collateral damage on the road is on the Brits because they failed to deliver Shawlens as scheduled. Washington has spoken to London and made that perfectly clear.'

'So the Brits are cooperating with the crash investigation? I thought they'd be screaming for my scalp.'

'I've cleaned up the mess, and they'll keep their mouths shut. Put that worry out of your head,' Katherine assured.

Katherine's deputy knocked on the door and then entered the room. She looked fresh, confident and eager to report her news. She handed a file to Katherine and then helped herself to coffee.

'What now? Wait for surveillance on Spock's garage to turn something up?' Spence asked.

'No time for waiting. We're on a very tight timescale. I have one further card to play. Ertha's card. An asset Ertha brought from Canada. Is the asset prepped for launch?' Katherine asked her deputy.

'Yes, we're good to go. A press conference is scheduled. All TV channels, all media outlets, social media, everything. Maximum high profile exposure right across the board,' she replied.

'This will bring you up to speed. You can read it on your way there,' Katherine said as she handed Spence the file her deputy had brought.

'Where am I going?'

'Scotland. Some place in the north called Fort Augustus,' Katherine replied.

Spence looked confused. 'Scotland?'

'Yes, back up the A1. When you reach Scotch Corner, turn left. When you reach the other side of the country, turn right, you can't miss it. Keep going north until you find men wearing kilts,' Katherine said.

Spence smiled. 'I think I'll be able to find it.'

'When the Shawlens business is in the bag, don't forget to bring back a case of single malt,' Katherine said.

'I won't forget. What resources do I have?'

'Your command vehicle is already on its way there. I suggest you fly up to Glasgow and meet them there. Fort Augustus is in need of a makeover.'

'A makeover? Into what exactly?'

'A village size cage-trap. For a Black Fox and her cubs?'

Twenty-Six

Darlington

Neither Gavin nor Zoe slept much after they returned to Zoe's house. Karen shared Zoe's bed and while Karen slept like a log, Zoe couldn't sleep beside Karen's restless legs. Zoe got up and camped out on her sofa just before four in the morning.

Gavin wrestled all night with the knowledge that Sharon Bonny had spied on him. He painstakingly searched his past for a reason but couldn't find anything. On top of that, the near death experience in the van re-ran continuously in his mind, and he worried about Zoe's family in danger.

He didn't understand why the CIA believed he had threatened their national security. He decided he would go alone to London and convince the CIA they had made a mistake. They had the wrong person. He thought it through and knew he had to get this mistake sorted before anybody else died.

Gavin heard Zoe pad down the stairs and go into the living room. He followed her and asked, 'Do you want any tea or coffee?'

'No, I'm going to have a couple more hours, put the light out,' she replied, and wrapped blankets around her body as she settled in the sofa.

Gavin sat at the dining room table and scanned the news channels on Zoe's laptop. He searched for some mention of the current threat to US national security. Desperate to understand why the CIA had wanted him.

He found traffic reports warning of major congestion on the southbound carriageway of the A1 because of the pile-up. In a separate report, he read that a helicopter had crashed on the A1 north of Scotch Corner.

While there were plenty of images of the mangled vehicles in the pile-up, images of the crash site were limited and confined to distance photographs only. He searched for video or mobile phone clips, looking for anything depicting the truth of what happened but found none.

Just after six in the morning, the house woke up when both Zoe and Karen arrived in the kitchen to prepare breakfast.

Gavin moved the laptop off the dining room table when the two women brought trays of food and coffee.

Zoe set out three plates of bacon, eggs, mushrooms and baked beans on the table beside three mugs of coffee. They ate their breakfast and Gavin told them what he'd found about the crashes on the A1. He complained that the truth had been covered up.

'I would be concerned if they didn't have a contingency plan to cover it up,' Zoe said.

'The police are reporting that gunfire in a gangland fight had ripped up the tarmac and caused the pile-up. They're saying a helicopter crashed,' Gavin said.

'Our Security Services will be cooperating with the CIA to keep the drone out of the media. It's no surprise,' Zoe said.

'I think I'd notice the difference between a drone and a helicopter,' Gavin said.

Zoe explained, 'No-one will see the drone. The military have a wrecked helicopter in storage ready to haul out for this kind of situation. Simply swap them over when they get to the warehouse for the crash investigation. I've seen the protocols for these swaps. If everything is in place it should go smoothly and no-one is any the wiser.'

'That's outrageous. The public should be told what's going on under their noses,' Gavin said, and sounded as if he had been deceived.

Both of the women disagreed with him and their expressions of disapproval made him look and feel uncomfortable.

Zoe said, 'The public get really hung up on ethics and emotions and religion and all the nice things that should define a nice world. Sometimes, it's better to keep the bad things out of the public psyche for the greater good,'

'I don't agree with that. People have a right to know what's going on in their country. They're not children,' Gavin said.

Karen spoke as if reading a policy document, 'Individual people are not children but the public as a whole behaves very much like a petulant child. You have to protect that child from knowledge that can harm, confuse or corrupt.'

'Who decides when to keep an incident secret?' Gavin argued.

'The buck always stops with an elected politician. They decide what is best for the public on many levels,' Zoe said.

'In schools, hospitals, social services, finances and many other levels, politicians decide what is best for the public,' Karen added.

'This is just another level,' Zoe emphasised.

Gavin shook his head. 'Okay, fine.'

He didn't agree, but he did note from the tone in both of their voices that he should stop arguing his point. He hurried his breakfast, took his coffee and the laptop with him. He climbed the stairs to his bedroom and sat on his bed to search other online news organisations.

He felt he couldn't argue with both of them. He thought, *if I tell them I'm going to London to sort out this mess, they'll stop me. I need to slip away and go by myself.*

In the dining room, Karen stretched over to push the door shut. 'Did he dream last night?'

Zoe shook her head. 'He didn't sleep much last night. I think he's still trying to get his head around everything that happened.'

'How long do you plan to wait for something to pop out?'

'Thus far, his last dream has been the most dramatic. It terrified him and he recalled a good bit more detail. I expect the next one will take him further and give us a clue to what's happening to him,' Zoe said.

Karen helped Zoe clear away and wash up the breakfast cutlery and crockery. They talked about what Toni had done to save them from incineration. Karen said she felt guilty that Sweet had betrayed them. Zoe told her Spence would kill Sweet to make sure he didn't betray the CIA.

'Anyway, how did you hook up with a bonehead like Sweet?' Zoe asked.

'Sweet had a great squat down by the river Tyne, and a couple of thugs wanted to take over his pitch, like. I'd been walking down by the river, looking for some odds and ends when I came across Sweet in the middle of a fight with them. He held his own, like, but I gave him a hand and they backed off. They came back mob-handed and he needed to get out, so he came back to my squat. We agreed to watch each other's back, nothing more, like. He's a dirty pig.'

'You deserve so much better, Karen.'

'I killed a man. It's life in jail or life on fail. There's nothing better for me.'

Silence fell between them as they looked at each other. Zoe felt sympathetic with Karen's feeling of hopelessness.

'I meant it when I said I'll start you up in a new life with a new identity,' Zoe said.

'Don't bother, boss, I don't want you to be charged with aiding and abetting.'

'Karen, you'll take on a new life and that's an order,' Zoe said, and they both laughed.

'Thanks, boss. So what's *he* like then?'

'Who? Shawlens?'

'Yeah, in the sack, like. Is he any good?' Karen looked keen to find out.

'Ha ha ha, interesting idea. I'm afraid I've not had that experience.'

'I thought you two shared a flat in Cosham? How did you pick up on his dreams?' Karen asked, and looked confused.

'I see what you mean. Yes, we shared for operational reasons, but we slept separately. When he has a nightmare, he screams like a baby. I'll admit I might have been tempted on a couple of occasions, but he does irritate me at times. To tell you the truth, I don't know what Emma Patersun ever saw in him,' Zoe said.

'You wouldn't mind, like, if I had a tumble with him?' Karen asked, and her cheeks flushed slightly with embarrassment.

'Oh God no, not at all. Fill your boots,' Zoe said.

'I've not had a good male between these legs for more than a year. It's driving me crazy.'

'That's a while. No decent men at the squat?' Zoe enquired.

'Sweet and the other scum at the squat were wild dogs. I want a man to make love to me. I want to be touched gently, sink into someone's arms, and feel loved again,' Karen said, and her desire came from her heart.

'Copy that,' Zoe agreed.

'Have you noticed his hands, they're so warm and soft?'

'Karen, he's an academic. He can probably spell manual work, maybe even knows what it means, but he doesn't do any.'

'I promise I'll be really careful with him.'

'Be my guest, but be sure to tread carefully. He's pining for the love of his life, and she died only a few months ago,' Zoe warned.

'Don't worry. When I take control of his body, his mind will follow.'

'Okay, when I think you're going to click, I'll get out and give you some peace. An hour ought to be enough.'

'No need to disappear for an hour, boss. I'm bursting for a good shag. Twenty minutes will do me fine.'

'I'd loosen him up first with a few drinks. Oil the works so to speak,' Zoe said, and smiled.

'I'll be so grateful. I've never been very good at masturbation, like. It takes me too long by myself. I need a male to get me going,' Karen said, and it sounded like desperation.

'Karen, please … way too much detail.'

'Sorry, boss, I wasn't sure how you'd feel about me making a play for him.'

'Anyway, I hope you slept well last night?'

'Oh, I had a really lovely dream. This thing we're in had ended and he couldn't go back to his other life. He had to go on the run. I had to take him under my wing, hide him. Keep him safe but not in the squats. He had money so we lived in a house like this one. Just like a normal couple. We started off in separate beds then one night, we fell for each other,' Karen said, and sounded enthralled.

'And here I thought the groaning while you slept had been a flashback to some post-traumatic stress incident,' Zoe mocked.

'When this is over, if I get a new identity, do you think he would be interested in me? I know I'm not much. I'm not his type right now, but I'm willing to go his way.'

Zoe saw Karen's heart on her sleeve. Her eyes lit up with expectation and Zoe felt responsible for her. She didn't want to give her false hope and she didn't want to disappoint her either.

'He's very lonely. I think you'd be good for him. You do know he needs a very gentle hand. His heart still belongs to Emma Patersun. It will be a while before he gets over her.'

'I know that. I want to help him move on. I'll be as gentle as a kitten with him. I can smooth his heartache and help him to find new love. Oh, I want that so much,' Karen said, and her eyes welled up.

'Okay, just one thing. If he flips into his nightmare and starts talking, break off and listen carefully to what he says.'

'Right boss, if he starts talking, listen to him. Okay, no problem, Just as well I'm a woman who can do three things at once.'

Twenty-Seven

After they'd finished in the kitchen, Karen followed Zoe into the living room. Karen pulled up sharp, gasped aloud, and then a big smile filled her face.

'Ohmigod, boss, it's the green lady,' Karen said, and rushed over to look at an old print hanging on the wall above the fireplace.

A dusty old print in a thin faded white wooden frame. A print of Vladimir Tretchikoff's *Chinese Girl*. Karen recognised her unsmiling face looking down to her left. Dressed in a Chinese gold-collared robe with her hands folded in the robe and out of sight. Her luxuriant black hair and skin a defining blue-green colour. All refreshed in Karen's memory.

'My Mum had one of those prints above her fireplace for as long as I can remember. I grew up with the green lady. I love her. I can close my eyes and I'm fourteen again in my Mum's house looking at the green lady. We used to discuss what her life must have been like, and what she'd been thinking,' Karen remembered.

'It came with the house when I bought it. It's a cheap mass-produced print. I'm not particularly struck by it,' Zoe said.

'Oh, boss, she's like a sister to me. Can I tell you what I see when I look at her?'

'Sure. I'd like to know what I'm missing,' Zoe said, and looked confused.

'Her hair and clothes are beautiful, so, she's refined, like a lady. Her expression is innocent, spiritual, like, and peaceful but serious. She's looking down at something, thinking, contemplating and you can't help but wonder what's grabbed her mind. I think—'

They heard a muffled scream and a thump on the floor upstairs. Zoe led and Karen followed up the stairs to Gavin's room. Zoe found him out cold on the floor, not dead but he'd fainted.

Zoe knelt down beside him and lifted his head off the floor. She slapped his face a few times until Karen fetched a facecloth dipped in vinegar. The pungent smell brought him back.

'What happened?' Zoe asked

'Emma … it's not possible. She's with the angels,' he said, and scrambled for words.

'What?'

'What did he say?' Karen echoed.

His face appeared white as if he'd seen a ghost. He sat up and tried to reach for Zoe's laptop on the bed. Zoe lifted her laptop and saw the browser still set on the BBC news channel. She replayed the piece, and it reported that Emma Patersun had escaped from the clutches of the criminal James Barscadden.

She skimmed through the text and read that Barscadden had killed Jim Patersun and that Emma Patersun and her sister Donna had previously been reported killed when their home had been razed to the ground.

It had now come to light that Emma and Donna had been kidnapped and held by the former food industry billionaire James Barscadden. In a dramatic new development, Emma Patersun had managed to escape and reach safety.

The news reporter said Emma's sister, Donna, remained missing. The news piece reported that Emma Patersun's parents were dead, and she'd been reunited with her aunt in Fort Augustus, in the Scottish Highlands.

A small video clip showed Emma at her aunt's house in Fort Augustus surrounded by media people and watched over by uniformed police. Emma looked overwhelmed and said very little in reply to a barrage of media questions about how she managed to escape.

She said she wanted to get her life back to normal. She repeated that her sister Donna remained missing and appealed for anyone who had seen her to contact the police.

A police spokesman stepped forward with a photograph of Donna and asked for anyone who knew anything about her whereabouts to contact the police. The police spokesman confirmed there would be a nationwide search for Donna.

Gavin got up, ran through to the toilet, and threw up his breakfast into the bowl. He collapsed beside the toilet.

Karen asked, 'Why is he in such a state? Isn't this good news?'

Zoe decided to leave him in the bathroom. She took her laptop and led Karen down the stairs and back into the living room. They sat down on the sofa and watched the news piece again.

Zoe explained, 'Emma Patersun is supposed to be dead. She and her sister were reported killed when their home had been razed to the ground by James Barscadden. Ever since her funeral, he's been racked with intense grief. Near suicidal.'

'Why?'

'Guilt. He survived and she didn't.'

'Whose funeral did he go to, then?' Karen asked.

'Good question, Karen. Who indeed?' Zoe said, and pointed to Emma on the screen.

'Is he gonna fall apart?' Karen asked.

'He's been devastated by her loss and I've tried to heal him. I'm not sure what impact this will have on his mind. He might have a breakdown,' Zoe said.

'Really?'

'He'd never faced the thought of life without her, even though he sat through her funeral and faced the inevitable. He didn't let her go.'

'You said they were childhood sweethearts, like.'

'He lost her once as a teenager and they were reunited earlier this year after eighteen years. He'd lost the most important person in his life, and then got her back but only for a few months before she died. She wasn't with him physically but he held on to her mentally and emotionally,' Zoe said.

Karen looked unsympathetic. 'I feel for him. But I don't understand what's going on. Why didn't Barscadden kill her? She looks great, for a captive who has just escaped. And why has she turned up now of all times?'

'Excellent, Karen. I'll bet the Redcaps are missing your investigator skills.'

'Didn't you tell me your lads eliminated Barscadden?'

'We tracked him and WRATH, and I engaged them at Ardwell Point off the Scottish coast. We took out the WRATH bodyguards but Barscadden and his second in command, Peter Bromlee, escaped in a coastal submarine.'

'A coastal submarine? Well, well, if you have to go on the run, you might as well do it in style,' Karen said.

Zoe paused the news clip on a picture of Emma Patersun. Karen looked carefully at the picture, and said, 'I'd say she's been well fed. She looks a bit ruffled, like, but her hair has been trimmed maybe only a month ago. Her highlights have been done professionally. Look at those nails, they're in good condition.'

Zoe agreed and said, 'I see what you mean. Her eyebrows and eyelashes have been done. If she's been held against her will, it certainly hasn't been harsh.'

'It doesn't make sense. If Emma Patersun can give evidence that Barscadden murdered Jim Patersun, why keep her alive?'

'I agree, Karen, it's not very likely for a man on the run. Is it?'

Zoe ran the video clip and Karen listened carefully to the questions and the answers. Karen shook her head with confusion and said, 'She hasn't said anything about her captivity. Has she been a sex slave? Has she been confined and locked up? Did they move around the country? The newspaper idiots aren't asking the obvious questions.'

'I wonder why she didn't get her sister out when she got away,' Zoe said.

'Smells like ripe old porky pies to me.'

'If my brother and I were captives. I wouldn't leave him behind. If she got away, why didn't her sister get away at the same time?' Zoe queried.

Karen shook her head and said, 'Someone needs to ask the critical questions.'

'What?'

'Who arranged her funeral? Who is in the coffin and how did they get there?' Karen said.

Twenty-Eight

They heard Gavin retching again in the toilet. Karen fetched a bottle of water and took it to him. His hands shook so she took the cap off the bottle for him. She knelt down and hugged his body for a minute before she returned to Zoe in the living room. Zoe and Karen sat opposite each other.

Excluding the different hairstyles, they looked like twins. Both physically fit and strong looking. Both dressed in black cargo pants and black vests with black bras underneath. Both had scars on their arms. Who needs tats when every scar has its own story?

'He's in a bad way. It's like shell-shock,' Karen said.

'His life has been turned on its head. His brain has probably crashed with confusion. One thing is certain. This whole story is a load of crap and it stinks to high heaven,' Zoe said as she switched off her laptop and closed the lid over.

'Copy that, boss.'

'They're saying Barscadden held her captive. Where? He's been on the run since his empire collapsed,' Zoe said.

'Why would he make room for her and her sister in his dinky submarine?'

Zoe said, 'I interrogated the crew of his yacht. No indications of captives and no mention of two women. He callously killed members of his secret cult, Gyge's Ring, because he didn't have space on his submarine. This story doesn't fit with what I know about Barscadden's situation.'

'This whole thing must be a ruse.'

Zoe thought it through. 'If her funeral had been faked to make her disappearance convincing; high level public officials are involved. My bet is she's been in protective custody since the attack on her home.

To protect her from Barscadden. That would be a Special Branch or Security Service job. They have the mechanisms in place to organise that kind of disappearance.'

'Now someone is dangling her in front of a media explosion. Why?' Karen queried.

'To lure someone into the open?' Zoe replied.

'Barscadden?'

'He is public enemy number one, and the Security Service is desperate to hunt him down, but he's way too smart to fall for that trick. He pays people to do his wet work,' Zoe replied.

'If not him then this must be about Gavin. I can't understand why the Security Service is bending over backwards to help the CIA.'

'Alan Cairn is the new head, he gave up my daughter to the CIA, and now he's given Emma Patersun to them. Either our government has agreed to sacrifice Emma to capture Gavin or Cairn is an asset working for the CIA,' Zoe replied.

'Jesus, he's not slow to step up to the next level.'

Zoe said, 'Pulling Emma Patersun out of protective custody and posting her face all over the media is totally disgraceful. Cairn has driven a coach and horses through all the rules and protocols for witness protection. It seems he can stoop lower than a rattlesnake's belly.'

'He's put a target sign on her forehead.'

'She's probably not the only one. Some other poor bastard will be shitting bricks,' Zoe replied.

'Who?'

'The assassin Barscadden contracted to kill the Patersun women. He double-crossed a very dangerous man, took his money and ran. I wouldn't like to be in his boots right now.'

Karen nodded to Zoe and said, 'That's his problem, at least we know we have to keep well away from Fort Augustus.'

'That's for sure.'

Zoe paused when they heard Gavin plod heavily down the stairs. She got up, and went into the hall to meet him. 'Gavin, how are you feeling?'

He shuffled into the dining room. Zoe and Karen followed, and the three of them sat around the table. He coughed loudly to try to clear dryness from the back of his throat.

He leaned his elbows on the table and supported his head in his hands. Karen got up from her chair and went to make him some sweet tea. He looked like he'd been through a wringer, and his hands still trembled.

He looked directly at Zoe and softly said, 'I need to speak to Emma.'

Zoe raised her eyebrows. 'Emma? You'll be arrested before you get anywhere near her house.'

'You don't understand, I am going to Fort Augustus,' he said.

Zoe raised her voice, 'No you're not. You'll be killed. We'll be killed.'

He pushed his clenched fists into his knees and fixed his gaze on the table.

'I have an overwhelming feeling. A powerful *déjà vu*. I must go there and speak to Emma. I must find out what happened to us,' he insisted.

Karen returned with a mug of sweet coffee and put it on the table beside him. She'd overheard their conversation.

'The boss is right. Fort Augustus is a kill zone,' she said, and tried to sound sympathetic.

He kept his gaze on the table and sighed loudly in frustration at the prospect of having to argue that he needed to speak to Emma. He sat back in the chair, crossed his arms tightly, and clenched his fists.

'I must talk to Emma. Find out what I did wrong. Everything will be okay. We'll get back together and everything will be fine,' he said.

Karen's heart sank. It wasn't what she wanted to hear. She wanted to shake him and tell him Emma had been set as trap bait to lure him to his death.

Out of the corner of his eye, he watched Zoe shaking her head from side to side. Her face fixed with a steely determination.

'You're in my custody and I'm not putting our lives at risk,' Zoe said, emphatically.

He looked up and swung his gaze around to Zoe, like a tank turret's main gun slowly traversing to face her.

'I've had this feeling in all of my nightmares,' he said.

'What feeling?' Zoe demanded.

'It's been there all the time, there's a door. I know it's there but I can't get to it. Emma can open the door and let me inside. If I can get inside the room, my nightmares will be over. Emma is waiting for me. She wants to open the door and help me to get out. I've always felt this but couldn't understand, until now.'

'It's far too risky, man, for you and for us, like,' Karen said, softly.

'Okay, Gavin. If it will put an end to these bloody nightmares, it will be worth a controlled risk,' Zoe said.

'What?' Karen looked aghast at Zoe and thought, *boss, what are you playing at?*

Johnson had told Zoe to tease out his nightmares. He said whatever the CIA wanted had been buried there. If Emma Patersun could unlock his nightmare, then like it or not, she had to take the risk.

Zoe got up from the sofa and faced Karen. She signalled with her eyes and a nod for Karen to follow and they went through to the living room and closed the door.

'Boss, what are you doing? We can't go to Fort Augustus.'

'We know it's a trap. Either real Emma under duress or an agent with a film mask and wig. But a few minutes with Emma could shock him in to remembering what the CIA are so desperate to keep secret. Whatever it is, it must be colossal to be worth all of this intense activity.'

'I don't know. We would be putting him in great danger.'

'I've done this sort of covert infiltration lots of times with spies and double agents. I can do it. Spence doesn't know it, but he's giving me a tool to unlock Gavin's nightmare,' Zoe said, confidently.

Karen looked concerned. 'Just maybe, that is exactly his plan.'

'Or, he isn't high enough up the chain of command to know it. Or, as you say, he knows fine well what he's doing. Either way, I can work around him,' Zoe said.

Karen shook her head. 'Boss, I don't like it, this doesn't feel good. Are you really sure you can pull this off?'

'Yes I am.'

'Okay, but we'll be real careful, like, just in case Spence knows what he's doing.'

'Of course. As always, not one but two steps ahead,' Zoe said.

Karen added, 'It would be good to bring this thing to an end. He needs to move on.'

'Better. If we uncover what's in Gavin's head then we'll have a massive bargaining chip. Something senior people in London can use to deal with the CIA. It will equalise the sides and bring the whole situation to a good end,' Zoe explained.

Zoe and Karen returned to the dining room, and Zoe said, 'Okay, Gavin, we'll go to Fort Augustus, but you must do exactly as I say without deviation. Is that clear?'

'Yes, of course. Emma will help me find the way,' Gavin said.

He got up from his chair and stood in front of the two women. He nodded to both of them but didn't say anything. He walked from the dining room to the living room to fetch the laptop, and then he went upstairs to his bedroom. He wanted to see Emma again in the press video.

Zoe asked Karen, 'I have no right to ask you but could you pose as a press reporter and slip a phone to Emma Patersun?'

'I'll do it but I'll need a new travelling face. Sweet will have given me up for sure,' Karen replied.

'Spence will have flooded the Newcastle area with his people to mount a search. They will have linked Spock to me and he'll be under surveillance. No matter, I've got my actor kit here for new faces,' Zoe replied as she fetched a suitcase.

Zoe had a suitcase that contained wigs, make-up, prosthetics and a whole range of other pieces that actors use to change their appearance. Karen had watched Zoe put the make-up on Gavin for the hostage exchange.

Zoe expected the Security Services would set up several facial recognition vans on the road to Fort Augustus. Spock had cloned the blue van of an electrical and plumbing supplies company based in Darlington.

Zoe searched their website for van drivers. She couldn't find a female van driver but she found a stock manager called Anna. Anna's picture on the company website wasn't good enough quality but her picture on Facebook proved much better.

Before they started out for Fort Augustus, Zoe would print Anna's face onto a special sheet of paper-thin latex-like plastic. Zoe would microwave the face print for ten seconds to soften it, and then carefully fit the facemask to Karen.

If you kissed Karen or touched her face, you would feel the latex, but out on the road, facial recognition cameras would identify Anna, the stock control manager as the van driver. Not her normal day job but needs must.

Zoe and Karen examined Anna's face and planned how to do the wig. They talked about what Zoe wanted Karen to do when she arrived in Fort Augustus. Zoe outlined her ideas and together they worked on the details of what they would need to do to get there and back.

Zoe gathered some gear from her house and took it to the large blue van parked in the lane at the back of her house. Spock had hidden the three backpacks Zoe had taken from the Prepper's store in the van.

She unlocked the back roller door and went inside the back of the van. Pulling the roller door down behind her, she switched on an overhead light. She opened up the backpacks and spread the equipment over the floor of the van. A plan had formed in her head. She checked what she had and noted what she needed.

When Zoe got back into the house, she found Karen sitting on the top step of the stairs looking bewildered. Karen held her two hands wide open, palms up. She nodded in Gavin's direction upstairs and mouthed, *I haven't said a word.*

Zoe climbed the stairs and followed Karen into Gavin's room. Zoe watched as he seemed to be having a mental episode.

On his hands and knees, he stared at the floor, and shuddered as if in some kind of trance. He sniffed loudly as if he'd been crying.

'Who's Siobhan?' Karen whispered.

'His sister.'

Zoe knelt down beside him and put her hand on his shoulder.

He didn't respond to her presence.

'Gavin, are you okay?' Zoe asked.

Still focused on the floor he said, 'How will I get there?'

'Don't worry about that,' Zoe said, softly.

Speaking to the floor in a quiet voice, he said, 'But, Siobhan, I've only just passed my driving test. I don't know the road, I'll get lost.'

Zoe looked up at Karen and they both looked confused.

Twenty-Nine

Zoe worked through the night on the fine details of the plan she believed would take them to Fort Augustus and back. She needed more equipment and she needed to pass a message to Spock. She sent a text to a new prepaid phone she'd given Spock's wife, Pat, on the first night at the garage.

Zoe asked Pat to meet in town at the indoor market located underneath the town clock on Prebend Row. Pat replied and confirmed they would meet at two in the afternoon.

Zoe scanned through her suitcase to find a suitable disguise. She chose her distinctive Bella costume. When complemented with an Aussie accent, it completely transformed Zoe out of all recognition.

Before Zoe went to meet Pat, Karen made a few last minute touches to Zoe's make-up and blonde wig. Karen tried to encourage Zoe to put on a Newcastle accent like her own, but Zoe stuck with her tried and tested Melbourne accent.

She didn't want to upset Pat by trying to mimic. Zoe told Karen to shift Gavin's mind off Emma Patersun, and joked that she didn't mean sex.

As Zoe walked through the town centre, she passed several pairs of American agents who didn't see through her disguise. *Clever, Spence, but not clever enough*, she thought. Spence's agents were dressed like Mormon missionaries, complete with short hair, black suits, white shirts and backpacks, but with one clear difference.

Instead of men in their late teens or early twenties, they were men in their thirties and forties who were clearly searching and scanning.

Both Zoe and Pat circled around the stalls in the indoor market before they met up. They stood inside the corner of a fabric stall surrounded by thick drapes and linings, hanging from displays. Anyone wanting to eavesdrop would need to be standing beside her. Zoe felt certain that Pat hadn't been followed into the market.

Pat carried two bulky carrier bags around with her. Bulky but light, the bags contained new pillows. Pat and Zoe liked and respected each other. They would have been good sisters in another life.

Three kids had filled out Pat's body and she'd become overweight. Spock loved Zoe like a sister and Pat felt comfortable with that. Pat didn't know the details but she knew Zoe had saved Spock's life and he would do anything for her.

She knew from his nightmares that he'd been in the darkest depths of hell when Zoe pulled him out. Pat owed Zoe for bringing the man she loved back home.

Pat told Zoe that a large camper van had parked outside Spock's garage. An odd van with its privacy curtains closed all day and all night. Spock had told Pat to tell Zoe he'd picked up a tail.

So far, no-one had approached the garage except for a pair of old Mormons who spoke to the mechanics. She said Spock had already destroyed everything that could link him to Zoe or the incidents in Newcastle in case they raided the garage.

While they browsed through rolls of fabrics, Zoe slipped a thick envelope into one of Pat's carrier bags. In the envelope, she'd placed a wad of cash and a list of equipment plus instructions of when and where Zoe wanted the equipment delivered.

Zoe leaned close to Pat, smiled and said, 'Tell him, absolutely no arguments about the last item on the list, or I'll kick his arse until its black and blue.'

*

In Zoe's house, Karen made coffee and cheese omelette sandwiches for lunch. She sat beside him at the dining room table. Close enough for shoulders touching as they ate, although they seemed like two strangers thrown together on a blind date.

She appeared keen but him less so as his mind dwelled elsewhere. She ate her food fast and he ate his food slowly—different upbringings.

Karen stared at the wall and wondered what they could discuss. She wondered how to tell him that she'd welcome a quick shag, without him thinking she'd become some sort of nympho.

If this Emma thing hadn't swallowed his mind, she would have seduced him, shagged him and slapped his backside when she'd done with him.

The whole thing skipped through her mind with gusto and she wanted to get started, but he looked far away. He didn't react to her signals. Reluctantly, she moved to the post-coital discussion with some frustration, given she hadn't actually had the coital.

'So then, Labcoat, how did you get into the lab coat business?' Karen asked.

'Please, don't call me Labcoat.'

'Zoe said you're a scientist. Scientists wear lab coats; what's your problem?'

'I manage the lab coats.'

'Okay, fine, so you have a nice clean lab coat,' she said.

'My name is Gavin.'

He got up and moved around the dining table to sit opposite her. He pulled his coffee and the remainder of his sandwich to his side of the table. Her jaw dropped at his rudeness and she swore under her breath.

He didn't even thank her for preparing his food—different upbringing again. He deserved a slap and in different circumstances she would have given him one. She paused, bit her tongue and started again.

'You don't sound very Scottish, like. I've got cousins from Glasgow. You don't have the same accent.'

'Lecturing to students has ironed out my accent.'

He didn't sound like he wanted to talk to her. He continued eating his food, drinking his coffee and avoiding eye contact. She dropped into her military police interview training.

'Don't like science much, anyway. It's too bloody scary,' she said.

'Scary?'

'The worst kind of scary,' she added.

'What? Did you have a weird science teacher?'

'I had a lovely science teacher. What I saw in the Iraqi desert, scared me out of my wits.'

He threw her a look of disbelief. 'What scary science did they have out in the desert?'

She shook her head. 'It's a long story. You don't want to know how science almost scared me out of my mind.'

'What scared you?'

'Well, I was travelling in a Snatch-2 Land Rover at night when we hit an iceberg rock,' she said, and dropped her voice into story-telling mode.

'An iceberg rock?'

'A huge rock with only a small bit showing above ground but when you hit it at speed; you break the axle. We had a long wait for support to arrive. We had to maintain silence, so I looked up at the stars. It's the scariest thing I've ever done.'

'Why? The sky on a clear night is absolutely beautiful,' he said.

'It's not what you see, it's what you think. Haven't you ever wondered what exists beyond our universe and what exists beyond that?' she enthused.

'No I haven't.'

'Where does it stop? When you reach the border of the outermost universe, what's beyond that. When you reach the border of that, what's beyond that? It can't go on for infinity, that's impossible. It must end and when you reach the end, what's beyond that?'

'I think the physicists say it will come back around on itself.'

'Okay, if it's circular then what exists outside of the circle?' she said.

'Just empty space.'

'But when you reach the edge of empty space, what's beyond that?'

'You're scaring me.'

'Is physics not your stuff?'

'No, I'm a biochemist.'

'Oh, right, a biochemist?'

'Yes.'

Karen looked thoughtful and racked her brain to find something she knew about biochemistry. Not much in there.

Then, like a light switching on, she latched on to something she recalled that did sound biochemical.

'What do you know about women's hormones?' she asked.

'What do you want to know?'

'How to control them, when they get, like, hot?'

'A cold shower does work wonders.'

'Thanks, I never knew that,' she said, sarcastically.

Karen thought of something else, but hesitated to ask. Something she did want to know, but didn't want to ask, in case he upset her.

'Have you ever done any work on cancer?' she said, and this time she sounded more intimate, more serious.

'No. It's not really my area of expertise.'

'My sister has stage four breast cancer. What does that mean?'

'Stage four.'

'Yes, what does that mean exactly?'

Gavin said, 'Stage four means cancer is advanced and probably has spread to other organs.'

'How long has she got before it goes to stage five?'

Gavin shook his head. 'There is no stage five, four is the last stage.'

'Huugh. The last stage. I don't know why but I thought there would be more stages. Four just seems … so few.'

'I'm sorry, stage four means the cancer has spread and is probably terminal,' he said, and he sounded cold and unfeeling.

It wasn't how he meant to sound. With his mind on other things, he wasn't fully engaged with her. He'd given her the very news she didn't want to hear. She regretted asking him.

She wanted to hear good news about cancer so she wouldn't feel guilty for not keeping in touch with her sister.

She raised an angry voice, 'Can't you get all your bloody biochemists together, and find a drug to beat cancer once and for all?'

'I'm not sure drugs will ever do it. We need our own body to fight cancer.'

'What do you mean?'

He bowed his head and closed his eyes. *I can't do this right now. She's not a student who already half understands. I can't concentrate on this just now*, he thought.

'Look. I'm sorry but it's really complicated,' he said in a patronising voice.

'Pardon me, Labcoat. Sorry I bloody well opened my mouth. I didn't know you had something bloody well else you need to be doing, like,' she said, and looked offended.

'I'm sorry, I didn't mean anything.'

'You *look*. I've put my neck on the line for you. I'm about to do it again just so you can meet up with this female who might mean something to you but means absolutely nothing to me. I mean, that's all I'm fucking doing for you,' she said and glared at him.

'I'm sorry. All right, bear with me. I think ... the best option for a cure ... is our own immune system.'

'Immune system?'

'The cells of our immune system can identify cancer cells and tag them to be killed, probably does that on a regular basis,' he explained.

'Why aren't they doing it to save my sister?'

'Our body has the tools. We have killer cells called phagocytes. These cells kill bacteria, viruses and recycle our own dead, damaged or dying cells. They can also kill cancer cells.'

'Brilliant, so it can be done,' Karen said, and her eyes lit up.

'Yes, but like real killers they need to be told who to kill. The cancer cells need to be tagged for destruction just as if they were bacteria,' he said.

'I understand, as always, it starts with the top brass issuing orders.'

'That's right. I often think of the immune system as a hierarchical police force. Police officers can identify and tag bacteria to be killed. Police inspectors identify viruses. Only a chief constable can identify and tag cancer cells to be killed. Problem is of course, chief constables aren't out on the streets all that often.'

'So, my sister's chief constable immune cell could tag her cancer cells and her phagocytes would kill them?' she said, and sounded excited.

'Yes. There are lots of examples around the world. People who had stage four, had prepared for the worst, and then cleared the cancer.'

'That, Mr Biochemist, is what I wanted to hear,' she said as she stretched over, placed her hand on his and squeezed it.

'Some called it a miracle, others a response to treatment, or change in a diet. Some say it's a survival mechanism. I believe in those cases, the patient's own chief constable immune cell finally got off its backside, got out and then did its job.'

'There's still hope for my sister then if her chief constable cell gets moving, like.'

'There's always hope. But don't get your hopes up too high. It may be that her chief constable cell is dead or damaged, and that's why she has cancer in the first place.'

'Could I donate my chief constable cell?'

'There's probably only dozens of these cells in your entire body. Trying to identify and find them among billions and billions of other cells is impossible,' he said.

'Nothing is impossible,' she replied, and looked deflated but not defeated.

'You sound just like Zoe. Did you serve with her?'

'No. I met her a few times when times were good. She's brilliant—an army gal through and through. Last time I met her we were in Afghanistan.'

'Did you see much action there?' Gavin quickly added.

'I had joined the Royal Military Police, the Redcaps. I loved every minute of it. I joined a military college at eighteen and set my heart, like, on a military career. We had plenty of work to do in Afghanistan and Iraq. We thoroughly investigated every allegation against a British soldier, and we were determined to uphold the highest standards. I'd say we succeeded.'

'Sounds like important work that the Redcaps have to do.'

'I helped bring many offenders to military court. I helped investigate dozens of sex attacks including nine rapes and over fifty sexual assaults.'

She sounded very proud of her service in the Redcaps, and he heard in her voice that she missed her friends and the work. He relaxed while she did the talking.

The conversation began to dry up when it seemed she didn't want to say much more about her work. Gavin didn't want to resume a discussion about cancer, so he put her back on the spot.

'What happened to put you on the run?'

That threw her for a minute. She wanted him to do all the talking. He'd turned the tables on her. Her training in interrogation would have enabled her to turn the tables back and put him back on the spot. She didn't want to upset him.

'It's complicated, like.'

She smiled, and he should have said *touché* but he didn't. She left him and went to the kitchen make a cup of coffee. She stared out of the kitchen window at the red brick wall that surrounded the back yard. She felt raw.

Unhappy memories hidden in the back of her mind had jumped forward. One moment, she had been bright, successful and loving her job. The next, she'd been broken and discarded by events outside of her control.

Thirty

Gavin sat alone for more than ten minutes. He knew he didn't want to fall out with Karen. He liked her and thought about what he might say to patch the rift between them. He went through to the kitchen, and with a sheepish look, he said, 'I'm very sorry. I didn't mean to pry in to your personal business.'

'It's no big secret. I killed a fellow Redcap. I have a murder trial waiting for me. I don't fancy it. So I'm on the run from justice. I know, ironic isn't it, I'm a Redcap OTR.'

'Oh, I see,' he said, dismissively, but didn't mean to be dismissive.

She shook her head. 'Do you? Do you actually *see* anything? You live in a different world. You know nothing about my life,' she said, and poked a forefinger at him.

He turned and walked to the living room. He'd tried, it didn't work and he wanted to be on his own. He sat down on the sofa and picked up a newspaper. It had been in Zoe's house for five months. She didn't follow him at first.

On reflection, she felt she'd shown him too much of her anger. She went into the living room but kept her distance. He still looked traumatised by the reappearance of Emma Patersun. She thought, *I don't want him telling the boss he doesn't want me to tag along. I'm supposed to occupy his mind. Well, I'll just have to do it.*

'Lab … eh, Gavin, sorry for snapping at you. If we're going to be friends, then you should know I did kill a man, but not an innocent man. He pushed me all the way to the edge of the cliff. One of us had to go over, and in the heat of the moment, I ended his life.

'But at the same time, my life and my future also ended. I think he got the better part of the deal, and every single day since, I've wished I could go back and let him kill me,' she confessed.

'What did he do?'

'He sexually assaulted me.'

'Why didn't the military judiciary punish him?'

She sat down opposite him and told him how the army system had let her down when she needed it most. Her unit had done loads of inquiries and heard traumatic stories of the desperate situations people got into.

She knew how these situations creep up, and had kept herself out of those traps. In particular, she believed she'd always been careful to make sure no males in her work circle had any reason to think of her as available in a sexual way.

'I just didn't see it coming, like. I'd just sent a text to my Dad for Father's Day. My unit had completed a major inquiry, We got a result, and we were all elated. We went to a Greenwich pub to celebrate. I drank vodka and orange, and all six of us had a great time,' she said, and then paused as if she didn't want to say more.

'What happened?'

Her face drained as she continued. 'Late in the evening we were joined by Jake Sarrone. A member of another Redcap unit. I'd met him several times before, and he seemed keen on my mate Maura, but Maura had brushed him off and didn't want to know.'

'Were you drunk?

'None of us were drunk. We were happy but not drunk when we piled into a taxi and headed for Maura's house. We drank some more, talked about jobs and some of the idiots we'd arrested. We all had a really good night … then.'

She paused and her eyes welled up. She hadn't talked about this heartache for a long time. Her emotions came rushing back.

'Do you want to leave it for another time?' Gavin asked, and hoped she didn't want to go on with her story.

'I'm okay. I woke up in the middle of the night with Sarrone trying to have sex with me. I went into Maura's spare bed fully clothed, and when I woke up, I found myself naked from the waist down. I felt sick. He'd undressed and tried to rape me. I punched him in the gut and pushed him off.'

'Bastard, did you report him?'

'I reported the incident to my CO, but he queried whether I'd been assaulted. I had stopped Sarrone before he climaxed. I had no evidence, no body fluids on my clothes and no defence injuries on my body. Sarrone told the CO that I consented, and the CO suggested that in a drunken state I may have consented.'

'Maybe the civil police should have investigated,' Gavin said.

'Officers aren't legally obliged to report sexual offences to the civil police.'

'That's wrong,' he said.

'When the CO spoke to Maura and the others, they said they heard and saw nothing. They took Sarrone's side. I felt alone, ashamed and embarrassed. Suddenly, I became one of the victims I had listened to so many times before. When I sat down with Maura on her own, she didn't believe me. Maura said if it happened to her she would have brought the roof down on him and beat him senseless. Why didn't I? I've asked myself that a hundred times. I don't know.'

'Was he charged?'

'After a couple of weeks, I reported back to the CO's office and he told me none of the others in my unit could support my story. No action would be taken against Sarrone. He ordered me to make no further complaints. I had to sign a disclaimer saying I wouldn't take the complaint further. End of.'

'Shit, that's not good. What if other evidence came to light?'

'I would have left it there but Sarrone wanted to make me suffer. He started a raft of disgusting tales, attacking my virtue. Telling everyone that I had slept with dozens of soldiers and it had been his turn. He'd taken a smartphone photo of my undressed body and passed it around. When I saw it I felt sick.'

'He obviously waited until you signed the disclaimer and couldn't do anything about it,' he said.

Karen looked upset but she continued. 'Then I did something really stupid. I got his address and went to see him. I thought I could get him to apologise or admit it or something. At least stop him spreading stories and the photo. He invited me in, we had a drink and then he turned on me. He told me he had more photos.

'He said he had a photo of my hand around his penis to convince others I had consented. I felt violated and disgusted. He laughed and said he had ten photos and he planned to release a new one every couple of weeks. We fought when I tried to take his phone. He tried to rip my clothes. We fought and I broke his neck.'

'I never believed for a moment you were on the run as a criminal. I knew it would be something like a crime of passion. A personal tragedy,' he said, and rested his hand on top of hers.

'Thanks, Gavin. It means a lot to me that you understand. I used to be a really nice lady. If you'd got to know me before I went OTR, I think we would have been good friends,' she said.

He nodded. 'When this is over, I'd like us still to be friends. If Zoe is going to fit you up with a new identity, I could organise a job for you in my lab. I could train you as a technician, if you fancy a new career.'

'Are you serious? Me? A lab coat.'

'You've got determination and motivation. I can give you knowledge and skills. You can join the battle to destroy the blood clots that cause strokes and heart attacks. It's a worthy cause, and I'd love to have you on my team.'

'Do you mean that, Gavin? Really? I don't know how I could possibly repay you. One thing I can guarantee—you would have the best damn technician in the world working for you, bar none,' she said, and a lump in her throat made her swallow hard.

'In time, I can see you as the lab manager. Leading my team of technicians and students. I think you'd be brilliant.'

'Thanks, I won't ever let you down, boss,' she said.

They got up and hugged each other and he held her in a firm embrace. He wiped a tear from her eye and he kissed her gently on the cheek. She felt he meant it to be sensual. Her cheeks flushed as vivid thoughts grabbed her mind.

She composed herself and said, 'First things first. We need to get you out of this mess with the CIA. Why do they want you?'

'Well… um. I don't know for sure. I had just finished a job for the Lambeth Group to investigate corrupt research in a university. Zoe found out that the CIA had put us under surveillance. Sir Milton Johnson told her we had to disappear, so we got out and raced up the A1 to come here. Zoe thinks there is something in the nightmares I've been having recently, but I'm not so sure.'

'What do you remember?' she asked.

'I'm in a boat, it's sinking fast and I feel I'm going to drown. I see figures that look like the demons in the movie *Ghost*. They want to take me with them. It feels so real, it's scary.'

'And you think a meeting with Emma Patersun will clear away the confusion. Is she in your nightmare?'

'Emma isn't there but I feel her presence. It's always been there in the room. I can't get inside. Emma can let me inside. If I can get inside the room, my nightmares will be over.'

'Doesn't sound like world-shattering, super secret stuff, the CIA should be in a knot about.'

'I don't think its super secret stuff. I told Zoe about a USB drive belonging to James Barscadden's Director of Research, Julie Blackhest. I copied all of her data onto a computer before she died. I thought Barscadden might have stolen something from the CIA and it's their data they want back. Zoe doesn't agree.'

'She's right, Gavin. This thing is a whole order of magnitude more than stolen data from a USB stick. That's for sure. The CIA doesn't play this hard on British soil unless the stakes are huge. I feel more comfortable now I understand your situation. We just have to keep you secure for a little while longer, until the next part of your nightmare unfolds and reveals what this is all about. When it's out in the open, then there is no point killing you to keep it secret.'

'Once I meet Emma, I'll know what's going on.'

'Where do you think she's been all this time?' she asked.

'They said Barscadden held her captive. That's why she couldn't contact me.'

'I think if Barscadden had her, he would have killed her. He sent someone to kill her because she could give evidence. Why keep her alive while he's been on the run from people like Zoe?'

'What are you saying?' he said, and sounded confused.

'Maybe there's another explanation we don't know about. Keep your mind open to other possibilities—is all I'm saying.'

'If she wasn't a captive, if she hid somewhere, she would have got a message to me. I know she would,' he said.

'If it had been me, I would have moved heaven and earth. At the very least, a coded letter or email to let you know I'm okay. I couldn't have lived with myself knowing you were grieving.'

'When I see Emma, we'll sort things out together. Everything will be fine once she has time to explain what happened,' he said.

Karen said with alarm in her voice, 'You understand this is a flying visit. Five minutes face time. You're not going to sit down with her for an evening, for God's sake.'

He looked disappointed and got up to leave. 'I'm going to have a lie down now.'

He climbed the stairs to his bedroom. She'd given him too much to process, and she'd sowed doubts. He needed to think privately about the past few months in case Emma had contacted him and he hadn't picked it up.

His lab technician, Christine Willsening, went through his mail and emails and filtered out anything she classed as junk. Maybe, Christine had missed something if it wasn't deliberately marked personal.

She wouldn't recognise Emma's handwriting on an envelope. She wouldn't recognise a personal comment on an email header. In fact, Christine would automatically delete anything overtly familiar or too personal from a stranger.

Maybe in all the hundreds of emails Christine had deleted without opening, she'd missed one or two from Emma. If Emma had sent something to him and he hadn't replied, then she would be livid with him.

He would be the one apologising profusely for not replying to her. The idea crashed through his mind like a lorry through a paper house.

Karen tapped on the door, opened it and said, 'I've come to say I'm sorry.'

*

Zoe returned to the flat and went to her room to change out of her Bella disguise. Karen joined her in the room.

'Everything okay?' Zoe asked Karen and nodded toward Gavin's room.

'Sure. We had a little problem. I've straightened him out, and now he's sleeping like a baby.'

'Why is he sleeping?'

'I might have drained all of his energy.'

'Good. I've given Spock two days to get what I want. A surveillance team are watching his garage. He needs to be very careful.'

'They'll put a tail on him,' Karen said.

'He's a smart old dog. While they have eyes on him, he'll have his mechanics do the running about town. They're always fetching and delivering car parts.'

'Will Spock be able to lose the tail?'

'I've given him advice but I'm sure he'll have no problem giving them the slip,' Zoe said.

Karen helped Zoe get out of her Bella disguise and Zoe noticed a new sparkle in Karen's face. 'What's put a light under your bush?'

'After this is over and I have a new identity, like. Gavin has offered to take me on and train me as a technician in his lab.'

'Great, I'm so pleased for you,' Zoe said as she pulled Karen close for a hug.

'He'll be my new boss.'

'No, Karen. No way. Get one thing straight from the beginning, you'll be *his* new boss.'

Thirty-One

London

Katherine sat alone in the communications room as final connections were made to the White House Special Situations Room. She looked calm but fidgeted with her clothes because she felt anxious to get past the conference call with President Cranstoun and General George Schumantle.

Reports and detailed accounts of what happened at Newcastle had already been sent to George by his army intelligence officers. She didn't have to get into those details, but there would be questions. She expected she would provide a summary, apportion blame if necessary, and then outline her follow-up plans to resolve the issue that so vexed her commander-in-chief.

'Good evening, Katherine, how are you?'

'Fine, Mr President, I'm good.'

Both George and Cranstoun observed her tired eyes, drawn face, unkempt hair and saw she'd not had much quality sleep. Cranstoun had intended to tear a strip off her, but when he saw her, he decided against it.

Earlier, the General's man in her office told him that she'd been outstanding in her handling of the events that unfolded.

'The clock has ticked on, Katherine. Seven damn days. Why is this so difficult?'

'I'm sorry, I don't have the news you want, Mr President.'

'I've read the reports, Katherine. There were a couple of good opportunities to end this thing. What happened?'

'I know, Mr President. Brits loyal to Tampsin interfered with our plans. They pulled her sorry ass out of the fire. We didn't foresee that betrayal but it won't happen again.'

'Do you know who brought down our reaper?' George asked.

'Not yet. Steelers and Cairn are refusing to account for their people in the field. I'm certain they know who is responsible. I'll find out one way or another,' she said.

'How are your people dealing with the fact that this operation is running in England?' George asked.

George's people had told him a senior group in the CIA London Station had serious concerns about 'shitting in their neighbour's garden'.

'The loss of life on the road has been a setback. It has produced some tension in the operations room. I won't deny that,' she conceded.

'We're way past that bridge now, Katherine. The death toll from the car pile-up is ten. More now won't make any difference,' Cranstoun urged.

'A few of my people were uncomfortable thinking of Britain as a war zone. They were worried about collateral damage and future interaction with UK personnel. I've corrected those opinions,' she said.

'Thousands of individuals die every day, Katherine. Great countries need to survive, provide values and a way of life for hundreds of millions. That's what really matters here. Sometimes, we have to edge the grass to keep the estate healthy.'

'I've made it plain that we cannot afford the luxury of compassion. I've emphasised the standing order is not apprehend and interrogate, but kill on sight. I'm prepared for whatever it takes, and I pray the loss of civilian life will not be too great. I'm confident my people will do what's necessary, when it's required,' she said, emphatically.

'I'm reassured to hear that, Katherine. Can you update me on this new asset you have deployed?' George asked.

Katherine reminded them of the last time she met with them in the White House. President Cranstoun had given her permission to collect an asset hiding in Canada. She'd despatched Ertha Odeele and a team to collect and transport the asset to England.

She didn't tell them, Ertha's inexperienced team had caused a medical emergency, termination of a pregnancy, and very nearly total loss of the asset.

'How much do the Brits know about the acquisition of Emma Patersun?' George asked.

'Nothing. I denied all knowledge of her abduction from Canada. The women have been kept completely isolated from any Brits. But since I've put her in play in Fort Augustus, I've had extreme histrionics from both Cairn and Steelers. I'd say they're having a quadruple coronary.'

'Good. Glad to hear it. This is their fault for not sticking to my deal,' Cranstoun said.

'Will Cairn and Steelers obstruct your operation?' George asked.

'I don't believe so. I've told them any lack of cooperation will be reported directly to their Prime Minister. Their jobs are on the line,' she replied.

'So why will this woman draw Shawlens out?' Cranstoun asked.

Katherine said, 'Emma Patersun and Gavin Shawlens were teenage lovers eighteen years ago. They'd been reunited a few months ago and looked set to rekindle their relationship. They were responsible for the exposure and collapse of James Barscadden's empire. In a fit of revenge, he ordered the death of Patersun and Shawlens. Someone tipped off the Security Service of an imminent attack, and they put Patersun in witness protection in Canada. At the time, Shawlens had been in hospital recovering from an injury.'

Cranstoun mused and asked, 'So, someone in Barscadden's organisation betrayed him. Why did he do that, I wonder?'

'Unknown,' Katherine replied.

George said, 'My agent, Sharon Bonny, had Shawlens under surveillance. She reported he'd been completely devastated by her death, and racked with guilt because he survived. She is certain he'll run to Fort Augustus to be with her.'

'When he's in the village, I'll surround them with a ring of steel. I'll scarify the place and finish the job. If there is collateral damage in Fort Augustus, then so be it,' she said.

'What resources do you have on the ground?' George asked.

'Spence MacAllisin has established a base in a secluded country house. He has two command vehicles and ten support vehicles. In total, I have 165 US personnel on the ground. Fort Augustus is perfect for our needs. Small population, isolated village with limited road infrastructure. I can lock the place down in six minutes. Once he's in our circle, he'll not get out. I'm absolutely certain of that,' she said.

'I have sent air support backup,' George added.

'Thanks, George. I'll have all the belts and braces you can give me.'

'I've deployed four Black Hawk choppers, one on each point of the compass. They are stationed not more than five minutes flying time to the village. There is a Delta Force team on board each one. Ready for you to make the call.'

'Excellent. My command vehicles have control of two reapers. One in high flight mode for pinpoint surveillance. The other is prepped for pursuit attack if I need it,' Katherine said.

'What about British Security Services?' Cranstoun asked.

'Not this time. Most definitely not this time. I've cut Cairn and Steelers out of the loop. They are restricted to liaison with local law enforcement. They're not happy, but they will cooperate.'

'Is that wise, Katherine? What if there is another civilian mess to cover up?'

'Tampsin has friends ready to help her. London is apoplectic with me for putting Patersun in play. They can't be trusted.'

'I agree,' George said.

'Why are they pissed off with you?' Cranstoun asked.

Katherine hesitated for a moment. She thought she had explained the point earlier. She didn't want to embarrass the President by asking what he didn't understand. She rephrased her explanation.

'Emma Patersun and her sister were in witness protection, hiding in Canada. Putting her out in the open has opened a can of worms for the Brits, but that's their problem. I have to focus on the fact Shawlens will run to her,' she explained.

'Are you sure he'll run to her?' Cranstoun asked.

'I think Tampsin will see what we're doing and refuse to take him to Fort Augustus. He'll slip out and travel there on his own. I have people monitoring all the public transport routes. With luck, they may catch him on the road, and it will be over,' Katherine reassured.

'Why is Spencer MacAllisin still on point?' Cranstoun asked.

'Spence worked very closely with Tampsin. He understands her tactical mind,' Katherine said.

'Not very well,' Cranstoun said.

'I'm confident Spence will win the day. He didn't fail; her friends interfered at the last minute. I stand by him,' Katherine asserted.

'How will you close the net?' Cranstoun asked.

'When he has made contact with Patersun, and he's in the trap, we will announce that a local resident has returned from West Africa with an Ebola virus infection. The village will be put under quarantine restrictions. Everyone in the village will be required to give blood for testing. No exceptions. The population is less than seven hundred. We can clear the village in less than three hours. If individuals are shot and killed while running away then it will be because they tried to spread the Ebola virus to the general population.'

'Good plan, Katherine,' George said.

'If there's anything else you think I should deploy, please let me know,' she said.

'I think you've got it covered, Katherine, good hunting,' Cranstoun said.

Cranstoun pressed a button on a handset to close the link with Katherine. The screen went blank and returned to the White House screensaver. He moved over to sit beside George Schumantle. He looked very worried.

'I thought she stood up to your grilling very well,' George said.

'She did. I'm not worried about Katherine. I'm worried about where this situation is heading. Don't you think this is getting a bit too close for comfort?' Cranstoun said.

'No. If Shawlens had recovered his memory, then he would have told Tampsin, and we would have London jumping on our heads. He still has no idea of POINT-K4. The fact Tampsin hasn't got us by the balls proves the secret is still hidden from him,' George replied.

'What if Fort Augustus accelerates his memory recall?'

'If Katherine should fail. I have a final sanction available that will remove this problem once and for all,' George replied.

'As I've told you, I want POINT-K4 to remain viable. I'm certain this country will have need of it in the future. I must be absolutely certain it cannot be saved before I'll allow your final sanction. That said, under no circumstances can it be exposed.'

'I understand, Mr President.'

'I sincerely hope so, George. If it is exposed to the world then the fallout will deflate the country, cripple our economy and destroy our credibility. The Great Depression of the 1930s will be nothing compared to what we will go through. I don't know how we could ever recover. No-one would trust us for tens of decades. My presidency will go down in history as the one that destroyed the country and our future. The risk is huge for us, George, just bloody huge. I think I've aged ten years since you told me about this POINT-K business.'

George opened his briefcase, extracted a thin beige folder and handed it over to the President.

'What's this?' Cranstoun asked as he picked up the folder.

'Something I've kept from you, but now you need to know.'

'What is it?'

'LuEllen has a sister. If the Shawlens business means we have to sacrifice LuEllen to keep the POINT-K4 secret safe. LuEllen's sister could take over in six to eight months.'

'And POINT-K4 would be available again.'

'Yes, in six to eight months.'

'Does LuEllen's sister have a name?'

'Yes, Mr President, her name is LuElldun.'

'Thank you for this contingency, George. Your country thanks you. Let's hope you don't need to use it.'

Thirty-Two

Fort Augustus, Scottish Highlands

The last time Emma Patersun drove into Fort Augustus to visit her Aunt Bessie, her thoughts were rich with wonderful summer holiday memories spent with her cousin Geena at Aunt Bessie and Uncle Dan's small farm. Emma loved to visit her Aunt Bessie and she loved all the animals on the farm.

Bessie kept nine milking cows and eighteen pigs. All the cows were given names and all the pigs were given numbers. There were numerous chickens and a pony called Sparkle. She remembered Sharp, the black and white Border Collie. A nippy working dog with a few scars on his nose from skirmishes with local foxes.

Bessie had a large kitchen and Emma loved helping in the kitchen. Emma liked to help her aunt with her baking or jam making for local fetes and garden parties. Bessie's farm chutney had become a fabulous local delicacy.

Emma and Geena had great fun. They fell into ditches, paddled in streams, jumped over cowpats and sometimes into them. They swung for hours on a tree rope swing, out and back over a stream. Bessie didn't mind the mess so long as they got undressed, washed and changed in the outhouse. Geena and Emma played and ran around the fields, often taking packed lunches on their explorations and adventures. Emma remembered her cousin with warm affection.

Geena's memories of Emma were of a scrawny city girl who thought the birds and the bees were pop groups. An obligate tell-tale, Emma always told Bessie when she asked questions about what they'd been doing. Emma had one redeeming quality, a hopeless desire to help with all of Geena's farm chores, and she allowed Emma to fill her boots, sometimes literally.

The only moment of recurring sadness happened at the end of the summer holidays when Emma's dad came to visit his sister and take Emma home. As always, he took at least six jars of Bessie's fabulous tomato chutney. The visits to Aunt Bessie stopped one summer just as the school holidays started when Emma's dad told her he'd found her a job as an office junior in a bank.

For Emma, no discussion, no choice, just the unexpected shock of walking out the school gate one day, and starting full-time work in a busy bank the next day. In fact, a lot of things changed for Emma that day.

*

When the police car turned into the road leading to Bessie's house, Emma knew this visit would be as far removed from those wonderful times as it could ever be. She knew Sharp had been put down after a fight with a fox left him badly hurt. She knew Aunt Bessie had given up farming when Uncle Dan died, but she wasn't expecting to see houses built on the land she remembered.

Twenty new houses with people and their cars had completely transformed the area. Bessie kept a large field behind her house but had sold everything else for residential housing. A small housing estate now occupied the surrounding fields, ten minutes' walk from the centre of the village, and just off the south A82 approach road.

Emma got out of the police car and ran to her Aunt and her cousin waiting at the front door. They hugged and cried while the police officers looked on. Two security people scanned the surrounding area.

'Come on away inside, lass, and sit yursel doon. I've made us tea,' Bessie said in her warm Highland accent.

Bessie led the way, followed by Geena with her arm tightly wrapped around Emma's shoulder. The two security people followed.

'Ah dinna mean you as well,' Bessie said, to the security people.

'Sorry, ma'am, we have strict orders. Ms Patersun does not leave our sight,' the security man said.

'Aunt Bessie, please,' Emma pleaded, and her distraught face gave Bessie no choice.

Bessie led them to her large kitchen. They all sat around the kitchen table like total strangers at a wake while Bessie poured tea for them. The security people said their names were Joshua and Caitlin.

'Emma, dear, I'm auffy confused. The police lassie said ye didnae die when your hoose burned doon. What happened to yeh, lass?' Bessie asked Emma.

'Ma'am, the reprobate James Barscadden kidnapped your niece. He made it appear as though she'd been killed,' Joshua said with a mid-Atlantic accent.

Bessie looked to Geena and said, 'Reprobate?'

'Criminal,' Geena replied to her mum.

'I'll need to remind that for my sudokit,' Bessie said.

'Scrabble, Ma, for your Scrabble,' Geena said.

'Scrabble babble, dinna fuss, lass, you ken fine well whit ah mean,' Bessie fired back.

Joshua and Caitlin were CIA agents Joshua Modamo and Caitlin Amster. They had been part of the team that abducted Emma and Donna and took them to the USA. They flew the sisters in a company jet to a private airfield in the south of England, and then drove them to a country house, somewhere near the sea because noisy seagulls used the house as a playground.

Before they arrived in Fort Augustus, Modamo had repeatedly warned Emma that Donna's life depended on her doing exactly what they said. Donna had killed one of them in Sarnia, and they kept her caged and bound like a wild animal. Emma worried they would kill Donna at the slightest provocation to avenge their loss.

Modamo didn't tell Emma that he worked for the CIA. He didn't explain why she'd been taken from her home in Sarnia, or why he'd brought her to England.

Emma had been visited at the country house by a nurse to check her health. After the traumatic loss of her baby, aborted and stillborn when they abducted in Sarnia; she'd been weak, unwell and emotionally drained.

The journey north to Glasgow took six hours and Emma felt ill for most of the time. They arrived at a large police station in the centre of Glasgow, and she became even more distraught when Amster told her they had another three-hour journey in a police car.

For the rest of the evening and the following morning, Amster or Modamo remained at Emma's side. When Bessie or

Geena asked Emma a question, the answer came from one of the CIA agents, so Bessie and Geena stopped asking.

Both Bessie and Geena were desperate to find out about Donna and about Emma's funeral but the agents intervened, and stopped Emma from speaking. The attitude of the two CIA agents created an uncomfortable tension, and Geena saw that Emma feared them.

The news of Emma's escape broke in the press that morning, and a large media pack descended on Bessie's house during the afternoon. Hounds desperate for any news on Barscadden. Emma faced the press while a police officer gave them an update on the search for Donna.

Emma pleaded for help to find her sister. She tried to look convincing but she knew Donna wasn't missing so her face didn't look as emotional or persuasive as it might have been if Donna had been really missing.

On the second day, more than forty reporters and camera operators jostled for pole position in front of Emma's face as they fired questions from all directions. Three large TV satellite vans dominated the road near the farmhouse. The barrage of questions about Barscadden and her abduction became relentless.

'Where were you held?'

'I don't know.'

'Were you tortured or abused?'

'No.'

'Where is James Barscadden?'

'I don't know.'

'How did you manage to get free?' No answer.

'Is your sister still alive?'

'Yes.'

'Are you afraid for your sister's life?'

'Yes.'

'How do you feel now you are free and your sister is missing?' No answer.

And a hundred other questions she couldn't answer. With only one policewoman at her side, the shoving and pressing media pack surrounded Emma, and harried her for scraps of information.

Watching from inside with her mother, Geena decided she'd seen enough. Geena had always been quick with opinions on anything and everything, and never one to varnish her comments or leave things unspoken. Geena had watched patiently but now she'd had enough.

'Hey. Are you blind or something? Can you no see she's terrified? Stop them harassing her,' Geena shouted at Modamo.

He ignored Geena and returned his gaze to the crowd outside. Again, Geena demanded Modamo do something to put an end to the reckless badgering of her cousin. He refused. Amster looked marginally sympathetic but she wouldn't budge either.

Geena stormed out of the house, pushed her way through the pack, grabbed Emma by the arm and pulled her back into Bessie's house.

Emma collapsed into a chair, sobbing hard and sniffing deeply through her tears. Her body still weak and her emotions still reeling from the loss of her baby. The policewoman remained at the front door. Modamo and Amster seemed unconcerned about Emma being bullied by the media hounds, and they continued to scan the crowd outside.

Geena sat beside Emma and they hugged each other while Emma sobbed. Bessie handed a handkerchief to Emma. Geena fired daggers at the security people for standing back and doing nothing to protect her. Geena wondered why they'd brought Emma to Fort Augustus.

Geena became suspicious from the minute she met them. Their actions and accents weren't British. They were American, early thirties, neat suits and sharp features. They didn't conceal the fact they were armed.

At first, Geena thought they were British Security Service officers because the local police were bending over backwards to cooperate with them. Now, she believed they weren't British Security Service.

Modamo seemed overly nervous as if he expected something bad to happen. He talked into a hand radio but too quietly for Geena to hear. Occasionally, he smiled through rows of uneven fish teeth. The only time one of them didn't stay at Emma's side was when she faced the press outside.

Emma had been very guarded about what she could say to Geena when either of the two agents stood near. Mindful of the fact they had Donna, and of their threat that Donna's safety depended on Emma doing exactly what they said.

Thirty-Three

Bessie's face became red with anger at all the people moving around her garden. Each day she'd told them to stop trampling on her plants, but they ignored her. Neither of the two police officers did anything to keep the media rascals off her winter bedding plants.

By the third day, Bessie had given up complaining, picked up her knitting, switched on the radio and switched off from the world. They had ignored her and so she ignored them.

When Emma had arrived, and Geena first saw her she couldn't believe how much she had changed. While her own thick legs, massive thighs and rhinoceros ankles were less pretty, she thought they were the hallmarks of a superior pedigree. The last time she'd seen Emma, she looked perfect as usual. Just like a fashion model.

Geena remembered Emma as a delicate beauty, slender with long legs and a pretty face. Emma stood two inches taller than Geena and had always been a size ten while Geena grew to a size fourteen. Emma's silky straw-blonde hair had always been cut perfectly to lie on her shoulders with the ends curled into her neck.

After Emma married Jim Patersun, his wealth added designer clothes and expensive jewellery to her emerald green eyes and distinctive Audrey Hepburn oval-shaped face. Always decorated with diamond earrings, gold bangles or a thick gold rope chain. Her voice plummy and honeyed compared to Geena's gruff and often stentorian tones.

Now, Emma looked radically different. Now, she had a plump shape with neat hair but not styled by a top salon. Her skin looked pale and blotchy, and she'd aged beyond her years. Slender Emma had gone, and her face had filled out much more. Her eyes looked worried and tired, and she wore none of her beautiful jewellery.

Desperate to find out what happened, Geena wondered why the police had said Donna is still missing. As far as Geena and the family knew, her cousin Donna died twenty years ago.

The whole family including Emma thought Donna had died because that's what Emma's father had told everybody.

Geena told Modamo that Emma needed to lie down and she escorted Emma upstairs to her old bedroom. Emma lay down on the bed and wrapped herself in a blanket. Amster came into the room and sat down to watch Emma.

'I'll stay with her for a wee while,' Geena said to Amster.

'I need to stay in the room. Sorry, I have orders,' Amster said.

'She's safe here. She'll sleep. I'll call you when she awakens,' Geena said, and lifted Amster's arm to help her up from the chair.

Amster stepped over to the edge of the bed, looked down on Emma's face, and said, 'I'm sure Emma wants to pray that her sister's situation doesn't get worse. I'll relieve you in forty minutes,' Amster said, and it sounded like a warning.

When the bedroom door closed, Emma unwrapped herself and sat on the edge of the bed. Geena sat beside her and they whispered to each other.

'Is Donna really alive?'

Emma nodded. 'Donna never died. My Dad lied to everybody including me. Donna's brain didn't develop normally, and she has the mental age of a ten-year-old girl. My Dad found out about Donna's disability when she turned thirteen. He put her in a children's care home, and then told the entire family she had died.'

'Ohmigod, Emma. A care home. Why?'

'I don't know. He never told me anything. It happened after I'd left the house to get married. He only told me Donna had died when I went to my Mum's funeral.'

'Where has she been all this time?'

'After the care home she lived rough on the streets,' Emma said as emotion sapped her voice because she didn't want to tell Geena what really happened to Donna on the streets.

'Oh, poor Donna. How did you find her?'

'She found me … when Barscadden tried to have me killed.'

Geena sensed Emma holding more of the story back. 'What's all this about Barscadden?'

'Barscadden killed Jim to steal his business. He tried to kill me to stop me giving evidence. People from the Security Service told me they had uncovered an imminent threat to my life. Barscadden had paid someone to kill us in my home. The Security Services faked our deaths and put us in witness protection. I agreed to be a key witness when they caught him and brought him to trial. Since the funeral, we've been living in Canada.'

'So, what about this story they're giving out about Barscadden holding you and Donna hostage, and you escaping and leaving Donna behind?'

'It's complete nonsense. They've made it up. They have Donna locked in a room at a country house in England. If I don't do what they say, they'll kill Donna. Don't say anything, please.'

'Don't worry, I won't. Are these two from the Security Service?'

'No, they're Americans. They brought the both of us from America.'

'America? Who are they then?' Geena asked, and looked puzzled.

'I don't know. At first, I thought Barscadden's people had found us but the police are cooperating with them. They must be some kind of government people.'

Emma explained how she'd been woken in the early morning by a group of American men and women, dragged from her house in Sarnia, and then taken to America. The two calling themselves Joshua Modamo and Caitlin Amster had been with them since the abduction.

'That explains why you look so awful,' Geena said, sympathetically.

Emma clamped her eyes shut and covered her mouth with her hand to stop a loud sob bursting out. Tears ran down her face. Geena hugged her while she sobbed quietly then Emma said, 'It's not that.'

'What did they do to you?'

They hugged again then Emma wiped away her tears. She patted Geena on the wrist to let her know she felt better.

'When they dragged me out of the house in Sarnia. Modamo pushed me and I fell heavily onto the sill of their car. I was almost seven months and I lost my baby.'

'Oh my God, Emma—a baby. After all those years trying for one with Chris then with Jim. You're blessed with one, only to have it taken from you—so cruel.'

'I've not had proper medical treatment. I'm still getting bits of liver in my pants,' Emma confessed.

'Liver?'

'They look like bits of liver. I think they're bits of afterbirth. I don't think the paramedic got all the afterbirth. I've been really unwell.'

'Was there nothing they could do to save the baby?'

'Every night I keep wondering. If they'd taken me to a hospital and the baby had been put in an incubator. It might have survived.'

'Do you know what you would have had?'

'A little boy,' Emma said, and burst into tears.

'Those bastards. I'll cut their bloody throats,' Geena said, and stood up as if she would go through the room and throttle them for what they'd done.

'Please don't do anything. They have Donna.'

'Why the hell did these people pull you out of your witness protection?'

'I don't know, they won't tell me anything. Maybe this will tell me something.'

'What?'

Emma slipped a mobile phone out of her pocket and said, 'It's not mine.'

'Where did you get that?'

'At the press briefing earlier today.'

During the scuffle to push microphones into Emma's face, no-one saw Karen slip a mobile phone into Emma's hand. Emma quickly popped it into her jacket pocket. When she opened it, she found an unread text message from Gavin Shawlens.

Geena said, 'I remember him. The deadweight kid you were dragging around for ages. I spoke to him at your funeral. You know he cried more than everyone else put together. I never did like him, too delicate. I always thought a hard day's work would give him a heart attack. What does he want?'

'I don't know exactly.'

'When did he get back in to your life?'

'Earlier this year Jim developed a project to extract a new food ingredient from fish. We needed a biochemist to do some work. Jim contacted Gavin and he agreed to do the work needed to get a patent. The project went well until Barscadden killed Jim, and tried to steal the process.'

'Oh God. What an evil man.'

'I gave a police statement and brought him and his business empire down.'

'Good for you. So, he tried to take his revenge on you and Donna?'

'Yes, but the Security Service found out. They did the swap so it looked as though we died in the fire.'

Geena's brain moved back to think about Emma's baby. She added up a few facts, some dates and an assumption in the back of her mind.

'Why is Gavin Shawlens not in witness protection?'

'You know, I've been wondering the same thing for months. He knows as much about Barscadden's involvement in Jim's murder as I do. He has his life back to normal.'

'Did he make a police statement?'

'I don't know. I don't think he did.'

Emma looked away and an uneasy silence hung between them.

Geena sensed something she hadn't been told. 'It wasn't Jim's baby?'

Emma shook her head and confessed, 'Gavin's baby.'

Geena looked disappointed. 'Oh, Emma—a lovely man like Jim Patersun. How could you cheat on him?'

'I didn't mean to … I had a business trip to Paris. Gavin appeared and … well … it got out of hand. I told him right after that I wasn't going to have an affair. I ended it.'

'Did you tell Gavin about his baby?'

Emma shook her head. 'No. I had to leave for Canada before I got the chance.'

Geena took the phone from Emma, read the text message, and said, 'He wants to meet you. What is he doing here? Is he expecting to find out about his son?'

'God, no. He doesn't know about the baby.'

Geena held the phone up, and said, 'Was he in the crowd outside?'

'I don't think so. I didn't see him.'

'Why did he pass this phone to you? Does he have something to do with you being brought to Fort Augustus? It all seems a bit squiffy if you ask me.'

'I don't know, Geena, honestly. I've been isolated in Canada. I don't know what's going on. When Jim died, I needed someone. We got closer. Maybe, he thinks we'll get back together.'

'Do you love him?'

'No, of course not. I've never really loved him, but he's—'

'What?'

'He's helpful and considerate. He does try really hard to please. He has many faults but he really does know how to kiss a girl.'

Emma thought back to her time with teenage Gavin Shawlens. When they first met, his lips were so young, and so energised with passion that every time seemed like his first kiss.

'Nothing like Chris, then.'

'Chalk and cheese. Chris had always been lively, unpredictable, on edge, wildly charismatic, but not a good kisser. I think his tongue and his penis thought they were a double act. But, if I'd been able to have children with Chris, I know we'd still be together. All his brothers have kids and he wasn't going to be the one with none,' Emma said.

Geena nodded. 'You did the right thing at the time. Once violence starts in a marriage; it's time to get out. Not ten years down the road when you're worn out and have much less going for you.'

'I wanted Chris but I knew it wouldn't last without kids,' Emma said.

'Why did you marry Jim? He wasn't very lively.'

'Jim wasn't chalk nor cheese. He had something much more important,' Emma said.

They both smiled when Geena rubbed her thumb repeatedly over the tip of the index finger and middle finger as if rubbing notes together.

'I still don't understand why they brought you to my mum's house?' Geena asked, and hoped Emma would tell her the truth this time.

Emma shook her head. 'I don't know. I didn't ask to come up here. I didn't know where they were taking me until we left Glasgow and took the A82. I've assumed it's about Barscadden.'

'You think they want to lure Barscadden here? Surely they don't think he'll come here with this media circus outside,' Geena said, and made a face as if she didn't believe it.

'I suppose that isn't likely, is it?'

'Barscadden didn't become a billionaire by making stupid mistakes,' Geena said, more harshly than she intended.

'Well, I have no idea what they're trying to do here.'

'What are we going to do about Gavin? Do you want to see him?' Geena asked as she held up the mobile phone in her hand.

'No. I told him eighteen years ago we were finished. He wanted to reignite the passion but I told him it wouldn't work. He's too clingy and too claustrophobic for me. The time we spent working on the fish project reminded me why I dumped him in the first place. I don't want to go there again.'

'Well, tell him exactly that. That's what I'd do.'

'When this is over, I'll have Donna to look after, and that will be tough enough for me. I don't need *two* high-maintenance dependants.'

'Tell him straight. Didn't he get the message when you told him eighteen years ago?'

'Yes, he did. I told him flatly and he ran off. I didn't see him again until he came to work for Jim.'

'Better tell him again. Get the monkey off your back. That will be one less hassle. Otherwise, he'll be hanging around thinking he still has a chance. He'll just get in the way.'

'Okay, maybe you're right. A quick chat and then he'll get lost just like the last time.' Emma said, and nodded her concurrence.

'I think it would be best.'

'Think I could just tell him over the phone?'

'No. He needs to see your face. See that you mean it. Meet him for a couple of minutes, then walk away and come back.'

'Come back?'

'You can't bring him here with all of this going on outside. Do you want him sobbing his heart out on my Mum's doorstep?'

'No, definitely not. You'll need to help me then.'

'You mean just like the old days but in reverse,' Geena said as she remembered how Emma covered for her when she slipped out late at night to meet her boyfriend.

The bedroom door opened and Modamo stepped in the room.

'Everything okay in here?'

'Yes,' Emma replied.

Geena said to Modamo. 'I've managed to convince her to have something to eat. She'll feel much better with some food in her stomach.'

Geena and Emma left the room. Modamo and Amster looked closely at Geena as she passed. Geena looked like a fiery woman but there were no fireworks.

Modamo and Amster exchanged looks, and believed Emma had kept her mouth shut about their story and her situation.

Thirty-Four

The kitchen clock had just reached eight in the evening when Geena and Emma finished the washing-up. They'd managed to eat a little of the food that Bessie had cooked for them, but they said very little to each other.

Amster haunted the dining room while they ate, and the kitchen while they washed up. Always within earshot.

Bessie settled down with a book but soon fell asleep in her armchair.

Modamo and Amster hovered in the kitchen and prepared a meal for themselves from a box of food they had brought. The CIA agents seemed like two ghosts wandering around the house, watching and listening, but hardly interacting with anyone.

A few minutes after nine, Emma and Geena returned upstairs to Geena's old bedroom. Amster put down the food she had prepared and wiped her hands as she prepared to follow the two cousins.

Modamo called her back and shook his head. 'Don't bother. If she planned to tell her cousin anything, she would have done it by now, and the cousin would have exploded in our faces.'

Geena peered through her bedroom curtain. Most of the media people had disappeared, except for one photographer, doggedly lingering around the front gate as if he expected something to happen.

Two of the satellite TV vans had left the area and the third had moved down the road. Geena sat beside Emma when the mobile vibrated. Emma felt so tense, she dropped it on the floor. Geena picked it up, accepted the call, and gave it to Emma.

'Emma,' Gavin called.

'Gavin, is that—' Emma whispered.

'Emma,' he repeated.

'Gavin, listen—'

'I need to see you. Please,' he said.

'Okay, I have something I need—'

'Emma, I'm at the Auchenhill Hotel. Can you drive over here? Geena can tell you where it is. I'll meet you in the car park. I love you, Emma,' Gavin said, and his voice racked with emotion.

'I know, but I've got to tell you … Gavin … Gavin?'

'What?'

'Shit. He hung up on me.'

'Didn't want to give you a chance to say no.'

Emma and Geena went downstairs and into the kitchen. Emma told Modamo that an old friend had called, and that she wanted to go out for an hour to meet him. Amster immediately refused.

Modamo asked for more details. Emma said her friend Gavin Shawlens had called and she had to speak to him. Modamo spoke with his boss on the radio and received approval for Emma to leave the house to meet Gavin Shawlens.

Modamo said, 'If he's an old friend, he's not a risk—so okay,'

'Emma, you can use my car. It's in the barn. I'll just get my mother upstairs to her bedroom. Then I'll get the keys to the barn,' Geena said.

Modamo said to Amster, 'You go with them to the car and make sure everything is okay. Take a flashlight, it's pitch black out there.'

*

In the CIA control room at Grosvenor Square; a strong feeling of jubilation filled the room. Spence had called from his command vehicle, disguised as a TV satellite transmission van, and parked near Bessie's house. He told Katherine, Shawlens had arrived in the area.

'Are you sure?'

'He's here. He's spoken to Patersun. They're going to meet at a local hotel. We've got him,' Spence's voice boomed through the speakers in the control room.

In the command vehicle, a CIA technician examined an IR image on his screen. It came from a surveillance drone circling high above Fort Augustus. The phone call to Emma's mobile had been made from a landline phone in a house on

Canal Side, not more than half a mile from Spence's command vehicle.

An overhead IR image revealed the house as empty, no moving heat signatures, but still, Spence despatched a team to check the house. The team discovered a relay that re-directed satellite mobile calls made to the house landline onto Emma's phone.

A CIA comms technician had triangulated the source of the satellite mobile signal to a van parked in a lane near the Auchenhill Hotel car park.

When Spence's command vehicle had rolled toward Fort Augustus, a comms technician had warned Spence that the low number of communication satellites over Scotland could make triangulation difficult. Spence had ordered another comms satellite to be tasked over the Scottish Highlands to increase the accuracy of mobile phone signal triangulation. It took eighteen hours to put it directly overhead.

'Listen up, everyone,' Spence called out over the background chatter in the command vehicle.

'The satellite call had been re-routed through a landline to evade us. Shawlens is not here alone. The Black Fox must have set that up for him. She probably thought the scarcity of satellites in this region would make triangulation difficult,' Spence said.

'She kept the call short and probably thinks we're trying to task a satellite movement now for the next call,' the comms tech added.

'We have the edge,' Spence confirmed.

Moments later, a surveillance drone pilot trained his drone on the van near the Auchenhill Hotel car park. Its IR sensors provided live IR images of two moving heat signatures inside the van. The pilot identified the van as an electrical and plumbing supplies distributer based in Darlington.

The drone IR video feeds were relayed to Spence's command vehicle, patched to London, and forwarded to the White House Special Situations Room.

Spence ordered the mission commander to send a team to the target vehicle. President Cranstoun and General

Schumantle listened and watched the video streams as the mission commander issued orders.

'Eagle Flight, this is Command. Immediate proceed to target—tango-one.'

'Copy that Command. Eagle Flight is in-bound to tango-one, ETA to tango-one, three minutes,' the helicopter pilot replied.

'Eagle Team, this is Command, you are cleared for weapons hot. Repeat—weapons hot.'

'Copy that, Command,' the Eagle Team Leader replied.

'One minute to doors open. Target is ten o'clock off our nose. Good hunting,' the helicopter pilot said.

'Eagle Team, prepare to go green.'

The matte black Sikorsky UH-60 Black Hawk helicopter with noise-cancelling motors and rotors, hovered over a clearing six minutes' walk from the Auchenhill Hotel car park. Ropes dropped to the ground. Six Delta Force soldiers of Eagle Team rappelled down to the ground.

They formed a single file then made their way to the target. They activated their helmet night vision cameras and the video streams were relayed all the way back to Washington.

'Command, this is Eagle Flight, Eagle Team is away. I repeat, Eagle Team have boots on the ground,' the helicopter pilot said.

'I want straight line deployment. Keep it tight. Double time to the target,' the Eagle Team Leader ordered.

Eagle Team approached the side and the back of the van. The Team Leader confirmed they'd found a dark blue electrical and plumbing supplies delivery van. One of the Team did a portable IR scan of the van and confirmed two moving heat signatures inside.

'Command, Eagle Team in position, two tangos confirmed inside the vehicle—holding,' the Eagle Team Leader said.

Spence waited for his technicians to ping the phone that had been used to call Emma Patersun. A technician confirmed the phone location inside the van. A vehicle check confirmed the van had been registered in Darlington. Spence gave the mission commander a green light.

'Eagle Team, this is Command. The Black Fox and her cub are in the cage. You are clear to engage.'

'Copy that, Command. Eagle Team. Fire on my mark, three, two, one—mark.'

Eagle Team opened fire with suppressed assault rifles. In total, they fired more than nine hundred piercing rounds into the van from two sides before the Team Leader hand-signalled them to cease fire.

The only sounds to echo in the cold night air were the *dint, dint, dint, dint* as bullets pierced the metal body of the van and the jingling of spent metal cases landing on the ground.

When they ceased fire, they were certain no-one inside could survive. The shooters had avoided firing on the fuel tank or the engine so the vehicle did not burst into flames.

IR images on the ground and from the overhead drone confirmed the occupants had stopped moving, and their heat signatures were fading. Even so, Eagle Team approached the bullet-ridden van with due care and caution in case the van had been booby-trapped.

'Command, Eagle Team is ready to breach the vehicle,' the Team Leader said.

Tension soared in the command and control vehicle and in Washington as the video streams from the Delta team showed the destruction of the van. No-one could have survived.

'Eagle Team, this is Command, confirm and identify kills.'

'Copy that, Command. Eagle Two and Eagle Four, switch to nine, open the can and spill the beans,' Eagle Team Leader said.

Two members of the Eagle Team put down their assault rifles and drew their 9mm handguns. Eagle Two and Eagle Four approached the van cautiously, searching for any devices, wires, or claymores attached to the doors. Slowly, they opened the two doors at the front of the van then they pushed up the back roller door.

All the doors were open wide and there were no obvious signs of a booby-trap. They peered into the van, searching for the bodies. Inside lay still and their night vision goggles showed extensive destruction inside the van body.

With handguns high, they inched forward. Eagle Two moved to the back of the van and Eagle Four moved to the front. The video streams from their green night vision cameras showed massive puncturing of the van body and extensive internal damage.

On the floor, underneath debris and fragments of wood, the outline of two bodies. Eagle Two looked at the blood-spatter pattern on the walls. Some of the blood splashes ran slowly down the walls.

'Two bodies confirmed. Repeat, two bodies down,' Eagle Two said.

The drone pilot said, 'Confirmed. Two static heat signatures, fading … fading … gone.'

Eagle Two flipped his night vision goggles away from his eyes. 'Extensive blood splatters on the walls and on the floor of the vehicle.'

'Confirmed. Hot blood is seeping from the van,' Eagle Four said.

He had crouched down and looked under the van. His IR video showed the fluid dripping from the van onto the ground. In the cold night air, the warm fluid gave off steam-like vapour when it met the cold ground. He took off his night vision goggles for a true image. He saw red blood.

Katherine said, 'Well done, Spence. The White Fox has triumphed over the Black Fox.'

Spence accepted the congratulations of the people around him. A part of him felt sad because he had enormous respect for Zoe Tampsin. He felt like he'd lost a close friend to friendly fire. It shouldn't have happened.

The people in Grosvenor Square let out a huge sigh of relief.

Cranstoun got up from his seat in the Special Situations Room and patted General Schumantle on the shoulder, before he walked to the door.

'Well done, George. I don't need to see the mess. I'll sleep soundly tonight.'

'Thank you, Mr President. I think we all will.'

Cranstoun stopped and turned to face George Schumantle.

'By the way, George, you can tell the Brits the deal is off. They get a big fat nothing. If they want to buy our nuclear deterrent, the price has just gone up.'

'Of course, Mr President. It will be my pleasure.'

Thirty-Five

In Bessie's living room, Modamo and Amster stood against the wall with their hands clasped behind their necks. Zoe held a handgun in each hand, pointed at their heads. Zoe told them to sit down. Karen tied their hands and feet with heavy-duty plastic ties

Emma, Geena and Amster had left by the back door of the house and walked along the path to the barn. Amster shone her flashlight on the door while Geena unlocked a padlock. Amster drew her weapon, and crept inside. A few moments later, Amster came out and told Geena and Emma they could enter the barn.

Geena went inside and Amster reported to Modamo that she had cleared the barn. Before Geena started her green Ford car, Zoe appeared behind Amster, put a gun to her head, and pushed her inside the barn. Karen followed and took Amster's gun and comms.

Zoe told Geena to cover her head and face with a large scarf as if hiding her face from the photographers. Zoe told Geena to take the car to the hotel as planned, and then before she reached the hotel to turn around and come back to the house.

Forty minutes round trip, and if she did exactly that then everything in the house would be fine. When Geena drove off, Emma headed to the back door of the house, followed by Amster, Karen and Zoe.

Modamo stood at the front door with Lockhert, a CIA agent posing as a photographer. They watched the car leave. Modamo reported to Spence that Emma Patersun had left in a green Ford car to keep her rendezvous with Shawlens. Spence told Modamo to return to the house, and he told Lockhert to stay outside the front door.

Modamo closed the front door, and as he turned he faced Zoe with a gun pointed at his head. Karen took his weapon and comms, and led him into the living room to stand beside Amster. When the two CIA agents were secure, Zoe whistled out through the back door. Gavin came into the kitchen.

Emma and Gavin came face to face across Bessie's kitchen table. They didn't run to each other, and they didn't hug each other. He seemed shocked by how different she looked from the last time he saw her. They stood apart. He froze and as always, she took the lead.

'Gavin, who are these people? What are they doing here?'

'Emma ... I've grieved for you ... every day, every single day since the funeral.'

'I'm sorry about that but it wasn't my fault,' she fired back.

'What happened to you?'

Emma rattled out her explanation. 'Donna and I were taken into witness protection. The police got a tip-off. Barscadden planned to raze my house to the ground. They organised the funeral. Took us to Canada. We've been hiding in Canada since the funeral.'

'I've been devastated for all those months. Why didn't you get word to me?' he said, and sounded more confident.

'They wouldn't let me. I've had strictly no contact with anyone. What did you expect me to do? Defy them and have Barscadden's people find us? I've moved on. You should move on. That's the way it is now,' she said, and her voice sounded harsh.

He raised his voice. 'Emma, I want—'

'I'll *tell* you, what I want. I want to know how *you* got your life back to normal and not me. Why is Barscadden not trying to kill you? Something else you haven't told me—eh? You've got your life back and I got given the nightmare.'

He saw anger on Emma's face and sensed their they wouldn't get back together. He'd seen that face eighteen years ago when she first told him they were finished. He suddenly felt very cold and alone. He took a step closer to her and she took two steps back—confirmation.

'I thought we were getting back together.'

Emma shook her head. 'I told you to think hard about what you want in life. We're not good for each other, long term. You're a fine man, but only in small doses, I'm sorry that's it. I tried to tell you, but as usual you didn't listen to me—did you?'

Karen smiled to Zoe. This sounded like music to her ears.

'Emma, please let me try to—'

'I've *said* all I'm going to say, please go. Go back to your good life. God knows what I'll have to face from now on. For sure it will not include you.'

Gavin looked and felt stunned. After what they had been through together, he had expected a very different reaction.

'Emma, I cried myself to sleep every night.'

'Well, I didn't and to be honest, I'm glad it didn't work out. I told you the last time you came here. We can't go forward together. Nothing has changed between us. Just go. Leave me alone. I don't want you. Do you get it, finally? I don't want you in my life.'

He watched in despair as she turned her back and sighed loudly with frustration. She spread her hands on the worktop, leaned on them and bowed her head.

Zoe and Karen had listened to them. Karen felt overjoyed.

Zoe looked disappointed. She had hoped to hear something that related to his nightmares and her setting him free. She stood in front of Gavin and said, 'Gavin, has this opened the door for you?'

'What?'

'Your memory. Do you have what you need to unlock the door?'

*

Eagle Two knelt down at the first body. He had flipped up his night vision goggles and moved them away from his face to get a real view of the body. Inside the van remained dark and he blinked hard to adapt his eyes from the night enhancement goggles.

He pulled a small torch from his pocket and waved it around like a wand. He looked at the blood splattered on the walls and he saw pools of blood on the floor. A blood splatter pattern he'd expected.

He reached down, picked up a severed head, and held it up for Eagle Four to see. With his free hand, he used the torch to push scattered papers and broken wood on the floor. He unearthed two life-size mannequins in boiler suits.

The mannequin head held up by Eagle Two filled the screens in Spence's command vehicle and in the operations room at Grosvenor Square. Eyes glared at screens, jaws dropped, and you could hear a paperclip drop on the floor.

The mannequins had been wired to simple pulleys that provided enough limited movement to fool IR cameras. Taped on to the chest and back of each mannequin, like a bulletproof vest, were a pair of rubber hot water bottles, both riddled with bullet holes. The bottles had been filled with hot tomato ketchup.

An explosion of anger took over and everyone looking at the screens screamed and swore. People stamped on the floor, kicked waste bins, and threw things off their desks. Others slumped back into their chairs. Spence kept his mind on the job and immediately ordered Lockhert to breach the house.

*

Lockhert ditched his camera, pulled a handgun from his jacket, and burst in through the front door of Bessie's house.

Modamo and Amster lay face down on the living room floor, hands and feet bound. Karen had knelt down to check on Amster's feet. In the kitchen, Zoe stood between Gavin and Emma.

Lockhert dived into the living room and landed on his side. He fired three rounds in quick succession as he dived through the air. He had aimed at Karen but he killed Amster.

Zoe leapt into the room from the kitchen, and before Lockhert could move his weapon to her, she fired a round into the side of his head.

Emma screamed and collapsed onto the floor when Lockhert fired his weapon.

Zoe pulled Karen onto her feet, 'Are you okay?'

'Fine. He hit the bottom of my vest,' Karen replied, and rapped her bulletproof vest.

Karen and Zoe rushed to the kitchen. Zoe stood between Gavin and Emma. No-one spoke. Karen stared intensely at Emma for a second then spun her around and tied her hands behind her back with a plastic tie.

She turned and pushed Gavin toward Zoe who'd opened the back door and looked outside. She grabbed Gavin and pulled him through the kitchen back door. Karen followed and the three scampered out into the inky black and cold night. No time to lose.

In the field behind Bessie's house, they ran to a low wall where they had hidden sets of navy blue seamen's sou'wester hats and long coats. The coats were cold enough to mask their body heat from the overhead drone Zoe expected had been tasked to the area around Bessie's house. Zoe trampled off to check the way ahead lay clear. Karen helped Gavin put on his coat and said, 'Are you okay, pet?'

'I'm fine. Thanks, Karen.'

She looked concerned for him. Their eyes locked and she rested her left hand on the side of his head and ran her fingers into his hair. He turned his head into her hand and kissed the palm of her hand, then her fingertips. She felt the deepest sensual feeling she'd had in a long time.

'Forget her. She's a wicked bitch and you deserve much better,' she said.

He embraced her and kissed her on the lips. A passionate and tender kiss as Gavin thrilled her with soft kisses on her neck and earlobes. Her arms wrapped around him to weld their bodies together. Oh, for a magic wand to transport them back to Zoe's flat. Time for just one more lingering kiss before Zoe interrupted.

'Come on, let's go. Karen, on our six,' Zoe whispered.

Gavin stroked his finger under Karen's chin, and said, 'I'd like to kiss you again. When we get back to the cottage?'

'It's a date. Can I tell you this first. I love your kiss so very much,' she replied.

Before he took off after Zoe, Gavin turned back. He and Karen exchanged looks of gleeful anticipation of the passion they wanted. Hot thoughts fired their minds and their bodies. *Zoe will need to cover her eyes and plug her ears*, he thought.

The empty holiday cottage they used as a base lay more than half a mile away through a small wood and over a stream. Zoe led them and Gavin struggled to keep up with her. He wasn't as fit as he thought, and the long coat made running more difficult.

Karen stumbled and fell to the ground when they reached the stream. She waded slowly across it, but couldn't pull herself up onto the bank on the other side. Gavin looked back and saw her struggling.

Gavin started to turn back, stumbled on a rock and twisted his ankle. He fell to the ground and let out a groan. Zoe tracked back and pulled him onto his feet. She struggled with Gavin, almost carrying him on her side as he limped heavily.

'Wait. Karen is stuck in the stream,' he said.

Zoe settled Gavin down then ran back twenty paces to Karen's side. Gavin watched Zoe pull Karen up onto the bank. Karen didn't get up so Zoe knelt down beside her. Gavin felt exhausted and he assumed they were both the same.

*

Two other agents ran from Spence's command vehicle to the house. They entered the house cautiously although they didn't expect Tampsin to be there. When inside, one of them untied Modamo and Emma. The other reported to Spence that Amster and Lockhert were dead.

Modamo reported that Tampsin, Shawlens and one other woman had escaped to the field behind the house. Spence ordered the spy drone pilot to concentrate on heat signatures in the area around the house.

An agent sitting beside Spence told him that Director Kaplentsky wanted to speak to him privately. He took a hand radio, selected a secure channel and went outside to walk and talk.

'Report,' Katherine demanded.

'Two of our people dead. Tampsin, Shawlens and Turnbell running. They can't be far.'

'Damn it all to hell, *Spence*. You are looking like a rank amateur. Jesus. People are beginning to believe the only real talent here is Tampsin.'

Spence shook his head. 'Katherine, I'm sorry, I don't know what else to say.'

'You need to get this woman. I want her damn head in my hands. This is turning into a bitch of a nightmare. That bastard mannequin head is not going to be a signature on my failure to get this job done.'

'I honestly thought I had the edge. I don't know if I can get the better of her. I really don't,' Spence said, and he sounded disheartened.

'Pull yourself together, MacAllisin. Get over it. Get the damn job done,' she ordered.

'Yes, Katherine.'

'They're not free. They're in the circle of steel. We know that. They must not get out. Get all your people in there and run them *down*.'

'The drone will be overhead in a few minutes. I'll have teams check every heat signature in the area,' he replied.

'Lock the place down. Bring the search forward. I want body to body searching to start an hour before dawn. Do you have enough hazmat suits?'

'There is enough for one person in a suit backed up with three wearing respirators. It will look convincing enough for the locals.'

'Get them on the streets as soon as they are ready.'

'What is Washington saying?'

He didn't want to say the word mannequin.

'Cranstoun left the Special Situations Room to go to a meeting before this unfolded. Schumantle has agreed not to tell him until he returns. We've got two hours to make this right.'

'I hear you loud and clear,' Spence confirmed.

'Okay, let me know when you're ready to start broadcasting the Ebola messages. I'll deal with the media splash at this end,' Katherine said.

Spence ordered roadblocks to be set up on every road that moved in and out of Fort Augustus. Large notices at the roadblocks warned of an Ebola virus outbreak and quarantine restrictions in and around Fort Augustus. Large notices were posted around the village giving the same information. Soldiers closed the Caledonian Canal and began to search boats waiting to pass through.

An hour before dawn, the villagers would be woken to the sound of loud hailer announcements from overhead helicopters and slow-moving vehicles informing them of the outbreak of an Ebola infection in the village.

They would be warned to stay indoors and await the arrival of medical teams to check for infection and give anti-Ebola injections. They would also be warned that anyone on the streets would be arrested.

Spence went over all the preparations, search patterns, people deployment looking for weak spots where the Black Fox would try to sneak past. He thought hard to try and predict her next move. She should try to break out and head south to central Scotland, big cities and more escape opportunities. Then the penny dropped like a dinner plate on a stone floor.

She had evaded him because he didn't understand her mission objective. She wasn't just protecting Shawlens. Like him, she had tried to find out why the US wanted to kill him. He couldn't predict what she would do next. That depended on Shawlens and whatever he had that made him a threat to national security.

Katherine, Washington or both had kept him in the dark about the threat, and that lack of understanding had stopped him from predicting her movement. While he remained in the dark, the Black Fox had the edge.

*

Pat had passed Zoe's instructions to Spock. She wanted an additional van, a mock-up of a commercial van. He chose a small white van with the livery of a Scottish-based satellite TV installation company. In the white van, Spock had stored everything on Zoe's checklist.

Zoe had anticipated he would need time to get everything so she instructed Spock to deliver the white van and equipment to Auchenhill Hotel car park in three days.

Then for the last item on Zoe's list, a compulsory item, Zoe had ordered Spock to use the remaining money to take his wife and disappear in the Scottish Highlands for two weeks. Pat rented a remote cottage on the Isle of Skye, and they headed there after Spock delivered the white satellite TV van to the Auchenhill Hotel.

At six thirty-seven in the evening, Karen drove the dark blue electrical and plumbing supplies van into the Fort

Augustus area. She arrived at the hotel car park and parked behind the white satellite TV van.

Gavin and Karen set up the mannequins in the larger blue van. Zoe prepared a mobile phone with a recorded message of Gavin calling to arrange to meet Emma.

Later in the evening, they'd driven the small white van to an empty holiday cottage on the outskirts of the village, entered the cottage and stored their gear. Gavin stayed in the cottage while Zoe and Karen went out to find a suitable house in the village to set up the second half of the call routing equipment.

By chance, they found what they were looking for. An elderly couple came out of their house beside the Caledonian Canal and got into their car. They wore traditional highland dress for an evening out at a ceilidh dance.

While Karen kept watch, Zoe had entered the house and attached the satellite call-porting device. Zoe set the device to receive a mobile call from the blue van then pass the call to the mobile phone that Karen had slipped to Emma. The call relayed a pre-recorded short message Gavin had made.

Thirty-Six

Karen lay on her back and opened her coat. Zoe examined the blood seeping around Karen's waist. Zoe ripped the Velcro fasteners to open Karen's bulletproof vest. One of Lockhert's bullets had hit the side of the vest and been deflected underneath.

Karen's blood flowed over Zoe's hand as she palpated the wound. Karen squirmed and her face screwed up hard against the pain. Zoe drew her hand back.

She pulled a fabric dressing from a pocket and ripped the dressing from its green packaging then tore through Karen's clothes to see the wound. She placed the gauze on her wound and Karen held it in place. Within seconds, the specialized granules formed a gel plug to stop the bleeding.

'I'm sorry, boss. You don't need this,' Karen said.

'Karen, you've got nothing to be sorry about.'

'Where's my Labcoat?' she asked.

'He twisted his ankle. Hopeless males, what can you do with them?'

'I planned to do a lot with him.'

'I've got a scar right about there. They told me I'd never have children. You know what? I survived and I have Amy,' Zoe said, and tried to sound positive.

'Ohhhh-mygod, this is bad. Must have been a right hot bullet. My guts are well ablaze,' Karen said, and her face looked terrified.

Silence hung between them as they stared at each other and remembered soldiers who'd fallen with gut wounds. Zoe opened a small flask for Karen to drink some water while she ripped open another fabric dressing coated with gel-forming granules.

'Where did it exit?' Zoe asked.

Karen shook her head and looked distraught. Tears welled up. She could feel intense flames and heat in her abdomen. As if she had a red hot poker in her side.

'I'll carry you. Come on. I've run up and down the Brecon Beacons carrying more weight than you can offer,' Zoe said, and pulled her up to a sitting position.

'Ahhwwll! Jesus, I can't … I can't move,' Karen squealed and flopped back.

She felt as if someone had poured scalding water over her stomach. Unbearable pain bleached all the colour from her face.

'I'll give you morphine for the pain.'

'Boss, you know I can't make it. We've both seen enough gut wounds.'

Zoe moved closer until their faces were no more than seven inches apart.

'Come on, Karen, dig in. Gavin is your man now. You can make it for him. Come on.'

'These last few days have been wonderful for me, the best I've had. Thanks for pulling me out of that squat. I hated every minute of it, living like a filthy dog with dirty thieves and druggies messed out of their minds. I'm so glad it's over. I'll die here on the field like a good soldier.'

'Karen, I'm not leaving you here.'

'I can't face torture. You know what they'll do to make me talk. I can't … please, boss. I can't suffer. Let me go and join them. They're waiting for me.'

Karen believed that when a soldier died a soldier's death, he or she met up with hundreds of fallen soldiers from the old regiment. Old friends, friends of old friends, friends of the old friends' friends. They would show her the ropes, introduce her to everybody and welcome her home with a big celebration of her life and service. Top seat at the table. She looked forward to it.

'Promise me one thing.'

'Of course, name it.'

'Look after my Labcoat. Tell him … tell him I would have been right proud, right proud to be his technician. He would have been right proud of me.'

'I'll tell him.'

'Come on, boss, it's time for last orders. Put the light out when you leave. I'll go to sleep like a good little lass. Be quick about it, like,' Karen said, and closed her eyes.

Zoe buried her face in Karen's neck and kissed her warmly. A tear rolled from Zoe's cheek onto Karen's neck. Zoe looked at the ring on her left hand. With her thumb and forefinger of her right hand, she moved a small slider on the ring. A tiny needle just a few millimetres sprang out from the ring.

Carefully Zoe pressed her ring finger into Karen's neck at the carotid artery, then carefully took off her ring and put it in a small plastic ring box. She hugged Karen while the drug coursed through her body.

It would take less than a minute to do its work. When she stopped breathing, Zoe lay Karen's head on the ground then arranged her coat and hat to make her look peaceful. She placed Karen's arms at her side.

'Aye, bonnie lass, you're a free girl now. Go and join them, You have fun with them. Give them my regards. I'll see you again when I get there. Away with you,' she said as emotion grabbed her voice.

Zoe wiped tears from her cheek, stood to attention and gave Karen a silent formal salute. Gavin watched and guessed what had happened when Zoe returned alone. As she helped him onto his feet, he knew not to ask about Karen.

When they reached their empty holiday cottage, Zoe pulled up sharp. She saw a black SUV parked in front of the cottage. Two men, weapons in their hands, circled and checked the property. Zoe told Gavin to sit tight and keep low.

The cottage lay on the opposite side of the village to the house on Canal Side where Karen and Zoe set up the phone call equipment. When they had broken into that house, Zoe carefully left trademark clues of a break-in, enough for trained eyes to notice.

The CIA agent reported by radio that the cottage had not been touched, and then they drove off in their SUV. She'd been careful to pick the cottage lock gently and leave no signs on the lock of forced entry. Zoe turned to Gavin.

'We're nearly there. How are you holding up?'

'Bloody painful—it's broken.'

'It's not broken. It's a bad sprain. You'll live.'

When Zoe opened the kitchen door to let him inside, Gavin collapsed on the floor and looked as though he might pass out. She took off his boot and sock, and looked at his bruised ankle. She rotated his ankle to make sure it wasn't broken.

He looked drained and exhausted. She reckoned the meeting with Emma Patersun had been more painful than two kicks in the face. He sat himself up with his legs outstretched on the floor and his back against a kitchen floor cabinet. Zoe got down and sat beside him.

'I need you to be more mobile. I'll give you a shot of morphine.'

'Morphine.'

Gavin sat closest to their first aid kit so he stretched over to reach it.

'Not that stuff. It's so weak it's useless for intense pain. I'll give you some good stuff.'

Zoe took off her left boot and sock. Stitched onto the side of the sock, she had a ring similar to the ring around her finger. She pulled the ring off her sock and rotated it in her hand to show him.

She rubbed a main vein on his leg. She compressed the slider on the ring and a short needle sprang out. She pushed the needle into his vein. Gavin remembered the warning Zoe gave him about touching her rings.

'Is that the ring you warned me about? Never to touch, ever, on pain of death?'

'Yes.'

'Why the big secret?'

'I'm going to tell you a story, and then you'll forget you ever heard it, right?' she said, and looked serious as if giving away state secrets.

Zoe spoke to Gavin as if telling a fairy story to her daughter. 'Okay, once upon a time, a brilliant major in the Royal Engineers had a talent for designing and building intricate pieces of smart kit for the army. Then during a tour in Afghanistan, he lost both legs to an IED.'

'Michael?' he asked.

'The top brass no longer wanted his engineering skills. Instead, they wanted him to push paper across a desk for the rest of his career, ignoring the fact his brain had remained as sharp as ever. So he refused, and they dumped him back in civvy street where he became a bespoke jeweller, designing and making fabulous but expensive pieces of fine gold and diamond jewellery for ladies of wealth and influence.'

'Not you, then,' he said.

'Your sense of humour is dreadful.'

'Sorry.'

'This major has a lovely sister, two years younger, but she's not very girly and doesn't need pretty jewels because her job is tough and scary. The major worries about his sister all the time because she deals with bad people who would kill her if they could. To give his sister an edge, the major designs and engineers rings with tiny high-pressure capsules and a short needle.

'The major makes these rings only for his lovely sister because if they were available to others then the bad people would know to take them off her and she would lose her edge. The major's sister has two rings called Deds and Meds. A Deds ring has a capsule of deadly botulin toxin and a Meds ring has a capsule of morphine.'

'Botulin toxin? How much toxin do you pack in a capsule?' he asked.

'Five hundred nanograms.'

'Five hundred. That's *enough* to kill an elephant and a bus load of people,' he said.

'I need it to work fast.'

'Hang on, botulin toxin causes paralysis. That guy in the Prepper's store lay out stiff as a board with no blood leaking. And in Prague, now I understand why the Czechs quizzed me about Herman Vindanson. They thought I had paralysed him. I'm impressed. Two quick and clever kills,' he said.

'Three. The doorman at the McVickin factory.'

'Well, he looked like an elephant and probably needed a few extra nanograms.'

'The morphine should be working on you,' she said.

'Okay, now I understand that night in the Cosham flat when you insisted I never ever touch your rings.'

'I sensed you felt insulted but I warned you for your own good,' she said.

'It did upset me but you were right to warm me off because even a tiny scratch from a Deds needle would have been enough to take me out.'

Gavin looked at the blood on Zoe's hands. He knew it had to be Karen's blood. She saw him looking at her hands. He hadn't asked what happened.

'Karen is gone, isn't she?'

'Gut wound. Lucky shot, deflected underneath her vest. You know about gut wounds, right?'

'Wish I could have said something to her. Held her hand, kissed and thanked her,' he said, sadly.

'I know. She's at peace now.'

'When this is over, I wanted her to train as a technician. I told her she could become my lab manager.'

'She told me about your offer. I'm glad you did that. She wanted that new life so much. You would have been proud of her.'

'Every time I hear a woman with a Newcastle accent, I'll think of her,' he said.

'So will I. A lovely lass with a big heart, and a first class soldier.'

Thirty-Seven

Gavin sat quietly in the dark while Zoe looked around the cottage. She'd found it available for holiday rent on the Internet, and from the numerous pictures of the property, she discovered what type of lock had been fitted to the back door.

Its location in the village, sandwiched between the Caledonian Canal and the River Oich, and well hidden by evergreen trees and bushes, would provide quick access to her intended escape route.

Zoe expected Spence would flood the area with agents to lock it down. They would have the village surrounded and would start a search at first light. She guessed they would use the pretext that James Barscadden had arrived to kill Emma Patersun.

She didn't know it, but in fact they had prepared a better story. That a local had recently returned from West Africa with an Ebola virus infection. Every vehicle, every house and outhouse would be searched.

The sharp dose of morphine made Gavin drowsy so he drifted off to sleep on the sofa. Zoe returned to the kitchen, sat at the table and stared at the three large black backpacks of gear sitting neatly side by side on the kitchen floor. She thought about Karen.

She rested her head on her arms folded on the kitchen table, and allowed herself to nap. She woke when Gavin groaned and moaned. When she went to his side, she found he'd come out of a deep sleep.

She checked the time, three in the morning, and told him they had to get ready. She dragged two of the large backpacks across the kitchen floor and started to unpack them.

The morphine must have loosened up his brain because he remembered something trapped in his mind. The expression on his face showed her he had recalled a memory.

'What did you get?'

'Eighteen years ago, I hadn't heard from Emma for ten days so I went up to her house. Her dad told me she wouldn't be seeing me anymore. I called her house a dozen times but her father always answered the phone. I couldn't understand.'

'So what did you do?'

'I waited outside her house the following morning, expecting her to go to work, but she never did. I panicked and waited until her dad went out to the shops then I went to the house. Her sister Donna told me she'd gone to their Aunt Bessie's farm in Fort Augustus.'

'So you made your way here?'

'Yes, I just passed my driving test and although I wasn't experienced, my sister Siobhan loaned me her car to drive to Fort Augustus. Bessie is well known so I soon found the farm. When Emma came to the door she almost slammed the door shut on me.'

'What a lovely surprise you must have been,' she said, and smiled.

'We had a blazing argument on the doorstep and at the end she told me she didn't want to see me again. She said she'd met someone else. Her new boyfriend drove a car so she'd taken him to meet Geena.'

'That would have been hard for you.'

'I felt physically sick. I drove the car up the side of Loch Ness and I did something stupid. I aimed Siobhan's car at the loch and floored the pedal. The next thing I remember clearly is the hospital in Inverness. They said I'd been in a car accident, left the road and ended in the loch. A few local people pulled me out and called an ambulance. This is all so clear now. I can't understand why I didn't remember it before.'

'Oh well, that explains these nightmares, the drowning, the flooding cabin and all that stuff.'

'I don't know what went through my mind. I had my sister's car, and I'd only just passed my driving test. I didn't know the roads.'

'Still nothing there to explain why the CIA want to kill you.'

'I don't understand everything yet. I'm missing something. I feel it strongly. I know it's there but I can't see it yet. Something behind the door. I thought I sensed Emma but I don't have that feeling anymore. Behind the door is odd, it smells more like a hospital ward.'

'Sounds like the hospital in Inverness might be worth a visit. First we have to exit Fort Augustus. Okay, let's get into these wetsuits,' she said.

He pulled a wetsuit from his backpack and struggled to put it on because he had a half-size smaller suit than he needed for comfort. He'd forgotten the knack to putting on a wetsuit.

'This wetsuit is too small,' he said.

'Gavin, try to relax. I'll help you get your suit on.'

When they stood in their wetsuits, Zoe checked the gear and the tanks. They carried their flippers and slipped out the back door of the cottage. Gavin stopped short.

'What's wrong?'

'Do we have to do this? I'm not really a confident diver. I've only logged fourteen hours. I've never dived in the dark,' he said with panic in his voice.

'This village is locked down. A cat won't be able to walk out without being questioned. If they stick to protocol, they'll announce an emergency and begin searching every house in the area. They'll have satellite and drones with infrared cameras picking up all the bodies. We must slip into the River Oich, head downstream to Loch Ness, and out of their trap. This is the only way their IR cameras won't pick us up.'

'My gear is not working properly.'

'It's fine. It's just a special diffuser to minimise bubbles. It does feel like there is a resistance; just breathe normally and you'll be fine. They'll have cameras on all the waterways looking out for bubbles. When they don't find us in the search, they'll know we went underwater but they'll think we headed south to get away from Fort Augustus. They'll concentrate their search there.'

'We're not going to swim up Loch Ness?' he said, half joking.

'Don't be silly. We track southeast for about a mile to reach the side of the loch. The B862 runs close to the loch and that's where Karen hid the white van. If we leave now, we have three hours before they start their search then maybe another hour before they trawl the waterways.'

'How long will it take us to get clear?'

'I think their ring of steel will be at least a mile in diameter. Karen has parked the white van just outside their perimeter. We have air for sixty minutes. The Oich is swollen with November rain and fast flowing. Fifteen minutes to flow down to the river mouth and into Loch Ness. Then we should do the mile in thirty minutes.'

'Let's get going then.'

When they reached the edge of the river, they fitted their flippers and cleared their masks. They found the river shallow at the sides and deeper in the middle, and the current wasn't as fast as Zoe expected. Although the water looked clear, they couldn't see anything in the dark. Zoe gave Gavin a three-foot tether to make sure he stayed at her side.

At some points in the river, the current flowed faster and their progress moved quickly, and at other points the river paused and slowed their progress.

They had been in the river less than ten minutes when she grabbed his arm and pulled him down and into the bank. She saw lights searching the river mouth.

At this part of the river, they found the river less deep, so they nestled under overhanging branches for cover and edged along slowly. The light beams danced on the river surface from both banks. When the lights passed, Gavin started to move up but she pulled him back and waited.

A minute later, they heard a rigid-hulled inflatable boat (RIB) pass overhead, and more lights from the boat played down into the water. Their hearts jumped into their mouths when one of the three grappling hooks dragging behind the boat caught Gavin's air hose and pulled the mouthpiece out of his mouth as it moved on.

Zoe quickly captured his mouthpiece in her hands as it swayed and jiggled in the water. It happened so fast he didn't have time to panic.

By the time he realised he needed air, she guided the mouthpiece back to his mouth. They knelt together, facing each other while she held his arms. She expected he would need a few minutes to recover.

They swam to the mouth of the river and out to Loch Ness. When Zoe felt they were clear, she surfaced to get her bearing. She saw spotlights on three RIBs search the mouths of the two rivers and the canal that flowed into Loch Ness.

They swam steadily southeast until they reached the most southerly part of the loch. When they arrived on a small shore, they popped up there masks, pulled off their flippers and hurried up the shore to a small clearing in the forest.

Ten minutes later, they found the B862. It had taken eighty-two minutes and they still had sixteen minutes of air left because the slight resistance caused by the diffuser forced them to breathe more slowly.

On the road, they saw the small white van ahead of them. Zoe pulled Gavin to the bushes for cover. They knelt down and Gavin helped Zoe remove her gear. She pulled her Browning from her waterproof backpack and fitted a suppressor. Before she crept up to the van, she told him not to move. She circled the van looking for evidence of tampering or surveillance.

Karen had left three sets of small twigs in a K pattern near the van to reveal any disturbance. The twigs were still where she left them. Zoe stepped out to the middle of the road and signalled Gavin to join her. He hobbled along the road carrying her gear.

Zoe helped him remove his gear then went into the front of the van while Gavin got into the back and stored the equipment. They sat down, relaxed, and gave out huge sighs of relief. Zoe looked around outside. Gavin stretched out, and started to take his wetsuit off.

'Oohhohhohho, it's cold,' Gavin said with a shiver in his voice.

Zoe put the van keys in the ignition and turned the key to check the battery and the fuel. They were both good, and she decided not to refuel at the local petrol station. A third of a tank would provide a hundred miles with careful driving. Zoe had siphoned fuel from the large blue van into a spare petrol can. Enough for an additional forty miles. They had enough fuel to get a good distance away from Fort Augustus.

'This is beach weather compared to a night out on the Brecon Beacons in winter,' she said.

The white van had been waiting for them for a long time and it felt as cold inside as it did outside. Zoe peered out the windscreen and said, 'Well, Fort Augustus. Nice visiting you, but it's time for us to take our leave. Thank you and a very good morning.'

'We can't leave, not now,' he said.

Zoe twisted around to look over the back of the driver's seat to see his face. 'WHAT? It's a bit early in the morning for academic humour.'

'There is something else. I know it. I can feel it. It's as if you asked me the name of my English teacher at school. I know I have memories of my English teacher but I can't remember her name.'

'I'm sure you'll regain your memory, but we've been lucky, very lucky. It's time to get out of the area. Once they realise we're not in the hot zone, they'll expand the net by five miles. They'll still have the resources to mount an intensive search. We need to be ten miles away before they make that decision,' she insisted.

'I want to go back to the place where I drove into Loch Ness. I left something there. I need to find it.'

She shook her head and said, 'No chance. No way am I going on a wild goose chase. End of.'

Thirty-Eight

In the back of the white van, Gavin struggled to remove his wetsuit top. His hands were numb and he shivered in the cold. Zoe reached over the driver's seat and extracted fresh clothes from a bag Spock had put in the van. She handed a pile of clothes to Gavin.

Zoe laid her body out across the front seats. She pulled off her wetsuit and ran a towel vigorously over her naked body to stimulate her circulation. Her back, her hair, her front, her legs, between her legs. The windows began to steam up.

She leaned between the two front seats. She wrapped her towel around her shoulders and pulled the ends down to cover her breasts. She rested her arms on the headrests of the two front seats and spread one knee on the driver's seat and one knee on the front passenger's seat.

'Look and see if my panties are in that pile of clothes I gave you.'

He rummaged around and found her black bikini pants. He handed them over and didn't avert his eyes from her neat, small triangular patch of dark hair.

Gavin missed the opportunity for a smart comment or even just a bit of friendly banter. His mind worked on what he could say to convince her to take him to the side of the loch. She turned around and leaned her back against the driver's door, folding her knees back to her chest to pull on her pants.

She said, 'The obvious escape is to scoot south but it's a long road. The chances of getting caught are high. They'll be expecting us to go east or west to the minor roads and single tracks. North would not be smart, single road easy to spot. Did you go up the east side or the west side of the loch?'

He struggled to pull off the top half of his wetsuit. 'I don't know. I'd borrowed my sister's car and she'd only just got me through the driving test. I didn't know the bloody stupid roads,' he said with frustration.

He managed to get out of the top half of his wetsuit and he quickly put on a t-shirt. He hadn't dried his body with a towel, so his t-shirt soaked up the water. More contortions on his face as he struggled with the bottom half of his wetsuit.

She told him to lie back in the van and put his legs through the gap between the front seats. She pulled off his boots and poured surplus water onto the floor. One at a time, she grabbed each leg of the suit and pulled it off.

Now, she took her turn to have a good look at his naked body. They both looked at each other for a moment and wondered if anything romantic would stir.

More concerned with his wet t-shirt, she threw her towel at his face and said, 'Get dried before you try to put your clothes on.'

'I remember the ambulance driver. I overheard him telling the emergency room doctor they picked me up on General Wade's Military Road. Can I look at the map?'

'It's on the east side.'

'Perfect, we're on the east side,' he said.

She shook her head. 'Not perfect. I've said I'm not going on a wild goose chase.'

'I know I can find the last piece of my memory. Don't you want to know what this has all been about?'

Zoe sensed increased confidence in him as if he wanted to take command, but he didn't know where to lead them. In life and death situations, the person with a plan, the equipment and the determination will win unless the opposition has a better plan. No plan and no idea what to expect is often a recipe for disaster. All of her instincts warned her he would get them both killed.

'Don't you *dare* question my commitment after what I have been through for you. We can't go searching in the blind. If you don't know exactly where to look, then that's it, tough.'

'I've had another *déjà vu*.'

'When?'

'Just now.'

She laughed in his face. 'I don't believe you.'

'I must go to the spot where I drove into Loch Ness. I left something there. It's my key to this nightmare. The last piece of the picture is there.'

She looked stern and said, 'You have no idea where this spot is. We need something to work with. If you don't have anything; I'm not going anywhere except out of the area as fast as I can.'

'I remember passing a graveyard.'

'On your left or your right?'

'On my left.'

She shook her head, showed him a look of disbelief and said, 'A graveyard on the east side of the loch. You're making this up.'

'No, I saw a graveyard.'

'Are you sure about this? If you were going up the east side, and it appeared on your left. It would be at the side of the loch. Doesn't sound likely if you ask me.'

'I'm sure but I only got a brief look as I drove past.'

'Of course you did,' she said with a sarcastic tone.

'Are we close enough to Fort Augustus for a signal?'

'Maybe.'

'Please. If I'm wrong then we'll leave and get out of the area,' he said.

Zoe fetched her laptop. The mobile phone signal proved too weak to connect to the Internet. She searched a cache of offline Google Maps on her laptop. She found Boleskine Burial Ground on the B852 between Foyers and Inverfarigaig.

'Okay, maybe you do have a reference point.'

When they were dry and clothed, Gavin stored the wetsuits in the back of the van. Zoe fetched wigs to change their appearance. His hair became dark red and neck length. Her hair became blonde and shoulder length. She wore thick spectacles with plain glass lenses.

*

Zoe drove the van north along the B862. They didn't meet any other vehicles, which at just after five in the morning wasn't surprising. The road led east and away from Loch Ness and climbed high up the side of the mountain for some distance.

When they reached high ground, they found themselves out in open moorland. Zoe suspected she'd taken a wrong turn. She stopped the van, got out and looked back toward Fort Augustus. She heard helicopter rotors and loudhailer announcements punctuating the morning silence. The search had started.

Gavin remembered the open ground and told her to keep going. They followed the road through a forest of tall Sitka spruce trees until the road started down through another forest, before it turned west back toward the loch.

'*Watch*,' Gavin screamed as Zoe swerved around a sheep trotting along the road.

'What's wrong with *these* Highland sheep? Don't they know the highway code?'

It felt like ages on the road heading east before the road headed north, and Zoe thought about turning back. Then they arrived at a fork in the road. The B862 carried on in the right fork. The left fork took them to the B852, known locally as General Wade's Military Road.

At last, Zoe's sense of direction told her she headed west in the correct direction back to the loch. The road led downhill steeply through more woodland.

When she saw a sign for Foyers, she knew the Boleskine Burial Ground lay not too far ahead. They'd only been on the road for thirty minutes but it felt much longer. They'd climbed up, then across the back and then down the other side of a mountain.

When Zoe reached the burial ground, she stopped the van to let Gavin have a look at the area. In the dark, he couldn't recognise much but he felt sure he'd been there before.

'The road I drove along ran very close to the loch side,' he said.

'Are you sure?'

'Like it happened yesterday.'

She drove further and found that the road ran directly parallel with the loch, and that it lay no more than a long jump from the water's edge. She slowed to allow him more time to take in the signs.

The more he saw the more confident he became, 'We're almost there.'

She slowed the van down to a jogging pace and drove through a little hamlet called Inverfarigaig. Early risers began to stir, and a few lights lit up in the sleepy houses.

He pointed ahead. 'I remember these houses. It's just ahead on the left.'

'You're sure?'

'Yes, this part of the road seems to cut through the side of the mountain.'

Zoe stopped just in front of what looked like a small lay-by except two large boulders blocked car access. The lay-by had become overgrown with weeds, bushes and grass but looked solid enough underneath to support a van.

Gavin stared at the grey rock face of the mountain jutting out on the opposite side of the road. 'This is it. I drove down here going too fast. I spooked a deer coming up from the loch side. It tried to run across the road in front of me. I swerved to the right but I saw the rock face. I swerved back. I hit the deer and I drove into the loch.'

'You were damn lucky,' she said.

'I *didn't* try to kill myself. I swerved to avoid a deer. I can remember it just as it if happened five minutes ago. I can feel the shock.'

'Shock could have caused a memory blockage or something,' Zoe said as she scanned around.

Gavin pointed over to the other side of the loch. 'The last thing I saw before the car sank was that castle over there.'

'Urquhart Castle? You remember seeing Urquhart Castle?'

'Yes, I can see the image in my head exactly as I'm looking at it now.'

Together Zoe and Gavin tried to move one of the boulders aside so she could drive the van into the space. They couldn't budge them so Zoe used the van to nudge one of the boulders to clear a path. He told her the boulders weren't there when he swerved into the spot eighteen years ago.

They looked around the lay-by and tested the strength of branches stretching out over the water. They both shuffled gingerly along the overhanging tree branches, over the dense undergrowth to look at the water's edge but couldn't see anything in the dark.

The rocky ground underfoot felt treacherous, slippery and dangerous in the dark. The overhanging foliage extended three metres, and the water lapped directly underneath with no shore. Zoe dropped a stone into the water, and from the sound she knew it wasn't shallow.

'It's deep enough. We're probably on the slope of the mountain. That's why there is no shore. What now?' she asked as he looked bewildered and confused.

They shuffled back along the overhanging branches. Zoe got into the van and Gavin followed.

She looked expectantly at him. 'Well?'

'What?'

'Do I need to ring a bell or something to catch the next *déjà vu*?'

Thirty-Nine

Loch Ness

A northerly wind blew down the loch, adding a sharp wind chill to the cold air. Ten minutes passed, and Gavin closed his eyes for the tenth time. He tried to concentrate, but he couldn't focus.

He felt sure that if he returned to the spot then something would help him to remember what happened next.

Zoe saw his frustration and she gave him a comforting squeeze on his wrist. 'Nothing?' she asked.

'This is definitely where my car went into the loch.'

'Maybe it's too dark. This place will look very different in daylight,' she said.

He looked uncertain and confused. Zoe felt they'd reached a dead end. She decided to give him a few minutes then she wanted to be speeding away. She rested her hands on the steering wheel, and her right hand moved to and from the ignition key ready to start the engine. Her mind flagged up something she didn't understand.

'Didn't you say your car sank like a stone until you hit the ground?'

'I thought it hit the ground but I clearly remember a banging metal noise. I'm sure I heard it before I blacked out.'

'I can't imagine anyone diving into the loch and following the car down to the bottom. Too deep. Even if it's sitting on a ledge ten metres down, it would still be too cold and too dangerous.'

'I remember being in the driver's seat when it sank. I remember being petrified,' he said.

'Someone must have pulled you out of the car before it sank, dragged you to the side and phoned for an ambulance. Someone must have seen what happened and rescued you,' she said.

'The next thing I remember I woke up in a hospital bed. A nurse told me they found me on General Wade's Military Road near Dores.'

'How did that happen? Dores is more than a mile further on,' Zoe said.

'I don't know.'

'Did you find out who rescued you?'

'No.'

Zoe said, 'None of this makes any sense. Mr Nobody is passing by when you crash, he pulls you out of your sinking car, and then takes you a mile up the road before he calls an ambulance. That doesn't sound right. Your mind is making this up. You're still upset with Emma. Time to move on. Let's get out of here.'

'These bits are real. I know some bits of the jigsaw puzzle are missing. If I just go into the water and come up again, I'll find the missing piece of my memory, just like I did by meeting Emma at her aunt's house.'

'We're leaving right now,' she said.

'I need to go down in a car to recreate my memory of the water filling up. I'll know what happens next.'

She looked angry. 'Are you crazy? That's stupid. It's bloody suicide.'

'Whatever this is about, it's in the car down there. I know I've left something in the car. I know it,' he said.

'If we commit this van to the loch, we'll be stranded. Stuck here. We'll be found and the consequences will be brutal. We should drive away and return better prepared another day.'

He looked determined. 'Zoe, I know you think I'm an academic idiot, and if truth be told you're right. You're absolutely right. I'm way out of my comfort zone here, and I'm floundering. But I know I'm right about this. I've never felt so certain about anything. I don't know how to explain it, but I know I've left something in the car that will end this nightmare.'

Zoe took a long deep breath and let it out noisily. There were a dozen good reasons why she shouldn't allow Gavin to talk her into driving the van into the loch. After everything they had come through, after losing Karen; to forsake all of that for one last act of insanity. She decided she wasn't going to do it. She reached for the ignition key and turned on the engine. The sooner they were away, the sooner he would see sense.

'We're leaving,' she said.

'I think it's in the boot of the car.'

'What's in the boot of the car?'

'I remember seeing it, and thinking, that's not mine. It's an aluminium case with a small American flag on the side.'

'Are you certain?'

'Yes. I can see it in my mind.'

'Shit. If there's something in the car that belongs to the US then we've bloody well led them here. Jesus, have they waited for you to lead them to what? Pandora's Box? Spence, you smart old fox. Wait a minute. Maybe there's still time.'

She got out of the van and listened. A helicopter in the distance sounded closer than before. Had Spence kept back and waited for Gavin to lead them to the sunken car? Her mind raced frantically.

The helicopter would be following a search pattern, and she figured she had fifteen minutes before the IR cameras picked up heat from the van. Putting the van into the water would eliminate the heat signature. They could run back to Inverfarigaig, steal a car and make their escape. She decided to go.

'Oh God. You'd better be right about this. If you are fucking with me, then so help me, I'll leave you in that car where you belong. Get the wetsuits and the gear.'

'Okay. Moment of truth,' Gavin said.

They helped each other into their wetsuits and diving gear. Eight minutes later, Zoe drove the van over the edge and into the cold water. Zoe switched on the headlights but they didn't help much. The battery shorted and they ploughed downwards in complete darkness.

Zoe had readied a hand-held waterproof torch to switch on when the headlights went. With ten minutes of air in her tanks, she believed she had enough for a quick search of the sunken car and a rapid swim back to the surface.

Slowly, they descended and two minutes later, the van settled with a clatter of metal banging. She couldn't see but they landed behind the remains of the old Ford Escort Gavin had driven into the loch.

By good fortune, the van landed on its nose at an angle of forty degrees, and a good air pocket had trapped in the top back corner. Zoe thought the van had settled on the side of the mountain. Their two heads popped up in the air pocket.

'I'll look for your car and bring back the case. Then we go topside and run back to Inverfarigaig for a new vehicle.'

'Okay. Be careful.'

Gavin kept his head in the pocket of air while Zoe slowly opened the driver's door and slipped out into the inky black water. She thought the metal banging occurred behind the van so she went out the back door to search by touch.

Tapping with her diver's knife, she found a metal structure and she thought she'd found Gavin's old car. She hit the surface with the heel of her diving knife and heard a dull sound of thick metal. With her gloved hand, she cleared away several inches of mud and peat.

She realised the metal wasn't thin and rusted as she expected from the old car, but heavy and thick. The van had landed on top of something else, something much larger.

So this is what the CIA is searching for, she thought.

The metal structure had been covered with silt and small rocks so it looked to be part of the side of the mountain. She felt her way along the structure until she found the side of it.

The side sloped and she followed it downwards. She banged it again with the heel of her knife, and again she heard the sound of thick heavy metal.

Oh my God. Is this alien technology, a spaceship? Is this what it's all about? Forty billion now makes a lot of sense, she thought.

She followed the metal shroud down and discovered a lower edge to the structure. The lower edge led into the mountain. She went inside and followed the metal wall upwards.

With the wall as a guide, she swam upwards and through the murky water until she could see light above her. The movie *Alien* flashed right through her head.

Don't touch anything. Don't pick up anything. Don't peer into anything that looks like an egg, she warned herself.

The patchy light looked artificial. She realised she headed up toward an underground moon pool. Carefully, she continued her ascent, and within a metre of breaking the water, she could see lights on walls.

She didn't know if a guard would be on duty so she moved around to the edge. She popped her head up and removed her mask. She found herself in a pool roughly the size of a tennis court.

She saw a wooden landing stage in front of her. She listened carefully and heard a motor noise droning and echoing in the cavern. A rough-sounding pump kept the air pressure at 1.25 atmospheres for the integrity of the moon pool. She saw an airtight door and she expected there would be an airlock behind.

The noise drowned the sound of Zoe moving around in the water. She looked around the walls of the cave and spotted one camera focused on the landing stage. Surfacing underneath and keeping close to the wall, she positioned herself to avoid being caught on camera.

She attached her mask and swam back to the van. Just in time because her air supply had nearly exhausted. Gavin heard her knocking against the van wall as she made her way around to the open front door of the van.

He became distraught with panic. No new insights had come to him. No final pieces had fallen into place as a result of bringing the van down into the loch. He expected she'd searched the boot for the aluminium suitcase, and found nothing because he'd lied to her.

He expected her to be livid, and he had nothing new to tell her. Her head popped up into the air pocket. When she took off her mask she said, 'Come on. I've got something to show you.'

'What?'

'Come on, my air is running out.'

They shared his air cylinder as they swam to the moon pool. They surfaced underneath the camera, positioned at three o'clock in the circular pool. For reference, she had set the landing stage at twelve o'clock.

'What on earth is this?' he whispered.

'Keep quiet, there may be microphones,' she whispered back.

They saw a wide range of equipment stored on the ledge around the pool, from the landing stage right around the ledge to about eight o'clock. They also saw a two-man mini-submarine tied up. It looked like an old torpedo from the Second World War but with two seats.

The door on the wall looked like an old sea closure door from a submarine situated at about one o'clock. They helped each other out of the water, removed their diving gear. She lashed it together with some webbing and secured it to the side of the ledge.

They climbed onto the rock ledge and Zoe opened her waterproof backpack to retrieve her Browning. She fitted a suppressor before she slipped it into a chest pouch. Gavin gave Zoe a boost so she could reach up and put a glove over the camera lens.

Gavin's wetsuit boots squelched as he walked, so he sat down and emptied the water from them. They both pulled off their wetsuit hats.

They waited patiently for nine minutes. Zoe began to wonder if the camera had been unmanned, then the circular door handle swirled around and the door opened inwards. A man stepped through the door. He had a toolbox in one hand. Zoe pushed the muzzle of her Browning into the man's neck. He recognised the cold metal on his skin.

'Don't speak. Put the toolbox down, gently,' she whispered into his ear.

Gavin came around from behind Zoe and faced the man. Gavin took a radio handset out of his hand, unclipped a cover and took a handgun from the pouch attached to the web belt around the man's waist.

Dressed in a US Navy uniform Type 3 of predominantly blue with some grey, he wore a matching cap, a shirt over a white T-shirt, and black leather boots. On the right of his shirt, a tape in silver lettering gave his name, ALKERTY, and on his left side, in silver lettering the tape said US NAVY.

The three of them went through the door into a narrow corridor. Gavin brought the toolbox. The Navy man re-sealed the door. At the opposite end of the short corridor, a vertical metal ladder led up through a circular metal tunnel.

Zoe looked up the ladder. It extended about three times her height to another airtight door with a circular centre handle.

'What is this place?' Gavin asked Alkerty.

'Quiet,' Zoe said to Gavin.

She knew Alkerty wouldn't answer any questions. She wanted silence in case Alkerty's buddies were nearby. She quickly assessed Alkerty; over six foot, early twenties with a strong muscular body. He looked like a bar brawler, and the type most likely to have a go.

She looked again at the ladder and decided Alkerty posed too great a risk. She pointed her gun at his head and told him to take off his uniform. Then, Gavin tied his hands and feet with red twine he'd found in the toolbox.

'Put his uniform on,' she whispered to Gavin.

'Me? What will that mean if I'm caught? Does it make me a spy or something? Maybe I should stay as a civilian,' he said, and sounded worried.

'If we get caught, we get shot. If you give me an edge we might survive,' she replied.

'I'm not sure about—'

'You're wasting time. Put the uniform on, and find something for his mouth,' she said.

Gavin slipped into Alkerty's uniform. He found some duct tape in the toolbox and used a strip to cover Alkerty's mouth. When Alkerty had been secured, Zoe sent Gavin up the metal ladder to unlock the airtight door and push it up.

Gavin stood on the ladder for a moment while he pulled the brim of the cap down on his face. He looked around before he climbed out and stood beside the airtight door. He signalled Zoe to climb up the ladder. While he stood guard, she headed for the cover of nearby dark shadows.

Both of them absorbed the unexpected sight. They were in a curved underground cavern. A few fluorescent light strips around the walls provided some light but the cavern appeared mostly dark and cold.

The cavern had enough headroom to stack eight London buses on top of each other over most of the surface. Zoe guessed the overall size to be similar to a football park. She recognised the faint smell of diesel from a generator. In the centre, she saw a large oblong-shaped pool of water.

Floating in the middle of the pool she saw a small submarine. A long wooden staging ladder with wire sides lay on the edge of the pool, ready for use as a bridge to the submarine. Either the submarine had just arrived or it would soon leave. Since no-one stood by to move the ladder out to the submarine, she figured it would depart.

Zoe's eyes tracked lines of cables, pipes and conduits on the walls but couldn't see where they led. She spotted one set of cables that ran along the wall and disappeared into an angled hole in the wall. *Communications and air supply*, she thought. The ground felt wet with water constantly dripping from the roof.

At one end of the cavern, she saw an office complex composed of six rectangular pre-fabricated interconnected cabins. Arranged in a block of three by two high. All the cabins had large glass windows but only the upper middle and upper left cabins were lit with fluorescent lighting.

The noise of a power generator beside the office block became clearer. Beside them were two prefabricated half-circle-shaped Quonset huts made from corrugated galvanised steel. From the amount of rust on the walls, it looked like these huts had been in place for many decades.

Zoe signalled Gavin to walk to the offices. He looked self-conscious and walked awkwardly in his uniform. Fortunately, no-one watched him because they would have known instantly that he wasn't Alkerty.

He tried to walk confidently with a swagger in his hips; the way he thought a Navy man might walk. She rolled her eyes and thought, *I don't believe it, he's trying to walk like Popeye. For God's sake walk properly—you idiot.*

Zoe skirted around the wall, darting from one deep shadow cover to the next one as she made her way to the offices. When she reached them, she spotted a prominent plaque with a brightly polished logo on one of the office blocks.

The logo showed a map of the world with the Atlantic at its centre and a trident in the middle. Around the map lay a banner with the words SACLANT on the top and RESEARCH CENTER on the bottom. On the sides were fish dolphins rather than mammal dolphins.

Zoe knew that SACLANT stood for Supreme Allied Command Atlantic. An organisation formed at the height of the Cold War and disbanded in 2003. Fish dolphins, she knew were a trademark of the US Navy.

Other markings on the Quonset huts, on metal shipping containers, on the office block and on the submarine left her in no doubt. She had stumbled into a secret US Navy base in Loch Ness. She smiled as she thought, *Nessie, you sneaky hump-backed bitch, what's this Yank doing under your skirt?*

She turned a corner and the smile disappeared from her face when she saw a shape she recognised and feared. A monster all right, but not one she expected.

Forty

Jerrid Penkmon sat at his workstation to type up the results of his latest systems check. He'd done this so many times, he'd dropped into automatic mode. His mind wandered to his wife Debbie and son Ryan waiting for him in Boston.

Then his brain outpaced his fingers, his typing got mixed up, and he backtracked to make corrections. Three steps forward, one step back. During the moment of typing irritation, he thought about this unusual posting.

No-one back home knew where he'd been posted, and he couldn't tell anyone. A niggling worry surfaced as Penkmon remembered the medical officer had told him his posting would only be two months due to the memory redaction needed to ensure security.

When Penkmon arrived, Commander Walterson had read the log, and welcomed him to his third posting to this base. Jerrid didn't recall the previous postings but believed him when he found some personal doodles he'd left behind.

He liked the idea that only he knew he wasn't where he should be. As far as his wife, his CO and his unit HQ were aware, he remained on the USS Maine patrolling the deep waters of some dark and dangerous corner of the world.

In fact, six days after leaving the Naval Submarine Base at New London, Connecticut, the USS Maine rendezvoused with a US naval vessel known as Nerrtoo somewhere in the Atlantic. Penkmon, Alkerty and Scudmore boarded the Nerrtoo for transfer to a base known only as LuEllen. The base wasn't listed on any US Naval register and it didn't exist on any official document.

As far as the Captain and crew of the USS Maine were concerned, Penkmon and the others were on TDY (temporary duty) elsewhere and would rejoin the boat in two months.

The Chief of the Navy who personally arranged the duty at the request of General George Schumantle, didn't know anything about Penkmon's TDY. The only formal records of this duty were made and retained by General Schumantle.

Most unusual for the Navy, there were no written orders and none of the plethora of naval documents that detailed every action and outcome of the personnel and equipment engaged in an operation. That didn't mean Penkmon and the others had no paperwork to do. They had plenty but it remained in LuEllen, and didn't see the light of day.

In a weird sense, Penkmon liked lying to Debbie and Ryan when they spoke on the phone once a week for twenty minutes. It wasn't like real lying where he tried to deceive and gain an advantage or control over something. They were white lies to conceal the fact he wasn't on the USS Maine.

Not like Alkerty, who'd recently finished a home call with his girlfriend Jackie just before he went to check the camera in the moon pool. He could lie to save the planet, and he liked Jackie to pick up things he'd said previously, so he could weave even more intricate and complex lies.

Of all the wives and girlfriends, only Walterson's wife fully understood the drill. She didn't ask about his work, his workmates or the boat. She kept her conversations strictly on family, friends, neighbours, neighbourhood, national news and the house. His home calls were completely stress-free and relaxed.

Behind Penkmon, a large glass window looked out over the pool and the light from his office lit the space outside and underneath.

Gavin entered a door in the middle bottom cabin and stepped into a dark corridor. All three of the bottom cabins were in darkness. Immediately to his left, steep stairs led to the office above. Zoe tapped him on his left shoulder and he walked up the stairs. The middle upper cabin appeared brightly lit, but empty.

Gavin stood still at the top of the stairs until Zoe tapped his left shoulder then he moved left to the door that led to the next cabin. Gavin stood at the door until Zoe tapped the back of his neck and crouched down behind him as he went inside.

'Did you fix the … who the hell are you?'

'Hands clear of the desk. *Now,*' Zoe said, and moved in front of Gavin.

The man also in the same blue-grey uniform got on to his feet and looked shocked as Gavin took his side arm. Gavin read the tape on Penkmon's chest.

Penkmon recognised Alkerty's uniform on Gavin.

'What have you done with Alkerty?'

'Resting for the moment. How many people manning this base?' Zoe said.

Penkmon shook his head. Gavin held the handgun on him while Zoe searched the documents and folders on the tables in the room to find the daily staff log.

Penkmon saw the man holding his gun hadn't flicked the safety off. His mind raced with thoughts of overpowering him to retake his side arm.

Zoe found and read the staff log. There were six men on rotating eight-hour shifts. Alkerty and Penkmon had been on duty for two hours. Two men were in the galley resting and two men were asleep.

'What's the status of your visitors out there in the pool?' Zoe asked.

Penkmon shook his head in defiance.

Zoe stood face to face with Penkmon. 'I have four SAS troopers out there ready to sink the boat if I tell them it's a threat.'

Penkmon shrugged and then Zoe said, 'Fine, they drown and it's on your head.'

'Okay, they're due to ship out anytime,' Penkmon said.

Zoe looked around and recognised the radio and SATCOMM satellite communications system. She saw a row of four screens embedded into computer consoles. A quick scan of the screens told her three were communications and one connected to the Internet for email.

She searched the shelves of manuals and books and found the current register of US Navy vessels. She noted the designation on the hull of the submarine outside. The DSV-NR2 known to her crew as 'Nerrtoo'.

She read the entry. Nuclear-powered ocean engineering and research submarine. Crewed by two officers, eight AB crewmen and two scientists. Remit, underwater search and recovery, oceanographic research missions, installation and maintenance of underwater equipment.

She stepped back in front of Penkmon. 'I'm content to let them go. When they call. You will respond as normal. If you alert them to my presence, my team outside will eliminate them. Do you understand?'

'It's not a warship. They're unarmed, save a few handguns,' he said as he looked at her military version extra thick wetsuit.

'Play ball and they can leave. Agreed?'

'Yes.'

'You've got direct comms with Naval Command Operations?' she asked, and nodded toward the row of communications consoles.

'Yes.'

'I'll be talking to your boss before I leave. But first things first,' she said.

The radio cracked then a voice boomed into the room.

'LuEllen, this is Nerrtoo. All checks complete. Time for us to take our leave. Thanks for the hospitality. See ya'all later, over.'

Zoe held the microphone with her thumb on the transmit button while Gavin held the handgun at Penkmon's head.

'Copy that, Nerrtoo. You have a safe journey. See you next time. LuEllen out,' Penkmon replied.

Gavin tied him up.

Zoe held the microphone to his mouth and told him to summon Paltec and Scudmore to the comms room with a fake story about a systems failure.

When the two men hurried into the room, Zoe held her gun to their heads while Gavin disarmed them, searched them and then tied them up. She made Penkmon repeat the process for Hitchen and Walterson. They scrambled up from the sleeping quarters cabin and into the same trap.

The five men sat knees up with their backs against one wall of the comms room. Gavin watched over them while Zoe returned to the corridor to fetch Alkerty. He looked shocked when he saw the others tied up and sitting in a row.

A neat row of sailors in uniform except Alkerty appeared odd man out in his T-shirt and shorts. Zoe picked up the log and checked the names in the log against the tapes on the uniforms.

'Alkerty, Penkmon, Paltec, Scudmore, Hitchen and Walterson. All present and correct,' she said.

Walterson said, 'I don't know what you folks think you'll achieve here. I can tell you the US Government does not negotiate with terrorists. Period.'

He looked the most senior in terms of age, and from the log she noted he had taken command of the base.

Zoe said, 'That doesn't make any sense. I'm British, Loch Ness is British. The only terrorists in the room are you six. I should shoot all of you for operating a secret military installation in my country without permission from the British government.'

Zoe waited to see if anyone would pipe up to say they had permission. No-one did.

'What is your intention?' Walterson asked.

'Obviously our two governments will have an almighty argument about this base. I'm sure an agreement will be reached on how it is managed going forward,' Zoe replied.

'If you are British then untie us. We're on the same side. We'll cooperate,' Hitchen said.

'I'm sure you would, but I know your boss would rather keep this base completely secret from the Brits. So, for the moment you'll remain secured until we leave. It we all remain calm, the worst thing you'll face will be some Brits bunking up with you,' she said.

Zoe collected and checked all the side firearms before she put them in a filing cabinet drawer. She extracted her SEM phone from her waterproof backpack, and switched it on. It hadn't been activated since Johnson told her to deactivate it at the start of her mission. She selected the camera app.

'Any of this familiar to you?' Zoe asked Gavin.

Gavin looked around the room. 'Nothing.'

'Why would he be familiar with this base?' Walterson asked.

'Long story, but he's been here before. That's how we found your base,' Zoe replied.

'That's impossible. Everyone who visits or does a tour here is redacted before they leave to ensure total secrecy.'

'Redacted?'

'Short term memory erased. It's a standard harmless procedure done automatically to ensure security. It's been an SOP for over fifty years,' Walterson said.

Zoe exchanged a knowing look with Gavin, and said, 'Redaction of memory. Now, *that* has just explained a whole load of things that we've been struggling to understand.'

'Where do you do this memory redaction?' Gavin asked.

'In the medical box,' Walterson replied.

'The what box?' Zoe said.

'It's what we call these cabins,' Walterson replied.

'I'll have a quick look around. You keep your eye on these men,' Zoe said to Gavin.

Zoe gave Gavin his SEM phone. Both phones immediately connected to the LuEllen Wi-Fi. No need for a password because normally there were no visitors. Since they hadn't been used, both SEM phones were fully charged.

Gavin looked through his phone to find out what he'd missed while it had been switch off. He had a lot of email from his technician, Christine Willsening. Too much to read so he scanned the subject headings. Before Zoe left the room, she stopped in the doorframe and told the US Navy men to behave.

Forty-One

Gavin walked around the Portakabin-type office and inspected the structure. He pushed the balls of his feet into the floor, and as he suspected the suspended floor pushed him back like a trampoline. He looked out of the window and admired the structure of the cavern. The small submarine had gone from the large pool.

'Are they Second World War British Nissen huts that you have out there?' Gavin asked.

'No, son, they're American Quonset huts,' Walterson replied.

'This cavern reminds me of the movie, *The Thing*. I can't remember if Kurt Russell survived in the end. There's nothing crawling about out there in the dark corners I should be worried about, right?' Gavin said.

No-one replied.

'How did that submarine get in here? In fact, how is this place even possible? I mean Loch Ness is above sea level?' Gavin asked.

None of them answered.

'If they redact you after each tour of duty here. How do you become reacquainted with the base?' Gavin asked.

No-one answered, but their reactions told Gavin he'd found something. He searched the tables and the bookcases and eventually found a very old book with the title 'LuEllen Base' on the front cover. It contained a detailed historical account of the formation of the base and included many black and white photos.

'Here we are. *Wow*. An underground lake,' Gavin said as he read the book.

Penkmon had a geology background and looked along the line at Walterson. He signalled with his eyes that he could take him. He mouthed, *he has my weapon, and the safety is on*. Walterson nodded back and gave him a go.

Penkmon said, 'A quarter of a mile below Loch Ness, there is a lake.'

'That's incredible,' Gavin turned to look at Penkmon.

'Not really, there are hundreds of underground lakes buried under the Antarctic. The largest is Lake Vostok, which is 160 miles long by 30 miles wide. LuEllen is 31 miles long and 6 miles wide, so its medium sized,' Penkmon replied.

'LuEllen?'

'L.U.L.N. Lake under Loch Ness,' Walterson replied.

'Is it directly under all of Loch Ness?'

'No, it extends from six miles south of Dores to about eight miles out in the Moray Firth, north of Nairn,' Penkmon replied.

'How did you discover it?'

Penkmon said, 'We didn't. The Nazis found it during the Second World War. They were probing undersea defences when they found the route from the Moray Firth into the south end of the lake and up a chimney into the north end of Loch Ness. They surveyed the loch and selected the rock formation on this mountain to establish a base.'

'A Nazi base? I wondered why there were pictures of German U-boats in the book.'

Walterson saw Gavin had let his guard down. 'They planned an advanced base to launch V4 rockets on London. They perfected underwater launch capability but the project required a major war effort by the Nazis. They sent Rudolph Hess here to assess the potential but his mission failed. We discovered the Nazi plans while we held Hess in Spandau prison.'

'Is the underground lake man-made?' Gavin asked.

'No, Nature built this one just like the Antarctic lakes using the most immense power,' Penkmon replied.

'Nature is really impressive, isn't it?' Gavin said, and he looked increasingly distracted.

Penkmon followed through. 'During the Ice Age, the ice at the bottom of a glacier melted when it came into contact the ground. Then the massive weight of the glaciers forced the meltwater to find a weak spot in the underlying rock.'

'To form a new lake?' Gavin asked.

Penkmon's excited voice said, 'Over thousands of years, pressure forced meltwater through the weak spot to form great whirlpools and potholes. Raging torrents scoured the ground underneath to form the underground lake.'

'Is that how they're formed under the Antarctic?'

'Yes, the same basic process.'

'How did the Nazis find a way into Loch Ness?'

'Over the centuries, the weak spot progressively collapsed and formed a long channel from the roof of the lake to the bottom of Loch Ness. The tunnel allows a good passage between the two, a chimney if you will,' Penkmon replied.

'Fascinating stuff. This would be a diver's heaven. Divers from all over the world would want to explore LuEllen. Has it been surveyed?'

'I've got all the charts, even the original Nazi sonar charts that led them to the chimney. I've got awesome radar charts of LuEllen. She's composed of two huge basins with a ridge between them. It's fantastic to see what Mother Nature has achieved with the application of nothing more than pressure. You won't believe the wildlife down there.'

'Wildlife? What wildlife?'

'I could introduce you to Nessie if you want,' Penkmon said.

'There is no such thing,' Gavin replied.

'True, she isn't a multi-humped sea serpent like those in the tourist brochures, but she is a monster from the deep. Nessie is a shark as big as a great white.'

'That's rubbish. There are no big sharks in these cold waters,' Gavin said.

'That's where you are wrong. The Greenland shark inhabits these waters and it can grow up to seven and a half metres long.'

'No-one has ever reported seeing a shark fin in the waters of Loch Ness,' Gavin said.

'The dorsal fin on the Greenland shark is small and floppy so it doesn't break the water surface like a normal shark fin,' Penkmon replied.

'How could a shark get into Loch Ness?'

'The Greenland shark is a deep sea creature. It has been found at depths of more than two thousand metres. Occasionally, one comes up through the chimney and into

Loch Ness. People who've seen what looks like an upturned boat on the loch, have actually seen a Greenland shark.'

'I've got plenty of photos I can show you and you can look at the German U-boat log,' Penkmon said.

'What's in the German log?' Gavin asked.

'They killed a six-metre Greenland shark and tried to eat it but the flesh is highly poisonous. Several of them died according to the log. There is a photo of the U-boat captain standing beside the shark. The remains of the shark head and jaw are in the Quonset hut. The shark mouth is a metre in diameter.'

'Can I see this evidence?'

'Sure,' Penkmon replied.

Penkmon swivelled around on his knees and butt to pull his bound hands from his back to his front. Still on his knees, he offered up his tied hands for Gavin to cut the bonds.

Gavin looked suspiciously at Penkmon, and said, 'I'm not doing that. Just tell me where to look.'

'The keys to the filing cabinet are in my pocket,' Penkmon said, and lifted his bound hands up above his head.

'Okay, stand up slowly, keep your hands up, come over here, and then kneel down again,' Gavin said as he held his handgun pointed at Penkmon's head.

Penkmon got up, and when close enough, he dashed forward and head-butted Gavin on the side of the head. Gavin dropped to the sprung floor with an almighty thud and his handgun fell on the floor.

Penkmon picked it up with his bound hands and flicked the safety off. He stretched his arms out, and clasped his bound hands around his handgun.

Penkmon said, 'There is a knife on the table over there. Cut these bonds, *now*.'

They all heard Zoe Tampsin's footfalls as she ran back along the corridor. She had set Gavin's phone to transmit audio. She'd been listening to their conversation while she searched the cabins.

Zoe appeared in the doorframe, and Penkmon swivelled his outstretched arms to point his gun at her head. 'Stand still. Drop your weapon,' he said to Zoe.

'Are you okay?' she asked Gavin.

Gavin looked dazed and disorientated as he nursed the side of his head. He needed a few seconds for his blurred vision to clear before he stood up straight. His pride hurt more than anything else.

Zoe examined his face. He would have a smacker of a bruise under his left eye tomorrow.

'Excellent work, Penkmon,' Walterson said.

The other men shouted woo-hahs and way-to-goes to Penkmon. He felt elated as he flashed his big grin to his buddies.

'Hey, dumb-nuts, get over there and cut these bonds,' Penkmon said to Gavin.

The other men got on to their knees and turned their bodies to present their hands to be cut free. Zoe still had her gun in her hand.

Penkmon shouted at her, 'Drop your weapon or I will fire on you.'

'Do as he says. No-one needs to get hurt here,' Walterson said.

'Drop your weapon,' Penkmon shouted.

Zoe stood back from Gavin. Her handgun pointed at the floor. She didn't comply with Penkmon's order. She turned her head to look at him. She raised her handgun up to waist height and then further as if to point it at him.

Her nerve shocked Penkmon, he had no choice. He had to fire on her. He didn't issue another warning. He aimed his gun at her head and pulled the trigger.

Forty-Two

Click … click-click-click. Penkmon snatched at the trigger and then looked at his handgun as if it were defective. Zoe aimed her handgun at Penkmon's head.

She said, 'You're as daft as a brush if you thought for one second I'd leave a civilian with a loaded weapon. Put the weapon down and get back in line. Move your hands behind your back.'

'Worth a try,' Walterson said to Penkmon as he sat down in line.

Zoe said to Gavin, 'What am I going to do with you? You're more trouble than a bag of monkeys.'

'Sorry, he distracted me with all this fascinating stuff about Loch Ness,' Gavin said to Zoe as he picked the handgun up from the floor.

'I'll admit, I found the story fascinating.'

'I didn't expect—'

Zoe patted Gavin on the shoulder, and said, 'Not to worry. I thought they would try something. I allowed them an opportunity. Now I know I can't trust them.'

'What? You expected them to attack me—'

Zoe smiled at Gavin and took the handgun from him. She replaced the empty clip with a full clip, chambered the first round and switched off the safety. She handed the gun back to Gavin.

She said, 'Loaded and ready to fire. Be careful, but if they try again, shoot to maim. Legs first, then the body. I won't be long. I'm nearly finished.'

Zoe had inspected four of the cabins. She found a power room with generator, tools, workbenches and stores. Another served as a medical and rest room with library, TV, video player and games consoles. A fourth cabin contained sleeping accommodation and a quiet rest room.

The last one she had searched contained the kitchen, dining and exercise room. She looked inside the Quonset huts and found stores of diesel fuel for the generator. She found she couldn't enter the sixth cabin. From a handwritten scrawl on the door, it had been labelled the launch box.

When Zoe first entered the cavern and skirted around the wall from one dark shadow to the next, she found a small-gauge railway track that ran behind the offices. On the track were a set of trolleys, and she discovered a cruise missile lying horizontal on them.

A large panel lay open and from the tools and parts nearby, it appeared to be receiving a repair or service. The entire missile had been covered by a clear plastic greenhouse-shaped cover with a zipped entrance. It kept dirt and dripping water from entering the open panel.

She followed the rail track and found it led to a row of three capsule launch systems built into the wall of the cavern. Each system contained one cruise missile, and a second cruise missile stood ready to be wheeled into the system when the first missile had launched.

Zoe understood the launcher mechanism. It would propel the missile up to the surface of Loch Ness, and when the missile cleared the water, the air rockets would fire and the guidance system would take control. Very similar to submarine launch systems. She returned to the comms box. Gavin had kept them in control, and no-one had moved an inch.

'The launch box is locked. I want the key code.'

'No way,' Walterson said.

'According to the log, you are the LCO. I know the launch control officer can't launch anything without codes from the President, so there's nothing to worry about,' she said, convincingly as if she believed it.

'You can see any other part of the base but not the launch box,' Walterson said.

'I'll use explosives to open it up but the vibration in this confined space … I'm not sure how much vibration the mountain could take before rocks above fall down. Obviously, I'm not going to do anything but I do want to see something,' Zoe tried to reassure him.

No-one spoke.

'Okay, cover your heads. I'll do it the hard way,' she said, and started out the room.

Walterson called out, 'All right, but only if I enter the keypad code.'

As she untied Walterson, Zoe warned Gavin that while they were separated they were vulnerable. She told him to ignore any requests for a drink or toilet. If anyone started to have a heart attack or began foaming at the mouth, then he should call out for her on the SEM phone. Gavin nodded that he understood.

Zoe followed Walterson out of the room and down the stairs.

'What's your first name?' Zoe asked.

'Chuck.'

'How long have you been in the service?'

'Twenty-three years,' he replied.

'Congratulations, that's admirable.'

'Are you Special Forces?' he asked her.

'You're not going to give me any reason to kill you—are you?'

'The other guy looked like he could be taken in, but you look capable,' he said.

'He's a scientist. Science babble will blind him every time. A good ploy from your guy, I'll give you that,' she said.

'You could have shot Penkmon, but you didn't. Thanks for that.'

'I expect you've seen your share of action?' she asked.

'I launched plenty of cruise missiles against Iraq and a few against Afghanistan as part of Operation Enduring Freedom.'

'What a complete mess we made in Iraq. Lots of very low-value targets were hit by you and by us. I don't know what the brass were thinking,' she said.

'I think there were too many agencies with their finger on the button. They proposed too many targets and most weren't evaluated or properly justified. We destroyed a lot of non-essential structures.'

'Copy that, Chuck. We did as well.'

'Why does your scientist guy think he's been here before?'

'He led me here.'

Walterson looked puzzled and said, 'I can assure you he hasn't been here. First thing I do when I arrive is check the log. It tells me I've been coming here twice each year for the past ten years. There is nothing in LuEllen's log about a visitor, especially a Brit.'

'What about eighteen years ago?'

'Obviously before my time but the logs are in the store. It would be easy to look back and see if he did visit,' Walterson said.

'Would he have been redacted before he left?'

'Absolutely, without a doubt.'

'That explains a great deal because he's been recalling fragmented memories that eventually led us here.'

'Memory recall is supposed to be impossible. So they told me,' he said.

'Well, we are here.'

'If you don't mind me asking, who is he? It's just I can't imagine any circumstances where a civilian scientist would be allowed into LuEllen.'

'He wasn't a visitor, more of a gate crasher. Eighteen years ago as a kid, and he arrived by car,' she said.

'Car? Oh, shit, the kid in the car, of course. That incident is in the medical log.'

'Why did you bother to rescue him?' she asked.

'Lady luck looked down on him. There were two divers working outside the moon pool entrance. They hauled him out of his car and brought him to the medical box. The officer in charge decided that if someone had seen him go into the loch and his body wasn't found, they'd search. We didn't want that in case they got too close.'

'So you redacted him and took him back to the surface.'

'Yes.'

Walterson opened the launch control box door and switched on the power. The systems rapidly set, checked and readied for action. The computer screens ran through their protocols and checks. The system had been designed for fast, all-systems boot up. Ready for rapid launch of the cruise missiles.

The control systems were much as she expected they would be with rows of control panel dials, key activated launch consoles and small screens for code input and verification. One console indicated battery power at ninety-six percent. If they had main power failure, they could still launch with a battery-operated system.

'So, this base has been here more than twenty years?' Zoe asked.

'More than fifty years. Around the time of the Cuban missile crisis, when it seemed Cold War communism would march from strength to strength. This would have been our Cuba equivalent, and the first line of defence if the Soviets had invaded Europe. We had eight ICBMs here before they were replaced with cruise missiles.'

'I don't understand. There were extensive nuclear systems based in England during the Cold War. Why this?' Zoe asked.

'The enemy didn't know about it so it wasn't on their first-strike target list. The British didn't know about it so none of your double agents could give it up to the Soviets. The Soviets had silos we didn't know about. This base is one of ours they didn't know about.'

'Impressive and reassuring. If the British nuclear deterrent is compromised, then this is a first line backup,' Zoe said, and made a face to show she felt impressed.

'What do you want to see?'

'I think you know what I want to see.'

Walterson sat at the LCO desk computer screen, logged in then typed in some details. The screen changed and Zoe read the heading on the page. *Targeting Module.* All the cruise missiles were listed down the left hand side of the page.

Against each CM number lay a user input box, and in each box, a set of coordinates had been set. Zoe examined them.

She said, 'CMXRP 238 is set for latitude 55.752 degrees, longitude 37.617. I do know that's Moscow. Where are the others headed?'

Walterson averted his eyes and didn't speak. She looked more closely at the screen and under each set of coordinates, but she couldn't work them out.

'I don't have authority to do that. I need to seek permission and receive a password.'

Zoe looked disappointed. 'Chuck, don't assume I'm an idiot. I can go use my SEM phone to connect to the Internet if I have to do that.'

'The target locations are input from Washington,' he replied.

'No they're not. Our system is the same as yours. You might as well reveal the target locations. I'll have them in five minutes from the Internet.'

Walterson pressed a few keys. The coordinates disappeared to reveal the target names.

CMXRP 234 St Petersburg
CMXRP 238 Moscow
CMXRP 239 Strasbourg
CMXRP 241 Paris
CMXRP 242 Berlin
CMXRP 247 London

Forty-Three

Zoe stepped back from the computer screen and stared intensely at the target names. Walterson moved the screen to the second page where there were another six missiles targeted at European cities. Walterson saw the shock on her face but didn't say anything. He didn't know what to say.

'Allies. You're targeting your allies?' Zoe screamed.

'I know how it looks. It's just a contingency for a worst-case scenario.'

'It's obscene. What scenario?'

'What if Europe and Russia merge to a super economic block.'

'Rubbish,' Zoe replied.

'I don't know much about the politics. We reserve the right to be ready to protect our people by any and all means possible.'

'It's one thing having a contingency plan in case of political upheaval, but nuclear missiles targeted at allies. Fucking unbelievable.'

'I don't think they would ever—'

'What's the payload on these missiles?'

Walterson refused to answer. She lunged at him, grabbed him by the neck and pushed his head down against the table in front of him. Her strong fingers squeezed his windpipe. The anger in her eyes told him she could kill him.

'One hundred and twenty kilotons,' he said, and she let him go.

'That's what, about six times Nagasaki?' she asked.

'Yes.'

'Nothing but the best for your friends?'

'Do you guarantee to always be our friend?'

'I've seen all I need to see,' she said, sharply.

Zoe's mind analysed the implications of this find as she followed Walterson out of the launch box. He didn't power down any of the systems he'd switch on. He agreed to take her there because he knew an unscheduled systems boot-up would be detected.

He felt smug he had outsmarted her, but remained careful not to show it. They didn't speak as she followed him back to the comms box.

'Everything okay?' Zoe asked Gavin.

'Fine. Did you find out what these guys are doing here?' Gavin asked.

She didn't conceal her anger. He assumed she wasn't pleased with what she'd found.

She pointed at Walterson and said, 'Tie him up good and tight.'

Zoe needed to think. This discovery had proved much more alarming than she expected. It wasn't about fighting terrorism or protecting new technology.

This base would attack Europe if it should ever become aligned with Russia and become a threat to America.

She closed her eyes to expunge the thoughts of a nuclear weapon going off in central London. She'd seen the training video simulations of nuclear explosion and the aftermath. She'd seen films taken after Nagasaki and Hiroshima.

She'd done the training on how to survive a nuclear war. She felt sick inside. She asked Gavin for his SEM phone. She showed the Americans the two phones.

'These are SEM phones with lots of tricks and gadgets. I'm setting this one to video your actions. I'll watch you on this one. If any of you move a muscle, *one muscle*, I'll come straight back here and crack every single fucking skull. *I'm angry*. If you won't behave. I will put you down. *Clear*?'

Her voice threatened, and the men realised she'd discovered the missiles were targeted at Europe. She fitted Gavin's SEM phone to the back of a chair so it could observe the men. Zoe switched the video feed to her phone and then she led Gavin out of the comms box.

'Where are we going?' he asked.

'We need to talk. This base is much worse than I could ever imagine. We are in seriously bad shit here,' she replied.

She took Gavin to the medical box. It looked like a small hospital ward with three hospital beds and various monitors, gas bottles and other medical equipment. Gavin stopped at the nearest bed and closed his eyes. He remembered the smell of old rubber.

'This is where it happened. I remember,' he said.

'Walterson told me your visit is entered in the log. When you drove into the loch, two divers were working near the entrance. They pulled you out of the car.'

'The demons I thought were from the *Ghost* movie.'

'They brought you here to the medical box to be resuscitated. When you recovered, they redacted your memory, dried your clothes, and returned you to the surface. They called an ambulance. I expect the CIA had you under loose surveillance to ensure the redaction remained.'

'Sharon Bonny,' he said.

'Probably just the latest in a line of monitors over the eighteen years.'

Gavin said, 'She did ask me a lot of questions after my transplant. I told her about my nightmares.'

'She must have figured out you were starting to remember this place. They decided to eliminate you to keep their base secret.'

'What do they do here?' Gavin asked.

'They have twelve cruise missiles with nuclear warheads targeted at London, Paris, Berlin, Moscow, St Petersburg and Strasbourg, and six other cities.'

'What? That's disgusting. What about the special relationship?'

'Special relationship? Don't be stupid, Gavin. There is no such thing. It came out of the Second World War alliance. Modern politicians use the phrase to make themselves look important.'

'I thought we had a special relationship like brothers in arms?'

Zoe shook her head. 'Less than ten percent of the US population have English ancestry. There are many more Germans, Irish, Italians, Africans and Mexicans. None are sympathetic to England. US politicians would never risk pissing off ninety percent of their voters for a special relationship with the UK despite the rhetoric,' she said with sharp sarcasm.

'I guess that would be silly.'

'Ever since the formation of the European Union, the Americans have been worried about a federal Europe led by Russians who control oil and gas for the whole region.'

'That would be a new world.'

'The gloom and doom politicians envisage a future world divided into four regions, America, Asia, Africa and Europe. The region with the best-placed hidden bombs will have a winning edge. This base gives the Americans a first-strike capability against Europe, and no-one knows about it.'

'You're describing a world like *Nineteen Eighty-Four*,' Gavin said.

'I'll bet that's where the paranoia has its roots. Fiction becomes fact and fact becomes policy.'

Gavin scratched his head. 'This is terrible. If we expose this base there will be huge fallout. The US will lose all credibility, and their economy will collapse. Our economy will collapse. If the CIA doesn't kill us, our Security Services will kill us to keep this secret. We have weapons of mass destruction under our own bed, and they're aimed at Europe.'

'If Johnson knew about it, he would have helped the CIA to kill you. He would have done it for them. Our side have no knowledge of this base.'

'We can't spill this can of worms. Our side can't allow us to expose it,' Gavin said.

'Correct. It would damage America too much. Our economy is too strongly tied to theirs. If they go down the sewer, we go down with them.'

Zoe and Gavin walked slowly out of the medical box and along the corridors back to the comms box. Zoe checked her video feed to make sure the men were still in place.

Gavin realised there would be no escape and no chance of getting back to a normal life. Until this day, he would have welcomed death as he thought it would reunite him with Emma, and he could be with her again. But now, with Emma alive and having rejected him, he didn't want to die.

'What can we do? We can't just leave as if we never found it?' Gavin asked.

'No.'

'We can't put the genie back in the bottle,' he said.

'That's the smartest thing you've said all day.'

'So, there must be another way,' he said.

'Well, if there is, I can't think of it, and I've been around the block quite a few times. Neither government can allow us to walk the streets with what we know about this base.'

'That doesn't mean we have to die,' he added.

'I tell you what. I'll make a deal with you. If you think of a way for us to survive this disaster. I promise you a night of such intense passion. You'll think you've died and gone to heaven.'

'Okay, it's a deal.'

'You're welcome to try.'

'I'll give it my best shot,' he replied.

'You watch over them. I want to have a look around outside,' she said.

She walked out of the room and imagined the aftermath of the base going public. North and South America would align themselves and push Europe into the arms of Russia.

Asia would quickly consolidate and Africa would be left to fend for itself until the time came to fight over Africa's resources. All of these ideas and the immense hopelessness of their situation gave her a thumping headache.

She thought about the irony. The Americans had put a gun in place to protect themselves from a future *Nineteen Eighty-Four* world. If she exposed their gun then the ensuing revulsion could end up creating the world they feared so much.

Her tactical and strategic mind analysed more than a dozen options. None of them were viable. Every way she looked at it, she came back to the same outcome. They had to die to keep the base secret.

If they disappeared, then both of their families would be brutally abused to draw them out. The risk of this base becoming public would be too great and too destructive for both the British and American administrations. Both families would suffer and Zoe couldn't allow that to happen.

She resigned herself to her fate. She smiled because she loved her job and had dodged many a bullet. Lots of exciting and exhilarating memories, but she always knew the day would come when she would meet the final bullet head-on.

She felt a little bit of sadness, a little bit of relief, and a little bit of regret. As a professional soldier, she didn't fear death. Death is inevitable and a good death is embraced for the release it brings. She thought, *when the time comes, we'll both join Karen, quick and painless, no nightmares guaranteed.*

She decided not to tell Gavin. No discussion and no prevarication. She had analysed all the options and made her decision. She planned how she would use her ring to end his life quickly and painlessly. In the medical box, she would give him botulism toxin instead of morphine.

Then her mind switched to Amy, Michael and her parents. Her thoughts dominated by the image of a nuclear explosion over London. She gasped and said, 'No! I will *not* allow this to happen.'

Forty-Four

Washington, USA

In the White House Special Situations Room, the door opened and a Secret Service agent led President Cranstoun into the room where he joined General George Schumantle and Admiral Grace Monklands, the Chief of the Navy. He carried a folder in his hands. He stopped at the table and slammed the folder down.

'What the goddamn hell now?' he shouted before he sat down.

'Shawlens and Tampsin have breached LuEllen,' George said.

'How could this happen? You said you'd contained the situation. How many damn shots do you need to hit this target?'

'I understand your frustration, Mr Presid—' George started.

'*No*, George, you *don't* understand. We are on the brink of a damn catastrophe and the best security brains have let me down. One minute you tell me you have the problem contained, then it's another situation, then you have it under control. Now, they're in the goddamn base. Learning all about LuEllen.'

'Yes, Mr President.'

'Move the warheads immediately to the sister site LuElldun,' Cranstoun commanded.

'That has already been done, Mr President. I moved them as a precaution when the situation shifted to Fort Augustus,' George said.

'At last, a glimmer of good news.'

'There is no risk of a nuclear detonation,' Grace said.

'Where is the CIA?' Cranstoun asked.

'Fort Augustus. Tampsin and Shawlens slipped through their net. I've not told Katherine about LuEllen. Do you want me to brief her?' George asked.

'No. Katherine has failed me. Keep them out of the loop. This is now a military operation. What are you doing to retrieve the situation?' Cranstoun said.

'A SEAL team is preparing to retake the base,' Grace replied.

'How many operational people do you have in LuEllen?'

'Six, but Tampsin has them under control,' Grace said.

'*She* is in charge of LuEllen? How much worse can this mess get?' Cranstoun said.

'Mr President, they are trapped in a box. This is where it will end,' George said.

'What are you waiting for?'

'There will be a firefight. Some of the men will be killed,' Grace said.

'So? Do you want me to be responsible for their deaths—is that it? Take responsibility for your own men, Admiral. Isn't that why I pay you the big bucks?' Cranstoun said.

'The men know that a SEAL team will be deployed from LuElldun. They know there will be no warning. They'll keep their heads down if they can,' Grace said.

'Bring this nightmare to an end, for God's sake, George. I want to be told the matter is ended.'

*

Admiral Monklands contacted the SEAL team preparing to retake the cabins. The team leader reported his team had arrived in LuElldun and were breaking out their gear. ETA to LuEllen ten minutes. The Admiral made her instructions perfectly clear. Retake the base and kill the two insurgents.

The team leader briefed his team as they crouched around a map of the LuEllen base and planned their attack. The leader stood tall with short black hair, and looked like the actor Ben Affleck but with a Texas drawl characteristic of the Lower South East.

He passed around a printout photo of Gavin Shawlens and Zoe Tampsin, standing side by side, captured from the comms room video feed and sent by Admiral Monklands.

Tampsin stood in front of a row of men who were sitting on the floor with their backs against the wall.

The SEAL team leader said, 'There are twelve of us and two of them. One professional and one civilian. We have surprise, superior skill and greater firepower. They have stupidity and weakness. They are trapped like rats in a box. I want to execute this operation with clinical precision and by the numbers.'

*

Zoe returned to the comms box. She'd been away forty minutes and Gavin began to worry something had happened to her. She told Gavin to check the bindings on each of the men. She said she saw Hitchen trying to work his hands free. She spotted him wriggling his shoulders on the video feed from the SEM phone.

'What now?' Walterson asked.

'What do you mean?' she asked.

Zoe read his tells and noticed a new confidence as if he had the upper hand. She'd seen those giveaway tells before. She sensed he wanted to tell her how futile her situation had become and how he would end the stalemate.

'I mean this is over for you two. You do see that?' he said.

'I don't think so. I'm in control,' she replied.

Walterson looked smug and said, 'Any minute, SEAL teams will overrun this base. They'll shoot to kill but if you set us free, I'll tell them I've retaken control. No-one needs to die.'

'How do they know?' Gavin asked.

'When you entered the launch box, the system made immediate two-way contact with our command centre. They heard our discussion,' Walterson said.

'*Shit.*'

Zoe had remembered the standard operating procedure. No-one could be playing around in the launch control box without the command centre knowing. It flashed in her mind at the time, but Walterson distracted her, and then her thoughts became overwhelmed with visions of a nuclear detonation over London. She hadn't forgotten about it. Zoe told Gavin to keep an eye on the men then sat down at the SATCOMM comms module.

She moved the mouse and clicked on a green transmission button. The screen flickered in to life. It split in two with her picture on top and the picture of a Navy officer on the bottom. He looked shocked at seeing her on the screen. On the top left of the screen a green icon flashed, TRANSMISSION.

Zoe said, 'Command centre, this is LuEllen. Who am I speaking to?'

'LuEllen, this is command centre, duty officer Matt Stinglehammer. Who am I speaking to?'

'I am Captain Tampsin, British Security Service. I have an urgent message for your commander-in-chief. Message reads, stand down Navy SEAL attack on LuEllen. Do you have the message?'

'Copy that, Captain Tampsin; FAO CiC, stand down Navy SEAL attack on LuEllen. Urgent transmission.'

She said, 'I'm in operational control of LuEllen. Any attempt to overrun the base will result in immediate detonation of a Perseus Two package and subsequent nuclear explosion. Is that clear?'

'Perseus Two package, immediate detonation, nuclear explosion. Copy that.'

'I want to speak to the Chief of the Navy about how best to avoid that scenario. Twenty minutes from now, check.'

'Copy that, Chief of the Navy, twenty minutes, check.'

'LuEllen out.'

Zoe flipped the mouse cursor and clicked on an END TRANSMISSION icon.

'Release Walterson. I want him to confirm that no-one has been harmed,' Zoe said to Gavin. Then she turned to the men and said, 'I'll speak with the Navy Chief and resolve this situation without bloodshed. Behave, and you'll be released by the SEAL team.'

She said if anyone tried heroics, she would have no choice but to execute all of them. She read all of their faces and believed she had done enough to convince them to sit tight and wait. She re-fitted Gavin's SEM mobile phone to a chair, positioned it in the middle of the room and said, 'I'll be watching through this video system.'

*

Twenty minutes later, in the White House Special Situations Room, General George Schumantle and President Cranstoun watched a live video screen. The main feed on the left took up a quarter of the screen.

On the right, three separate feeds ran down the side of the screen, and along the bottom six screens showing the video outputs of the SEALs making their way through a cavern tunnel that led from LuElldun to LuEllen.

On the main feed from LuEllen they saw the row of Navy men tied and sitting against the wall in the background. Cranstoun asked where they were and George told him they were in the comms room. Zoe Tampsin stepped into the foreground of the picture.

'Good evening, Mr President, General Schumantle. I assume the Chief of the Navy is away on leave,' Zoe said when she looked at the picture on her monitor.

'I have the Chief on standby. She'll be informed of any actions she needs to take,' Cranstoun said.

'I understand,' Zoe replied.

In fact, Admiral Monklands sat in a corner blind spot outside of video camera capture range. She had a direct link to the SEAL team leader. She wore headphones to hear him but she could speak normally because a noise filter removed her voice from the transmission sent from the room. She could talk to Cranstoun and her voice would not be heard in LuEllen.

Cranstoun said, 'Now, Captain Tampsin. If I have been reliably informed, it seems we have something of a Mexican standoff.'

His comment threw her for a second. A Mexican standoff involves three opponents, none of whom wants to fire first because if first fires on second, third will fire on first, so no-one wants to fire first. She thought he might be confused.

'It would seem so, Mr President,' she replied.

Gavin Shawlens stepped into the picture and stood beside Zoe.

'I believe you know Dr Shawlens,' Zoe said.

'Not personally but I'm aware of his unique position in this situation. I can guess why he's wearing that uniform,' Cranstoun said.

'Can I speak to Lieutenant Commander Walterson?' General Schumantle asked.

Zoe waved a handgun. Walterson stepped into the picture and stood beside Gavin.

'Commander, are your men safe? Is the base secure?'

'The men are unharmed, sir, the base is—'

Zoe interrupted, 'I'll answer any strategic questions, General.'

Gavin moved Walterson sideways until they both were out of the picture.

'Captain, what is a Perseus Two package. Why do you have it with you?' George asked.

'It is an IED of sufficient energy to destroy this base. I didn't bring it. I found six cases of C4 left over from your demolition work together with a handy box of cables, detonators and initiator boxes. Any fool can rig it up when you leave all the necessary components lying around. Perseus Two is a name I thought of to get your attention,' Zoe said.

'I see you more than live up to your reputation, Captain,' George said.

With a severe look, she said, 'Taking my daughter only served to make me more determined to run this thing down.'

BOOM! The building shook with an almighty crash followed by the rapid *thud, thud, thud* of suppressed machine gun fire. The video feed the President and the General were watched jolted to the left then righted itself. The video appeared unchanged with the men still sitting against the wall as if nothing had happened.

Zoe's face came back into the video picture. She looked shaken and angry. She raised a black hand-held initiator box in front of the webcam so it filled the entire screen. It had three wires trailing for firing a detonator. She pressed the red button.

A BANG followed and the video picture shuddered violently. Everyone heard a large explosion outside the cabins. The video feeds from the SEAL team scattered and then most of them went blank. She held up another initiator box with two trailing wires.

'*Stand down*,' she ordered.

Forty-Five

Admiral Monklands spoke directly to the SEAL team leader and ordered the men to withdraw with their wounded. Four of the SEAL men had been caught in the blast Zoe set off. They were injured with blast wounds but not seriously. She had set a charge to shock and disable rather than kill.

Gavin went with Walterson to the comms box, and found a thick pall of dust and paper fragments in the air. So thick, they could hardly see their hands in front of them. They waved their hands to clear the dust from their faces. Dry particles caught the back of their throats and made them cough.

Broken glass and furniture littered the floor, papers scattered up in the air and everywhere. Some tiny bits of paper were still floating back to the floor.

Looking through a broken window, Gavin saw twelve heavily armed men dressed in dark combat uniforms and black beanie hats. A few stood guard while others attended to wounded lying on the ground.

Four of them looked to be seriously injured. They covered their heads when an avalanche of dust and small stones fell from the cavern roof.

Gavin picked his SEM phone up from the floor. It had re-connected to LuEllen and he still had access to the Internet and email. He called Zoe on his phone and told her a grenade or something had been thrown into the room and there were bullet holes in the wall and white dust everywhere.

Walterson attended to his men and shouted out that all of his men had blast injuries and two of them were dead from bullet wounds. From the positions of the bodies, it looked as though a stun grenade had landed on the floor, and some of the men got up and tried to move away. When they were on their feet, they'd been cut down.

Zoe told Gavin to bring Walterson back to the launch box.

Zoe switched off the video projector function on her SEM mobile phone. She had attached it to a chair and it displayed a video recording of the comms box onto the wall behind her. The video showed the men sitting down on the floor in the comms box.

She had expected an attack and recorded the video earlier to fool them into thinking she would use the men in the comms box as a shield. The signal received in Washington simply reported it had come from LuEllen. The SEALs had attacked the comms box.

Zoe altered the zoom on the desktop computer webcam camera so Washington could see her standing in the launch box and not the comms box.

Cranstoun gasped and George Schumantle stared at the screen as if he couldn't believe the picture. Grace Monklands simply covered her eyes with the palm of her hand. The SEAL team leader had told her what had happened.

Zoe spoke loudly. 'General, your attack failed. You have killed two of your own young men. Others are seriously wounded and need immediate attention. I knew you would attack my position so I used this technology to re-direct you to the comms room.'

She held her SEM phone in the air. The secure encrypted modular phone issued by the Lambeth Group for satellite communication also had an app for video projection.

'Stand your men down,' Cranstoun said to the Admiral.

Zoe spoke commandingly, 'I'm sorry you've lost good people. They didn't deserve to die. If you insist on playing hardball with me—be prepared to suffer consequences if you lose.'

Cranstoun said, 'I'm sorry we underestimated your determination, and not for the first time.'

'If you challenge me again, you will fail. Attack options are no longer valid. I press this button with the last twitch of my body. Loch Ness goes into orbit.'

'Zoe, what do you mean?' Gavin asked as he and Walterson entered the room.

'General, *Am I clear*?'

'*Clear*,' George replied.

Zoe raised her voice a few notches. 'Have the SEAL team tend their wounded and recover your people in the comms box. If I suspect for a *second* they are moving on my position.

If I see them approaching my C4 explosive. I detonate instantly. You've been warned. There will not be a second warning.'

'I have ordered them to stand down,' Cranstoun said.

'Mr President, I assume my government do not know about this base.'

'Correct.'

'Mr President. Why are your missiles targeting London and your allies?'

No-one spoke and a long silence hung in the air. Zoe prepared to repeat the question when Cranstoun spoke.

'Europe is heading for unification. In time, the current Russian President will be replaced by a Gorbachev mark two or mark three. Russia will become Europe-friendly. Europe and its loyalties will shift east. I believe it's no more than a decade or two away. If a Russian-dominated Europe should ever decide America is the enemy, and it may never happen, but if it does, we will protect our people by any and all means.'

Zoe replied, 'In that situation, my concern is for the maverick president who goes berserk and uses these weapons to kill friends, family and colleagues.'

'That can't happen at this level,' George said.

Zoe said forcefully, 'General, you and I both know history is littered with insane politicians and crazy military commanders. We only find out they were mad *after* they have committed their atrocities. No system is safe from these people, and human history just loves to repeat itself because we always fail to get the message.'

Cranstoun replied, 'Okay, Captain Tampsin, I hear your concerns. We could argue the point all day but we are where we are. You have your view. I have mine. We disagree. Surrender yourselves to the SEALs and I guarantee you'll not be harmed.'

'That is not going to happen. We will be killed one minute after we surrender. That is guaranteed,' Zoe said.

'Maybe not,' Gavin said to Zoe.

She said, 'Gavin, wake up They want this gun pointed at Europe. We don't get to walk away from this. It's our duty to protect our families from the threat of nuclear attack. Even if it means we have to die.'

Gavin asked, 'General, could we be redacted to erase the last few days?'

'Yes,' George replied.

'Gavin, you're not thinking. If we are redacted, they will resume operations. I will *not* allow this base to pose a nuclear threat to London. What if the President's scenario unfolds in ten years' time and we're living in London? Do you want your family to deal with the aftermath of a nuclear explosion?'

'No.'

Zoe looked and sounded fatalistic. 'Our two lives are a tiny price to pay for the security of tens of millions of innocent people. This base must be destroyed while we are here to see it destroyed. We go down with the base. No choice. End of.'

'I don't want to die,' Gavin replied.

Zoe sounded unsympathetic. 'You died eighteen years ago when you drove your car into the loch. They managed to postpone it, that's all. Don't be so worried. You're not alone this time. I'll be with you. Alec died for you. Karen gave up her life for you. Now you'll give your life for millions of others.'

Zoe's determination shook Gavin as he believed he only had minutes to live. He approached Walterson but he looked too distraught to offer any suggestions or alternatives. Gavin left the room and walked along the corridor. He stopped and banged the heel of his fist into a wall. He felt like running away as fast as he could. He went back to the comms room and sat down with his head in his hands.

An hour ago, he'd sent an email to his technician and friend Christine Willsening, telling her he would see her soon. She replied saying she would organise a big party for his return. He'd sent a reply saying 'okay, see you later'. He sat with his phone in his hand and thought about sending her another email to say he wouldn't be back after all. Walterson came into the room.

Walterson said, 'She has told me to leave the base. She's a soldier, and she wants to go down with the base. She said you can come with me.'

'I don't want to die in here,' Gavin replied.

'Come on, I'll lead you out,' Walterson said.

'I should tell her that I'm leaving,' he said.

In the launch box Zoe said, 'Mr President. I'll give you ten minutes to get your people away from this base then I'll detonate the cruise missile that I have under my control.'

'I don't believe you would detonate a nuclear device and kill millions of Scottish people,' General Schumantle said.

Zoe frowned and shook her head gently, 'General, I'm so disappointed, you still want to patronise me. Thank you for extinguishing any remaining hope that you could be trusted. I know the warheads have been removed. But all the missiles and the fuel in this confined space will magnify the explosion. In fact, the C4 and the fuel depot alone will be more than enough to obliterate this base. Trust me, I know a thing or two about explosives.'

Cranstoun shouted, 'You are *not* in control of my base. I'm in control.'

Admiral Monklands passed a paper note to General Schumantle. He read it and passed it to Cranstoun. It reported that the SEAL team had evacuated the dead and wounded, and they were on their way to LuElldun.

Cranstoun got up to leave the room, and said, 'I call the shots. We're done here. *Execute*.'

*

Within a few seconds, a loud siren sounded in the cavern. It lasted for exactly ten seconds. Walterson and Gavin ran out of the comms box.

'*Evacuate. Evacuate*,' Walterson shouted along the corridor to the launch box.

Zoe followed Gavin and Walterson out of the cabins, and found they were alone. The SEAL team and the casualties were gone.

They ran over to the tube that led down to the moon pool. Walterson arrived first, just as the first explosion detonated in the roof at the far the end of the cavern and brought down thousands of tons of mountain rock and a huge volume of water from the loch.

Gavin helped Walterson to pull on the handle.

'It's stuck.'

Zoe arrived and pushed Gavin out of the way. She pulled up a metal bar she'd put in place to prevent anyone from entering from the moon pool. When the three of them were in the tube, the second explosion in the middle of the cavern brought the large middle section of the roof down.

The percussion threw them off the ladder. The airtight hatch on the tube hadn't sealed and it sprang back up to the open position. They picked themselves up as dust and water flew down through the hatch.

Zoe opened the airtight door as water flooded from the moon pool through the door. Walterson and Gavin waded through the rushing water. Frantically, they untethered the two-man submarine as the water level in the pool surged upwards. Zoe followed them.

The water had reached waist-height when Walterson waded to a locker and pulled out three re-breather masks. Small closed-circuit breathing systems. They provided a small supply of oxygen, and scrubbed carbon dioxide from the exhaled air. They were good for ten minutes underwater.

Zoe checked the submarine's battery, less than twelve percent. Not enough to head back to Fort Augustus or north to Inverness.

'We are not going anywhere in this thing,' Zoe shouted above the noise of rushing water and crashing stones in the cavern.

'We just need to get across the loch to Urquhart Castle,' Gavin shouted.

A third explosion rocked the mountain and the water level in the moon pool rushed faster upwards.

'We need to go now,' Gavin shouted.

'The airlock is failing,' Walterson shouted above the loud noises of the mountain falling above them.

Zoe helped Gavin and Walterson push the submarine away from the ledge around the moon pool. Zoe climbed onto the front seat and activated the controls. Gavin took the second seat and Walterson straddled the back and secured himself with webbing to the backrest of Gavin's seat. The submarine submerged just as the moon pool flooded.

Water surged up to fill the moon pool and Zoe used full power to dive the submarine down against the upward force. Zoe counted fifteen seconds to be certain she had cleared the structure. Then she levelled off and headed up to the surface at an angle of thirty degrees.

The submarine pushed up through the surface then splashed down hard. The engine failed and the submarine sank, leaving the three of them to bob around in the water. A fierce wind blew down the loch, and made the bitterly cold water choppy. Zoe still wore her wetsuit but the two men in cotton clothes began to lose heat rapidly.

They took their re-breathers off and saw two helicopters hovering over Urquhart Castle. The helicopters spotted them, turned and headed directly for them. The three of them heard the helicopters above them but couldn't look up.

A commercial RIB skimmed over the loch from Urquhart Castle and pulled up beside them. The skipper's mate pulled them on board and wrapped gold-coloured foil around their heads and shoulders as the RIB returned to the castle.

Zoe looked ahead at the small pontoon on the grounds where small cruise ships on Loch Ness allow visitors to embark for a tour. When they were less than a minute out from Urquhart Castle, they saw a huge crowd of people on the north lawn waiting at the pontoon. Zoe thought, *tourists in November?*

The three of them were numb and turning blue with cold when the RIB brought them alongside the pontoon. The deafening noise of excited people made it difficult to hear what individuals were saying. Slowly, they clambered off the RIB and onto the pontoon.

With glazed and watery eyes they faced a wall of people shouting and pointing, but it all sounded like a single indiscriminate noise. Impossible to focus on it. Security men from Urquhart Castle's visitor centre arrived at their side and wrapped blankets around them.

Zoe prepared for the worst. Gavin Shawlens smiled and waved at the helicopters. Zoe looked confused. She looked more closely at the helicopters circling their position. They were news helicopters with cameramen pointing cameras at them. In both of the helicopters, the news correspondents sent reports back to their newsrooms.

'Ladies and gentlemen, it appears we have been the victims of a gigantic hoax. The Loch Ness Monster has *not* been sighted. I repeat, the Loch Ness Monster has *not* been found.'

Another said, 'Three hoaxers have just landed at Urquhart Castle to give themselves up.'

When the three walked off the pontoon onto the grass, they were immediately surrounded by media people with microphones and cameras, and a barrage of questions. All demanding to know who'd been responsible for the hoax, and why they did it.

Four official-looking people arrived with a stretcher. They quickly stretchered Walterson away to the visitor centre and out to a black SUV waiting in the car park.

Zoe grabbed Gavin's hair and pulled his head close to her. She asked him, 'How?'

'Chr-Chr-Chr-Christine Willsening. I sent her an-an-an email. Her brother is-is-is-is an editor on-on-on a newspaper. He-he-he-he'll be furious but who g-g-g-g-gives a shit?' Gavin said, through teeth chattering from the cold.

Gavin and Zoe pushed slowly through the media pack back along the path toward the visitor centre. The media were desperate to get a story. They started to behave like a mob when they sensed neither Gavin nor Zoe would answer any questions. Zoe and Gavin continued to move forward until they were met at the entrance to the visitor centre by Spence MacAllisin.

Gavin and Zoe stopped and faced him. It looked like a confrontation so the media hounds surrounded the three as if they were expecting a fight to break out. The news crews pointed their cameras and microphones toward them. Zoe scanned the people around her. She spotted at least a dozen CIA people waiting and watching.

'Please come with me,' Spence said.

One reporter asked, 'Are they under arrest?'

Another asked, 'Will they be charged?'

Others shouted, 'Which one of you is Dr Shawlens?'

Another, 'Where is the scientific evidence that you found?'

Another asked, 'Did you actually see the monster?'

Zoe listened to them and needed to think fast.

Gavin hadn't told her he'd contacted Christine and told her to tell her brother that a scientific team led by Dr Gavin Shawlens had found the Loch Ness Monster swimming on the surface near Urquhart Castle.

Zoe wasn't prepared to face intense media frenzy. Her body wasn't as cold as Gavin's because of her wetsuit. His teeth were chattering loudly as intense shivering tried to generate some heat. She felt cold but not shivering enough to make her teeth chatter.

'What did you hope to achieve with this hoax?' a reporter asked.

Zoe announced, 'Listen. I don't know anything about a hoax. Someone has misled you. Dr Shawlens, my friend and I were enjoying some private leisure time on the loch, when we got into difficulties. We were not searching for anything. We have no scientific evidence of anything. We sighted nothing and we don't know anything about a hoax. As far as I can see, someone has played a hoax on you media guys.'

'Were you leading a scientific team to find Nessie, Dr Shawlens?' some reporters shouted to Gavin.

'No-nooo-no,' Gavin said, and shook his head from side to side.

Zoe said, 'Whoever told you about a scientific investigation on Loch Ness has played a hoax on you. Nevertheless. We are grateful you people were on hand to come to our rescue. That's all I can say.'

A policeman said, 'No more questions. These people need medical attention. The police will release a statement when they have completed their investigations.'

Spence MacAllisin stepped forward and offered his hand to Gavin as a smile creased his lips. Spence shook Gavin's cold hand first then Zoe's hand as he said, 'Welcome back.'

Forty-Six

Saffron Walden, Essex

In the small town of Saffron Walden, like many towns, late evening produced a quiet and calm air as clock hands moved ever closer to bed time. But one Georgian house in particular, Kineerdly Beechgrove, seemed resolutely oblivious to the demands of clocks.

A grand six bedroom house, and sumptuous home for Nicholas and Penelope Orcherd and their two daughters, Camilla-Anne aged eleven and Catherine aged six.

Penny looked every inch an attractive and easy-going thirty-four-year-old natural blonde with shoulder-length hair and a rich husky voice. She capped a wonderful sense of fun with a hearty infectious laugh.

Nick looked a bit older, he'd reached forty and had a thin face with chiselled cheekbones. He kept his hair short and neat. He liked to look good in his well-tailored immaculate smart-casual outfits, mostly Barbour country gent styles.

The Orcherds ran a successful antiques business from a large shop in Saffron Walden. The children were already in bed as usual although Camilla-Anne had only just fallen asleep. Penny tidied up and moved wine glasses and cups to the kitchen.

Nick did the rounds, checking windows and doors. When he walked through the utility room and into the garage, he found two men wearing black donkey jackets, collars up at their ears with black baseball caps and semi-transparent Tony Blair masks on their faces.

One of them flicked a handgun to usher Nick back into his house, and then to the drawing room. The man with the gun told Nick to call Penny back into the room. The men stayed out of sight until she returned to Nick's side.

The man with the handgun told Nick and Penny to sit down on their sofa and keep quiet. He warned them they did not want their children running down from their bedrooms. The man with the gun nodded to the other man.

He took surveillance detection equipment from a bag and began to scan the room for bugs and video devices. He moved progressively from room to room. After half an hour, he came back to the drawing room and reported no finds. He then put the equipment back in the bag.

The man with the gun raised a two-way radio to his head, pressed transmit and said, 'Clear.'

Ten minutes later they heard a van reverse up their drive. A third man entered the drawing room wearing the same disguise as the other two. He sat down in a chair opposite Nick and Penny and the man with the gun stood behind him. The man in the chair took off his mask, cap and put them on the seat. Nick and Penny recognised him immediately.

James Barscadden. The man standing beside him also took off his cap and mask to reveal Barscadden's right-hand man, Peter Bromlee. The third man, Duncan Blackie, Barscadden's loyal driver and personal bodyguard, took off his mask.

Penny took a sharp intake of breath and then covered her mouth with her hand. Barscadden looked thinner in the face, and he had a thin grey beard.

Barscadden said, 'Lovely house, Nick. We've been admiring it from your neighbours, the Browns, up the road. I have to say their house is classier, and they have top quality wine in their well-stocked cellar. Well, they did have but they won't need it in the future. We've been watching your family come and go for five days. Very orderly, very organised and precise.'

'What are you doing in my home?' Nick asked.

'Sorry about the theatrics, Nick, but we do have unfinished business and unfinished business is not good business,' Barscadden said.

'We didn't torch the Patersun's house. We don't know who did it, and we don't know anything about how they escaped and turned up in Scotland,' Nick said.

'You're both still alive because I know you didn't have a hand in that ruse. I already know that someone in the Security Service planned and organised the fire, and put the Patersuns into witness protection. Probably for some future trial they think they'll have,' Bromlee said.

'How perfectly convenient for you to keep my money when you didn't complete the contract. I paid for the Patersun women and Shawlens. I understand Shawlens is still alive, is he not? So the three of them are unfinished business as far as I'm concerned.'

'This business is on me. It has nothing to do with Penny or my children.'

'Well that's as may be, but I'm most disappointed in you both. You were the best team we had in WRATH. How many successful additions to our Rehab programme, Peter?'

'Exactly, 196. Sorry, 193. There are three outstanding items,' Bromlee said.

'Not counting the sixty grand paid in advance for the last three. How much have I paid the Orcherds?' Barscadden asked Bromlee.

'Over two and three quarter million, give or take the odd ten grand,' Bromlee said.

'We didn't do Shawlens or the women because you changed the rules and tried to deceive us,' Penny said.

Barscadden looked insulted. 'I certainly don't recall anything of the kind. How, precisely?'

'We have never done a woman. We were widow-makers,' Penny said.

'All of the people we took for you were violent, male, sexual predators. The Patersun women and the Shawlens man were not in that category,' Nick said.

'Are you saying, that after delivering 193 men to their death, you have suddenly developed scruples over a couple of women?' Barscadden asked.

He shook his head and looked back at Bromlee with disappointment on his face.

'I don't do women. None of the animals we collected were normal human men. They were violent beasts, doing unspeakable things to women and children. Shawlens isn't one of those beasts. I checked him out,' Penny argued.

'So, you decided to make up new rules and chose not to tell me,' Barscadden replied.

'When Peter recruited me into WRATH, I agreed to deliver violent animals to your Rehab factory so they could be put down and have their organs recycled. I had no problem with that. But the Patersun women and Shawlens were a different matter,' Nick said.

'I see. Well, since we're drawing up new rules, I have a new one. I paid in advance and you kept my money. You'll complete the contracts, and I'll hold your children as insurance. This time, I require conclusive proof of death for all three. Failure to complete or insufficient proof of death will result in the permanent disappearance of your daughters.'

'*Please*. Don't take my children. Take me instead,' Penny pleaded.

Peter Bromlee signalled to Duncan. He put his mask and cap back on his head then went upstairs to the bedrooms. Five minutes later, Duncan came downstairs carrying Catherine in a blanket. He walked from the hall into the drawing room, and he deliberately walked past Nick and Penny so they could see their daughter.

They caught a whiff of the chloroform Duncan had used to put Catherine to sleep. Duncan took Catherine out to the black van in the drive and put her inside. Eight minutes later, he carried Camilla-Anne by the same route and put her beside her sister. More chloroform lingered in the drawing room. Nick put his arm around Penny and held her close.

Barscadden said, 'Finish the contracts. I recommend head shots in a public place with lots of surveillance video and camera phone video. Brains on the sidewalk should do it—if you want to see your children again.'

'What you ask is impossible,' Nick said.

'You are very good at this type of work. I'm sure you'll find a way to prevail. Don't be so glum. I'm allowing you to keep the sixty grand,' Barscadden replied.

'That is more than generous,' Bromlee said.

Duncan came back into the drawing room. His masked head nodded to Peter Bromlee. Peter tapped Barscadden's shoulder; time to leave. Duncan stood beside Peter Bromlee, and pointed his gun at Penny and Nick in case they tried to do anything to stop them leaving.

Barscadden picked up his mask and hat then pushed up from his chair. Bromlee put his mask on and his cap.

Barscadden beamed a large smile to Penny and Nick as he pulled his black gloves tightly onto his fingers.

'Well, it has been nice visiting you two. I do hope you complete our business quickly, so I can return your lovely daughters to this fine home,' Barscadden said.

Everyone turned to look at the door leading to the hall. They heard someone walking heavily on the herringbone-style parquet flooring.

A woman with long hair and dressed in an expensive tennis club tracksuit and white trainers, stopped in the hall at the living room door and faced the drawing room.

'Okay, I'm off now. Play nicely,' the woman said.

Peter Bromlee raised his handgun toward the woman but before he could fire, Duncan shot Bromlee in the head at point blank range. He stepped forward and pulled Barscadden's collar, to drag him back into his seat.

Penny and Nick stood up and Penny ran over to the woman, kissed her and hugged her. The two women turned around to face Barscadden.

'Mr Barscadden, I don't believe you've met my sister Cassie, and my brother-in-law, Robin.'

Robin took off Duncan's mask and cap and threw them to the floor.

'I've moved the girls to my car. They'll stay at ours for tonight. They'll be fine once the chloroform wears off. It'll be fun explaining how they magically transferred to our house in their sleep. I'll leave you all to clean up this appalling mess,' Cassie said before she turned and went out the front door.

Barscadden turned around and stared intensely at Robin for a few moments. He sighed loudly then shook his head with annoyance.

'How foolish of me. You are slightly shorter than Duncan, and you're wearing different shoes. Very foolish indeed, not to have noticed. Ugh,' Barscadden said with regret.

'I'm rather upset you killed the Browns. I liked Barbara, we met regularly for coffee because her children are all grown up and living abroad, and she felt lonely. She used to phone me twice a day just for a chat and keep in touch. Find out when Camilla-Anne would next be playing. She attended all of my daughter's rehearsals and concerts. When the calls stopped suddenly last week, we did discuss me going over to see if she needed anything, didn't we?' Penny said.

'Yes we did, but Emma Patersun had come back from the dead. I knew sooner or later Peter would want to chat about that.'

'Forget Patersun and Shawlens. We have new business to consider. I have over two hundred and forty million in twelve pouches of diamonds in my safe deposit box. Allow me to go free. I'll give you six pouches. You know that above all things, I am a man of my word.'

'Oh jolly hockey sticks and berry tarts. That would just set us up for a superior life, Nick,' Penny enthused.

'The trouble with that idea, darling. When he's free, he'll give someone a hundred grand to kill us. Diamonds won't buy many strawberry tarts when we're dead.'

'That is certainly a risk you need to consider. I would owe you for sparing my life. I would be in your debt. In any event, you could easily afford to hire people to do the same to me. Checkmate, I think.'

'Darling, after we split it with Cassie and Robin, we would have sixty million. We could open another two or three shops. A manor house and a Rolls Royce car. My dream come true. Oh my God, what a fabulous opportunity. Lady of the manor sounds so exquisite, don't you agree, Robin?' Penny said.

'I know Cassie would be in heaven with that kind of money. We could build a fabulous life for all of the family. My parents are in a crap retirement home. I'd love to move them to something better,' Robin said.

'Ooohhh, Nick. We can't turn it down, please, we simply can't,' she squealed.

'How easily disposable?' Nick asked.

'Each pouch contains five thousand two-carat diamonds. Weighs two kilograms and is worth roughly twenty million.'

'Twelve kilos each. We'll need a rolling suitcase,' Robin said.

'How would this handover work?' Nick asked.

'You accompany me to my bank. I'll collect the diamonds, give you six pouches then we go our separate ways. I'll have to trust you, of course, but I'm a good judge of character,' he replied.

'How far do we have to travel?'

'Not too far from here. Norwich.'

'It's a very tempting offer. With that kind of money, we could hire a team of bodyguards to keep us safe. What do you think, Robin?' Nick asked.

'Sixty million is an awful lot to money to explain away. I'd need to rack through my family history. Find a long-lost wealthy relative who could have left it to me in his will. Okay, you're on. I'll go with you to the bank as backup.'

'Looks like we have a deal,' Nick said.

Robin lowered his gun from Barscadden's head and walked around the sofa to face him. Barscadden quickly grabbed a small handgun from inside his pocket but before he could point it at anyone, Robin shot him in the head.

'Damn it, Robin,' Penny shouted.

'Risky move,' Nick said.

'Not really. Takes two to three seconds to get a hand into a pocket, grab a gun, pull it out and aim it. And always there is a dramatic change in facial expression, just before they go for it. He pulled slower than most. Besides, I knew what he planned the moment he started taking his gloves off.'

'Why did you wait for him to draw?' Nick asked.

'I had to give him enough rope to find out what he would do with it. Now, we know what he always intended.'

'What about those lovely sparklers? Do you think he has them in Norwich?' Penny sounded disappointed.

'We'll never know. Where is Duncan?' Nick said.

'In the back of their van outside,' Robin replied.

'What are we going to do with all these bodies? We don't have a Rehab factory to take them to for disposal,' Penny asked.

'If they killed the Browns, then we could take the bodies over there. I can say I got a tip-off, went to interview the Browns, but they were already dead. I got the drop on Barscadden and took him out.'

'You single-handedly got the drop on Barscadden, Bromlee and Blackie?'

'Why not? Everyone knows I'm the best shot in my section, probably the best in the whole of the Security Service.'

'Won't there be an investigation, or at least lots of questions?'

'There won't be a great forensic investigation to show how they died. Who cares about that? They'll accept my explanation and be glad to hear it. Why would I not tell the truth? Everyone at the Security Service will be overjoyed that the Barscadden saga has finally ended. It's been quite a running sore for all of us,' Robin said.

'This outcome is probably for the best. If he found out that you faked the deaths of the Patersuns, and put them into witness protection. He would come back with a vengeance,' Nick said to Robin.

'Why *did* the Patersun woman come out of witness protection?' Penny asked.

'All I can tell you is they were abducted and used as pawns in an operation.'

'Really, Robin. That's not very sporting of your chums,' Penny said.

'Not my people. Another agency. People who are altogether more ruthless.'

'Well, she won't have to worry about Barscadden anymore. She'll be relieved about that,' Penny said.

'I think we all will,' Nick said.

'Boys, shall I fetch champagne glasses? I've got some lovely Bollinger Special Cuvée.'

'To celebrate what?' Nick asked.

'Obviously, darling, the end of Barscadden.'

Forty-Seven

London

Zoe Tampsin opened her eyes. They were blurry, and she took a minute to regain control of her eye muscles so she could focus. She looked around and saw two hospital beds side by side. A medical treatment room, and a nurse helped Gavin Shawlens walk around the floor.

He walked unsteadily with a stoop. He had one hand clamped to his forehead and his mouth gaped open. He wore an army tracksuit top and bottom. Zoe raised her arm and found she wore a similar tracksuit.

An excruciating headache hit her like a car crash. Her hands leapt to her head as if to stop it from exploding. She sucked a huge noisy breath and let it out slowly.

Toni Bornadetti had also been at Gavin's side, but left him and went to Zoe's bedside.

'Boss, how do you feel?' Toni asked Zoe.

'What … happened?' Zoe struggled to say.

'Don't you remember?'

'My head is crushed. I can't concentrate. I can't remember.'

'Do you remember arriving at Loch Ness?' Toni asked.

'Where am I?'

'You're safe. We're in Babylon House. The medical room.'

'Do you remember how you got to Urquhart Castle?'

Zoe frowned. 'Urquhart what? No.'

Zoe heard a door open and close but couldn't see who had come in the room.

'How long have I been out of it?' Zoe asked.

'Try to take it slowly. You're recovering from extreme hypothermia,' Spence said as he stepped into her field of vision from the other side of her bed.

Zoe turned her head to face Toni. 'What's going on?'

Spence said, 'Zoe, relax. Let me explain. Milton Johnson had the wrong end of the stick. We know that now. Look, no-one is after Gavin Shawlens.' He nodded to Gavin and the nurse.

Zoe looked fearful and said, 'What happened?'

Spence put his hand on her wrist and said, 'You were right all along. Gavin wasn't a threat, but as usual, someone in the Pentagon got their knickers in a twist. You know how paranoid we are about national security. The train departs leaving all the smart people still on the platform. If we had taken Gavin before you got involved, we would have quickly established he didn't pose a threat to our national security. But the whole thing about Gavin and the Russians just snowballed. Milton Johnson wound himself into a destructive knot, searching for something that wasn't there. His determination made us even more paranoid. We got into a spiral trying to find out what he wanted. Fortunately, you kept Gavin alive until we all came to our senses.'

'What about?'

Spence interrupted her and said, 'Everything is straight between our governments. We were both at fault. We both made mistakes and there has been loss of life on both sides. I'm very sorry about Alec Haymarket. Michael has kept your daughter and your family safe, and your friend Spock is fine. Both sides have learned lessons and put mechanisms in place to make sure we can't go down this road again.'

'Toni, my family—are they safe?'

Toni leaned toward Zoe. 'Yes, they're back in their own homes. When you want, you can call Michael. He has Amy with him.'

Spence squeezed her wrist and said, 'I'll get on my way. I just wanted to let you know that you and I have no outstanding issues. We part today as friends—am I right?'

Zoe fixed her eyes on Spence's face. 'We're on the same side. Sometimes we lose friends to friendly fire. It hurts but it doesn't change us.'

Spence smiled and left the room. He believed Zoe wouldn't seek revenge over the death of Alec Haymarket.

Toni said, 'I've just been telling Dr Shawlens about James Barscadden. The Security Service got a tip-off and found Barscadden in Saffron Walden. Barscadden and two of his people are dead. He's no longer a threat to Dr Shawlens or

Emma Patersun. They can get on with their lives and start a new life together.'

'No, we can't,' Gavin said, loudly.

Toni turned around to see the anger on Gavin's face, and said to Zoe, 'Or maybe not. Boss, Alan Cairn is the new boss at the Security Service. He wants to speak to you as soon as you are able. Do you want to speak to him?'

'Not now, Toni, he can wait until I feel better.'

'What about Karen?'

'We found her. She's with her family now. She'll receive a proper burial,' Toni said.

Zoe rubbed her eye. 'I want to attend the funeral.'

'So do I,' Gavin added.

Toni nodded. 'I'll make the arrangements.'

'Thanks,' Zoe said and then she closed her eyes.

*

'Thanks for giving me heads up when Tampsin turned up at Urquhart Castle. I became so distraught when they got away from Fort Augustus. I really needed that closure,' Katherine Kaplentsky said to George Schumantle as they watched Zoe on a video screen. The video stream had been sent from Babylon House to Grosvenor Square.

'I thought she wouldn't accept a handshake from anyone else,' George said.

At Urquhart Castle, Spence had delivered a drug to Gavin and then Zoe while they shook hands with him. They didn't feel it because of the cold. They collapsed, seemingly from exhaustion and hypothermia, and were stretchered away to a waiting ambulance.

'It was important they were drugged immediately after they were taken at Urquhart Castle. Less time for them to consolidate their short-term memories. Probably the cold worked in our favour. My technician checked and double-checked their redaction before we released them to Steelers. They have no memories that will compromise our POINT-K secret. As far as they'll remember, they drove up the east side of Loch Ness, lost control of their vehicle, ended up in the loch, and were picked up by a boat. They don't even remember Walterson,' George said.

'What about the kill order on them?'

'Rescinded. The Brits would immediately become suspicious and begin an investigation starting at Loch Ness. They are content with the current picture,' George said.

'Thank God this is over and the POINT-K secret is safe. The Brits are remarkably sanguine about all that went down,' Katherine said.

'Cranstoun has relented. He's giving them an under-the-table discount on their nuclear deterrent. That has shut them up.'

'He'll be mightily relieved this crisis has been averted.'

'Yes, he is. What is this business about Barscadden?' George asked.

'Barscadden had become a business magnate with his own private army called WRATH. They were responsible for horrendous crimes. He killed Patersun's husband then tried to have Shawlens and Emma Patersun killed. He escaped justice, went on the run, and Emma Patersun had to go into hiding with her sister while he remained at large. The Brits have spotted an opportunity to use Barscadden as a patsy. He's being blamed for everything that requires an explanation. The SAS had destroyed WRATH and now the Security Service have killed Barscadden. There will be no trial or investigation. Case closed, and the Brits have come out smelling of roses for taking down an evil billionaire and his corrupt empire.'

'And we are completely free of any involvement?' George asked.

'As far as the public is concerned, yes. The Brits have used the Barscadden incident to draw a black veil over what happened.'

'Thanks, Katherine.'

'You could have kept me out of the loop in Fort Augustus. Allowed the military to gain all the credit,' she said.

George replied, 'Cranstoun said we need to resolve the differences between us and work as one. Some in the military would have danced a jig to see the CIA damaged. I don't believe that a weakened CIA will serve the country effectively. Competition is good for retail businesses but not for the work that we do. We must find a way to better cooperate and coordinate our efforts.'

'I agree, and I'll work with you to make it happen.'

'You're the lawyer, Katherine. Maybe you could start by drafting a new policy. Let's call it AB3C. A better communication, cooperation and coordination.

End

Author

I hope that you enjoyed this book.

If you did enjoy it, I'd be thrilled if you could post a review. Reviews are very helpful for indie writers and the feedback is most welcome.

My website can be found here: http://gordonbickerstaff.blogspot.co.uk/ or you can find me on Twitter: @ADPase. Sample chapters of each book are available to download.

If you would like to comment on any of the characters or the stories then feel free to contact me. Characters, stories and writing are works in progress and I would be delighted to hear of any suggestions that might make them better.

If you would like to know more about the author then visit my author page: http://goo.gl/rLFrV9 or my website above.

Thank you for reading my book.

Gordon Bickerstaff

Deadly Secrets

The truth will out…

Gavin's life will be turned upside down when he joins a company to work on a product that will revolutionise the food industry. His initial gut instinct is to walk away until he discovers one of the company directors is the former love of his teenage life.

The financial implications are global and incredible. Powerful individuals and countries are prepared to kill as they compete to seize control of the company. Corruption at high levels, a deadly flaw in the product, and the stakes jump higher and higher.

Against overwhelming odds, Gavin must rescue his former love from the hands of an evil cult as they prepare her for a living nightmare.

'... doesn't have twists - it has hairpin bends'
'... an intricate fast paced modern day thriller'
'... will appeal to readers who like intricate plots'
'... plot kept me guessing what will happen next'
'... weaved it all together masterfully'

Everything To Lose

The chase is on...

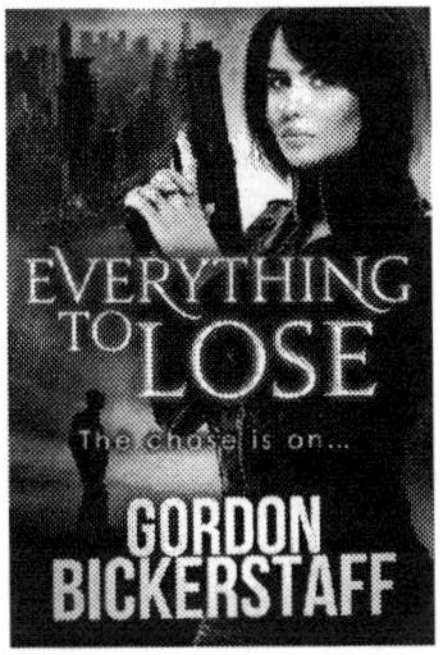

University researchers claim their new product will boost the performance of every athlete in the world. The Lambeth Group send Gavin Shawlens to investigate the claim.

The product is stolen, top athletes disappear and the research team are unaware that their product has a dangerous side effect. Gavin must stop the product launch before more people die horribly. When Gavin disappears, Zoe Tampsin, from the Lambeth Group, must find him before he becomes the next victim.

As if Zoe doesn't have enough on her plate. Past events in Gavin's life catch up with him. A powerful US general has decided that Gavin must die to prevent exposure of a 60-year-old secret capable of world-changing and power-shifting events.

Toxic Minds

The damage is done

'There's a special place in hell for women who don't help each other'

Madeleine Albright

Alexa Sommer had it all - stellar career, beautiful home, successful children, and a devoted husband. Then came meltdown and divorce. Her children's love turned to hate. She is forced out of the job she loved. Desperately, she tries to rebuild her life around a new job, but her work is controversial. Her enemies want her work stopped, and a few of them prepare to take their protest to the ultimate level.

A handful of Alexa's new colleagues have a compelling reason to want her sacked. Only one colleague can help her. Gavin Shawlens has nothing to lose - his train has already crashed, and his career is finished. He is all Alexa has on her side as a perfect storm of dreadful nightmares bear down on her.

'Come on Alexa, don't give in - fight back.'

Tabula Rasa

The end is nigh ...

A thriller for fans of Michael Crichton, Lee Child, Tess Gerritsen and James Patterson.

A hundred years ago, a wealthy family of visionaries prophesied the devastation that global warming would bring to world food supplies in the 21st century. They decided to prepare for the worst, and embark on an ambitious plan of revolution.

Lambeth Group agents, Zoe Tampsin and Gavin Shawlens, prepare to investigate the unusual death of a government defence scientist. Someone is determined to stop their investigation before they get started. Zoe uncovers two unfamiliar words, Tabula Rasa. The only other clue is the curious behaviour of the dead scientist's son, Ramsey.

Posing as a couple, Gavin and Zoe enter the secret and dangerous world of Ramsey's aristocratic guardians, headed by philanthropist billionaire, Lord Zacchary Silsden. What Gavin uncovers, shocks him to the bottom of his soul. Does he have the courage and the conviction to interfere in the greatest revolution the world has ever faced? What Zoe discovers about Gavin—words can't describe. Zoe is faced with an impossible choice, but one thing is certain, she will not hesitate to do her duty, no matter the cost.

28598039R00180

Printed in Great Britain
by Amazon